Vagabond Skyline

A Novel

by

T.I. Rotkiewicz

ISBN: 978-0-578-61085-6

Any references to historical events, real people, or real places are used fictitiously. Names, characters, and places are products of the author's imagination.

Front cover image by Lynn Lepko.
Lettering by Sam Parrett.

Printed in the United States of America.

First printing edition 2020.

Rocklynn Press

For all who carry a song in their heart and believe in the power of romance with a little dance.

Introduction

A different world from less than ten years earlier, the *New York Daily News* proclaimed, *"Ford to City: Drop Dead!"* Although President Gerald Ford did not say the words literally, everybody knew he felt it. Manhattan, a vibrant and gloriously glamorous city, had been stripped of her beauty in the sixties. The troubles started as far back as post-World War II when populations changed over to the suburbs. People no longer had a love for the city. It was only with time businesses would follow, shutting their doors and moving out. Slowly, decay sprouted, carrying an array of drugs and crime. Adult related businesses proliferated along the once-booming Times Square. A change in immigration, racial tensions, labor strikes, and riots began to pull the city apart. If that wasn't enough, in the seventies, New York City was bankrupt, financially, and spiritually.

It wasn't until the latter half of the decade that those in New York City realized they would have to make the changes to become the healthy, vibrant community it once had been, since they would receive no outside help. President Ford had refused to bail the city out of bankruptcy. Incoming president, Jimmy Carter, a breath of fresh air to the citizens, could do little himself. It would take years to turn around the decades of blight, crime, drugs, and festering emotions to move towards change.

There were those, the dreamers and doers, who wanted success and pursued to have it. Slowly, Manhattan returned to a state of glory. Clubs, in particular, shined brightly on the scene, creating word-of-mouth excitement. Hungry artists from near and far craved to take a bite of the Big Apple.

By nineteen eighty, Manhattan would become a rock star of sorts, enjoying the fame and infamy it had in its heyday.

Beauty in decay.

It's a city filled with pockets of glory, tragedy, laughter, joy, merriment, mystery, and crime. A kaleidoscopic world unto itself. A progressive amalgam of contradictions. Transvestites in stiletto heels trot along a neon jungle juxtaposed with men dressed in crisp suits of name brands, scuttling along the sidewalks near skyscrapers. Christians espouse the virtues of Jesus Christ on the same street corner as a triple X theater. Fortresses of glass and concrete fill the rest of the spaces. Fleets of yellow cabs drift aimlessly through the grid-like layout of the land.

The city embraces its return to being ahead of the curve of every other metropolitan in the world. It brings together men, women, black, white, Latino, Asian, straight, and gay. Disco era refugees sway and move to the songs that make memories in the clubs along the East Village. Within the West Village's meatpacking industry, men clad in leather and flannel, bump, grind and sweat together under a fiery red glow. Along SoHo, artists hide away in loft basements, burning the midnight oil to complete another success, vying to be the next big thing. Subways run from one location to another, carrying passengers, their belongings, and the latest graffiti in every car. They are the bowels of the Earth, a name given by those who travel them. It's the holy terror of being robbed by some street gang aiming most likely for somebody in a suit. A haven for all those on the move, whether it's the Hasidic Jew from Brooklyn, the businessman hiding his face in the pages of *The New York Times*, the black man in a jean jacket and bandana holding his portable boom box, the young woman with layers of blush and eye shadow attired in the latest trends. Cafes and delicatessens that have existed since beyond the city's financial collapse bustle with customers, ordering hot coffee and sandwiches. Tourists go to the Metropolitan Museum of Fine Art and receive the gift of beat poetry by a homeless writer outside the front steps. Central Park plays host to its drama of memorials and mayhem over the years.

Where residents of the Tri-State Region fill taxis and flood Grand Central Station like eager immigrants seeking new land, only, it's the same yearnings that those who already know and experience daily. It's those in search of such luminary neighborhoods as Little Italy, Hell's Kitchen, Chinatown, the Bowery, St. Mark's, Greenwich Village, the lower east side, uptown, downtown, and midtown.

Manhattan is the mistress of artists, songwriters, and movie makers. The muse of film directors such as Martin Scorsese, Woody Allen, Sidney Lumet, and John Cassavetes. She is the city that is King Kong's tragic end from high atop the Empire State Building. The hip image of a sleeveless T-shirt-wearing John Lennon that could knock any picture of James Dean from a wall. She is the postcard of perfection featuring the majestic skyline with her famed stars, the twin towers jutting into the sky from downtown, the Empire State Building along the center, and all of the co-stars and bit players of the uptown.

Somewhere within the confines of filth, crumbling buildings, and a menagerie of eccentric personalities, romantics dream of finding a fairy tale they can call their own.

Chapter 1

Along the darkened streets of Manhattan is a man on a mission. His profile gets caught under the watchful eye of glowing red neon. His wild hair is partly lit, showing a wash of pink from the sign above. He twists around to see a building that reads *27* on its graffiti-ridden front. Quickly, he pulls out a small folded piece of paper from his light-colored suit. Furrowing his brows, he compares the number to the one scribbled on the scrap piece of paper, reading *24B*. His eyes follow a row of darkened buildings. Businesses closed for the night. Grated metal gates and accordion doors fill the landscape. The only signs of life are a few buildings remaining open. A small coffee shop empties as two people walk out. He does a double-take at one building across the street. Perhaps the right address was nearby? He walks over to compare numbers again. *30.* For a third time, he checks the opposite side where the odd numbers are. An idea strikes him. He goes to peek around the corner of a small alleyway. Nothing is there. Hope seems lost as his whole body slumps in disappointment. Glancing down at the sidewalk, he moves along down the gloomy path.

***

At Seventeenth Street, a beige, four-story building of concrete and glass sticks out from the older designs assigned to neighboring retail businesses. It is here that the Japanese firm San-San Industries keeps its U.S. headquarters, housing database inventory for a quarter of the nation's electronics retail market. It's also where spreadsheets for large firms are created to stay organized and save money in an ever-increasingly fast-paced world.

On the fourth floor of the building, all remains quiet at the department of the JPL Group. Connie Ayers, a thirty-two-year-old database processor, punches at the keys of an Apple III. She has the girl-next-door appeal, only slightly more mature. A perky brunette, her face is a pleasing, though not overly made-up image of beauty. She is mostly devoid of the latest fads, although modern enough. Her green eyes reflect that of the bright green letters flashing by with each tap of the keyboard. She scans her hours' worth of work. Connie then hears noises from nearby as she concentrates. She furrows her brows as the computer cursor key gets stuck. Under her breath, she mutters, "What is with this thing?" Her eyes give a steadfast glance to the right, acknowledging the steps. "Ted? When are we getting new computers? This thing is messing up again. I've got three hours worth of processing done, and I'm having a hard time with this stupid machine." She grits her teeth and smacks the side of the monitor.

Ted answers her from afar.

"When the boss decides to invest in them."

"Ha!" Connie abruptly rejoices. "That did it!" She hits the save button. "Just gotta show 'em who's boss." She breathes back with a sigh of confidence and checks the time on her Mickey Mouse watch. Sliding in a floppy disk, she waits for the information to save as backup. Popping it back out, she says, "And that is it! I am done for today!" Connie gets up, puts her jacket on, bids adieu to the few co-workers doing overtime. After she walks out the door, somebody tacks up yet another notification on an already crammed bulletin board in the office.

Outside, Connie breathes in the crisp evening air. Light traffic passes by. Taking a look around, Connie sees something to the left side which piques her interest. She walks in that direction, following the need to satisfy her curiosity.

She stops directly in front of a parked white van displaying airbrushed art inspired by Alberto Vargas. A voluptuous pin-up girl adorns the side entrance. Connie attempts to use her hands as blinders to block out the reflection so she can peek through the passenger's side window.

"Huh. Nice."

Then she sees a lone man standing at the corner who immediately catches her attention. He doesn't look to be anybody she recognizes from around the area.

She steps nearer, noticing his physical appearance — an attractive fellow with three tones of tousled, carefree and wild curly blond hair. The lightest covers the top, medium gold in the middle, and a brown shade down to the collar. He's of average height from between five foot ten and five foot eleven. Trendy though casual, he looks like he could have stepped off the set of a music video, in a light powder blue blazer with matching slacks, a visible dark pink shirt peeks through underneath. The oddest thing is, he wears black Ray-Ban Wayfarer sunglasses. At night? What was he hiding?

Connie says to herself, "He looks interesting." She calls out, "Excuse me? Sir? Is that your van?" She starts walking up to him.

He points to himself, then turns to see the vehicle she's talking about, peering over the rims of his sunglasses. With certainty, he answers quickly. "Uh, no." Glancing over, he thinks about something. "It might be the band's van from two blocks away."

Connie says, "Well, whoever's it is, it's nice!"

He answers with a shrug, "Not my thing. Um, I think there's a parking ban going on because of filming. Don't hold me to it. But, if you look…," he walks over towards the side of the San-San building. "…there are signs posted with something on them."

"Oh, I didn't know that." She bites her bottom lip, wanting to engage in making small talk with the attractive stranger in her sights. Even his voice is a pleasant mid-tone, almost Long Island-sounding, a tinge strong on the "s" pronunciation. Maybe he was from there? "Are you an actor?" she asks him.

Immediately, he lets out a loud laugh. "Me?" He grins wildly, shaking his head. "That's a first!"

Connie tries to backtrack, unsure if it's an insult, even though she likes his laugh. "I mean, you kind of look like you could be."

He glances up at her. "An actor? No. I'll take it as a compliment, though," he answers with a huge smile. "Are you?"

His response makes her laugh a little. "No. Nowhere near."

"You have that Diane Keaton and Molly whatshername look? The young girl that's in a new film, the redhead? I don't know? Some *Ridgemont High* type of movie I detest, coming out next month. I read about her in a magazine recently."

Connie lets out a laugh. "Molly Ringwald? And Diane Keaton?" She looks down in shyness. "You have an active imagination. To have a total stranger tell me I look like either something out of a Woody Allen film or one of those teen movies? Wow. Just, wow. And, I'm not twenty."

He can tell she's flattered and pours it on. "Would it have helped if I said, a young Elizabeth Taylor?" He grins mischievously.

"Now, you're stretching it!" she giggles back. Connie seizes her humor and says, "Only, I can't think of anybody you resemble."

He tilts his sunglasses in the awkwardness of the compliment.

Connie glances at her watch. "As much as I've enjoyed this back and forth thing, I have to get going. Long day at work tomorrow, and I need all the rest I can get."

"Ah. Not a night owl," he remarks.

"No. Not with the work I do. Weekends are a different story." She smiles back. "Well, enjoy your night. Bye." Connie begins to walk away when she hears him.

"G'night."

She turns and sees his head tilted at a funny angle, with hands in his pockets.

Connie giggles back, not knowing what to think of the stranger, other than he's a bit of an oddball character who has a lot of charm and somewhat flirty in a subtle way. She bites her bottom lip, thinking of their exchange while hailing a cab.

The next day at the office, Connie continues to type. A woman drops a stack of papers on her desk. Ted puts his hand on the top of her computer, tapping a beat. Her eyes bob up.

"Yes?"

"Nothin'," he smiles back. "I just like to fool with ya."

Connie shakes her head and types more.

"That's obvious, Ted."

Suddenly he remembers something. "Hey, before I forget... Don't know if you noticed, but there's a parking ban going on about two blocks away. So, traffic might get a little hairy if you know what I mean."

"Yeah. I found out last night. I talked to somebody about it already."

"So, you wanna be an extra? I can get you an issue of *Backstage*."

"No, thanks, Ted. I'm not cut out for acting."

"I don't know if it's really acting or standing around."

"The same from my angle."

Ted finishes tapping out the beat with his fingertips as he tells her, "Suit yourself." He begins to turn away.

Connie bites her bottom lip, with a thought on her mind.

"Ted? Can I ask you a question?"

"Sure."

"Do you think I look like Diane Keaton or Molly Ringwald in any way?"

Ted answers back with a smile, "Oh, I thought you were going to ask if you looked like Bo Derek. Then I could say you were a ten!"

Connie groans and rolls her eyes. "Oh, brother. You're no help." She gets up and drops off some papers on another desk while shaking her head in disbelief.

Ted follows her and says, "Hey, you wanted to know. Besides, why would you ask?"

Connie turns to him. "Curiosity. But, of course, I'll get a wise-ass remark from you."

"Is it that important?"

She glances around before answering, "No." Taking a deep breath, she says, "I'm leaving now. T.G.I.F.!" Connie answers, putting her jacket on. "I will see you Monday, like normal. Goodnight."

"Goodnight, Bo," Ted smiles back.

Connie rolls her eyes, slipping away down the short corridor to the main door.

Getting off the elevator, she sees the old, grizzled janitor. "Goodnight, Richard."

He turns to her. "Goodnight, Miss. Ayers."

Connie walks out of San-San, checking her watch. The beeping of a horn grabs her attention. A bicyclist zooms in front of a car, with the driver angrily throwing his fist in the air. She gives a glance around when the stranger she had talked with the previous night, walks the same path. He wears a nearly identical outfit but in different colors, still sporting the Ray-Bans.

Connie calls out, "Hi!"

The stranger turns to see her and waves back with a smile.

She trots over to him.

He grins, "Hey, yourself! Molly, right?"

"Nope," she answers with teasing flirtation.

"Well, I'm pretty good with names...," he pushes up his sunglasses, "...but I'm not gonna be able to get it if you don't give me a hint."

"I don't know what kind?" She thinks for a moment. "What's with you and the sunglasses at night?"

"It helps me stand out," he giggles. "It's not like I'm Stevie Wonder." With that, he illustrates the famed singer's swaying side to side movements with a spot-on impersonation.

Connie bursts out laughing. She tries to regain her composure, but only leads the amusing stranger to do the same. Soon, both are in laughing fits. Coming down from the hilarity, Connie manages to say, "Oh, that is bad!"

He smiles back, "I'm a huge Stevie fan and have listened to his music for years. I couldn't resist. I wish I had his talent." Looking down, he pulls off the sunglasses. "But, uh, I do have sight." He produces a broad grin, and reveals a pair of dark amber eyes distinctly of European origin.

Connie is caught off-guard, mesmerized by his looks without being hidden. She thinks for a moment, "I'm just going to tell you." Holding her hand out, she says, "Hi, my name is Connie. Connie Ayers."

He puts his hand out in a similar fashion with a grin, shaking hers. "Nice to meet you, Connie. Philip Reinhardt. Most people call me Phil. Philly's another one. Then again, I've been called worse." He rolls his eyes at the thought.

"I think Philip is a great name. It has an air of sophistication."

Philip animatedly answers her with a tinge of British flair. "Tea and crumpets if you will?" he giggles back.

"Yeah!" she answers, playing along. Growing serious again, she says, "So, I was trying to think of what you might be — your occupation. You can't be a plumber," she smiles. Closing her eyes, she tries to imagine what he is, "I can't see you as someone in the sports field." She opens them. "You're in the entertainment field, somehow."

Philip looks at her, slightly surprised by her guess. "Uh, yeah. How did you come up with that?"

"I used to work at Howard Johnson's midtown. A lot of people would come by, and I got to know on-sight what jobs they had by what they wore. For you, the giveaway was the hair. It's meticulous. Not everybody goes around with three colors, either. The suit, and of course, the sunglasses to show how important you are." She squints. "I'll go even further. You're into music, aren't you?"

Philip raises his brows in surprise. He puts on a big grin. "Have we met before?"

"No. I don't think so."

"Gee. I didn't think I glowed like neon."

Connie lets out a nervous laugh. "OK. Maybe a little bit." She continues giggling.

Out of curiosity, he asks, "What color?"

"What? Neon?"

Philip nods his head, "Mmm. Yeah."

"Uh, yellow. Maybe orangey."

"Oh, good. I was afraid you were going to say red. That's like saying you look like a cheap motel."

Connie laughs hard. She catches her breath between giggles. "Um, in all seriousness, you look like one. Somebody in the biz. Besides, your little Stevie Wonder imitation was perfect!"

Philip looks away with a big grin, then turns back, "What else can you tell?"

Connie turns her attention to him, wanting to look more deeply into his eyes. She then figures her stare would be too odd and creepy for a stranger. She shrugs her shoulders and says, "Nothing. Nothing else. Why? Should I?"

"Just asking," expertly, he flips on the pair of sunglasses like a gunslinger. Philip gives her a huge smile, exposing two rows of near-perfect teeth. A charming sight, indeed.

Connie grins back, shaking her head in amusement. "A musician for sure." She glances out at the street, putting a hand to her hair. "Well, it looks like I'll be getting going. I'm so pooped out from working so much this week. It was nice seeing you, or should I say, bumping into you again?"

She hails a cab. One pulls up. Looking back at Philip starting to walk away, she mutters to herself, "He is cute." She gets inside. Before the cab pulls away, she rolls down the window. "Philip! How do I find you?"

He stops, spins around, and sings his answer in the form of The Spinners' "I'll Be Around."

Connie cannot get over this guy. Either he's a real ham, or he's incredibly charming.

Philip spins back around with hands in his pockets, strolling down the street.

She rolls up the window, still shaking her head in disbelief.

"Very cute."

The following Thursday, Connie leaves her office at the same time. She looks around at the wide sidewalk in front of the building. Furrowing her brows, she checks her watch. Would Philip show up again? She glances out at the traffic, moving to a rhythm. A thought crosses her mind. Maybe she scared him away by guessing too many things about him? At the same moment, a couple crosses her path. She jogs over to the side of the building where passerby appears. Nothing other than the usual people in work attire released from the daily zoo. No guys dressed in Ray-Bans and unconstructed suits.

Who was Philip Reinhardt, and why did he fascinate Connie so much in two chance meetings? Aside from being a snazzy dresser, he had a wicked sense of humor and a lot of confidence — killer smile. Sweet laugh! Charming and spontaneous. A bit of a crazy character. He seemed to stand apart from other guys. Not overly flirty. Beautiful in a different way. Softer than typical macho men. Almost childlike in demeanor, and high school senior coolness. Philip couldn't be that young, though. His strong reaction to the van she pointed out was slightly peculiar. He was involved with the music business in some capacity. But what? Executive? Musician? Manager? Someone behind the scenes found on the credits of an album?

It disappoints Connie that he's not around. Then again, he was probably busy.

At least that week.

She goes to hail a cab.

* * *

Another week passes in that same déja vu haze. Get out of work. Check the time. Walk towards the street to catch a cab back home.

Then it happens.

Philip stands at the corner.

Connie is a little surprised, though pleased. She walks up to him with his back partly turned.

"Hey stranger," she says in a playfully sly tone.

Philip turns around quickly to face her.

"Uh, hi. What…," He asks in a confused way that tells her he's shocked to see her show up again.

Did he think she was following him?

Connie hesitates for a moment.

"Oh, I work here." She throws her head in a way to angle at the large building in back. "I didn't want you to think that I was like a stalker or something."

He says with a grin, "I was beginning to wonder what was going on."

"Me too," she giggles back. "Same place. Same time. Same people. I mean, what are the chances of that happening? Three times? Spooky! It's not like I believe in coincidences."

"Fate?" Philip asks. "Maybe I need to check my horoscope?"

Connie laughs.

"I don't know if that would do anything? I mean, yeah, it's weird. There's like several million people in this city, and this happens." She puts her hand out.

"What do we do?" he asks.

Connie answers, timidly, "Take advantage of it?" She bites her bottom lip.

Philip gives an awkward laugh. "Ah. I don't think it'll go very far." He checks the time on his watch. "I gotta go," he answers with a hasty breath, as though wanting to make a quick getaway.

A disappointed Connie watches Philip walk down the street until he's shrouded in the darkness past an unlit lamppost.

"You're not the first guy to run away from me," she says to herself.

Connie wonders though if she scared him off by being a little too bold. What was she hoping would happen after only talking with Philip three times? Take advantage of the moment? That was probably the dumbest thing to come out of her mouth in a long time. He was in the music business, and with that a bevy of beauties who would grab his attention. Prettier, talented, and possibly more willing to move faster. But, a feeling had overcome the computer operator. She wasn't normally flirty, but something about him made her a little bolder.

There would be another time.

She was sure of it.

"Connie, you have to watch yourself out there," Gary advises, as an army of computer tapping surrounds them.

A Xerox machine zaps out an identical copy of the latest front-page work listing.

Connie turns to Gary. "What do you mean?"

"Haven't you paid any attention to the local news? Yeah. There's a lot of girls getting mugged or robbed on the streets. Gotta watch out for street vermin."

Connie walks back to her work station with Gary following her. She organizes a large number of papers neatly on the desk. "Gee, thanks, Gary." Looking out at the other work spaces, she thinks. "You know, it's either you or Ted I get to hear these things. Don't you have a girlfriend? Doesn't he by now?"

Gary asks her, "What? You think we're homos or something?"

"I didn't say that. I'm only indicating you must have somebody else you can tell these things to."

Before he can answer, she spins around to face him. "Why me? What is it about me that you or Ted find so fascinating?"

"You can take it, Connie. You dish it right back. Some other girls might get all pissy about what we say. Besides, they're all taken."

"You mean, I need to find a man to get you off my back? What would you prefer? A guy about six-three with bulging muscles? Or like a nerdy kind of guy who wears a tie and big glasses?"

"Whatever makes you happy, Connie. I'll be happy for you."

Connie puts her long jacket on, picking up her pocketbook from the floor. She looks at him, unamused.

Gary catches her staring, feeling uncomfortable by it. "What? What are you looking at me like that for?"

"I'm looking at you like street vermin," Connie answers, tossing her keys and catching them with one hand. She walks past the workstations and out the door.

"Ooh!" A voice from behind a nearby computer pipes up.

Gary turns to see who reacted, then shakes his head in defeat.

Connie leaves the building. She tosses her head up to the night sky. Facing the street, Philip appears carrying a black guitar case. She bounds over to the end of the sidewalk.

"Hey!" she calls out.

Philip turns around, knowing it's Connie. "Oh, hey. Look, I really need to get going. Can't be late."

Connie answers aloud. "You're a guitar player."

"How didja guess?"

"Gee, I don't know. That guitar case might have something to do with it. You are a musician."

Tight-lipped, he says, "You got me." He looks out into the distance. "I really can't be late."

She turns to him. "What if I joined you? Not that far, but I need to go in the same direction. No cab this time." Glancing at him, she knows he's feeling awkward by her persistence. Maybe it was wrong of her, but she wasn't about to let him go that fast. "Look, it's not like you're the first guy to run away from me," she answers with annoyance.

Perhaps it was her slight pushiness that makes Philip feel guilty, or how she said others would run away. Maybe he knew that feeling? Thinking for a split second, he says, "Come on," with an angled nod.

The two walk along the sidewalk, getting to know one another better.

At least that's what Connie is hoping.

"So, where are you from?" she asks.

Philip checks for traffic in all directions. "From?" He briefly gets distracted as passing vehicles speed by, then crosses with her trailing behind. "East coast."

"Gee, talk about vague. That's only fourteen states. I'm trying to detect your accent. Long Island? New Jersey?"

"What would make you think that?" he asks in curiosity.

"You kind of have that Springsteen thing going on. Your way of talking and a mystique. Something about you, and I can't put my finger on it. I could be wrong."

He snickers back, "You've got an active imagination. There are only a few things I've got in common with The Boss. New Jersey is not one of them. Yeah. We're both east coast guys, like about a million other musicians." He checks his watch. "Ten more blocks to go in fifteen minutes. That'll never work." Philip shakes his head, looking out at traffic. After watching several vehicles pass by, he hails a cab. Connie gets in, followed by the guitar case nearly hitting her in the jaw. Lightly, she puts her hand on it to lower the item away from her face. Philip gets in. Awkwardly, they sit next to each other. Two nearly perfect strangers separated by an instrument case horizontally overlapped between them as if it were a sprawled out sleeping child. Connie looks out the window, realizing the street she intended to split from him has passed by. They continue until the cab pulls up to a darkened street, all except a few low-lit light posts overhead. Philip gets out and looks back at Connie, who exits after him.

"Was Caddy in your way?"

"No," Connie answers without knowing who he's mentioning. Then it occurs to her. "Wait, who's Caddy?"

"You'll meet her."

"I'm not that tired. Are you telling me, Caddy is your guitar?"

Philip grins back, "Yeah."

She looks around, realizing how dark and desolate the street is. A rat runs by them, giving Connie the ick-factor. There is nothing more than litter on the sides, graffiti scrawled doors and a whiff of urine in the air.

"Where are we?" she asks a little startled.

"The classiest place around."

Connie does a full rotation. Her eyes swing back and forth.

"You took me to a slum?"

"I'd like to think it's nicer than that. At least the inside."

Philip walks over to a dark beige building with white graffiti scrawled of an armpit. Triple lines underneath indicate the stench. He presses the buzzer, waiting for the click.

Connie eyes the artwork. "Classy," she shakes her head.

He opens the door, leading a guiding hand for her to step inside first.

She looks around, realizing the interior is far more pleasant than the exterior.

Philip walks up a set of stairs, through a short hallway and into a room that looks cozy enough to be a lounge. A soft couch, coffee table, and a set of lamps provide a kinder atmosphere. Connie looks at a poster on the wall. A beautiful woman illustrated wearing a beaded gown in the Art Nouveau style of Czech painter Alphonse Mucha perched on the wall. A platinum RIAA plaque is on the adjacent wall next to the control room. Philip puts his guitar case on the coffee table and opens it. Inside, he gently pulls out a light pink Fender Stratocaster guitar.

Connie leans over to take a better look at his prized instrument. "Oh, wow," she marvels. "It's pink!"

Philip grins back widely. "This is Caddy. She's been my girl since seventy but was born at the Fender factory in sixty-four. That was before they sold the company to CBS the following year. Her color was a little lighter before. That was called shell pink. I named her Caddy because I wanted a color that stood out. You know? A little more oomph," he emphasizes with a clenched fist. "Brighter. She's a pink Cadillac shade I got with the custom paint job. Hence, her name. I do need to get her re-fretted, though. She's gone through a lot with me." He takes a deep breath. "I told you I had a few things in common with Springsteen? This is one of them. We're both Fender guys. No other electric guitar will do."

"Nice." Connie answers before asking, "What is re-fretting?"

He points. "It's where these lines…metal bars on the neck need to be taken out and reshaped. I'll have to give you the whole anatomy of a Stratocaster. Guitar strings are actually coiled wire. When you play it enough over time, the so-called strings or wires hit the frets, that they get filed down in the process. It's metal on metal action. I should get it done before she starts giving me serious problems. Buzzing, or sounding flat. Sound stuff. It's a tedious task that needs to be done by a professional. I wouldn't begin to know, and I'd be afraid of breaking her! I don't want to do that," his eyes widen.

"No. Of course not!" She answers with the same amount of fear.

Turning her attention to the next room, Connie asks, "Is that a recording room?"

Surprised at her interest, Philip says, "Yeah. It is. Wanna tour? I can show you around. I'm guessing you've never been in a studio?"

"No."

"Well then, let me tell ya about it."

Philip leads her to the control room, where a casually dressed black man gets up from his chair parked next to a large console. Chewing gum, he manages a smile. The guitarist puts his hand out, "Connie, this is Jermaine, our head engineer. He bullies us if he doesn't like the way something sounds."

Jermaine takes a deep breath, shaking his head.

"Jermaine, this is Connie."

Connie smiles back, shaking Jermaine's hand.

He says, "Pleasure to meet you. Are you backup?"

"B...?" she attempts to comprehend.

Philip says, "No. She's not a singer."

"Oh," Jermaine answers, mildly surprised.

"I'm just showing her around."

"OK. Are you aware you're half an hour early?"

"I thought it started at nine?"

"Nine was yesterday. Nine thirty today."

Philip nods his head in understanding. "Thanks for letting me know. I'm going to continue showing Connie around."

He shows her the studio, crammed with equipment. Connie's introduction is to a world of mixers, sequencers, compressors, consoles, equalizers, recorders, and five different microphones. In the middle of it all, she releases a yawn. Her eyes grow heavy, but she tries not to show her fatigue in such a fascinating setting — a real music studio.

"That's Achieve Recording," he says with pride.

Going back to the lounge area, Connie sits down on the couch, struggling to stay awake.

Ten minutes later, two men walk through the door. Perry Leonard, a tall man of black and Latino origins, carries a guitar case, and the other, Mitch Evans, a small, sleek, dark-haired man, taps out a beat on his knee with drumsticks. They walk by Connie, who smiles at them.

"Are you backup?" Perry asks her.

"No."

Perry and Mitch look at each other. They walk over towards the door. Mitch says quietly, "New publicist. Gotta be."

"Mmm. I'll say she's an interviewer from a magazine. Girlfriend is out of the question."

Connie overhears the conversation, but can't comprehend the last line. What did that guy mean? Sure, it was too early to tell if something could develop between her and the guitar player, but out of the question?

Perry continues, "Mitch? Whatever happened to...? He stops to remember the guest. "I'm not going to get into anything. It's his life."

Mitch opens the door to the recording room, letting in Perry and himself. They close it behind them.

Connie furrows her brows in confusion. She shakes her head and sinks to the arm of the couch. Another yawn overcomes her.

Inside the recording room, Perry unlocks his case, pulling out a black Fender Precision bass guitar. Mitch goes over to the drum kit, checking it out.

Perry fixes his bass strap. "Hey, Boss? Who's the lady outside?"

"A guest," Philip answers, wiping down Caddy's strings.

Mitch begins guessing.

"Backup?

"No."

"Publicist?"

"No."

"New assistant?"

Philip glances at the ceiling briefly. Closing his eyes at the line of questioning, he continues to fiddle with Caddy's tunings.

"She's a female, so she's gotta be something," Mitch pries.

"Yeah. She's a guest," Philip replies affirmatively.

Perry checks his tunings and further asks, "What happened to—"

Philip cuts him off immediately, "That's over." Slightly miffed, he goes over to a piece of equipment to turn it on, then flips switches.

Everybody remains silent from the awkward moment.

Mitch hits the snare, followed by the toms.

"I wonder if he changed the tone?"

Jermaine answers over the intercom in the control room, "Mitch, I'm not taking any guff from you."

Mitch sinks in the chair. His eyes dart back and forth. "I didn't know that was on."

"Phil turned me on."

Philip bursts out laughing while strapping on his guitar.

The three get down to business and go through lines before doing a take.

"Let's take it from where we left off yesterday with just the vocals. Then we'll try with everything else," Philip says.

Time goes by with one-hour spinning into another. To the outside world, the three musicians cannot be heard from soundproofing foam muting all of their activity. Even Connie is oblivious to the music and laughter in the next room.

Jermaine wipes his eyes and stretches when he enters the recording room.

"Fellas, that's all I can take for tonight. We've got the weekend ahead, but I have to get things done with the family. I don't know what you want to do."

Perry asks, "What time is it?

"Five. I'm gonna close up shop," Jermaine answers before going back to the control room.

Philip looks ahead, then tells the other guys, "I'll be right back." He opens the door to the control room, closing it after.

Jermaine flips switches off, and turns down knobs. He looks back at Philip. "You can do what you want. Just lock up. Oh, and the princess you brought with you turned into Sleeping Beauty early on." Philip glances back at him, a little surprised. "Yeah. Go ahead and see for yourself. I gave her a blanket. Don't think she heard anything. Those walls are pretty much soundproof. I don't know why you brought her here if you planned on leaving her in the other room?"

Philip can't answer, as he has no idea why he took her there himself. He walks back to the recording room through the control door.

Perry finishes locking the case for his instrument. He turns to the drummer, "Mitch, where are we gonna catch a cab?"

"At five in the morning? I have no idea. At the corner?"

"I was thinking, we're gonna have to walk a little further."

"Got a flashlight? We'll need it, so we don't run into any used needles."

Philip looks at the two, uneasy by their exchange.

Perry asks, "You comin', Boss?"

The guitarist turns his attention in the direction of the lounge.

"I'm gonna stick around for a little longer. See if I can get a few parts done on my own."

"OK. Well, see you later."

"Yep. Bye."

Perry and Mitch leave the studio.

Philip walks out of the room and sees Connie curled up on the couch, fast asleep. Jermaine shuts off the light in the control room and stops when he sees the guitarist looking at the sleeping guest. He waves goodbye, then heads down the stairs.

The guitarist realizes how late it is. Not wanting to wake Connie up and send her on her way home at such an early time, he considers the circumstances. It's not the best neighborhood, and certainly not right for a lady to walk alone, even to catch a cab. There's something about her that makes him want to do the right thing and wait until daylight. He shuts off the light in the lounge and returns to the recording room for a few more hours.

Connie gets to catch up with Philip the next week, where they walk along the city streets in a more pleasant area. As charming as one would expect Manhattan to be, including the stench of urine, and the sights of hundreds of people taking to the sidewalks, moving about. Connie looks at Philip, realizing how good he looks in the daylight.

She turns to him and asks, "Where are we?"

"We are on Fifth." He looks at her. "You don't get out much, I'm guessing?"

"Does my naiveté show?"

"I didn't think it was about being naive. Just not knowledgeable on neighborhoods. That's all." Philip raises his brows.

"So, where were we last week? Alphabet City?"

"No. Lower east side. Maybe not the best area, but the studio is fine. Ah, that's why I felt like I owed you. To go to a better section."

Connie glances down. "Hey, I'm really sorry about falling asleep like that. I missed everything going on. I was so tired and didn't even know it!"

Philip gets distracted by a man who he locks eyes with. He averts his attention quickly.

Connie stops for a moment. Philip can't be sure if she's caught the glance. She looks up. "Look, I know I'm a workaholic. It's not like I do it for the money even. I don't get out much. You're right. That's why I need to change things." She looks down out of guilt. "I'm not going to put in so much overtime. That way, I can hang out. You know? We can have more fun."

He answers her with immediacy, almost fearful. "You don't have to do that."

Connie's taken aback by his response. "OK," she says in an understanding though confused tone.

Philip notices the reaction on her face.

She walks next to him silently.

He tries to remedy the situation. "You can do what you want. Just do it for the right reasons."

"And what are the right reasons?"

"What you honestly want, more than anything."

"How astute," Connie answers dryly.

"Some things aren't always easy to explain."

Shaking her head, Connie says back, "Um, whatever you say."

They continue down the street, among the crowd.

Chapter 2

The clicking of computer keys fills the office, until the Xerox machine chimes in with rolling thunder. Green letters track through everyone's screens in an almost synchronized manner. Pages pour out of printers, as though they were soft-serve ice cream dolloped at the edge of desks. Several fall to the floor, beckoning their masters to pick them up at once.

Maria, a pretty, olive-skinned Puerto Rican with heavy violet eye-shadow, grins as she looks over at Connie, who's in a daydream.

"Whatcha doin' Connie?"

Connie sits up, startled, clicking hard on a button. She rubs her eyes and yawns.

Maria continues, "That's what I thought. By the way, what's been goin' on with you lately?"

"What?" Connie answers, confused.

"You've got your head in the clouds. And I've seen that shit-eating grin on your face like all the time lately."

Denise, a tall black woman, walks by the two ladies sitting close to each other.

"I'll bet it's a man."

The commotion alerts Ted, who joins in on the action.

"What's goin' on, ladies?"

Maria rolls her eyes, walking towards the line for the Xerox machine. Denise goes back to her desk quickly.

Ted glances around, noticing how the two women clear the area.

"What's the matter? I put deodorant on," he lifts his arm, taking in a heavy whiff. Again, he looks around. "Well then, I'll just see how Connie's doing." He goes over to her, noticing how awkward she reacts to him being next to her computer. "How ya doin' Connie?"

"I'm fine, Ted."

"Couldn't help but overhear Maria. You know, she's right. Something different about you lately."

"It's only your suspicious mind playing tricks on you."

"Ooh. Nice Elvis reference," Ted leans over. "So, who's the boy on the playground that's caught your eye?"

"What?" Connie answers in confusion.

Ted leans his hand over the computer and presses down on a couple of keys, producing the words, HE IS CUTE. Again, he hits a key. This time the same sentence continuously crawls down the screen, creating a pattern all its own.

"Whoa!" A voice from behind answers, watching the screen up ahead.

A startled Connie stumbles over her words. "How did you... I didn't..."

"Connie. I know how to do these things. It was easy to recall the last bit you wrote. So, who is this guy that's got your tongue, or whatever else he might be able to capture?" Ted answers assuredly.

She rolls her eyes.

"It's nothing, Ted. Absolutely nothing."

"Defensive."

"You're making something out of nothing."

Gary saunters by, looking at Connie then Ted. "What's up?"

Connie rolls her eyes again, "Oh, great."

Ted answers, "Connie finds a guy cute."

Gary glances her way.

"Anybody I know?"

"No," Connie answers sharply. "Now, can I get some work done? First, it's Maria and Denise. Now, it's you two."

Arnold Edwards wanders through. As the office boss, he's a stockily built man who wears glasses down to his nose. Neatly dressed in a short-sleeved button-up shirt, his tie flaps about over a protruding belly. He rubs the back of his thick neck and brushes the top of his head, and whatever little hair is left. He stands over one of the workers. "Do you know how many inventory lists we have to go through? Can you imagine how many of these we'll get for the Christmas rush?"

Bryan, a tall black man, answers quickly, "That's months away, Mr. Edwards."

"No, it's not, Rodgers," Mr. Edwards sticks his neck out defiantly. "It may seem it, but it's not. Months roll by before you know." He turns to all of the workers, making sure they hear him. "We need productivity, people! We're the best ones in the building, so much so that we'll be having visitors."

Maria stands next to the Xerox machine, loading a page. "Who's that?" she asks.

"Corporate, Delgado. Suits directly from Japan. So, I want everybody to be dressed with perfection and professionalism when they do come here."

"When will that be?"

"They'll get back to me on that. I don't know yet." He walks through another row, meeting up with Connie, Gary, and Ted. Addressing Connie, he asks, "So, how's my busy little bee doing?"

Ted once again answers for her, "She's found a cute guy."

Mr. Edwards doesn't quite know what to say, "Yeah, well, let me know when the wedding is so that I can send you a nice fruit basket."

Connie watches the scene unfold awkwardly. He walks away. Suddenly, she thinks of something and gives chase with a slow trot past co-workers into the boss' office. Closing the door, she addresses him. "Mr. Edwards? I need to talk to you about something. Um, the overtime I've been putting in? I'd like to have fewer hours if that's possible? I'm just looking for Thursdays and Fridays. That's all. The rest of the time, I'm free."

He briefly glances down, then back at her.

"OK."

"That...that's all?" she asks in confusion.

"Yeah. You're the one who wanted overtime every day. It's not my business why you would want it. Hey, I'm happy to get out at the normal time myself. You, Gary, and Ted are the ones who stay behind."

Connie backs away, holding her palms together.

"Thank you, Mr. Edwards. It means so much to me."

She leaves the office.

He looks up, peering from the rims of his glasses before pulling them off to massage the bridge of his nose.

On a bright, sunny, calm day, Connie explains to Philip the merits of having a good computer. They come across a newsstand, stopping by to take a look at what there is to offer. The dark brown chicken-coop-sized box is full of magazines. Signs offer cigarettes and lottery tickets.

"You'd think that these machines would be so great, like the commercial they aired during the Super Bowl. Sure, it has a great graphic interface. If you know how to use it."

Philip pulls out his wallet while Connie talks. He looks at the vendor and says, "Newport." The musician presents his license as verification. The vendor nods back. Philip takes out a bill and looks at the magazines.

Connie continues, "I know it's just listings, but they've got us over a hump working on this stuff. Anyway, I'm chewing your ear off about the merits of the Apple Macintosh computer system. Well..."

He checks out the various titles, ignoring his acquaintance's concern over the latest computer technology. *People*, *GQ*, *Cosmopolitan*, *Time*, *Newsweek*, *Life*, all of them pass by him. His eyes scan more choices of; *National Geographic*, *Shape*, *Sports Illustrated*, *Motor Trend*, and loads of sports-related publications.

Connie says, "Oh, I wound up getting less overtime on Thursdays and Fridays so we..." her voice trails off more indefinitely, noticing he's not paying attention to anything she has to say. "...could hang out...more."

He leans in to pick up a copy of *Billboard*. Flipping through it, he checks listings of what's hot on the charts. The vendor hands him back change, which Philip shoves back into his pocket along with the pack of cigarettes. He returns the magazine and picks up *Musician* instead. Scanning the pages, he can't find much in it and places the magazine back. Something else catches his eye instead.

Oblivious to his choices, Connie continues to try and make small talk.

"I was so surprised the boss went along with it. I won't tell you what led up to me asking. It's still embarrassing for me. OK. I'll admit it was my fault." She puts her hand out for greater emphasis.

Philip pulls out a magazine that has his full attention. He shuts the outside world off, with the inclusion of putting Connie on mute. Slowly, he looks at the cover and flips through until he stops to examine it further.

Connie looks slightly over his shoulder and says with disdain, "Oh, you're one of those guys that's into doom and gloom. Isn't it enough that they have the local news on about four times a day? Then, later at night, it's world news. I mean, how much are we supposed to take?"

He looks up, staring past the peeled paint on the stand's facade. Closing his eyes, Philip takes a deep breath. Putting the magazine back on the rack, he walks away. Connie quickly trails behind, attempting to catch up with him.

"What happened?"

"Nothing," he answers quickly. Pulling out the pack of cigarettes, he rips through the cellophane. Fishing out a cigarette, he digs in his deep pockets only to produce a lighter. He lights it in a flash, takes a long drag, and closes his eyes. Philip says, "You're a nice lady, but I don't know if you really want to hang out with me."

Connie glances at people passing by when answering back, "What's wrong with that?"

He shakes his head, "I come with a lot of baggage."

"So? Nobody's perfect."

Philip gives a weary sigh as he takes another drag from the cigarette. "I'm not what you think or what you're hoping for." His eyes meet the ground in shame. "There's more to me than what you would ever imagine."

She furrows her brows. "I don't get it?"

Philip closes his eyes with a certain amount of discomfort. "Are you sure you want to do this?"

"Hang out with you? Yes, to everything."

"OK. Don't say I didn't warn you."

"I won't," Connie answers with utmost certainty.

Philip looks at her, slightly surprised by her reaction.

"Alright, then. Buckle up," he answers with a raised brow.

The two explore Greenwich Village with further depth. Philip shows Connie around different studios in a window-shopping manner. When they come across Electric Lady Studios on Eighth Street, Philip explains, "All of the studios look pretty bland from outside. Not like what you would imagine. They do that as not to create attention. If they were to be outlandish with bright colors popping everywhere and all the artists visible through windows, people would be flocking over here as if it were the latest Macy's window display. Nothing would get done. Time costs money because studios charge per session or sometimes per hour."

Connie sees her reflection staring back at her. Everything seems so exciting. Learning about studios, and simply being with her new acquaintance. Or was he a friend at this point? Could he be more?

Philip continues to talk about Electric Lady Studios.

"Now, with this one, Hendrix had it built for himself in seventy. That was unheard of at the time, an artist having their own studio. Of course, that would be short-lived. He only got to use it for ten weeks before his death in London." He takes a deep breath, "Time can be short. Too short." Getting back on track, he says, "Anyway, Stevie Wonder, Bowie, Patti Smith, Clash, AC/DC, Stones... They all recorded here."

Connie turns to him, putting her hand on his arm.

"Will you be around next week?"

Philip looks at her, slightly surprised by the excitement and physical approach she chooses to take. His answer is apprehensive. "Um, no. Not Friday. My schedule is full then."

"I know it's not my business, but more sessions?"

Philip methodically plans his wording. "Mmm. Work is more like it. Yeah." His glance falls upon Connie's hand on his sleeve.

Her eyes drop down to notice what he sees. Quickly, she retracts her arm back. "Sorry. A little too touchy-feely. You said it's not what you think. So, I'm just guessing that's one of the things. You don't like being physical."

"It's not...," he tries to find the right words. "It's not that. It's um..." biting his bottom lip. There's no way he can adequately explain things to her. "Never mind. Let's say it's difficult to think of."

"OK. I won't push it anymore if I've overstepped my bounds. I guess I'll go back to overtime. No big deal."

"I'll be back," Philip reassures her.

Connie eyes the sidewalk as she begins to walk away.

"Yep."

Philip suddenly has the urge to follow her a little way.

"Listen, Connie. We can still hang out the next day. That is if you want to?"

"I don't want to be a burden to you, or push you into some ridiculous guilt trip."

"You're not," he shakes his head. "Besides, you said you were willing to put up with me, and I'm going back on my word. That's something I don't do. I made a mental note, and now it's time for me to fulfill that goal. I need it. Come on. Let's plan this out. Next Saturday, at the usual rendezvous point. Is ten too early for you?"

"No," Connie smirks.

"OK. Ten it is. In front of the building."

Connie nods back in understanding.

They part ways, with each stealing glances at moments neither knows.

Keeping his promise, Philip turns up in front of the San-San building on the following sunny Saturday morning. Connie is only too happy to see her new friend again. They take in the sights and sounds of midtown, blending in with everybody else. The two walk along Seventh Avenue.

Connie says to him, "I'm surprised you were willing to go here. You know. You industry types."

He grins back, "What? I'm not a hermit!" Glancing back and forth as they cross the street, he tells her, "Besides, sometimes I'm up for a little people watching. Good to see what's happening outside in the world." Pulling off his sunglasses, he raises a brow, answering like a game show host. "You just got schooled, young lady."

Connie stops and snorts out a laugh. Looking at him makes her burst out in laughter again. They continue their journey when they come upon a gathering of people nearby.

Connie asks in curiosity, "I wonder what the brouhaha's about?"
Philip looks ahead. "Well, it could be a brou. Or it could be a ha ha. Any way you put it, it's going to be funny."

She snorts out another laugh. "Figures you would come up with something like that."

They hear a deep beat while getting closer. Philip's ears perk up.

"Oh, I know that sound. It's a Roland TR-eight zero eight. It's a drum machine that got discontinued as of last year. Let's check it out." He puts on his sunglasses and looks for an area from which to view. Several guys nearby wearing graffiti-backed jackets give a glance his way.

Connie looks over, seeing a young black teen sitting up on his hands and feet. Three others adjust large flattened TV boxes, spreading them out like newspaper for training a puppy.

"Street musicians?"

"Nope. Break dancers. They're just getting warmed up."

Several more youth move to the beat of the boombox situated a foot away, blaring.

A black teenager is wearing Cazal 607 glasses and Addidas sneakers as he barks out, "To yo daddy!"

Two NYPD officers watch the action next to Philip and Connie. One is tall with dark hair and a mustache. He chews gum while making remarks to his partner, a small Hispanic man.

"Wonder who's..." he looks over. "Should have known. The Robinson kid. He acts all ghetto."

"Which one, Sam?"

"The one with the big glasses and the bigger mouth. His dad works on Wall Street. How do ya think he got those glasses? He's on the upper west side. Good guy. Teaches kids how to do this kind of dancing in the Bronx. A lot of fun to watch."

Two Puerto Rican kids wearing blue jean vests approach the dancers. Robinson looks at them cautiously.

"Wanna shot?"

One nods back in agreement.

Robinson says, "Aww, right! East Harlem wants a piece!"

One of the boys drops down in a stooping position. Immediately, he twists and turns one side to the other in a quick succession of moves. While he spins, a young black boy wearing overalls walks over, putting a stop to the

Puerto Rican's dance moves as if he owns the block. He waves a hand. The older boy steps back in shock. The child stares at Robinson, who retaliates with a barrage of insults.

"Aww no. Get back on yo tricycle, boy. We ain't needin' no OshKosh B'gosh Sesame Street-wearing-toddler. This is for adults only!"

Somebody from the crowd quietly mutters, "Hurricane Harry."

Robinson's friend tinkers with the boombox, fast-forwarding the tape. Harry snaps his fingers in a commanding sign. He can't be any more than eight or nine years old. His small, wiry frame wiggles with anticipation. Robinson stands off to the side, arms crossed in a sulking manner. The big beat of "Planet Rock" by Afrika Bambaataa & the Soul Sonic Force gives life to the rhythm young Harry awaits.

Sam says, "Big mouth is about to get schooled by a nine-year-old."

Connie peeks between several people.

"Oh my God. He's just a little kid."

Philip stands in the back, next to the two cops.

Little Harry begins to do the electric boogaloo, waving his hands, popping in jerky motions. He gets down and twists his body to and fro as though he were the human version of the Rubik's Cube. The boy exhibits more finesse than an Olympic skater, spinning on his back, then his head, like an out of control top. Harry flips as though he were born with springs on his feet. Everybody stands with mouths agape at the juggernaut of switchblade-fast moves, earning him the name of 'Hurricane.' He finishes with a kip-up and polishes his hands off as though it's all in a day's work.

"Word up to yo momma! Look who be wearin' diapers now!" The boy crows valiantly.

Robinson pulls off his glasses, handing them to the cop with no hesitation.

"I'm gonna get you, little punk!" he sputters.

With long strides, he walks over to the boombox, then stops to fishtail his way back towards the brazen young boy. He puts his hand out. "I'm not going to battle you, kid. You're too good. Put it there."

Harry gives a hard slap connection with Robinson's hand in recognition and respect for his efforts. They hug it out.

The audience begins to disperse. Connie finds Philip among the small number of people left.

"Did you see that?" she grabs onto his sleeved arm in excitement. "That little kid! All those moves!"

Philip glances down at her touch. An edge of hesitation is in his voice. "Yeah." Wiping any thoughts, he continues with, "Did you hear what somebody said? Nine. I know what I did when I was nine. I collected frogs and rode my bike. These kids are far and a long distance away from Saturday morning cartoons and breakfast cereal." Stopping for a moment, he says to her, "Connie, there's something I need to tell—"

They're interrupted by a loud bang from nearby. Two cabs have collided. Smoke billows from the engine of the one who rear-ended the other. Philip yanks Connie from harm's way. The drivers from each vehicle get out, checking the condition of their yellow workhorses. Both begin screaming in their native tongue, one in Russian, the other in Arabic. The Russian kicks the tire of the offender, while the Arab man freaks out over the mess his engine is in. They continue to spew a tirade of unknown words, occasionally peppered with expletives in English.

Philip and Connie continue down the street as they hear the roar of a fire engine closing in on the scene.

She turns to him. "What were you starting to say? You needed to tell me something?"

Philip feels words but is unable to speak them.

"It can wait."

It's been nearly two months since Connie met Philip, and although things had progressed, they were not in the direction she had wished. He was attractive and smart. Even better, Philip was a gentleman. An all-around nice guy, but he never showed any sign of wanting to get serious with her, only weird jokes. She wished he would give her a nudge — the little okay, so reciprocation would be accepted. Connie couldn't be sure if Philip maybe already had somebody, and was loyal to her. Perhaps he had just gotten out of an awful relationship, and it was too soon for him to find another. Maybe Philip didn't want to perceive Connie as a rebound and needed the necessary time to heal. He didn't wear a ring. Always a good sign!

Then again, maybe he was separated. Philip seemed to have an issue with being physically touched. Perhaps it was from a painful experience when he was a child. Abuse? Molestation? Could she help him? Probably not. He stated that he had a lot of baggage. What did that mean? Did he have a deep dark life? Past? Current? Philip had become disturbed by the news magazine at the stand. She could try and find what it was, although that might have been a previous issue compared to the new week. What was with this guy, though? Connie ran every possible explanation as to why Philip hadn't made any moves on her. One thing crosses her mind — a possible hidden reason.

He just wasn't into her.

Philip and Connie head down to SoHo, past the coffee bars, boutiques, shops, and little galleries. Connie makes a move to take his arm in escorting fashion. His eyes slowly swing to her when she's not looking. Connie sees something that sparks her attention. A gallery shows Pop Art through the large window.

"Ooh! Let's check it out! Looks like fun," she expresses gleefully.

They walk in, disengaging from each other to check out individual artwork. Connie investigates the small bio attached to the wall, reading the words. Philip looks at some of the offerings by various artists. They stay close by each other, in case one has an opinion.

"Pretty cool. Especially Keith Haring's work. Very linear, and well, interesting." She gives a smirk at the colorful figure with an elongated male appendage in clear view. A couple of pictures down, she finds similar works.

Philip looks at the same image Connie had only moments ago. He closes his eyes, glancing down at the floor. Averting his sights from the artwork, he sees the other two near it. The sexual content makes him take a step back.

Connie reads another bio, when she feels a light breeze, and hears echoed footsteps on the hardwood floor moving further away. She turns in time to see Philip quickly walking out the door. Connie rushes out, looking back and forth. Slowly she glances back, where he stands next to a coffee shop's wall with his head hung low.

Connie asks him, "What just..."

Philip shakes his head and raises his brows. He steps away from the wall. "It's not my thing."

"That's an understatement. I know some of the art is a little provocative." She takes a deep breath while he remains silent. "I'm not even going to ask what brought that on."

Philip reacts quickly. "It's nobody's business. OK?" With his hand out, he signals to stop. For a moment, he thinks, knowing how confusing things must look to Connie. "Sorry. It's not easy." He steps away, ruffling a hand through his hair out of irritation.

Cautiously, Connie asks, "Do you want to talk about it?"

He answers her with his back turned. "No."

Quietly, she makes a mental note. "Galleries are off the list." Glancing back at him, she asks, "Do you want me to get some coffee?"

"Yeah. OK," he says with ease.

"How would you like your coffee?"

"Black."

"OK. Black it is. How about a pastry to go with it? Cheese Danish? Croissant?"

"Sure."

"Which one?"

"Cheese Danish."

"Alright. Black coffee and a Cheese Danish coming up," she smiles cheerily, leaving to go inside the coffee shop. Walking in, she stops at the counter and puts in an order.

"Hi. Yeah. I'll have a Cheese Danish, croissant, black coffee, and a coffee with cream and su—" She turns her head off to the side, spotting Philip through the window talking with a woman who has a young child in tow. Her attention returns to ordering. "Uh, cream and sugar." Again, she looks out the window from where she stands. Philip looks to be talking animatedly to the woman, who pulls out a small notebook from her pocketbook. He writes something down as he explains to her. He then gives her a quick hug, and she walks hand in hand with the child down the street. Connie's attention turns when her order is ready. She picks up the items, still keeping an eye on Philip.

Philip has his back to the window when she walks out.

"Hey."

He turns around to see her hands full. Immediately, he helps her out.

"Better watch it. That coffee is hot!" Connie giggles as he takes the paper cup.

He retracts his hand, waving it.

"See? I told you it was hot!"

His eyes go wide. "You weren't kidding, huh?" he giggles back.

Connie shakes her head at his amusing reaction. "OK. Now, where are we going to go?" She looks around when she sees a bench nearby. "Right there."

The two sit on the bench while sipping on coffee and indulging in baked goods. Connie breaks off a piece of the croissant daintily before popping it in her mouth. Licking her fingers, she asks, "So, who was she? The woman you were talking with?"

Philip looks at the Cheese Danish when he says, "She needed directions." He takes a big bite.

"You hug everybody who needs directions? I mean, it's alright. An old girlfriend?"

He stops chewing and closes his eyes with a hint of anguish.

"I don't, and no, she's not," he answers, resuming his chewing.

Connie looks at him, digging deeper by saying, "It's not like I'm jealous or anything. You can be honest with me."

"Connie, believe me when I say, she's not an old girlfriend."

"OK," she looks down at the remainder of her croissant. "It's just that your whole demeanor changed after she asked for directions, from right before I went in and got the food."

"I simply needed the time to think, and sometimes little things mean the most."

"Oh. OK," Connie answers in the way of pretending to understand.

They continue to eat. Philip's eyes swing her way as he takes another sip of coffee.

At the office, Connie types out a list, bouncing her sights from a packet of papers to the computer screen. She scans the type with a finger pressed on the arrow key. Shaking her head, she audibly says, "Sixty-two pages."

Bryan answers her from in back. "Multiply that by two, and you'll get what we're in for the holiday season on every order." He shuffles pages while continuing. "The more electronics that are going into production, we'll see the results. It's all part of the daily grind, Connie. That's progress for you. Wonder if it'll reflect our paychecks?"

Denise shakes her head at a nearby workstation. "Pfft. Probably not."

Connie begins to print out the order. She glances over at Denise while biting her bottom lip.

"Denise, can I ask you a question?"

"Sure! What's up, Connie?"

"Um... What do you do with a guy you're interested in? I mean, do you wait for him to ask you out, or can the woman lead?"

"A date?" Denise asks loud enough.

Connie looks around, hoping nobody else hears their conversation above the sound of the printer.

"I knew it!" Maria shouts. "It's about Mr. Cute, isn't it?"

Connie has a hard time trying to stay serious. Her nose crinkles as she answers with a grin, "Yeah. He is cute." She raises her brows mischievously.

"Spill the beans, girl!"

"We've only hung out for a little while. Mostly after work."

"What does he do?"

"He's involved with music. I think he's a session player. I don't know, but I kind of like hanging out with him. Just chilling."

Denise takes Connie by the arm, "What you need to do is bring him to the nicest restaurant. Blow your entire paycheck on him. I'm talkin' caviar, champagne, the best bottle of wine you can afford, a big ol' steak dinnah."

Maria adds in, "You never wanna go with something you don't know. Like, take sushi or anything Asian. If you don't know how to eat with those little choppy things..."

"You mean, chopsticks," Denise corrects her.

"Yeah. Yeah. See what I mean? You'll look like a fool, and he'll take you for bein' stupid."

"Don't want that," Denise shakes her head disapprovingly and wags her finger. "Especially on a first date."

Patti goes over to hear the conversation.

"Did I hear someone say, their first date? Connie, was that you? Listen, you've got to take him out to a movie. It is the quintessential date. Hold on." She walks over to the countertop. Grabbing a newspaper, she rustles through the entertainment section and movie listings. "Let's see what's playing. *Beat Street*, *Ghostbusters*, and *Gremlins* is being released this week. The thing is, don't bring him to a movie that's already been released. Not even what premiered last week. Gotta stay current because you never know within a week if he saw those already."

Bryan says, "If you need a man's perspective, we like to be touched. A hand on the arm, or sometimes even a light feel of the chest, sort of a lean. It lets us know you're interested. It gives us ample time to make a small move, maybe. It's certainly a plus!"

Connie looks over at him in shock of how much attention she's garnered from merely asking for advice from Denise.

Stephanie steps up to her. "If he's cute, yeah, that's fine. But, if you find him seriously hot? You procreate with him to carry on that hotness."

Connie gives a confused expression. "Uh, Steph? Isn't that what you did with Jeffrey and Kyle's dads?"

Stephanie stares ahead and states, "I have to get my kids after school," then walks away.

Connie closes her eyes at the absurdity of advice she's been barraged with.

"Guys, I appreciate what you're doing, but I think I can handle the situation."

Ted calls out, "What did I miss?"

She rolls her eyes and grumbles, "And things were going so good."

Bryan answers back, gleefully, "Connie's looking for dating advice."

"Really?" Connie answers, turning wearily away.

Gary arrives back from lunch, glancing around at the co-workers who suddenly grow quiet and stare back at him.

Ted yells out, "Connie's goin' out on a date!"

Gary calls out, "That's fantastic!" He rushes towards them.

Connie rolls her eyes, quietly uttering, "No. No. No. Not Gary too."

Both Ted and Gary surround Connie, double-teaming their co-worker with a hug that engulfs her.

"Aww! Our little girl is growing up!" Gary answers proudly.

Smothered between two bodies, Connie answers to the scene in a muffled tone, "Good grief." She pulls away from the two. "I'm not a kid, guys! I've done this before. I just want to get it done the right way. I don't even know if he'll like me, like that." Her eyes meet the floor with a hidden sense of rejection already placed in her mind. In a mere whisper, she says to herself, "I don't know if anybody would."

Ted tries to be more serious. He throws an arm around her shoulder.

"Hey, just remember, if he hurts you in any way, he'll have to answer to us."

She glances down again with a growing smile, shaking her head at how these guys know the right thing to say when she doubts herself.

"OK. Deal."

"So, what does this guy you're so high on do?"

Connie bites her bottom lip.

"He's in the entertainment field."

"That's a pretty big field," Ted indicates.

She closes her eyes when answering, "He's into music, like...a lot."

Gary says, "Ooh, impressive."

Ted grins back, "Ya know what would be even more impressive? If he were like, a rock and roller. That's where the fun is. I was seeing this hot little number with a band at a club out in Jersey a few years back." He wriggles his brows, suggestively, "She was spunky."

"Spunky?" Connie squints back.

"Yeah, she could make the earth shake."

Connie puts her hand up. "Stop! I get the picture. And it involves bleach in my eyes because I don't want a visual." She returns to her workstation and turns to face all of her colleagues while addressing everyone in the room. "Hey, I just want to thank everybody who inserted themselves in my conversation with Denise. I'll consider all of your advice and sort through every option suggested." Awkwardly, she says, "OK. Everyone can go back to what they were doing. Thanks." Putting a hand up as though to wave, Connie puts it to the back of her head instead. Sitting down in front of the computer, she hides her face within the palms of her hands. "Oh my God," she says to herself.

Philip and Connie exit a cinema, joining the evening revelers and bright neon lights awakened in darkness. Shaking her head, a smiling Connie admits, "I did not expect that. I thought it was going to be a more serious science fiction kind of film."

He answers, "Kinda gotta figure with that cast it wasn't going to be too serious. You know, Bill Murray and Dan Aykroyd bein' from *Saturday Night Live*, something was up."

"I didn't think of it that way. Associating something like *Caddyshack* and *The Blues Brothers* was furthest from my mind." Connie glances around at couples walking around them. She tries to ignore her own growing feelings for the musician. "What was that great line Murray's character, Venkman said? What led to it? Um, something about, forty years of darkness, volcanoes, and earthquakes. Then…,"

"The black guy. What was his name? Zed?"

"I think his name was Winston."

"He said something about the dead rising from the grave. Then Venkman said…,"

Both say it at the same time, "Human sacrifice. Dogs and cats living together. Mass hysteria!" They laugh, realizing how each can remember the same thing.

Connie puts her hand on Philip's arm, giving a little squeeze. Playfully, she says, "Ghostbusters!" Swaying slightly from giddiness, she indicates, "We need to do this more often!"

Philip has his hands on her sides, giving an off-sided glance at the same sight of couples wandering the streets with a hint of awkwardness.

"Um, yeah," he tries to look Connie in the eyes. "There's…, There's something you need to know." Philip feels her arms snake around his back, drawing him in tighter.

A big smile creeps across her face.

"You can tell me. I can keep secrets." She edges her face closer to his.

"Uh, I know a thing or two about secrets," Philip answers, taking a step back.

She laughs, "Shy, huh?" Her big grin shows.

A group of people walks into them, pushing Connie directly back to where she wants to be. Her hand lands against his chest. She lets out a laugh.

"Something tells me that a higher power doesn't want us to part."

"It sure looks that way," he says with a sense of surprise, eyeing upward.

Connie's gaze falls on his face.

"So, why should we?"

Philip looks up again, only to get startled by a sensation. He puts a hand out to test if it was his imagination. A large drop splotches like a spitball, landing at his foot. She feels a drop too. Unable to say anything, they turn to see other people looking up at the sky. A man nearby flips up his umbrella, encasing him in dry safety. Three young women with their hair teased, run by, shrieking in horror from Mother Nature's wrath. A taxi pulls up with the windshield wipers swaying to a beat. The women pile into the vehicle, getting whisked away.

A loud crackle immediately grabs Philip's attention. He and Connie, along with everybody else on the sidewalk, get caught in the whiteness of a passing flash. The soft drops turn larger, landing harder and more frequently. Soon, a downpour follows. A variety of shrieks and screams line the streets. Several people run in the opposite direction. Philip and Connie turn to the door they had just exited only moments earlier. It's crammed with bodies determined to stay dry. Philip grabs Connie's hand, and they make a run for it. With every white flash, the two pick up their pace, running faster. High above, the brightness of veins lengthens across Manhattan's landscape. Screams echo as the danger of getting struck by lightening frightens everyone. Puddles get splashed. Neon reflects on the streets.

Connie lets out a laugh, enjoying the run, and doesn't feel threatened at all, not since Philip has a firm grip on her hand. She tries to take a breath between giggles but finds it difficult from the fast pace. Instead, she breathes in droplets that make her cough. While the two races for shelter, she suddenly breaks into "Singin' in the Rain." Philip turns his head in the confusion of her glee. Another deep boom and crackle give him a reason to pay attention ahead. His sights are sporadically on the buildings they pass by. There are no awnings or shelter in sight. A block down though looks to be salvation at last. Connie has a tough time keeping up, somehow never losing her footing. Philip takes a hard left past several locked storefronts with gates to a particular spot vacant of rain refugees. He stops short of hitting the door under an awning. Connie clutches her chest, sweeping away her doused tresses that have amassed in a mess. Philip begins to scrub at his three-toned hair with furious hummingbird speed, trying to dry it quicker. Connie makes little effort to do the same. Rather than being annoyed, she's full of giggles and laughter, loving the atmosphere of everything.

A thousand things run through Connie's mind that set the mood. The rain had made her feel excited, and the possibility of having Philip as a potential boyfriend was exciting. A musician! A guy who didn't mind her company. Everything felt so good. It felt like Valentine's Day, the pitter-patter of a heart overtaken by something special. Flowers. Chocolates. Teddy bears with 'I Love You' on the tummy. It is holding hands and stealing kisses — tight hugs. Candlelit dinners. Park benches with flowers in bloom. Central Park. Horse-drawn carriages. Vacations in far-off exotic lands full of adventure and memories. Movies. Loads of black and white classic films. It was Holly Golightly, and Paul Varjak caught in the rain without the cat, in *Breakfast At Tiffany's*. Perhaps it was the Ghostbuster, Peter Venkman, and his off-beat romance with Dana Barrett, culminating in the climax of saving her from the perils of Gozer, minus the sticky sweetness of an ending.

It was rain, not an explosion of marshmallow remnants strewn in the city. A warm night that made the feeling all the more exhilarating.

Connie giggles uncontrollably, walking over to Philip, she drops her hand on his chest. He looks at her as though she's completely drunk.

"Oh, this is so great," Connie answers, biting her bottom lip. "You, me…," she puts a hand out, "all of this." Her eyes lower as she leans into him. He looks away with a grin.

"Yeah. I'm going to see if the rain has let up," Philip says as a distraction.

Going to check how things are outside of the awning, Philip knows full well it's still pouring. The rain comes down in steady sheets from the covered shelter. People continue to run by, in the same predicament he and Connie had experienced a short time ago.

Connie can tell something is off, with Philip's concentration on her distracted many times. It's not the reaction she had hoped for under ideally romantic circumstances. She crosses her arms, eying the dry pavement under her feet. Connie steps into the recessed doorway. Her fingers hitch onto the blackened gate as a form of support while her mind begins to wander. She begins to believe the musician has a problem with her, but what would it be?

She takes a different approach.

"You know, I was just thinking…," she begins with the same chipper giddiness, "how we were running?" Her eyes fall on Philip, who remains at the edge of the awning. She takes a step away from the entrance. "Boy, you sure are fast! I could hardly catch up," Connie laughs. "I'm guessing you must have been one of the school's best track runners!"

Philip slowly turns, listening to her carry on. It only makes him feel more awkward.

"What would that be? The one-hundred-meter dash?" she asks. "Wait! If it's not track, then it has to be football. What were you? Captain of the team?"

He closes his eyes, feeling the shame take over while inhaling deeply. Exhaling with calmed nerves, Philip slowly shakes his head and puts a hand through his drying hair. He follows it with a nod, as though something is eating away at him and a need for release.

Connie continues, "I'm sure you could run the distance. The whole nine yards!"

"I'm gay."

"It's gotta be…" her voice trails off, realizing the words. She stares at him motionless. A sensation of heat throws her body temperature into overload from the shock. Every romantic thought. Every movie. Every forever after ending. Valentine's Day gifts. All of it crumbles like a demolition site. She can't even locate her heart — no lump in her throat. No tears shed.

Her eyes slowly turn to him. He glances up at her with seriousness etched in his beautiful brown eyes.

She blinks back to a state of reality, unsure of her own words until they spill out.

"Sure. Yeah." She answers affirmatively, rubbing the back of her head, as though it's part of her thought process. "Why not? Of course! Whatever!"

Connie figures it wasn't easy for him to say those words. What made it worse was the way she automatically had treated him. She was throwing herself at Philip repeatedly and never once considered his feelings or emotions. Here he felt a little bad for the way other men would run away and even broke down by bringing her to the studio with him.

Sheepishly, she looks at his wilted expression.

"Would I be crossing the line by asking if you want to get some coffee?"

Philip slowly looks up at Connie, surprised by her reaction. He nods back in agreement.

Connie goes over to check how the weather is fairing. The downpour has ceased. People come out of their hiding spots, retracting umbrellas.

Slowly, Philip and Connie emerge from the awning's safety to join the world again. Unlike before, she studies him for any signs of homosexual traits. His walk is straightforward and determined in a masculine way. Nothing is mincing or prissy in his style. Philip only displays the archetypal, straight male.

A steaming hot cup of coffee arrives next to Philip, another to Connie. She waits for the waitress to walk away before asking Philip, "Do you want to talk about it?" Her eyes scan the nearly empty diner as she rips open a packet of sugar.

"Black coffee? It's what us guys in the industry live off of," he answers with a playful laugh.

"You know what I'm talking about," Connie says with a slight giggle.

His grin disappears. "It's not something I'm prone to talking about," he says back. "I only do it when I have to warn somebody who might have a problem with me, or if there's something in common, like a potential partner. It's tough to explain to people who possibly can't understand or are afraid that I'm instantly going to go after them." He takes a sip. "I think some guys think we'll go and hump their leg like a dog. It's not like that. We don't think of sex every second of the day. I've heard it all, including, 'Oh, those perverts have about two hundred or more partners a year.'" Philip laughs back. "The truth is, Gene Simmons probably has seen more action than I have so far in my lifetime." He twists the cup in amusement. "As if we're not picky in what type we're looking for. You know, like you would find an attraction to someone dark-haired or blond. All the typical things. We're the same. Generally, we tend to seek the same overall body type. That way, we can share the same insecurities and issues. Neither of us feels as awkward about ourselves, and nobody's going to judge. Opposites don't always attract."

Connie asks, "What about some of the guys I've seen on the Lower West Side?"

"Connie, not all of us are Village People material. Some are willing to do things at clubs, bathhouses, in bathrooms, and movie theaters with really gross floors." His eyes widen. "Probably the reason why I won't go to CBGBs to even see a show. Anyway, I prefer my adult activities behind closed doors. Not everybody needs to know my business. If you're wondering, no, I don't go to rallies or parades. I don't walk around in a tutu down Christopher Street. I don't hang around drag queens and transvestites. I have no interest in looking like a part of a Coney Island freak show. I like to blend in. I am what I am.

That's all there is to it. Like I said, not everybody knows, and I like my life private."

"Does your family know?" Connie asks hesitantly.

"Next question," he answers quickly.

"There are obvious differences, though, right?"

"Same feelings. Same emotions. Same pain. Same thrill of being in love. No difference there." Philip takes another sip of coffee. "Physically? Yeah," he grins. "Obvious. I'm sure you know."

Connie takes a sip.

"You don't have to tell me," she answers with an uneasy smile.

"Um, so..." he says among the awkward silence. "Yep. That's what it's all about. Oh, and about being captain of the football team? You won't find me anywhere on Super Bowl Sunday. Not into football, and I hate beer. I prefer a nice wine or champagne."

They each finish their cups of coffee. Before Connie can pull out a couple of bills, Philip does it instead, then leaves.

Connie rushes over to open the door, glancing around. He is nowhere in sight. "Philip?" she gently calls out with no response.

Down the street, Philip stops in front of a window display to see his reflection staring back. His eyes drop to the dampened sidewalk. Taking a few steps over to the entrance guarded by a black security gate, he lets his fingertips curl against the cold metal. Leaning the rest of his body against his arm, he closes his eyes. There is both relief and sadness. He knew deep down, though, he broke Connie's heart.

CHAPTER 3

On the sixth floor of a high-rise office building in Midtown Manhattan, Al Shockley, the lead singer of Petunia Prank, sits in a chair. Looking to be in his late twenties to early thirties, he plays with the straight fringe of his charcoal bowl haircut. Licking lips that resemble the sheen of black licorice, he attempts to unnerve the hapless Barbara Hecht-Ross. Barbara's chubby hands stop writing. Her dark mascara-made eyes peer up at Al, who's busy either sucking on his finger or fishing for leftover remnants around his teeth. Whichever it is, she's annoyed by the singer's perverse need to make that weird suckling noise or smacking of the lips. He stares back at her, waving his tongue. She closes her eyes and returns to writing.

Philip shows up, wearing his sunglasses, and closes the door.

Al stops tormenting Barbara and looks up.

"Oh, look. It's Philly Joel. Looking for your uptown girl?" He answers in the most effeminate way.

Philip says, "Al," as he takes a seat next to him.

"You're such a big shot, Phil. We all know that you have a thing for the ladies. You know, I could do you in five minutes."

Grinning back, Philip answers with mock astonishment, "Five minutes? Come on, Al. I thought you could go a lot longer than that!"

Al rolls his eyes, "You have no idea the joys of Crisco," he rolls out his tongue.

Philip pulls down his sunglasses to peer briefly at the singer.

"Um, no thanks. I like to separate my cooking ingredients from personal pleasure."

"Suit yourself, pretty boy. You left the hairdryer on too long again."

"At least I don't look like I robbed a beauty salon."

Al leans over, "Knock. Knock. Phil, come out of your closet."

Barbara answers, testily, "Honeymoon's over."

Both Al and Philip face Barbara.

"Now that I have your attention. I had a good reason to call on you two. You're my at-risk clients," Barbara looks on her desk, picking up a magazine. She hands it to Philip. He slowly takes it, pulling off the sunglasses. "You look like you've seen it before," she answers, taking in his disturbed expression.

Al yanks it away from Philip's hands to read, "What is this? Scare tactics?" He tosses the magazine back on the desk without reading it. "Darling, I do what I want with whom I want, when I want. You certainly are not my mommy. That article is to sell more magazines. That's all."

"So, it has no truth to it? Al, you didn't even read it to make that judgment," Barbara shakes her head in disgust.

"Judgment? Who the hell are you to talk about judgment? You're doing it to me right now. Do I look like I'm going to get sick?"

"Al, it's not a matter of physically looking ill. Do you know there's a dire need for information and protection?" Barbara holds up the magazine. "This tells us all we need to know so far. It's a retrovirus they're calling HTLV-III. It's AIDS. The medical industry is hoping that a vaccine will go into production in two years."

"OK. So, you're a health expert now. I don't see a Dr. or MD. next to your name in any way. And, two years? What are we supposed to do in the meantime? Sit on our hands? Remain celibate? That would go over really well. 'Oh, Honey, we can take our clothes off and maybe touch each other, but nothing further.' That's a real mood killer. Do you know what it's like to go inside a candy shop and not be able to try any candy? No. You can probably eat a whole jar, and it looks like you already have."

Barbara says with caution, "Al, there are over three thousand people infected, with the numbers growing every year. I find that alarming, and you should too. There are choices you can make to become a victim or not."

Al sits up in the chair. "The choices we make?" He shakes his head in absurdity, glancing at Philip, who remains silent. "You think you know everything. Choices? It's not like I can get the gay cut out of me. You have the choice to be a fat pig. You can go and get weight loss surgery or stop eating garbage. No operation can stop my chances of being infected, or experiencing the hatred people have against me, the churches who think I'm possessed, or because I look funny." He throws Philip a look. "I can't speak for Hall without Oates, but you don't know what it's like. Going through high school, not understanding why I was not experiencing normal feelings with girls. Instead, I found myself watching the guys during football practice, how they moved with strong, sinewy brawn, or seeing the boys' swim team, with their perfectly sculpted bodies and tight shorts that made me fantasize about what I could do to them. How about getting my head dunked in the toilet, just for looking at the captain of the football team the wrong way. Or how about constantly having to run home without glasses because guys kept crushing them. Always trying to find excuses to tell my mom why she had to buy another pair, on a cleaning lady's salary. So, you can take your choices and eat it."

Unmoved by Al's story, or penchant for being rude and abrasive, Barbara stares coldly at him.

"I didn't ask to see you here to hurt your feelings. You are my clients. I have a responsibility to see to it that you fulfill the financial obligations of your label, without breach of contract. That's all. What you choose to do behind closed doors—"

Al immediately cuts in, "That's right, sweetheart. We're everywhere!" He throws his hands up in greater emphasis. "It's been that way for fifteen years now. Get used to it!" He lets out a hard cough.

"That reminds me. Your video has been banned from every station playing clips. They won't even play it after nine or ten. They've deemed it too suggestive for both the lyrics and the visuals. Crisco, bananas, pickles, whipped cream. The drag queen. Even your depiction of champagne."

Philip pays full attention to the manager's acidic tone. Her biting remarks cut quick to the bone. He knows she's doing it on purpose, hurting Al. She is dishing back pain, which he served first. The best way was through his music and words.

Al stares bitterly at Barbara with hurt etched in his eyes.

"Bitch."

He gets up from the chair and storms out. A resounding thud from the office door puts an end to the conversation.

Philip stares down at the sunglasses, in which he unwittingly toys with the arms. Looking back up, he nods again. "That went well." His sight bounces to the magazine on Barbara's desk, avoiding eye contact with her. "You know he's right."

"I didn't do it to be nice, Phil. I did it because I care," Barbara answers in a cautious, though stern, tone.

"There's nothing we can do to stop from getting it."

"How long have I known you?" she inquires.

"Since the last year with Deacon."

"That would be seven years."

"Yeah. I don't think it was fair of you to throw that bit about his being banned was necessary. I know why you did it. It wasn't right, though. An eye for an eye in the dishing-out department?"

"Phil, I care. I wouldn't have called both of you in the office if I didn't. It is a grave matter, and I'm worried. I can't do anything. Government officials, Mayor Koch, President Reagan, are doing nothing about this. They're not saying one word on the subject. Somebody has to look out for guys like you and Al. I know how it affects you, and yes, it should be scary. There are too many people beginning to disappear, and many are in the arts community. Art world. Music world. Did you know the avant-garde artist Klaus Nomi was suspected of having died from it last year? He sang opera and wore those weird outfits in black and white. I'm sure you've seen him before."

"Japanese makeup? Odd-looking guy? Not quite glam? He did the song 'Total Eclipse.' That one?" Philip ponders.

"See? I knew you would know who I was talking about. Yes. The same one. Anyway, I heard he died alone. Nobody wanted to visit him at the hospital because they thought what he had could be contagious. Phil, he's one of many growing stories. Young men all over are dying and getting abandoned by their families. It's horrendous!"

Philip thinks for a moment. "How old is Al?"

"He's twenty-six. Younger than you. I know his story is different than yours. You didn't go through everything he did."

"True. I didn't even know who I was at that age or what I was doing then. Some of it is a blur for other reasons."

"Hazy?"

"Yep. Too much rock and roll." Philip answers as he gets up with a lot on his mind. He begins to turn around when Barbara remembers something.

"Oh, before I forget. It looks like you've got a slot with Spandex Shades' *Radical Moon* tour. Have you heard of them?"

"Yeah. I've got their first album, *Shasta Nights*."

Barbara picks up a sheet of paper. "OK. Well, it's looking to be about three weeks, at least. You'll have the west coast. Golden, Phoenix, Albuquerque, five dates in California, Portland, Seattle, and Vancouver. I think I got them all." She hands the page to Philip. "You can check it out yourself. Do you know who you'd bring?"

Philip scans the page. "Yeah. Claire, Perry, Mitch, Ross, and uh, a new guy, Tim from New Haven. He's got an amazing resume."

"Just be prepared. Also, you might consider getting a new look."

"Huh?"

"What you're wearing? It's like everybody's got a suit. Rod Stewart, Billy Joel, Daryl Hall, even McCartney."

Philip walks over to the door and looks back. "Yeah, but not everyone's got a pink Strat." He grins and raises his brows while turning the knob.

Connie sits at her workstation, typing and alternating her sights from a package of papers to the computer screen. Maria walks by, glancing at her.

"So? How'd it go with Mr. Cute?"

Denise goes over to her workstation and sees Maria at Connie's space for the interrogation.

Connie answers, unaffected, "It was OK."

Maria leans in, "Just OK? Come on, Connie. You can tell me." She looks around. "Us."

Denise pops her head up to join in.

"Uh-uh. You mean, Mr. Very Cute. I'd like to see further evidence if he is what you say he is," she leans in. "So, tell us? You know you can't keep us hanging on."

Maria checks one of her fingernails as she answers, "So, you're doin' him now, right?"

Connie rolls her eyes.

"I'm not doing anybody for your information. Things simply didn't... Look, it's just not going to work. We're too different."

Denise interjects, "He's married, and the divorce isn't final. Uh-huh. Tell me about it. Been there, done that. If he ain't done with her yet, he never will."

Connie's eyes glance over.

"He's not married."

Denise's eyes grow big. "I ain't gonna get in your business, honey."

Stephanie wanders over, "He could be playing you, until the right one comes along with a cheap slut who wears tons of makeup, tiny mini skirt, and stuffs her boobs into a size A cup when she's a cow in D. Then tries to turn the kids against you."

Bryan pulls out a package of papers, shaking his head, walking over to the Xerox machine.

"Steph, everybody knows you're all about drama. Your still sore Kevin re-married, and Kyle wanted to go to Disney World with them." He turns to Connie. "There's plenty of fish in the sea. All you have to do is wait, 'cause sometimes the best ones haven't found their way to shore yet."

Connie smiles, close-lipped, holding in a laugh. She lets it out.

"Bryan, when did you become so philosophical?"

A bright flash takes everybody by surprise at their seats.

"Hey, Shakespeare," Maria calls out. "You didn't put the lid back down on the Xerox machine!"

Connie glances over, amused that her life is so interesting enough that co-workers lose concentration of what they're doing.

Ted and Gary walk-through. Connie notices the two and immediately groans in dread.

"There's our lady in love!" Ted says aloud.

Gary adds in, "So, how did it go?"

Connie answers back, plainly, "It didn't work."

An incensed Ted takes a step forward.

"What? Did he hurt you?" He puffs out his chest. "I'll take care of this guy."

"No, you won't." Connie quickly states. "He did not hurt me. He is a gentleman, but things won't work with us." She stares at Ted. "That's all."

Mr. Edwards storms out of his office, waving a package of papers.

"Delgado! Bainard! Which one of you two took this order? I know one of you wrote this!"

Maria walks up to see it.

"Oh, that's not mine. I don't write g's like that." She steps away.

Mr. Edwards stares coldly at Stephanie.

"What?" Stephanie answers defensively. "Why are you looking at me that way?"

With a beckoning finger, Edwards says, "Come into my office, and we'll talk."

She walks away in a huff. The office door closes behind them.

Connie briefly looks at the door.

Denise shakes her head.

"Connie, having a relationship not work out isn't the end of the world, like Bryan indicated. Look at it this way, you could be like Stephanie. Sure, she used to be one of the best, then she became a lazy-ass worker. Got two kids from one-night stands, with one father who is now her ex-husband, that's re-married to a woman she despises."

Maria squints at the door before turning her attention back to Connie and Denise.

"I think there's something else going on with her."

"What's that?" Denise asks. "You think she's playing, hide-the-salami?"

"I'll make a bet with you," Maria answers assuredly.

Denise's lips turn into a grin. She slaps Maria's palm in solidarity. "You got it. Speaking of salami, how about a hot pastrami sandwich, with a big-ass plate of juicy deli pickles from Katz. I haven't been there in a while."

"OK. Yeah. It's only fitting. I'm sure Steph is looking for her next meal," Maria remarks in seriousness.

"Oh my God," Connie snickers. "You two are terrible."

Denise says, "See? It could be a lot worse."

"So, I did something at work last week. I told some of my colleagues that I was getting to hang out with somebody. Of course, they asked a thousand questions and gave me loads of advice. Dinner. What movies to go see." Connie glances down at the sidewalk. "Then, after Friday..." her voice trails off. "Things changed." She says with a shrug. "When I went back to work on Monday, everybody wanted to know how Friday went."

Philip listens, intently.

"What did you tell them?"

Connie stops to look at the musician in the eyes.

"I told them the truth." Again, she eyes the sidewalk for a second, then allows herself to stare at him with serious intent. "That things wouldn't work...for us."

He is surprised by Connie's words and incredible willingness to not release his secret, Philip eyes the sidewalk, gathering his thoughts on how to deal with her honesty. He had also noticed after disclosure of his sexual preference, Connie had physically grown detached from him. Gone was the reassuring touch to his arm, or squeeze of excitement. That little bit of human warmth had turned into a barrier of acknowledged wariness.

Philip decides to test her.

"Yeah. OK." He playfully leans to her. With one brow raised and a grin, he asks, "So, did you tell them how many times a day we were doing it?"

Connie stares at him with her jaw dropped.

"Oh my God. Not you too!" She snorts out a laugh, unable to contain it. "I thought my co-workers were bad. Now, I have to deal with you?"

Philip lets out a laugh.

"Really?" she asks.

It only makes him laugh harder.

Connie rolls her eyes, muttering, "Men. All the same." She starts walking on, leaving Philip to catch up with her.

His test failed. Not once did Connie give him a playful slap, or put a hand to his arm. It was a void that hurt more than anything, but he wouldn't let it show.

After all, what did he expect when he made things clear?

Connie was OK with it.

They continue to walk down Seventh Avenue, not hand in hand, but side by side. Connie feels motivated to say something to Philip while passing by the Fashion Institute of Technology.

"Can I ask you something?"

"Yeah. Go ahead."

"Besides the session work you do? What are some things you're most proud of outside of music?"

Philip thinks for a minute, repeating her words in thought. "Some things I'm most proud of outside music. Hmm. OK. I've got one. Try this on for size. I have the distinction of being popular among the kids in my neighborhood. They treat me like a rock star," he grins wildly.

Connie blinks back in confusion.

"Halloween," he says.

"Oh?"

"I tend to attract the six to fifteen-year-old set. You know how nowadays they've got these little packages of candy bars about this big?" He illustrates with his fingers. "Those are nothing. It's a crock of crass commercialism to spend more and get way less. I'm old-fashioned. I believe the only thing that you should give is the regular sized ones."

"Yes!" Connie emphatically reacts.

"So, that's what I do. I give out the full-size Hershey bars. The young kids don't know much about music or my involvement with it. However, I'm the ultra-cool guy who gives out the candy bars." Philip says with pride. "Their dentists thank me later."

Connie laughs.

He breaks into a wide grin.

"Last year, I got the sunglasses at Saks Fifth Avenue, and it inspired me to do something for Halloween. I got dressed up, and...my...," he hesitates with uncertainty. Looking back at her, he realizes there is nothing to hide. "My partner at the time said, 'You're nuts! I don't want anything to do with this!' So, the killjoy got to hide in another part of the house, and I got the couch."

"You got the couch? OK. Now, You've got me really curious. What was the costume?"

Philip grins. "Are you familiar with the movie *Risky Business*?"

"Tom Cruise?"

"Yeah. You know the scene where he's in the living room?"

They cross over past Twenty-Seventh Street.

Connie stops him. "Wait! You don't mean...? No. You're not telling me where he does the slide and sings along to 'Old Time Rock and Roll?'" She thinks for a minute. "Oh, wait. You got the couch because..." Her concentration is on thinking of what would annoy somebody.

Philip cautiously attempts to jog her memory. "What else is the movie known for?" He puts on his Ray-Bans, arching his brows. A smile creeps across his face.

Connie stares at him with her jaw dropped. It finally strikes her as they near the crosswalk. "No. You didn't! The shirt, socks, and shorts?"

Philip nods back, placing the sunglasses back in his pocket. "The whole nine yards. They were ridiculously short shorts. Like, incredibly uncomfortable to move around in," he giggles again.

She laughs back, "You earned that couch! I'm trying to picture you like that."

"Hey, I wasn't going to be obscene about it! There were young eyes. I didn't want to corrupt the youth," he laughs.

They continue to walk in silence. Suddenly, Connie bursts out laughing.

"I got a visual now!" she giggles. "You're going to have to tell me how the kids reacted."

Philip says, "The kids were fine. They got their candy. It was their mothers who lined up, past the driveway."

"No doubt!" Connie laughs hard.

Philip eyes the sidewalk with a hint of disappointment.

"Only, my partner would disagree with having fun...at all."

Connie shakes her head, smiling, not realizing how strongly he feels.

At the crosswalk of Twenty-Eighth, she notices Philip is not by her side. Glancing back, she sees him staring down, as people walk around him, oblivious to his pain. His thoughts revolve around his latest failure. Saddened for her buddy, Connie walks back to him.

"You look like you could use a hug." She puts her arms out, forgetting about the strict physical boundaries they both set. "Come on."

Philip obligingly steps up to her, wrapping his arms around her. A chance to feel warmth he thought was lost. A hug could feel so good, and he wasn't afraid to show his gratitude for one. Connie feels him tighten his body against hers.

He closes his eyes, letting feelings of inadequacy spill out.

"I tried to hold on to both, but I lost him."

His hug changes with the position of his hands. A little too close to her lower back. Maybe it was just an innocent way of relaxing his fingers.

Connie pulls away immediately. Realizing the hug is too long for her taste, and those fingers were almost in the no-go zone.

Philip takes a step back. Noticing her reaction, he puts his hands out in a way to show he'll back off. She looks at him, wide-eyed and wary. He brushes back the top of his hair in awkwardness.

Once again, the two remain with an invisible wall between them when it comes to anything physical.

Taking a turn onto Thirty-Sixth, Connie sees a record store.

"Oh! I forgot this one was here. I'm so used to going past the shop near where I live. As you can tell, I don't always go down this way."

"Hmm. Yeah."

Philip glances at the window, which causes him some alarm. He guides her away from getting any closer.

Connie lets out a laugh.

"What? Oh, I get it. You're sick of seeing the projects you did sessions for."

Again, he displays the same uncomfortable manner he showed her the previous week. Something agitates his thoughts as if he were keeping other secrets.

"Um, yeah. Well, you know what they say, 'Absence makes the heart grow fonder.'"

"I take it, you don't like to be reminded of some sessions?"

He changes the subject quickly.

"I'm sure there are other things to do besides visit record shops. Kinda gets monotonous."

Walking further along Fifth Avenue, Philip puts his hand on Connie's shoulder.

"Hold on," he says.

She turns around.

"Connie, there's something I have to tell you."

"Well, you told me about your secret already. So, I'm guessing this has nothing to do with that."

"I won't be around in August all that much...if at all. Three weeks tops."

"Busy, huh?"

Philip bites his bottom lip.

"Yeah."

"It's not my place to ask why, so I'll leave it at, busy."

Nodding back, he answers with, "Sounds good."

Connie looks at him.

"You don't seem like you want to do whatever it is that will keep you away for those three weeks."

"No. I do want to do it. Maybe I need a change of scenery? It's not the act of doing it. I have no problem with that. I feel like I'm going back to the same emotions as previously. Something I did some years ago, but I've grown from the experience. I think I can handle it better. It doesn't change what goes on after everything is said and done."

Connie says with concern, "Will you be alright?"

"Yeah. I'll be fine."

"OK," she glances back the opposite direction. "Want to go back the other way pretty soon? There isn't much here."

It's the same old daily grind at JLP Group. Everybody in the office types the latest orders. Ted realizes he's completed the newest account. Getting up, he goes to the copy machine. Knowing it won't turn on properly, Ted shuts it off, then switches it back on. Knowing the thing will take forever, he picks up the latest copy of a newspaper, flipping through it. With furrowed brows, he comes across an article that confuses and intrigues him at the same time.

Lou gets up. Maria stretches. Denise yawns. Connie finishes up her latest account, before joining Ted.

"Hey, anybody heard this story?" Ted asks, reading it aloud.

Robin Hood of Manhattan - A young gay man, named Tim Boscane became so deeply moved after visiting a terminally ill friend at a hospital. He witnessed patients that were nothing more than skin and bones, brought on by the recently named AIDS. Saddened by what he saw, he went in search of items at high-end department stores and boutiques, where he promptly stashed accessories away in his jacket, totaling a cost of $10,000. He brought the stolen goods to various hospitals, donating them to patients. "They wanted to be stylish to the end and with that having dignity." Many of the items were scarves, socks, and hats, as many patients lacked in body weight." He is currently awaiting a trial date. The stores are seeking restitution.

Ted shakes his head. "Too bad he didn't have the foresight to include condoms."

Denise breathes out in annoyance, "Come on, Ted. Have a heart! The guy was trying to help other people. Why can't you take it at face value?"

"Now this vigilante is going to pass it around to everybody. Chances are, he'll do it in the jail system, if that's where he's going. After he visited all those infected people, it'll happen."

"You don't know that. Nobody knows how it spreads."

"Oh, come on, Denise. We know how it's spread and among who. I don't understand how any guy can be attracted to…, You know? Other men, and do that stuff with them. I don't need any guy getting sweet on me. I'm not into that."

Connie eyes her co-workers hesitantly as she thinks about what Philip told her. She turns her attention to Ted.

"Have you ever thought, maybe they have a preference?"

Ted looks at Connie. "Yeah. Other guys!"

Connie briefly closes her eyes. "I'm not talking about the obvious. What I'm saying is, maybe they have a preference for certain things. You know? Dark hair? Blond hair? Slim? Things like that in a male way. Traits you would be attracted to."

"Oh, hey. I dig the ladies exclusively. Size C will get my attention. Maybe a B cup."

"Really, Ted?"

"Are you sure they don't measure by the inseam?"

Connie rolls her eyes. "Isn't it at all possible for two people to have an attraction to each other? Should it matter what they are? Doesn't everybody deserve to be loved?"

Lou pipes in, "Yeah. A man and a woman! That's the way God intended it to be."

Connie tries to reason with them. "What if we could all simply love who we want? Without judgment. Without boundaries. What if it's all the same?"

Ted answers with some concern. "You're getting a little overly philosophically weird, Connie. What gives? Are you leaving us to become some psychologist or something?"

"No, Ted. I'm not leaving San-San. I'm just saying maybe we need to understand other people who aren't like us."

"You're voting for Mondale, aren't you?" Ted smirks.

Philip and Connie walk to the east side of Manhattan, taking in the sights of shops along the way. She admires some of the displays. Philip doesn't share her interest in shopping. As much as Connie tries to put up an emotional barrier between her and the musician, evidence from the reflection shows an attractive couple wandering the streets.

Connie turns to face him.

"Did you hear the story about the guy who's like you, that stole ten thousand dollars worth of clothing accessories, and gave them to hospital patients?"

He grins. "You're asking me if I heard the story because this guy and I share the same preference?"

Connie answers apprehensively, "I'm not saying, you're all the same. I'm asking what you think of the situation. He gave the stuff to dying patients."

"Yeah. I heard it on the news the other day. Um, what I think? There's a difference between charity and being a criminal. As nice as the gesture was, he broke the law. As with a lot of businesses, somebody will have to pay it back if he can't. The average shopper will have to foot the bill for this guy's actions."

"So, you don't feel he should have done that?"

"Connie, not to sound cold, but all we can do is live for today. Enjoy life while we have it. We can't worry about everything on this planet, or we're going to drive ourselves crazy. You come up with one more reason to freak out, and it's unnecessary anxiety. Yeah. I feel for him. I feel for the patients, of course. But, there is a right way and a wrong way of going about things. You know?"

Connie looks down when she comes up with something.

"Can I ask you an honest question? Maybe it's weird."

"You never know if you don't ask."

"What kind of parent would you be?"

Philip groans. "Oh, you know that's not going to happen."

"If things were different. You know what I mean?" She giggles back.

"Me, as a parent."

"If it's too much, I won't push..."

"Terrified," he grins at the thought. "How about you? Considering you have about a ninety-nine point nine nine nine percent chance of having any in your lifetime."

Connie shakes her head. "No. Kids are not for me. Just the idea of childbirth makes me want to jump on a ceiling. I hear so many women talk about how it's so rewarding and not that bad. I can't help but have nightmares about that one time I experienced a horrific case of constipation."

Philip lets out a hearty laugh. His attempt at trying to calm down fails miserably.

The sight of her buddy cracking up laughing proves contagious, as Connie soon joins him.

Philip says, "Now, that's a new way of putting things!" He emphatically states, putting up a finger. "Gee, Connie. Thanks! I'll never be able to get that vision out of my head."

Connie looks down at the ground. She shakes her head at a thought, ceasing her laughter.

"I'm not fit to be a parent. As it is, my track record with guys isn't so hot."

Philip says with a wide-eyed appeal, "Neither is mine!"

A smile briefly crosses her face as she grows more serious. "I look at figures like these," she points to a storefront window. An enormous photo of a shapely woman wearing a bikini stares back at her with tropical blue eyes and perfectly rounded breasts.

Philip furrows his brows, taking a good look at the display.

"It's a photo. The eye color isn't even real."

Connie begins walking away, unable to face the window any longer. Philip catches up with her immediately.

She says, "It's what men want. They want a perfect body with all the curves. I don't have that. I've been told numerous times that I have a pretty face, but the rest isn't much of anything. I have this flat little body, where I can't even go to the beach because I don't fill a bikini top the right way. I'd try to wear something form-fitting, and the guy I was with chose... He was too busy looking at another girl because, well, who wants someone who looks like an under-developed girl? I know I shouldn't say this. But, I figure since you are...," She gestures with a hand out. "You won't care." Connie closes her eyes. "There was a guy I thought I was getting along with great. I had been seeing him for a little bit, and finally, when we were ready to spend the night together, he told me he preferred the lights off, so he could use his imagination. I felt worthless, not loved." She courageously puts on a smile through the pain. "Sometimes, I wish I could look different or be more attractive. Just something."

Philip glances down at the ground, then takes Connie by the arm to stop her.

She feels the tug back.

He looks at her in seriousness. "Don't do that to yourself. You don't want to change anything. Look what happened to Karen Carpenter. She didn't like what she saw in the mirror and went into an early grave for it last year. I'm not saying to the point of extremes, but it's better just to be yourself. The worst thing you could do is be fake. That's when you become miserable. Whether you look happy on the outside, you don't feel it inside. I mean, yeah. I have certain things about myself I don't particularly like, not necessarily in the mirror. I chalk that up to the choices I've made. I don't make things easy for anybody."

Connie looks at him, realizing how sincere he can be. It's refreshing to talk to a man who doesn't act like an over-bloated, egotistical jerk.

They come upon a small market, selling deli fare, beverages, and grocery needs in a pinch. Outside of the shop are neatly wrapped flowers and fresh fruits in cardboard containers. Philip quickly goes over towards the window. At first, Connie is surprised when she thinks he's going to pick out a bouquet of roses. In reality, he goes to the fruit section. Picking up a banana, he spontaneously uses it as a microphone and starts to croon Billy Joel's "Just the Way You Are" to her.

Connie looks on, shocked. She pulls the banana away from him, putting it back in the box.

"You are crazy!" she says in disbelief.

"Mmm. Only a little." He answers.

She shakes her head, trying to get more serious.

"OK. Flipping the subject back to you. What do you look for in a relationship?"

A slow grin appears across his face as he answers, "A decent human being."

Connie tilts her head in a confused manner.

"Sure. You want to find a great guy."

Philip repeats his answer with, "No. A decent human being." He raises his brows. "That's all."

Connie hesitates, trying to understand.

"Um, OK."

"Yep." He thinks of something else. "You asked about my thoughts on kids? I didn't tell you this, but I have a niece. She'll be eleven in August."

"You're an uncle!"

"Yeah. A big regret I have is not being able to see her that much. I was hardly around when she was born. That's what happens when your priorities take over everything, including family." He looks up, picking his words carefully. "I was traveling...a lot then. One of my older sisters became a single mom and made things work. My parents loved having a little one around the house. There are five of us. The oldest is my brother, who's six years older than me, then the oldest sister, four years. Then, my other sister is two years older, and she's the mom of my niece. I'm the fourth. The fifth is my younger sister by about nine years. A little bit of a gap there."

"Wow!" Connie answers. "And here I am, an only child."

Soon, the two wind up in Greenwich Village after stopping for a quick dinner of hot dogs.

"I don't know how they do it," Philip remarks. Looking straight ahead, he and Connie are within short walking distance from Washington Square Park.

Just beyond the Washington Square Arch lies a juxtaposition between the bombastic fury of a drumming busker and the near-library-silence of chess players across the way. In between are a group of youths blasting the latest in hip-hop on a boombox, laughing, and clapping. Several kids do some mild versions of breakdancing. In the bright June sun, a grizzled man, patches of wiry gray hairs mixed in his beard, shuffles past with a dirty pillowcase slung over the shoulder of his spotty trench coat. A tourist couple busies themselves in taking pictures next to a section of graffiti on the arch, as though it were a focal point for their gratification. A group of people watches a man perform magic acts, oohing, and ahhing at his antics.

The entire thing looks like a peculiar circus of sorts.

Philip finds himself drawn to watching the drummer, and in particular, the eye-catching gold-speckled kit. A young man with wild dark hair, attired in an open vest, looking every bit the seventies cliché rock star commands a small audience. Flailing sticks in dramatic fashion, he plays in such a way that Philip furrows his brows. He shakes his head with disapproval. Peering over the rims of his sunglasses, Philip remarks, "Nice kit. Too bad he doesn't know how to play." He glances around. Connie follows his lead. "Uh, that would get some poor sap a big hit at a pawn shop."

She looks at him, not understanding what he's getting at.

Returning the puzzled glance, he explains. "With a kit like that, here? He could get it ripped off by a junkie. By the looks of it, there's plenty of them here."

Connie gives him an unnerved swing of her eyes, then scans the area where there are lots of people.

Philip crosses his arms, paying attention to the drummer. Every so often, he twists his frame in the direction of other activities around.

"See over to the right? The lady with the backpack? She's shooting up. She figures nobody can see her."

"Oh my God," Connie mutters under her breath. Rather than keeping her eye on the subtle cringe-worthy scene, she watches the drummer.

They step up closer with the rest of the small gathering of people.

Philip tells her, "He's probably seen plenty of zeros on a check with nothing in front of it."

"Oh," Connie groans, shaking her head.

"Can't keep a beat."

"Mmm-hmm."

"Makes love the same way."

Connie stifles a laugh, turning her head.

The young man at the kit attempts to look cool. He gets blank stares, and a few look on in awe, oblivious to how bad he is. A couple walks away. Philip observes a nearly empty box with the words 'Bobby's Booty' scrawled on it next to the kit. He shakes his head.

"Bobby's a pirate. Hmm. Might account for the missing arm action."

Suddenly, Bobby gets up from the kit, swishes back his hair, and surveys the audience.

"Who wants to try and do what I just did?"

Philip mutters to Connie, "Take off the training wheels?"

Again, Connie holds in a laugh.

Bobby points to a guy with spikey hair, who shakes his head and walks away. Disappointed, he attempts to find somebody else. His sights fall on Philip.

"How about Mr. Preppy?"

Connie makes the mistake of turning to take a look at Philip, who wears one of his usual oversized jackets with the button-down shirt. It doesn't help that he wears Ray-Ban sunglasses either.

Bobby asks, "Hey, aren't you a little too old to be dressing up like that?"

Philip shoots back, "Shouldn't you stop changing in the dark? That whole disco ringmaster look has been over for some time. I have better stuff in my closet and believe me, that's where it's staying!"

"Don't you want to impress your girlfriend?" Bobby goads.

Philip looks at Connie. She angles at him. Girlfriend? Maybe he would correct the talentless smartass.

"Oh, I know. Your sweetheart isn't getting any from you. That's why you're here to learn from the best." Bobby answers.

Philip has had enough. He yanks off his jacket, handing it to Connie.

"Here. Hold this."

"You don't have to do this," Connie urges.

He pulls off his sunglasses, placing them on top of the jacket she holds. Adjusting his belt, he walks over to Bobby and takes the drum sticks from him.

"Got a key?" Philip puts his hand out.

Bobby reluctantly digs in his pocket, handing over the key.

"You're out of tune," Philip indicates while tightening the lug nuts all over the kit. "You're really out of tune." His eyes go wide. He works his way like a mechanic, tapping the various heads once he's satisfied enough with the sound. Dropping the key on the ground, he situates himself on the stool. Without further ado, Philip takes a swipe at the crash cymbal, going full force on the drums.

Connie takes a step back in a state of shock.

The sparse crowd grows as passerby point and become drawn like moths to a flame. Even a few of those watching the magic show turn their heads. The only people who remain unaffected by the commotion are the two men fully concentrating on their next move on the chessboard. A slight tapping from one's foot is the only sign of approval among strategizing.

What the hell? Connie thinks to herself Philip is not a run-of-the-mill guitar player for sessions. There's something more. It's in the way he plays and makes it look easy.

Too easy.

Philip keeps going while two women smile and drop bills in the box. A kid goes over and lets some change fall from his hand. A group of men dig into their pockets, throwing bills in with the others. In the meantime, Philip has done everything a professional drummer would do in the spotlight. Not the usual, but a rock steady beat that could be familiar if people knew particular pieces of music. It was as if he wrote them himself.

He winds down with an obligatory crescendo on the cymbals, before striking the snare to finish things off.

The crowd gives a resounding cheer as though they were at a big concert.

Philip gets up from the kit, takes a bow, and hands the sticks back to the stunned Bobby.

"Call me when you're with the Registry."

He goes to fetch his jacket and sunglasses from an awestruck Connie.

A man approaches him.

"Wow! That was great. Do you play often?"

"Drums aren't my primary instrument," Philip answers while putting his jacket back on.

"They're not?"

"No siree."

"What is?"

"Guitar."

"Do you have anything released?"

Philip takes a glance over at Connie, who eyes the ground, trying to gather her wits after that performance.

"Ah, no."

"Wow! Well, you're great!" The man blubbers over. "I mean, terrific!"

"Thanks," Philip grins. He looks at Connie again. "Ready to go?"

She nods back in agreement.

They head out of the park. Bobby finally comes to from his frozen state of shock. He picks up the box, seeing a bunch of money inside. Staring at the two people disappearing, he slowly shakes his head in wonder.

At the office of JLP Group, everybody works diligently. Pages flip by as the copy machine hums. Coffee flows from the dispenser. A resounding army of fingers clicking keyboard keys fills the empty spaces.

The sound of the boss's office door closing puts every worker on high alert. Heads turn. Gary holds his coffee mug in one hand, papers in the other, standing like a mannequin. Maria's eyes swing over to where footsteps lightly traverse the thinly carpeted floor. Bryan takes a heavy breath. Denise keeps her focus on the screen, ignoring the ensuing drama ready to unfold. Ted peers up from his computer, remaining silent. Connie's eyes survey her workers, not fully aware of what is going on.

Stephanie walks by, holding a small cardboard box. She returns to her workstation. There are no words spoken, as Stephanie fills it with all her belongings consisting of knick-knacks, photo frames, and a drawer stuffed with pens, makeup, and personal mementos. Dumping the whole drawer, she picks up the remnants from the floor as all eyes are on her. Stephanie turns around, surveying all of the eyes looking down. With the box in her arms, she rushes out of the office. The door closes.

Gary takes a deep breath as he clears his throat, returning to his workstation.

"I can taste that pastrami now," Denise remarks, breaking the silence.

Ken raises his brows. He says, "It happened."

"It was only time," Maria remarks unapologetically.

Connie looks over at her. "What was?"

Mr. Edwards appears in front of all the workers. Just as quickly, he makes a hasty disappearance back into his own office.

After the interruption, Connie asks again, "What was?"

Suzanne answers from further away. She walks over towards the front rows.

"You didn't hear? Gary, did you know?"

"I knew something was going on with her," Gary admits slowly.

"Stephanie kept screwing up the Trenton and Rutherford accounts. Mr. Edwards gave her at least a half a dozen chances. He felt bad for her and thought she needed more. Plus, she's got the two boys who are in the crossfire of her bitterness against their fathers. If that wasn't enough, Edwards found out his younger and much better-looking brother..., a very much married man was having an affair with somebody else," Suzanne informs them.

"Not Stephanie? Tell me it wasn't her." Connie says, cautiously.

"It was. The story goes, they met at some singles bar. He was getting bored at home. Edwards found out and was understandably shook up about it. He loves his sister-in-law and the kids."

"Is that why she was let go?" Gary asks.

"No. Steph can't be let go for screwing the boss's brother. Do you know what kind of lawsuit she could lodge against the company? The termination was due to the New Jersey accounts, and her over-all lack of professionalism."

"Damn! Steph was one of our top people," Ted remarks.

"Well, she liked horizontal action more," Maria answers.

Denise is off in a dream world as she says aloud, "A big plate of pickles."

Bryan looks at Maria and Denise angrily.

"What's the matter with you, ladies? Don't you have any respect for somebody who's getting the ax? Denise be talkin' 'bout pickles, and you, Maria, with your sexual innuendos."

Maria turns to him just as pissed off.

"You think I'm gonna have respect for a home-wrecking hussy? You're crazy!"

Gary closes his eyes to the squabbling between Bryan and Maria. Eying Connie, he says, "This is what you miss when your head is in the clouds. I knew something was going on. I didn't know it was this big. Goes to prove, everybody has secrets. There's no telling what's in anybody's closet."

Connie looks off to the side, thinking of Philip and how well he played those drums. She was sure there was more to him, besides his secret personal life, but what could it be?

CHAPTER 4

Under the watchful eyes of street lamps and neon signs burning brightly, the nightlife scene awakens. A variety of young people pour onto the sidewalks in search of their evening salvation. Derelict buildings sit in the dark, rotting away with only graffiti to give them some sense of life. The few livelier ones are those that have groups of people in front, talking, laughing, and smoking. These are the clubs containing everybody from teenagers to near forty-year-olds.

Philip walks by a crowd of people in front of a plain dark building that shows the name 'Scribbles' on the front wall. Connie is a few steps ahead, wearing her evening best and trendiest, a red silk jumpsuit by Regina Kravitz, under a long black cardigan. She leads him to the door. Upon entry, they are met up by more people dressed in the freshest fashions, hairstyles, and accessories. A man attired in a suit and polka-dot tie waves patrons in as he holds a clipboard. Connie holds up two fingers, joking with the doorman. She swiftly turns to Philip, who gives a small smile. He looks around. She guides him to walk in front of her. They step inside a thrilling atmosphere of lights and loud music.

He turns to her. "So, tell me again? How did a nice lady like you find a place like this?"

Connie giggles back, taking off the cardigan, "This is a club that I frequent with my friends." Walking over to a small room, she leaves the sweater, quickly rejoining Philip. "It's just a place to—" she stops abruptly to glance over. "Oh, hey! There's High-Top. Oh, you have to meet him. He's a great DJ!"

She takes him by the hand, leading the guitarist over to the DJ booth. There, they meet up with DJ Marlon "High-Top" Evans, a smaller black man in tinted Foster Grant sunglasses. The DJ peers over his rims at the guitarist who signals to him behind Connie's back. The two men shake hands.

Connie says, "High-Top plays all the great new tunes courtesy of WLIR and how fast they get imports from the UK."

High-Top answers, "Straight off the boat!" He lets out a laugh. "Sometimes we get records directly from the artists themselves," the DJ makes eye contact with Philip.

"I'll let the two of you become acquainted," Connie glances over to the front. She exits the DJ booth, stepping down to meet up with some other people.

Philip surveys the scene below.

High-Top asks, "So, Phil, haven't seen you in some time. Where have you been?"

"Uh. Around. Hey, thanks for not saying anything."

"No problem, man. The last time I saw you, you were platinum blond with those little skinny ties. You were Mr. New Wave for a time. You used to hang out at the Garage with Campbell."

"Not anymore. People change. Styles change, Marlon. Just like you're not manning the disco floor anymore."

"So, Connie doesn't know?"

"No. I'd like for it to stay that way as long as possible."

"That's too bad, man. You know people dug that song."

"Different times. What can I tell you?"

"Yeah. Hey, I saw your boss, Barbara, down on the dance floor. Don't know what she's doin' diggin' this scene."

Philip looks down, seeing if he can spot her.

"She digs everything."

On the floor, two women who are smartly dressed talk with Connie. The blonde, wavy-haired Sally greets her quickly. Cynthia rolls up the sleeves of her close-cropped jacket, revealing her milk chocolate toned arms before hugging Connie.

"Hiya, sweetheart!"

Sally says, "We were wondering if you'd be here today. You haven't been around for a little while."

Cynthia begins pointing to various women around the club.

"There's Monica, Jean, Gretchen. I think I see Dommy and Stevie on the other side. They've missed seeing you too."

Sally puts a hand to her hip. "Hey, you've got to come clean with us! Jean said you came in with this really cute guy. Tell us. Is that why you've been hiding out?"

Cynthia leans in. "I heard he's fine!"

Connie is briefly at a loss for words. "Wha—" She stops herself. "Oh. Well, it's nothing."

"Yeah. Right." Sally answers, incredulously.

"Come on, girl. You can tell us. Who is he?" Cynthia nudges.

Connie turns to look up at the DJ booth for Philip, who's not there. "He's somewhere in the building."

She then spots him talking with a few guys in an animated fashion. He laughs, which makes her feel better that he's more comfortable with the club's atmosphere. One guy hands him a pen while another pulls out some photos. Philip leans in, taking a better look. He shakes his head in astonishment.

Sally stretches to get a more unobstructed view.

"Oh, wow. What a doll! Where did you get him from, and does he have a twin?"

"You make it sound like I got a new puppy. Where did I get him from? Come on!" Connie grins mischievously. "I met him in front of San-San after work one night. That was all."

"I need to hang around your neck of the woods sometime."

"What about Jeff?" Connie inquires.

"Jeff, who?" Sally smiles back. "Jeff is with his brother in the Adirondacks for some fishing." Glancing back at Philip, she squints. "You know what? Your new guy kind of looks familiar to me. Where have I seen him before? That face. What did you say his name was?"

"Oh, it's Philip."

"Hmm. I don't know," Sally shakes her head.

Philip shows up, full of pep and energy.

"Where do we put our jackets?"

Connie says, "In the coatroom off to the left. It's a little room."

He pulls off his long jacket, exposing a very colorful short-sleeved striped shirt as he says, "This guy I was talking with said he has one of the first-built Stratocasters from the Fender factory in Fullerton. A fifty-four. What are the chances of meeting somebody who has one of those? Unreal! I've got a sixty-four, but that can't compare. Huh? Rock and roll!" He lets out a laugh, then disappears.

Connie shakes her head, unable to wipe the smile off her face.

"He's crazy," she remarks to the two women hanging on to her every word.

Cynthia says, "You like him. That's obvious."

Connie tries to avoid the answer, knowing full-well he's gay, and nothing will change that. "He's OK. I mean, we're just friends. Nothing serious."

"Not yet," Cynthia says slyly.

Philip goes over to Barbara.

"Funny seeing you here! What's up, Barb?"

"I'm just here to see what's happening. Have you seen any new or potential acts?"

He holds up his hand, "I'm not an A&R guy. If I had the power to predict, I'd have already found somebody who could put up with me, or know that I would meet somebody like Connie."

Barbara looks at him.

"Who's Connie?"

"Just a lady I met."

Barbara throws her head back in agony, squeezing her eyes shut.

"Please tell me this has nothing to do with our conversation a couple of weeks ago."

Philip answers with furrowed brows, "No." Looking back out on the dance floor to see what's around, he says, "I met her a few months ago...on a street corner of all places." He looks over at Connie. "She doesn't know."

"What you are?" Barbara asks in confusion.

"About what I do. Occupation-wise. She doesn't have to. I'm hoping I can hold her off for a little longer."

"People talk, Phil. Anyway, which one is she?"

Phil angles with a nod of his head.

"Over there. The one in red."

Connie looks over to see the heavy-set woman talking with Philip.

Gretchen, a pretty, frizzy auburn-haired lady with heavy lavender eye shadow, smiles while holding a drink. Sally and Cynthia are nearby.

"That's his manager," Gretchen points.

Connie looks confused.

"Manager? I don't know too much about the music industry, but I wasn't aware session players have managers. I thought they simply get a call."

Gretchen stops stirring her drink.

"Session player? Uh, Connie, where did you meet this guy?"

Sally answers her instead. "She said she met him on a street corner."

Connie gives Gretchen a challenging stare.

"In front of the San-San building. After work."

Gretchen briefly glances back at the guitar player, now having fun with a couple of girls on the dance floor. They enjoy the beat of Madonna's "Holiday," even though it's obvious he can't dance.

"Phil Reinhardt? Um, that's no session player. That's a bona fide rock star. He was with Deacon's Alley."

Cynthia goes, "Ooh!"

"What?" Connie answers, bewildered.

"He did a signing for his new album, *The Afterglow* last month at Tower Records. It's slowly been climbing the charts," Gretchen informs her.

"No. I didn't know," Connie looks at Philip through what she can see on the dance floor.

"Where did you think he was from?"

"Jersey," Connie stares at him.

"Moorestown is where the band originated from. That's how they got the name, Deacon's Alley."

"Band?" Connie replies in confusion.

Sally excitedly answers, "That's where I've seen him! I have one of their albums."

"Lehigh County," Gretchen says.

"Isn't that in Pennsylvania?" Sally inquires.

"Allentown," Gretchen looks directly at Connie. "You can ask him yourself. Yep. Philip Emmett Reinhardt. The fourth of five children, born November twenty-eighth, nineteen forty-nine to Emmett and Patricia Reinhardt. He's known for having a pink guitar."

"Connie, you need to get out of your parents' basement with their Tony Bennett collection," Sally remarks.

Philip pops up between Sally and Cynthia and says, "There's nothin' wrong with Tony Bennett." He steps from behind them with hands to hips in a less than masculine way. Putting his hand out, he asks, "And who are these lovely ladies?"

Cynthia lets out a laugh. She follows his lead, copying his moves.

"I'm Cynthia."

Sally introduces herself with a smile, "And I'm Sally."

Philip glances over at the DJ booth. He disappears for the time being. Connie notices him talking with High-Top and all of the hand gestures he gives.

Cynthia nearly squeals in excitement.

"Oh my God! He is a doll! So adorable!"

Philip returns to the women, peeking between Cynthia and Sally's shoulders. He says to Connie, "I'm gonna take these lovely ladies hostage." The guitarist mischievously sticks his tongue out. Again, he steps out in front of them. With hands to hips, he points to each of the women. "Tonight, you're Shirlie," at Sally, "and you're Pepsi," he directs at Cynthia.

Both women look at him, awestruck and thrilled.

He pulls them both by the hand. Connie shakes her head, watching all three disappear into the crowd. She says to herself, "Gay and famous," while walking over to the bar near the wall. Making her order, she turns around, nearly colliding with Barbara.

"Oh, pardon me!" Connie pushes back her hair in awkwardness, still feeling the remnants of shock from finding out Philip's full-blown rock star status.

Both women know of each other, but try to conceal their knowledge. Barbara breaks the silence between them.

"Phil is a great guy. He's a real sweetheart, very much a child at heart. You know he's gay, right?"

Connie nods her head in agreement.

"He has this sense. It's like a sixth sense he possesses. I've heard that guys like him have it. A kind of intuitiveness where he can pick up on things. Behaviors, body language, traits. Those eyes of his don't miss anything. Little things that we may not think of, he has it stored away in his cerebral cabinet. Phil is sensitive. He gets hurt a lot, but very headstrong when he wants something. He likes a good challenge, but at the same time, he can adapt to situations. I've known him for seven years. He continues to surprise me with his growth."

The snapping of fingers starts, "Wake Me Up Before You Go-Go," by Wham! At the further end of the dance floor, Philip strikes a pose before reacting to the song's infectious energy. Sally and Cynthia join in, laughing at their horrible go-go dancing. Shaking and shimmying, he leads the way for others to do the same, bringing about a synchronized gathering.

A long, loud wail breaks the laughter among the bright bursts of light and booming beat.

Barbara and Connie turn their attention to where the sound originates.

"He sure can be the life of the party!" Barbara comments.

"I can see that." A smile slowly spreading across Connie's face.

Barbara looks at her with seriousness as she states, "Be a friend to him. That's all he's looking for, 'cause they're hard to come by."

She then leaves.

Once the song ends, Philip hangs on to both Sally and Cynthia, unable to stop laughing.

High-Top spins "1999" by Prince, as the action on the floor continues.

Sally comments, "Oh, George has had enough for now!"

Cynthia lets out a laugh, "Poor Andrew."

"I know. There is none!"

Cynthia and Philip laugh harder at the thought of lacking one Wham! member. All three go to the bar, making orders.

"Phil, you want anything with whiskey?" Sally asks him.

"No. I don't go that hard."

"So much for a nice cocktail."

Immediately, the three burst out laughing. Philip can barely stand, leaning his head against the bar's top. Connie overhears them. She stifles a laugh.

Sally says, "I know just the thing Phil would love. How about a drink with cognac?"

Philip calms down. A sly grin appears on his face. "What do you have in mind?" he asks in an innuendo-filled tone.

Sally answers him in a teasing sensual tone, "Oh, a little something called, Between the Sheets."

"Oh God," Philip drops his head against the bar again, laughing hard. He pounds at the top, overcome by hilarity.

Cynthia remarks, "Poor Phil. He's not coming up for air anytime soon."

Connie shakes her head, glancing back at her buddy, who has the drink placed in front of him. Slowly, he comes out of his laughing stupor.

Gretchen approaches him after he takes a sip of the drink.

Looking at the martini glass, he remarks, "That's good."

"Phil, you used to do some gigs in Lehigh with The Town Allens."

He nods back cautiously. "Yeah. We did a bunch. Mostly high schools and some proms." Looking at Gretchen, he asks, "Do I know you?"

"Probably not. But, I'm sure you know Pete Fincher."

"Finch? Yeah. He ran sound for us, even when I joined Deacon's Alley." Glancing over at Connie, he realizes she might now know more about him. "We did one memorable show in sixty-nine. I was almost twenty, and it happened in Lackawanna. Valley View. They had recently consolidated a few locations, and the kids went crazy. They loved us. I remember we were asked to do a gig at Northeast in seventy, but I had just joined the band in Jersey, and Finch left the other guys too. He became Deac's number one roadie for all seven years. Some crazy times we shared."

Gretchen says, "I know Finch. I met him back then."

"Where are you from?"

"Emmaus."

"Emmaus? That's nearby. What year did you graduate?"

"Seventy-one. I was a sophomore when you guys played the dance at our school. A few of us managed to sneak in and watch you play. I talked with Finch that night. We lost touch. I went to Ivy in Pittsburgh afterward, then SVA here in Manhattan. Met up with him earlier this year. He does sound for this club. That's how we reconnected."

Connie listens on. Philip quickly notices her presence, then continues.

Philip asks, "Here?"

Gretchen nods back in agreement. "Yep."

He shakes his head in a sense of awe. "Small world. Anyway, I think we played just about everything east of the Susquehanna, except Philly. That was when I left." Philip takes another sip of his drink. "This is surprisingly good. Well, with a name like that...," he laughs. "What else can you remember or tell me?"

"You used to have a light blue guitar, didn't you?"

"Yeah. It was a sonic blue one. You know just about every musician at that time wanted to be a Beatle. I wanted a Fender Stratocaster like George Harrison. That's the guitar he repainted later on with the crazy colors and named it Rocky. So, I saved up and got enough to buy one. It was a great guitar too. We had a gig in Palmyra, and everything was stolen after the show. That guitar was one of the items taken. Somebody found a busted amp on the street a few blocks away. This was when we were scheduled to play a whole slew of shows. I didn't have another electric guitar to use. I tried to get by for two shows in Reading with a borrowed one, but it didn't feel right. I needed a reliable guitar and was scraping by financially. I figured it would cost too much to buy a new one. I liked the Strat. There was one option left for a starving artist," he grins. "I went to a pawn shop and did something crazy. I had a perfectly good Martin acoustic but knew there was no way I could play it at live gigs. These weren't coffee shops, and, uh, I didn't want to put anybody to sleep. Ya know? We were loud rock and roll. So, I was checking out this pawn shop, and I saw one guitar there. It was a Fender Stratocaster in shell pink. The shop owner told me that somebody found the guitar abandoned in the back of a furniture store and brought it in for some needed cash. He figured it was good enough, but no guy was going to want a pink guitar. I raised my hand and was like, 'I will,'" he giggles. "I didn't think twice and traded in the Martin for the sixty-four Strat. I totally loved her sound! A few gigs later, I got the call I was wanted for Deacon. Just before that, I went to LA. Visited the Fender company in Fullerton and begged these guys for a re-paint. I asked them if they could still get a custom pink Cadillac color because they used automotive paint. I was lucky enough. Caddy got her name and her color from there. I knew I wanted something that would stand out from other players. Unlike the blue one, I don't let Caddy stray far at all. She goes on planes, buses, taxis with me. No trunks or compartments."

Gretchen says, "Oh, wow! I never knew about that guitar. I just figured you liked pink."

"That, I do."

For the rest of the night, Connie consciously makes sure Philip has all the freedom he needs. She dances with several random guys, pretending to enjoy their company when knowing full-well the man she wanted was far and apart of higher status than she ever imagined.

In the wee hours, patrons from the euphoric rush of good times and dancing, stumble out into the city's sleepless streets. Connie and Philip follow suit, donning their outer apparel, stepping out to meet the overnight activity. With a lot on her mind, Connie stops in front of a gated storefront. Philip takes her cue, doing the same. Unable to hold back her thoughts, she begins talking aloud. He pulls out a cigarette and lighter. Lighting the end, he senses the turbulence in the air.

Connie steps back, cautiously retracing the steps of her friendship and the words spoken at any particular time. Meticulously, she pieces everything together.

"Right from the start. Music industry. Guitar. Even that drumming. East coast. Not New Jersey. Session player? Nope. A rock star from Allentown. Boy, I sure know how to pick them!" she marvels in mock joy. Connie glances at him with hidden shame, "I...I don't know what to think or what to say? How many gold records?"

Philip stares up at the night sky's fading light. He moves around like an antsy toddler, agitated by what he hears. Taking in a hasty drag from the cigarette, the guitarist ruffles his hair uncomfortably.

"A few," he answers.

"Quite frankly, I'm baffled by everything. I mean, I thought I met a pretty cool guy on a street corner. That's all," she continues. "Just an unencumbered friendship. Nothing to question." She waves a finger. "But that doesn't happen to me."

Philip closes his eyes, feeling her hurt tone.

"Nope," Connie shakes her head. "I find a guy who's preference is," she holds in a breath while a couple walks by. She briefly watches the traffic pass before continuing. "People like himself."

Philip exhales a column of smoke, as he quickly interjects, "Other human beings."

Connie rubs her eyes out of frustration.

"Oh, great. Semantics. Just what I need. Corrected grammar. Other human beings. People. Whatever. Your kind, not mine." She points to him. Turning away, she looks up at the sky. "If that's not enough, I find out you're a rock star. Wait. Not an ordinary one. What was it that Gretchen called you? A bona fide rock star. You sure are full of surprises, Mr. Reinhardt. I'll give you that." Her tone turns to anger and hurt. "All this time, I was talking about the dumbest things. I would be yammering away about work, Halloween, family stuff, bathing suits, even kids. What was I thinking? You were probably bored senseless, only trying to humor me. God, why didn't I see this coming? So embarrassing."

Philip eyes the sidewalk. Tight-lipped, he nods in agreement. His thoughts turn to what he wants to say as either a make-it or break-it moment.

She says, "Honesty seems so overrated when you can lie."

Quietly, he mutters, "I didn't technically lie."

Connie rolls her eyes. "You never quit, do you?"

Philip takes one last drag on the cigarette, throwing it down fiercely, stomping it out for good measure.

Immediately, he states, "Who do you want to see?"

"What?" Connie answers, puzzled.

He angles with disgust. "Who do you want tickets for? Who do you want to meet the most? Prince? Van Halen? Bowie? His comeback is pretty amazing! Bananarama? Duran Duran? Wham! Culture Club? Lionel Ritchie?"

"What? No."

"Oh, wait. You've talked about Springsteen before."

"No. I don't...,"

"I know what it is. Like everybody else, you're dying to see Michael Jackson."

"No. You're—"

"OK. How about backstage passes? It's the least I can do for you."

"Stop!"

"Hey, today's your lucky day. I am your genie. Rub the lamp, and you can get countless wishes," he smiles sarcastically.

"Just stop. Please. Now you're acting cruel," she answers while shifting her body in discomfort.

The traffic rushes past them. Connie feels her head spin from lack of sleep and fighting the urge to scream. Taxis beep, wanting to get by sluggish pedestrians crossing the street. It only adds to her agitation. Connie wipes back her hair again. She squeezes her eyes shut.

"I DON'T WANT ANYTHING FROM YOU!"

Philip blinks in wide-eyed shock by her outburst. He pulls back, tight-lipped.

Connie takes a deep breath. Calmly she says, "I never did."

Turning away from her, he looks down.

"I'm used to it by now." Philip goes over to lean against a nearby wall. "That's why I didn't say anything." He gives a hint of a smile.

Connie looks at him, wanting to understand.

"It's what to expect in this business. It doesn't matter what they are, men or women. Always the same. People are more interested in what I do than who I am as a person. For guys, it's the relationship aspect. They can see how far it'll go until the problems happen. For the women, they realize things won't go far, but they'll try for the friendship thing, and still, it's about favors."

"How many times does it happen?"

"Eight or nine times out of ten," he answers, looking down. "If I say I'm a professional musician or was with a band that had a few hits, that's when it happens. I get asked by somebody I'm with for one night, 'Hey, do you know...,' and they rattle off a name or two of who they want to meet. The evening is ruined as it is because they want to know what I've done. Then I don't feel like a human being, but someone else's lottery ticket. It's particularly tough when you're in the mood to make love, and what you get back is, 'My sister's birthday is coming up. She's a big fan of...,' Of course it's never me. They want tickets or backstage passes. Sometimes, even to meet their favorite artist. I remember one particular instance where I spent the night with someone. I was in the bathroom, just getting out, and there was this guy's little sister. She didn't care what was going on with her brother. She had stars in her eyes. It was incredibly painful and pathetic at the same time. I knew what it meant, and I couldn't do it again. Being over the age of thirty and single, you start to recognize it as desperation."

Connie turns away, shaking her head.

"I'm sorry. I'm so sorry that I ever said those awful things. I didn't know."

Philip looks at her when she decides to face him.

"I'm not bored senseless when you talk. Quite honestly, I find it rather refreshing to talk with somebody about the simplest aspects of life," he raises a brow. He grins, "There's nothing wrong with being treated like a human being. I made certain decisions that would affect my life in one way or another. I don't want my life broadcast by the likes of Rona Barrett or *Page Six* of the *New York Post*. What I do professionally takes precedence over the personal. I can repeatedly have my heart broken by a person. With music, it never lets me down. If whoever I'm with can't understand that, then the relationship fails, and one of us moves on or finds someone else to fill the void."

Connie looks out at the passing traffic. She checks her watch.

"It's about four in the morning. I think we should get going."

"Yeah. It is a bit late," Philip answers in agreement.

She twists her body with hesitation and says, "Listen, I know this might sound cliché, but I'm not out to get you. Friends aren't easy to come by in general. Sometimes we need the simple fundamental of understanding those who aren't like us." Stopping, she thinks for a moment. "OK. So, same time as usual next week?"

He nods back in agreement, then waves down a cab. Walking over to the opposite side of the vehicle, he opens the door for her. Connie gets in. For a minute, he stands by before saying, "Thanks." The musician smiles at her while his eyes show the look of satisfaction. He closes the door, giving it a light tap. "Go ahead."

Philip watches the taxi speed away. He closes his eyes and takes a deep breath.

The next weekend, Philip and Connie exit a shop.

"Would I be tempted to dress up like Prince?" Philip laughs. "It takes a lot of confidence for a man to wear some of the things he would, especially with his height. He's like eight inches shorter than me. Garter belts and high heels? Nope. The attraction of wearing underwear on the outside, eh, isn't there for me." He thinks for a minute. I'm not really into those weird fads. I think the music should do the talking. I mean, sure, you can dress up crazy, but if you don't get an audience moving, then what good is it? Too many artists live and die by their outrageousness. At least their career does. It's not to say I haven't done things maybe I shouldn't have." He glances down. "Some people have a gold tooth or two. Most of the time, they get them due to a bad drug problem. I have one, a gold tooth that is. It's a little towards the side.

"How did you acquire it?"

"Uh, playing too rough," he answers, then gets tight-lipped. "Anyway, you know there's a lot of crazy fashions people go through."

"What do you mean, playing too rough? You mean you smacked yourself with the guitar?" she asks.

"Not on a stage," he answers, turning his eyes away.

"Not on a st—" her brows go up. She stifles back a breath. "Well, I guess you really are a rock and roller!" She bites her bottom lip. "Would it be too personal if I asked you what kind of stage wear you used?"

"When I first joined, I always wore a suit. You know you want to look your best to impress? That carried over into Deacon's Alley. I was inspired by Hendrix and how he dressed, so I got a few velvet suits. The other guys in the band followed my lead, but then we learned the hard way when it came to outdoor festival gigs. Uh, velvet doesn't work too well in ninety-degree weather. We started getting into a routine during the second half of our shows by whipping off our jackets and throwing them down as if to say, 'Now we're gonna get serious!' It was a very angry and sexual response that got the audience into a frenzy. I didn't know how the new guitar would be for the experience, but Caddy was a big hit with the ladies. They totally were turned on by seeing me playing a pink guitar. The other guys in the band wanted to get extra security for Caddy. They referred to her as the Chick Magnet. At one point, somebody suggested everybody in the group get pink instruments. Our leader was like, 'Don't you dare!' That idea didn't go over so well. Caddy remained the only pink instrument for the duration of the band's time. After nearly dying from heatstroke onstage for the first few months, we started to wear lighter and more breathable material. There's a reason why Elvis wore those jumpsuits. Polyester holds up under spotlights."

Connie asks, "So, you weren't outrageous?"

"No. I've always chosen substance over being flashy. I'm not Elton John or Freddie Mercury. That's not to say I haven't had my moments of showing my rock and roll roots. I have. As a matter of fact, I did have a different look about four years ago. I discovered New Wave. I had my hair dyed bleach-blond, a little shorter. My partner at the time designed skinny ties, the shiny kind. I had a drawer full of them, and I'd wear one everywhere I went. Lots of guys were wearing them. I call it my Blondie period. I was so drawn to Debbie Harry, that I wanted to be the male equivalent of her. After the relationship ended, so did my interest in New Wave." He raises his brows to her, "So you see? There are different styles I've had. I'm sure the one I have now will change as soon as I get bored with it."

"I think it looks fine, if you ask me," Connie answers in apprehension.

He thinks while eyeing her.

"Wanna get a bite to eat? I can sure use it!"

"OK," she smiles back as they walk down the street.

"I don't come around here that often. Funny to say that when I used to work over there," Connie says, while pointing to Howard Johnson's further down Broadway.

Philip takes notice at a triple X theater marquee. Lowering his head, he shakes it in the sense of preposterousness. Looking back up, he nearly crashes into an older man with a dark suit, proselytizing Christian beliefs with a sign.

Philip gains a little more speed to keep up with Connie, who is unfazed by the sight of sexual displays glaring through shop windows.

"Ah, here we are," Connie points to Playland, the long-standing arcade center. She opens the door, playfully smiling back at her friend. Philip follows her into a cacophony of audio mayhem and lit up arcade games. Pinball bells and whistles sound off, causing lights to flash.

"An arcade?" Philip asks her.

"You don't want it to look like a date, do you?"

"Tr—" he begins to answer back, getting distracted by one of the pinball machines. "Hey! I haven't seen one of these in a long time!"

Connie looks over to see what he's talking about.

"I have to confess." Philip grins.

"One of your many?" Connie quips.

"I don't remember which one. All I know is, it was a pinball machine. Come on. I'd do this on the road with the guys in the band. Oh, and I think the last time I played was a few years back, somewhere in Chinatown. You ever play?"

"Pinball was never a big thing for me."

Philip suggestively raises a brow. "Want me to show you how? It's all in the hips," he says with mischievous glee. Getting close to the machine, he gives a sharp twist of the hips, watching Connie's reaction.

She gives a deep breath, shaking her head.

For good measure, he gets her going with heavy gyration and a thrust. He lets out a loud laugh.

Connie groans in disapproval. She mutters under her breath, "Typical male." Turning away, she walks towards the video arcade section, leaving Philip alone to do whatever he wants with a pinball machine. Walking by games like *Space Invaders*, *Asteroids*, *Centipede*, *Pac-Man*, *Donkey Kong*, and *Frogger*, Connie finally decides on which one she wants to play.

At the same time, three boys show up at the arcade. All look to be pre-teens and are white, Puerto Rican, and black. They put their backpacks down and join the sparse crowd. The dark-haired boy studies Philip while he plays pinball while the other two hang around the Atari games. The black youth looks Connie up and down admiringly from the back. He goes to her left side to play *Pac-Man*, or pretend to. His Puerto Rican buddy checks out *Frogger* on the right side of her.

Connie's eyes slowly tilt one way, then the other, feeling she's being watched.

Philip keeps missing with the flipper. He notices the kid to his right looking on. Turning his way, he tells the boy, "Go ahead. It's all yours."

Connie keeps her concentration on the object of the game. She aims for the spaceship to shoot at all the colorful asteroids. Beeping sound effects accompany every shot. She turns the ship around, expertly firing at every size asteroid vertically crawling up the screen.

Philip goes over to her. Both boys quickly step back and watch from a distance away.

"I see you have some hip action going on," he mischievously teases, draping his arm over the top of the game's cabinet.

She jolts the controls, trying to get at every asteroid she can shoot at.

He says, "Pretty fierce. I wouldn't want to be that asteroid!"

Without making eye contact, she answers him. "I'm at twenty-three thousand five hundred and sixty-seven points." Again she shoots at a fresh batch of asteroids coming up. "What happened? Get bored of getting it on with the pinball machine?" She bites her bottom lip, staring at the screen in concentration.

"You're the one who brought me to Sexland."

"Playland," she corrects him.

"I was referring to the entirety of Times Square."

"I'm sure there's something here you can play." A moment later, she says, "Thirty-six thousand five hundred eighty. I want to see if I can get this puppy up to sixty thousand."

"Well then, you're barking up the wrong spaceship."

Connie snickers back, "You're so awful."

He giggles back, going over to the *Pac-Man* game.

"Amateur," she says with a smile, noticing his choice.

Philip pulls out a batch of change from his jacket pocket. He loads a quarter into the machine. Looking at the screen, he readies himself as though he's about to pounce.

"You know how to play, right?" Connie asks.

"Sure. I'm a pro." He answers in a pseudo-macho tone, then laughs. "OK. Let's go." Keeping his eyes on the screen as the ghosts are released for Pac-Man to devour. The sound effect of sirens and other noises gives way to Pac-Man getting attacked by his foes instead.

Connie shakes her head at the recognizable sound effects. "Uh, Mr. Pro? You just got eaten."

"Ah, I gave them that one. I'm just warming up."

Again, Philip begins to play, and still, the same sound goes off.

Connie protests, "You can't even play *Pac-Man*!"

Philip answers quickly, "Hey, it's not as easy as you think!"

"Yeah. Not when you're getting killed like that!"

A man in a business suit hurriedly walks in. Loosening his tie, he glances around at the variety of games and occupants.

The two boys continue to watch the exchange between Philip and Connie, enjoying the volley of words and laughter. Their buddy goes to join them. The boys are fascinated by Philip's appearance of looking like something from MTV, but also his child-like demeanor. At least the black youth is taken by Connie's playing skills, making him pay attention to how high her score soars.

Philip glances over to see the audience of three boys standing nearby, watching him and Connie.

"Uh, Connie? I think we're being watched," he tells her.

"They probably figure you're an overgrown kid."

"Oh, I figured they could tell I suck at being an adult."

He shakes his head, walking over to another machine. "*Q*bert*. Hmm. I'll give it a whirl. Can't be any harder." He loads a quarter. Looking at the screen, he reads the directions. "Fatal plummet." Sucking in his teeth, he quietly taps on the console and says, "Yeah. That's all I need." Philip works the controls quickly, realizing Q*bert is not working the right way and plummets off the cliff. Taking a deep breath, he says, "Fatal plummet is successful. Yep." While he shakes his head, the Puerto Rican boy addresses him before he can properly grieve.

"Excuse me, Mister? Do you have a couple of quarters to spare?"

Philip turns to look back, dumbfounded by the kid's brazen question of money. He digs in his pocket. Connie glances over briefly.

"Here," he drops a few quarters in the boy's hand.

"Thanks!" the boy answers, handing a quarter to each of his two friends.

They wander off to find a game of their choosing.

Philip looks at the boys walk away. "Yeah. No problem." He glances at Connie. "They know an adult by the fact we carry money in our pockets." Shaking his head, he grins at the thought.

Suddenly, they hear a loud thud, and a man's voice booms, "Son of a bitch!"

Several people turn to see the man in the business suit kick one of the machines hard. Connie's eyes swivel away from the *Asteroids* game momentarily. She shakes her head.

The three boys wander towards the front. They giggle while watching the frazzled man move on to another arcade game. He stares at them with an icy vengeance. Running a hand through his hair, he goes over near Connie and looks her up and down. She feels his eyes creepily watch her back. Instead of showing him any attention, she keeps her eyes on the game and looks up further to see the score. Luckily, he walks away, only to be near Philip. He hears snickering in back, turning to see the boys. That's all this guy needs. To be laughed at by some kids. Situating himself next to a game, he pops in a quarter at the *Centipede* machine.

Philip continues to tend to *Q*bert*.

The man next to him kicks the machine hard, muttering under his breath.

"No reason to get violent. I know it's frustrating, but it's just a game," Philip says quietly. He hears the all too familiar sound of failure from the *Centipede* game. The man pounds his fist against the control panel and shakes violently.

Philip leans closer with a grin, "Seeing red?"

The enraged man grabs Philip by the jacket collar, shoving him against the arcade game cabinet.

Before Philip can even react, Connie steps between both men. She puts her right hand to his chest, with the other to his attacker.

"Don't you dare even touch him!"

The man grits his teeth, looks at Connie and releases Philip from his hold.

"You want a challenge? Take me on!" Connie points to herself.

Slowly, the frazzled man steps back and looks around, retreating out of the building.

Philip closes his eyes and exhales deeply.

The three boys watch with jaws agape. The black youth utters in amazement, "Now, that's the kind of lady I wanna marry when I grow up!"

The Puerto Rican kid shakes his head. "She's got balls!"

"Wow!" The third boy says.

Connie's eyes scan the room, knowing they've caused a scene. She walks out of the building quickly. Philip follows her.

Within a few steps, he says, "You didn't have to do that. I know what you're thinking. I can't handle myself and need somebody to—"

Connie swiftly turns and cuts him off. "I could have beaten his ass at *Centipede*." She knows he thinks it's about him and a lack of masculinity. Taking a deep breath, she looks at him with a slight pout. "Come on. Let's get out of Sexland."

With the mid-July heat, Philip and Connie go to a club in the Village. They walk in while English Beat's "Mirror in the Bathroom" is playing. Connie looks at all of the patrons on the floor. Black, white, Latino, Asian, straight, gay, flashy, subdued, trendy, and artsy, all have converged for a night of dancing magic. Magenta and green lights flicker in time with the beat. Philip finds a table for the two of them. He signals to a brightly dressed waitress about drinks. Connie already finds herself moving to the music, standing in place, propelled by her hips wagging.

"I'll have a Coke," she advises. Her movements sway with more emphasis. She turns to Philip. "Are you going out there?"

He hesitates for a second. "Nah. You can go ahead."

"OK," she leans backward. "Suit yourself!"

Connie goes out to the dance floor as the beat turns into the Human League song, "Love Action (I Believe in Love)." She nearly bumps into a couple. Rather than being awkward, they all laugh in recognition of their closeness. The couple invites her to dance with them, which she joyously accepts. Seeing Philip sitting at the table, she bops her way over to him. Pulling off his sunglasses, she puts them on herself. They begin to slide from her face. She takes them off. Leaning over his shoulder, she says, "They don't fit me." Connie puts them back on him before sashaying away.

He shakes his head with a small smile.

As time goes on, the music starts to release Connie's inhibitions. She goes back to dancing by herself when a young guy attempts to assert himself. Connie notices he can't even keep up with the beat, ruining the sexy sway of INXS' "Original Sin." She stops to watch the man who looks like he's convulsing. He doesn't even notice the sour glance she gives. Her eyes wander over to an interracial couple who are deep into the song. Envious of them having a good time, she couldn't get Philip onto the floor. Not this night. She would have to do it alone or find some great guy for herself.

Philip continues to watch her from the table, occasionally taking a sip of his drink. Connie comes over to have her soda. A song awakens her senses. "Furs! Oh, I love this one!" She quickly rushes back out to the dance floor. Several people walk away, unable to latch onto the beat of "Heaven."

Connie spins in place, putting her arms out as if she were catching the rain. She sways to the drumming that sweeps her away. All the while, her eyes are closed, letting the feeling engulf and energize her. She goes through the motions to the lyrics with the same passion as a ballet dancer. The music drives her body to movements that make Philip take notice. He pulls his sunglasses down to peer at her from the rims. It's the primal need to feel the energy of the beat. She twists and turns as though under the will of a supernatural force. It's an electrified feeling that she's plugged into.

Philip's eyes never leave her, even when the next song starts up, and she starts moving again.

From behind, two men walk up to the table. Both look nearly identical, other than the bone structure of their faces. Each has short dark hair and neatly trimmed mustaches.

"Burt, hon, will you look who's here?" One man says to the other.

A distracted Philip turns the other way when he hears the voice.

"Burt, Randolph. What's up?"

Randolph answers with feminine quality, "Surprised to see you here."

Philip slips his sunglasses off, pocketing them in his jacket. "It's a pretty good variety of music."

"New Wave?"

Burt's eyes meet the glass of a partially finished soda with a straw sticking out of it. He asks in a similar tone, "Isn't that a bit kitschy?"

Philip answers with little defense. "It's not bad." He changes his thoughts. "So, what's going on with you two? Lookin' for trouble?" he giggles back mischievously.

Randolph fishes in his jacket pocket. "Well, we managed to score some much sought-after prime seats to *Les Miserables*." He produces two tickets, placing them on the table. "And we would like to offer these to you."

Philip looks at them. "Uh, nice. But, um, I'm flying solo these days."

"So we heard. Listen, there's somebody new that works with Burt, who just moved into the city. He can use some help getting around the Big Apple."

Burt adds in, "You can even show him a good time."

Philip puts his hand up. "Oh. Wait. I know where this is going."

Randolph asks, "How else can you mend a broken heart? Besides, he's terribly cute."

Burt gives Randolph a hard nudge.

"Well, he is! I'm not trying to push you off the bed!"

The two men laugh.

Connie comes back to the table, where she finds the three of them talking. Burt notices right away that she picks up the unattended drink, delicately sipping it with a straw. Connie turns her attention to Philip. "They play a lot of good music here!" she enthuses.

Burt and Randolph stare at her as though she has just interrupted the most important conversation in the world.

Philip looks back at the two men.

"Connie, this is Burt and Randolph. Guys, this is Connie."

Neither Connie nor the two men make any move to extend their hands for a greeting.

Philip turns his head in her direction. "Alright?"

Connie graciously gives a small smile. "Hi."

Randolph says, "Couldn't help but notice your moves, sweetheart. Did you get those from Uncle Vinnie's?"

Connie takes a careful sip of her drink. Licking her lips, she gives him a look as though to understand a secret code. "No," glancing at Burt, she squints at Randolph. "But you look a little familiar to me. Are you an EMT by any chance?"

Burt snorts.

Randolph turns around at his partner's reaction.

Philip remains silent.

"No," Randolph answers with stone-like masculinity.

"Are you sure?" she asks in a state of confusion. "Because I thought you might have…, Well, I thought maybe you played the part of an EMT. You know, like those…, What do you call them? Singing telegrams? The kind who do them for old people with the boombox to raise their heart rate."

Burt lets out a groan.

She turns to him instead. "Maybe it was your partner. I couldn't be sure." Picking up her jacket, Connie excuses herself from the table, leaving the club.

Randolph stays quiet.

Philip gets up and walks away.

Burt waits until the musician is out of their sight when he says, "The closet-y type. You just know there's a football jersey waiting to fall out." He turns to his partner. "Did you see the way she squirmed?"

Randolph replies, "Probably readjusting her maxi pad."

"The little bitch had some moves," Burt answers with a smirk.

Both of them start laughing.

Outside, Philip looks around when he sees Connie a little ways away from the club. He trots to catch up with her.

"Hey, are you going to just leave like that?"

"Your friends can use some bedside manners," she answers stiffly.

"I know they're more open about who they are, but you didn't have to go off on them like that. I've known those two for some time. Look, I'm only saying this because you seem a little bit judgmental regarding them." His eyes go wide. "You're the one who's talking about bedside manners, and I didn't even introduce Burt and Randy as together."

Connie looks at him. "I don't judge people by how they look. It's how they act that I notice. I didn't put my hand out because I already saw the look on their faces when I approached the table. They resented me on sight. You know why? Because I'm a woman. Of course, you would defend them. They are...," She looks around to make sure nobody else is around. "...your friends."

Philip rolls his eyes and shakes his head.

"That look reminded me of being in junior high school. It's the you-don't-fit-in look. Prejudice goes both ways, buddy," Connie advises.

Philip looks down in guilt.

"Do you even know what Uncle Vinnie's is?"

He shakes his head, no.

"It's a strip club on the west side. Your so-called friends think that a woman who likes to dance must like strange men to shove bills down their thongs. It couldn't possibly be because somebody like me, actually enjoys music. Nah. It has to be for some other nefarious purpose," she snorts back. "You can treat people whatever way you want to. You have a license to do what you want because I'm just a regular person, not a business associate you meet with at a fancy restaurant."

Philip glances down at the sidewalk.

"You know what? I think you should take those two tickets. One for you. One for your ego." She turns to look down the street. "As far as I'm concerned, this night's done." Connie walks to the corner when she spots a cab getting closer.

Philip takes a deep breath, beginning to walk toward her when the cab pulls over.

"Connie," he says.

It's too late for apologies, as she gets in the car.

The taxi disappears into the night.

He puts a hand in his hair, then turns to walk away.

Returning to the club, Philip goes back to the table. He looks at the two men. Sliding the tickets back to Randolph, he says, "I don't want them."

Taking out his wallet, he picks out a few bills and drops them on the table. Noticing the waitress nearby, Philip points down, then leaves.

Burt and Randolph watch him walk away.

Burt remarks, "He likes the little vixen."

CHAPTER 5

Connie walks out the door of San-San, glancing down at her opened pocketbook. She begins to look back up when her eyes meet his. Neither says anything. Wanting to step forward, Philip stands in her path. She stops and shifts her weight on one leg.

"I have to apologize for what happened last night," Philip answers with guilt. "I don't hang around Burt and Randolph often at all. I only talk to them when I see them. I know how abrasive they can get. I went into defensive mode, and that wasn't right. Sometimes we condemn the worst things when we're guilty of treating people the same. I'm quick to project when anybody can turn around and do the same to me. Instead, I took it out on you, and I'm sorry about that. I'm not used to doing this apology thing. Stuff ends typically, and that's it. I walk away with a clear conscience but scarred from experience. I'm not doing it this time."

Connie inhales deeply, showing her patience is running thin.

He continues, "I know you probably think my apology is garbage, and I can't blame you. But, you have no idea what I've seen and heard. There is a hostility that has even shocked me. I know the stigma. I live with it. If I'm defensive, then there is a reason. It's challenging to juggle a public persona and a very private and much-detested life not many people know. It's especially tough when I'd bring a female friend to meet my family, or go it alone when I know full-well that the person I want to be with, I can't. I know they wouldn't be accepted. My parents will ask when I'm going to settle down, and I always have to tell them, 'I'm too busy with my career. You're not going to get grandchildren from me.' I'd rather say that than be treated like a leper. I love my family with all my heart, but I'm not going to hurt them with what I am. So you see?"

Connie crosses her arms, looking down at the sidewalk, then up at the sky. She doesn't know how to feel. Guilty of her shame at leaving the club in anger? Or was it her anger in being discounted by other people, who she perceived as far more important? In a way, she wants to be sympathetic but doesn't want to come off as anybody's welcome mat. Pushing back her hair in discomfort, she shakes her head.

Forgive him, or not?

Philip bites his bottom lip, knowing he screwed up. He reaches in one of his oversized jacket pockets and steps up to her. She looks at him. He hands her a card-sized envelope. Connie furrows her brows in puzzlement while accepting the item.

"What is...? You got me a card?" she asks.

"Open it."

Connie opens the flap, sliding out a card. Her frown instantly changes to a creeping smile at the sight of a sweet though sad-eyed basset hound with daisies in front of the large paws. Flipping open the card, it reads, "*I'm sorry...*" Accompanied, are his words half printed, half cursive.

Connie - That I hurt you.
Can you forgive me?
P.S. (the daisies are as close to flowers I can get!)

Connie wipes a tear from her eye, stifling a laugh. She closes the card.

"OK. Forgiven." Putting the item back in the envelope, she asks, "Did you really get this yourself?"

"Uh, do you need the receipt?" he asks, before producing a smile. "Yeah. I did. At least I hope I did. Twins don't run in my family."

"You actually went to the store and got this yourself. Not a personal assistant or hired help?"

"No," he giggles back. "Send a butler to pick up a greeting card? I'm not that spoiled!"

Connie shakes her head in wonder.

"It's just that, I've never received a card...from anybody. You know, like this." She places the card in her pocketbook. "Thank you."

"You're welcome."

She asks, "So, what do you want to do?"

"I have an idea. Come on."

He hails a taxi.

Ten minutes later, Philip and Connie arrive at their destination.

The Lower Manhattan skyline looms overhead as Philip leans against the railing while looking out at the wonderment. Lights hang along the perimeter of the Brooklyn Bridge. Ripples of light shine against ebony waters below. Buildings, faded orange from the light pollution are dotted with white and yellow squares of windows within. High up, the sky casts a navy curtain over the city.

Connie walks along the railing dividing the Brooklyn Heights Promenade from the East River. She joins Philip, overlooking the business district's structures. Parts of Wall Street and the twin towers of the World Trade Center jut to the sky in majestic glory. The landscape looks like a larger-than-life diorama.

Philip says, "Sometimes I come here to get away from this crazy city. I did it when I first arrived over a decade ago. I don't know? To me, it felt safe. From this distance, it looks like any old metropolitan city. Dirty. Old. Building after building. Then you realize how much fun it is. And of course, there's plenty of architecture, museums, art, theaters..."

"Shops," she adds in.

"Shops too. But it's amazing what you can find here."

"There's no other place like it. Maybe that's why we love it so much," Connie says. "You look around right here, and it's a great setting for romantic couples."

"Anything really," he smiles.

She looks back at him with a small smile.

"Yeah."

Suddenly, a spotlight shines on the water little ways down the river from up high. The sound of a motor rumbles. Philip and Connie look up to see a police helicopter looming above. Two NYPD boats scurry to the lighted area.

Philip shakes his head.

"That doesn't look good. Um, strike the part about me saying, it seemed safe. Let's get outta here."

The two walk away.

Connie and Sally sift through a variety of clothing on racks at Trash and Vaudeville. Sally is less enthusiastic about the apparel, grimacing at some outfits. Connie intently pulls out a purple striped jersey.

"What do you think?" she asks, placing it against herself, twisting her body to model it.

"I think it's fine if you're seeing a rock star," Sally answers, fishing for a response.

Connie rolls her eyes, shoving the shirt back on the rack.

"Does he know you come here?" Sally asks.

"He doesn't care. He doesn't like to go shopping," Connie says back, flipping through hangers of clothing.

Sally furrows her brows, "What's with men having an aversion to shopping?"

"I don't know." Connie's eyes fixate on a black and silver metallic blouse. "They're built that way." She picks up the hanger. "What do you think of this one?"

"Great..., If you're sleeping with him," Sally nonchalantly glances around.

Connie flares her nostrils, jamming the hanger back, among other shirts. Angrily she turns to her friend, "Oh my God. Really?" In a huff, she says, "I am not sleeping with Philip. All we do is hang out together, and ninety-nine percent of the time, we talk. That's all."

"You don't do all the normal things couples do? Eat? Go to the movies?"

"Yes. We eat, like normal human beings. And yes, we did go see *Ghostbusters*."

Sally puts her hands up, "Oh, how romantic!" she answers sarcastically.

"What do you suggest we see, smarty-pants?"

"*Purple Rain* is supposed to start playing pretty soon. It's sure to have music in it."

"OK. I'll bite. Who's starring in it?" Connie asks with disinterest.

"Prince," Sally sways while answering.

Connie starts to walk towards another section of the shop with Sally following close behind. Knowing she's there, Connie throws out, "We're not a couple. We don't date. It's strictly platonic."

"Oh, that's too bad. I was hoping we could double up. You and Philip, me and Jeff."

"Not gonna happen," Connie answers while checking out a rack of skirts.

"Does he do that thing a lot of famous people do when going to a restaurant? You know...," Sally speaks in a deeper voice. "Do you know who I am? That kind."

Connie looks back at her, shocked.

"Oh, no. No. Philip does not do that. He doesn't act like a pompous jerk. We've only gone to diners, delis, and an occasional hot dog stand."

"Boy, you really are avoiding anything romantic."

Connie exhales deeply. She takes off her pocketbook to rummage through it. "I want to show you something." She picks up the envelope inside. "Here."

Sally pulls the card out. Her face lights up. "Awww! It's so cute! A hush puppy, and with daisies. "Oh, it looks like the face of, 'I'm sorry.'"

"Read what's inside," Connie smirks.

Sally reads it. Her expression changes. She hands the card and envelope back to Connie with no words.

"Are those the words of a pompous jerk?" Connie asks with assured confidence

"No. Not at all."

Connie puts the card back in her pocketbook. "He gave that to me after a little angry episode I had with him. It was a one-sided deal." She gives a slight smile.

"Are you in love with him?"

"No," Connie answers stiffly, before walking away.

Sally rushes to catch up with her.

Connie turns around quickly.

Sally stops herself from saying anything. She changes her tune.

"Something occurred to me. What if Philip goes on tour? I mean, are you going to go with him?"

"No. I'm not. Besides, I know he won't ever ask me. Plus, you know the kind of work I do. I don't go on vacation."

"That's the problem with you, Connie. You work for a company that services half of the east coast. You make like a jillion dollars, and you don't like to have any fun."

Connie answers back, "I do. Just locally. Take right now, for instance. I'm looking for clubwear. That makes me happy."

"Happy for you is leading a single, solitary life with a rock star as a buddy, and sitting in front of a cranky computer, typing out inventory lists for people who probably enjoy fun in the sun."

The two women glance over accessories such as large hair bows, long mesh gloves, and broad belts.

Sally takes a long glove and slaps Connie on the shoulder with it.

"Remember, I tried to invite you to Costa Rica with me?"

Connie thinks before saying, "I kind of remember."

"I asked if you wanted to go snorkeling."

"Oh. OK. Yeah. I do remember. You know I don't do crazy things like that."

"I know, alright. I know you're turning into your mother! You listen to her music already. Or am I getting confused with your dad?"

Connie turns around defensively to answer, "I listen to plenty of new music!"

"You didn't even know Philip was a rock star."

Connie ignores Sally's words, becoming transfixed to the display counter glass display.

She asks the sales clerk at the register, "Excuse me, can I see the bracelet? The one in the back?" Connie points to the item as her mind wanders.

Sally looks over at her friend, finding interest in an item that shocks even her. The sales clerk takes out the black bracelet to show Connie, who looks at it like it's more precious than metal.

Sally shakes her head.

"What are you going to do? Start dressing up like Madonna? Maybe you want to start going to Danceteria too?" She watches the exchange. "Connie, it's one of those silly rubber bracelets. They call them Jellies. Are you sure you want to get something like that?"

"Oh, wait!" Connie steps away from the counter to grab the black and silver jersey she saw earlier. Returning to the register, she says, "And that."

Sally hums the Madonna song, "Holiday," while her friend gets rung up.

Connie says, "I'll take that," before the bracelet goes in the bag. She drops it in her pocketbook. Sally looks on in befuddlement at how much the item is a priority to Connie.

"Are you gonna get some mesh gloves with that?"

"Nope."

"The next thing you're going to tell me is that you want to go see breakdancers."

Connie turns to her with a smile.

"I already did that," she answers with raised brows.

"What? You went to see breakdancing?" Sally asks in astonishment.

"You don't think I have fun."

The two women begin to exit the shop. Connie opens the door.

Sally abruptly says, "Can I touch your forehead?"

Connie giggles as they leave.

"What categories do black artists dominate?" Philip repeats Connie's words as they venture around Fifth Avenue.

"Mmm-hmm," Connie nods back. "I figured I would ask you since you're the expert."

"Let's see. There are blues. That's broken down by region: Texas, Delta, which is Mississippi, Chicago, Louisiana, Piedmont, or Appalachian. I'm sure I missed a few. Jazz, R&B, soul..., You've got STAX, which is more funk-based soul than say Motown, which is more along the lines of R&B. Smoother. In other words, it's Otis Redding versus The Temptations. They all have a specific feel to them. STAX is Redding, Booker T & the M.G.'s, Rufus and Carla Thomas, Isaac Hayes, Sam & Dave, Albert King, Eddie Floyd, Johnnie Taylor. On the Motown side, yeah, there's The Temptations, Smokey Robinson, Stevie Wonder, Four Tops, Martha Reeves, who I had a massive crush on as a kid. Gladys Knight, uh, Jackson 5, Marvin Gaye, Diana Ross and the Supremes. The list goes on. Then you've got pop, rock and roll, disco, hip-hop. Then you break it down into region or sub-categories, like..., OK, there's, Spanish Harlem. That's where you'll find artists like Ben E. King, The Drifters, Coasters. Brill Building kind of music. The prominent songwriters from there wrote for them. Stuff like, 'Stand By Me,' and 'Under the Boardwalk,' is from that type. I guess you can say that every label has or had its sound. Phil Spector's Wall of Sound gave us a lot of great black lady singers and groups. On that end, there's the Ronettes, Crystals, Blossoms..., Well, you get the idea."

Connie reluctantly nods again in agreement, not truly knowing what he's saying.

"And then there's Philly soul," Philip answers with a slight smile. "Patti LaBelle, Harold Melvin & the Blue Notes, Spinners, Trammps, Lou Rawls, The O' Jays. The earliest version of Chic was part of it, but they were from here, I think." Philip looks around. "Anyway, I don't think music has color," he answers in brief distraction, glancing ahead. "It's how you feel."

The two come upon the New York Public Library with its Beaux-Arts architecture, paired with two life-sized marble lions bookending the main stairs.

Philip rushes over to one of the lions.

"What did Mr. Beauregard tell you in Mythology and Literature class?" he asks Connie while arching his brows in mischief.

"What? I didn't have a Mr. Beauregard."

"Ah-huh. That's the problem right there. Ya missed it. It was on the test."

"Wh... What did I miss, and what test?" she asks in perplexity.

"I guess I'll have to tell you. You know about Medusa, right?"

"Medusa's Angel? The band that plays at the..., I'm trying to remember the name."

"Medusa. The lady with the snakes? She needed a better hairdresser for sure."

"Oh! That Medusa," Connie stifles a laugh.

"Anyway, you know the story about these two," Philip points in back to the lions.

"Patience and Fortitude? No," Connie answers, slightly puzzled.

"Word has it that these two managed to cross paths with Medusa and made the mistake of looking at her," he glances up at Fortitude. "And here they sit to this day."

Connie eyes Philip suspiciously.

"Wait. How many times did you see *Clash of the Titans*?"

Philip laughs, walking away. Connie goes to join him.

"You didn't answer me," she says.

"More than once. You?"

"Once was all I could stand. Medusa gave me the creeps! I thought I was going to turn to stone!"

Philip laughs again.

"So? What's next?" he asks. "The park?"

"In the back? Yeah."

They head over to the spacious Bryant Park, where Philip takes in the sight of green grass on the central lawn. Park benches surround the outer perimeter.

"An improvement," Philip quips. He turns to look back at Connie, who trails behind.

A few feet away, a group of two men and one woman glance his way and point. One man shakes his head. The woman animatedly nods her head enthusiastically. She walks over to Philip.

"You're him! You're Phil Reinhardt!" She cups her mouth with both hands. "Oh my God," she muffles her trembling voice. "We love every one of the Deacon's Alley records. All four of them." Again, she covers her mouth and nose. "I can't believe this. What are the chances of something like this happening? I know you're from Pennsylvania. Todd and Ralph are New Jersey. Keith was from Washington, originally. Oh, but this is amazing. Are you in the city now?"

"No. Elsewhere," Philip answers back readily.

"Still, it's...," she puts her hands up. "It's incredible! My name is Andrea." Glancing over in the back, Andrea points to the two men. "Oh, and that's my husband, Steve, and his brother, John. When we were dating for a time, their grandmother had just passed away, and all of us were wondering what to do after the service, and then we found out Deacon's Alley was playing that night in Tulsa."

"Seventy-four," Philip answers with assurance.

"Yes, it was."

"I remember that show, I think. That was the one where the girl in the front row started doing a striptease. Her bra landed on Todd's bass, and he couldn't take the thing off fast enough. Not like many people had a problem with it. Security started freaking out. They threw her a towel and tried escorting her out of the arena."

"We were on the other side of the stage, so we missed the whole thing. I know the audience shifted."

"Yeah. There was a tug-of-war between security and some young guys trying to keep her there. We thought we were going to have to stop the show. The stage manager told us it was OK and to keep going."

Connie stands a little further back, able to hear the conversation. Feeling uncomfortable that fans know more about her buddy than she does, intimidates her. She fidgets with the inside of her pocketbook nervously.

Quietly, she utters, "It's stupid. He won't care. What was I thinking?"

Philip lets out a laugh. Andrea finally gets her husband and brother-in-law to join her in the conversation.

Steve says, "How did I miss that?"

"You were in mourning," Andrea reminds him.

"Oh, that's right. Well, my spirits could have been lifted if I'd known."

"I'm sure," Andrea answers before thinking of something, turning back to Philip. "The only thing I have for you to sign is my notepad. I carry one on me all the time. Can't always walk around with albums!" she laughs.

Philip giggles back, "True."

Andrea picks out a pen.

"Have you heard anything from the new album?" Philip asks out of curiosity.

"Oh, yes! Of course! If I don't listen to the album, then I have the tape in the car. I love the title, *The Afterglow*, especially the second track, 'Object of Affection.'"

Andrea hands over the notepad and pen to the musician.

Philip says, "Yeah. We should be filming a video for it soon, Or so I've heard."

"That's great!" she answers excitedly.

Connie watches Philip sign for the fans.

The three people finish their conversation with the musician, congratulating him on the new album and wishing him luck before parting ways. Philip watches them walk away gleefully. He's happy to make somebody's day because they made his by acknowledging the music.

Walking over to a park bench, he plops down. Looking up, he notices Connie's expression of awkwardness.

"What?" he asks.

She stays quiet.

Choosing to stand up instead, he answers with, "That sometimes can happen."

Connie turns her back, thinking of what she wants to do or say next. Again, she fidgets in her pocketbook. Spinning around to face him, she hesitantly says, "Um...,"

He looks at her attentively.

For a moment, Connie feels like she could have a crush on him, with the giddy, heart-galloping innocence of a child. Stopping herself, she continues, "There's something I want to give you."

"Me?" he answers with his expressive almond eyes going wide.

Connie slips her hand in the pocketbook, pulling out the item with a clenched fist.

"Turn your wrist over."

Philip turns his hand over.

She shakes her head.

"No. Palm down. Now, close your eyes."

Connie takes the small item and tries to fit it over his much larger hand than she anticipated.

Closing his eyes, he grins at the feel of her fingers sliding up his wrist.

Connie bites her bottom lip, hoping he'll like it.

"OK. You can open your eyes."

Philip looks down.

"What...," he starts to say, lifting his hand to inspect it. A broad grin appears on his face. "What's this?" Philip stares at the skinny black rubber bracelet sitting on his wrist. "Oh! Now I look as pretty as you!" he answers in less masculine glee.

Connie giggles.

He playfully teases, "Is this like a proposal or something?" His brows arch up.

She laughs back, "No, silly. It's just a little something I picked up. All the cool kids are wearing them these days."

"Oh, really? Cool kids? So, I'm officially cool now, right?" He holds up his hand in front of her.

Connie hesitates, giggling again.

"You're cool already. I don't know. I thought of you and.., It's just a little friendship thing. Ya know? You can wear it if you want to think of me or if you happen to get lonely. Something like that," she shrugs. "I don't know. Maybe it was silly..."

She notices immediately that Philip's expression has changed from his usual jovial, playful kid-like manner to deeply pensive and reflective.

He takes a deep breath. Connie looks at him before deciding to join him.

Philip gently picks up the bracelet on his wrist, rubbing his fingers between it. He wipes an eye, staring down at the item.

"I don't normally receive gifts. Well, besides birthdays and Christmas."

"How about Valentine's Day?"

"No. I get the keys back."

Connie glances down in shame for asking such a question.

Philip shakes his head, ruffling his hair before smoothing out the wild, untamed mass of two tones. Again, he looks down at the bracelet.

"Before meeting you, I met somebody at a club the same night who gave me an address. I wondered where it would take me. I looked around several times in the same area until I realized the address didn't exist. Then, I wound up at the corner, and..." his voice trails off. "Here we are," he gestures with his hand out, summarizing the outcome in a sheepish tone.

Connie slowly turns her attention to squealing children playing tag.

Philip looks in the same direction, reminded by his unattainable quest for love and joy.

"I'm looking at priesthood soon."

Connie gives him a sharp glance.

"Celibacy?"

"Priesthood, not sainthood," he shakes his head. "More like a break. I haven't been with anybody for nearly six months. I'm not looking either. I need to work on myself first."

Connie places her hand over his in the form of understanding and compassion.

"Just think of me as a bookmark until the greater chapter comes along and gives you what you need. Everybody should be entitled to happiness."

A smile crosses Philip's lips as he says, "Thanks."

After a little while, Philip becomes restless.

"Wanna split?" he asks her.

"Yeah. I'm not much for sitting around at parks," Connie answers with a wrinkle of the nose. "What have you got in mind?"

"We're basically on Forty-Second Street. We can always explore the other side of Times Square."

"Ooh, isn't that dangerous? The last time we went there, you called it Sexland."

"Yeah. For a good reason. Because it is."

"What are we going to do then? Take a taxi?"

Philip raises his brows as he says, "I have something better in mind."

Moments later, Philip and Connie run through the streets, hand in hand. They breeze by buildings. Beyond the defunct Bond Clothes, and Xanadu. Past the proselytizers with the signs, the streetwalkers willing to take on the daylight, the homeless shuffling with bags. Every dingy adult theater whizzes by in their path. Connie's heart flutters to every beat and breath she takes. Philip's hold tightens at each stop for crossing. Taxis zoom by. The two take off, weaving around the stoplights deterring oncoming traffic for only brief intervals of time. At the cross-section of Broadway, Philip leads the way down Seventh Avenue. They pass the TKTS booth, where their pace slows down long enough to catch a breath before speeding along. Connie lets out a laugh as she joyously runs. Philip looks up at the large vertical Manny's sign ahead as he takes a turn onto Forty-Eighth Street. Connie jogs to a stop and catches up with him.

She laughs between heavy breaths from running.

"Forty-Eighth?"

Philip leans over with hands to knees as he catches his breath.

Connie continues, "We could have easily crossed through Fifth or Sixth."

Breathing hard, Philip answers, "Wouldn't've been fun."

She looks around at the buildings along the street after walking by the Cort and a parking garage, noticing a distinct feature they all have in common.

"You planned this, didn't you?"

Philip laughs.

"What if I said, yes?" he asks with raised brows and a giggle.

"I should have known," Connie sighs.

Philip does a full spin on his toes, putting a hand out to emphasize the surroundings.

"It's Music Row. The Street," he answers gleefully.

Connie shakes her head.

"As I said, I should have known."

Philip breaks into a quick-paced walk, taking in the window displays of Manny's Musical Instruments, Sam Ash, Alex Music, and Rudy's Music Stop. Along the way are also a variety of repair shops, and sheet music stores.

"You can't see them, but there are various studios along here. Legacy Studios is in that building," he points.

Up ahead is an unmarked box truck. Two men carry out a large keyboard and stand from Sam Ash. They place it next to the opened back of the vehicle. Philip watches them figure out paperwork. Like a moth to a flame, the musician finds the instrument to be tempting. He walks over without words, waiting for the two men who busy themselves near the front instead. Connie watches him, unsure of what he'll do. And he will do something, as she's acquainted with his spontaneity.

When the moment is right, Philip goes over to the keyboard, turns, and pretends to play it behind his back.

Connie laughs, shaking her head in disbelief.

The two are interrupted when they hear the two men say they have the location. Philip makes a quick getaway, tip-toeing away.

As they walk away, Philip does a little spin.

"You know, people have called me Philly Joel."

Connie bursts out laughing.

"Oh, really?"

"Yeah. I know a thing or two about keyboards."

"Just like you showed me with the drums last month?"

Sheepishly, he looks down.

"Something like that."

They head out of Forty-Eighth, out onto Seventh Avenue, where they talk about anything and everything.

"You know, when I first came here, it was a total culture shock. Manhattan is truly a melting pot. We didn't have this kind of diversity in Allentown. Not to say I'm some country bumpkin or uh, hayseed. It's just, you know, there's no other city like this. The whole thing felt miles away from home. You're all alone here if you have nobody, no family or friends. It's a strange feeling like you're in a completely different world. Yet, it's only three hours away from home," Philip says, turning to Connie.

In turn, she says, "An hour away for me."

"From?"

"Mount Kisco. I wanted to get away from the dullness of life that was strangling my very existence. I didn't want to stay and run into all of the other kids from my graduating class and have them always ask me how I'm doing. I know my mom was disappointed. My dad knew I had to find my way. I moved here, in seventy-six when things were starting to happen. I mean, it was dirty and nasty. Not as bright as now."

"Bright?" he giggles. "Really? I don't know if I could call a bunch of triple-X theaters, prostitutes, drug deals, homeless in virtually every park, and empty buildings throughout the city as bright."

"Well, if you lived in Mount Kisco, you'd find Manhattan far more vibrant," Connie answers assuredly.

"Um, OK."

"So, what made you move to New York City? The music scene?" she smiles.

"I figured if there were one place I could truly be myself, it would be here."

"What happened?" Connie asks out of curiosity.

"I chose not to make it public. Instead, I wanted to focus on my music. What I could give artistically."

As they pass Fifty-Fifth Street, Connie catches a glimpse of AVIS Car Rental. She gives Philip a glance, who remains oblivious to her sights on him.

Biting her lip, she asks, "What kind of car do you have?"

"You come from left field with these questions."

"Well, I'd like to know more about my friend."

"I've got a sixty-nine Chevy Corvette Stingray L88."

"In pink, of course," Connie teases.

Philip grins back, "Classic black." He shakes his head at her response. "They never made them in pink. Not that I would want one. What did you think I had?"

"I don't know? A Rolls Royce?"

"I'm not Mick Jagger or Michael Jackson. I don't even have a chauffeur! OK, so on the rare occasion, I'll rent a limo, but not a Rolls Royce. What am I gonna do? Pop out with a fluffy boa and wear sequins?" he giggles. Changing his voice playfully to go deeper, he says, "I'm like any other red-blooded American boy. I like a good muscle car...," he flexes a muscle for hilarious emphasis. "...with a big-block engine, and five hundred and fifty horsepower."

Connie laughs at his antics.

He prods her harder to laugh.

"That's because I lack in Trojan power," Philip bursts out laughing from his own absurdity.

Both try to calm down, but can't, as another wave of laughter hits them simultaneously.

Finally, Philip can explain.

"I got the car in seventy-four. Before that, I wasn't making much money. None of us were. When you make it big, you think big. I was always fascinated by muscle cars. Maybe it's a testosterone thing? When we were touring around Pennsylvania, we'd see these big trucks hauling high-powered corvettes on the highways to either Nazareth or the Pocono Speedway. I'd say to myself, 'When I have enough money, that's the car I'm going to get.' I thought it was just a pipe dream. A guy out of Kutztown was selling his because he felt it was too much to drive. I bought it from him and was zipping down the turnpike and every highway in the state. I got five tickets the first week, which is unbelievable," he grins.

"Oh my God! Five in one week?"

"I didn't get to the best part. So, I'm driving with my older brother, Patrick, and I get pulled over on a Friday afternoon in Fredericksburg. I hand over my license. I know the deal. He looks at me and says, 'Hey, didn't I give you a ticket on Tuesday?'" Philip bursts out laughing again.

Connie joins him.

"We drive away afterward, and my brother says, 'What the hell did he mean by that?' I said, 'Pat, check the glove compartment.' He opens it, and about a half dozen speeding tickets pop out. It was a sight to behold. I still have the car. It's sitting in the garage. Of course, I don't drive like I'm twenty-six or twenty-seven anymore."

"I'd like to hope not!" Connie giggles.

"I discovered quickly speeding tickets can cost you. I can't remember exactly how much I owed, but the police departments knew me. Anyway, that car made it on the cover of our last album. Pretty good deal."

The two laugh again as they draw closer to Central Park.

Connie turns her attention to the spacious park.

She points, "Central?"

"Nah. I have a better idea," Philip answers. "Harlem."

Connie looks at him as they walk by a small portion of Central Park's south side.

"You want to walk to Harlem? Do you know how long that'll take? We walked from Greenwich Village already. It would be at least another forty blocks. We won't get there until dark."

Philip looks around, turning in place to see nothing but large non-descript condos and corporate buildings of earthly hues as far as the eye can see. He gives her a frown.

"Eh, maybe you're right. OK. So, where do we get a taxi?"

Connie steps out as she awaits the oncoming traffic. She hails a yellow cab heading their way.

"Well, that was easy," Philip says in mock surprise.

"Come on," Connie waves him over, getting inside.

He follows her, and together they are whisked away.

Philip announces, "Uh, East One Nineteenth."

The cab zooms, making its occupants know this won't be a slow ride. Jolting at stops, they whiz by buildings and businesses along the way. Connie feels her head hit the back of the front seat with the sudden stops at traffic lights. Philip's eyes go wide for a minute.

He quietly mutters, "Shit! I'm not going to give him a tip." Just as quickly, he gets his head thrown back to the seat. "Damn!" he manages a little louder while trying to get up. For seven minutes, Philip and Connie endure a hellish ride from the south end of Central Park, all the way to the north and beyond. Finally, they get let off. Philip tosses several bills and shuts the door.

The cab speeds away, shocking the musician who holds back from uttering a barrage of expletives in the company of a lady.

"That's why I don't like taxis," he answers, shaking his head. Walking ahead of her with some annoyance from the harsh ride, he chooses to stay silent.

Connie senses his quietness, respecting his personal space, and pissed off state. She walks behind him. They go further up into the city when coming upon the smaller Marcus Garvey Memorial Park. At the corner, they catch sight of five young black men standing next to the fence of the parking lot belonging to the New York College of Podiatric Medicine on 124th Street. The two slow their pace as they hear the group doing a doo-wop version of the classic Drifters tune, "Up On The Roof." Philip's mood changes drastically from the cab drama to upbeat upon hearing the music. He mouths the words.

Philip looks in surprise.

"Well, I can't exactly call the air fresh and sweet here."

Connie lets out a laugh.

He giggles.

The men spot the couple walking towards them. One of them waves over the other group members to follow him. They line up and walk over towards Connie, surrounding her while crooning "Why Do Fools Fall in Love?"

Two bookend her, singing the chorus while the younger of the bunch does lead. Philip steps back to watch with a sly smile. He enjoys seeing Connie happy and loving the music he so adores. The group follows her to the end of the parking lot's perimeter. The whole thing feels so charming to Connie, who has never experienced anything like it before. Doo-wop in Harlem. She would hold on to this moment for all time. Her smile breaks into infectious laughter, which captures Philip differently. His eyes ease on her. Looking down at the sidewalk, he thinks as the group finishes the song. During the conclusion, he claps heartily over their performance. Something strikes him as he rubs his chin in thought. The group smiles at Connie. Philip steps out in front, between her and the young men. He turns to one of the singers who seems to be slightly older than the rest.

Pointing his finger at the young man, he says, "That was great. can I talk to you for a minute?"

"Yeah. Sure," the man says.

Philip angles to him.

"Come into my office."

The two walk away from everybody else. Philip glances back at Connie. She looks back at him in peculiarity at his sudden need to talk with one of the singers. She notices his gestures, followed by him taking out a small notebook from his jacket pocket. He clicks on a pen, jotting something down, then hands it to the young man. Connie feels slightly out of place as she's left alone with the other singers. They chat among themselves. Philip trots back to Connie, putting on his sunglasses.

Turning to look back at the men, she asks him, "What was that about?"

"Business," he smiles.

"Oh. You mean like to have them on your next album?"

Philip thinks reflectively before answering quickly, "Yeah. Something like that." He begins to walk away.

Connie continues to follow after him until she catches up. He turns to her and walks closest to the curb in a gentlemanly manner as they cross onto 125th Street. As they pass by Carver Federal Savings Bank and a row of retail shops, Connie grows more awkward being in this particular neighborhood. She felt safe enough with Philip by her side, and she trusted him. But where was he taking her?

She asks him, "Where are we going?"

"You'll see."

They cross Adam Clayton Powell Jr. Boulevard.

Philip points straight ahead.

"We're almost there. I can see it already."

Before she can ask, Connie sees the iconic vertical sign just beyond the Volunteers of America Thrift Store and Mike's Jewelry.

"The Apollo?"

"Yep," he answers while pulling off his sunglasses. "This is where the magic happened back in the heyday. It played host to all the greats. Duke Ellington, Count Basie, Staple Singers, Ray Charles, Otis Redding, Sam Cooke, Aretha Franklin, Wilson Pickett, and of course, James Brown were all here at one time or another. When I was a little kid, I used to hear about the Apollo when my parents would bring me to a show because they knew I loved that kind of music. Black artists. Whoever was playing at a local theater or in Philly would mention it as one of their stops. So, I got to know the Apollo as this mythical place that was miles away from home. It became my version of Disneyland. That's where I wanted to go. One time when I was about eight-years-old, and the teacher asked us, 'Where do you want to go for summer vacation?' I remember this one kid said he wanted to go to the Smokey Mountains. The girl next to me said, 'Hollywood.' When it came to my turn, I said, 'The Apollo!' The looks I got were something else. They looked at me as if I said, Mars."

Connie smiles as she asks, "So, do you want to go inside?"

He looks at the marquee.

"Nah. I just wanted to show you a piece of musical history that meant something to me."

Connie stifles a laugh.

"We walked how many blocks, and took that taxi cab ride from Hell? You're telling me now that you simply wanted to show me this?" She shakes her head. "You're something else."

"If it helps, I think it was worth it," Philip says in his charming way.

She looks at him with an unbelieving expression.

"OK. What are we going to do now? Take a cab back to midtown?"

"Yeah. I guess."

"You wouldn't mind after the last ride?"

He shrugs, "No."

"You are a glutton for punishment."

She steps out to hail a cab. One pulls up, and they are taken to midtown. Before long, Philip and Connie are dropped off at Forty-Eighth Street.

Stepping out of the cab, Connie says, "It's starting to get a little darker out. Want to grab a bite to eat?"

Philip answers her eagerly, "Sure. I think I can go for that." He then grows quiet.

"OK. I think I've got an idea where we can go. Want to go through, what did you call it? Music Row?"

"Sure," he nods back but remains lost in thought.

They begin to walk when he stops.

"Wait. Connie, I need to tell you something."

"It's not another secret, is it?" She looks up in thought.

"No," he shakes his head. "Remember when I told you I would be away for most of next month?"

"Yeah."

"What I didn't tell you is that I'll be on the road. I'm on tour for the west coast."

"Yeah. You told me you weren't sure about certain things."

"Playing on a stage is great. Getting to be up close and personal with the fans is fine. It's what goes on afterward. I haven't done it in a long time, and I don't want to go through some of the same destructive habits I experienced that led me to stop in the first place after being in a band that big. The road isn't as romantic as what people are led to believe. Ya know? Hotels can get awfully lonely at times, especially when you're alone. It's tough in my situation to find companionship. It's never been easy, and I'm not so sure I want to go on another merry-go-round."

"A merry-go— Oh. That's what you mean." Connie answers looking down. "Now it's my turn. What did I tell you earlier today? About thinking of me as a bookmark? Maybe that time will come earlier than expected. I'm not going to stop you, and quite frankly, I have no right to say anything. This is what you do. If this is the end, so be it. I don't want to be a third wheel when you find true happiness. Because there's an excellent chance, you will. So, let's just enjoy the time we have left."

Philip looks down, nodding in agreement.

"Come on. Let's start now," Connie smiles, leading the way.

He follows behind until he catches up with her.

The two walk down Forty-Eighth when the shop lights come alive in neon and brightly lit white porcelain. As they come upon Music Row, Philip takes Connie's hand, then lets her do a spin directly in front of the window display of Sam Ash.

Connie lets out a joyous laugh, skipping and running the rest of the street with Philip after her. They stop at the end, taking in the view of Broadway's lit signs and displays before crossing over and winding down their destination in front of McHale's Bar & Grill.

Connie opens the door for him.

"I hope you have a big enough appetite for what they serve here!" she smiles.

After being served, Philip looks down at an oversized burger on his plate. He picks it up quickly. Before he can dig in, though, Connie finds it necessary to break his concentration on the attack.

"With this tour, do you have to get into road shape?"

"Road shape?" he asks with one brow raised in peculiarity.

"Yeah. Like, do you have to work out?"

Philip drops the burger back on the plate, shaking his head.

"Where do you come up with these things? Oh, wait. I know. *The Rock and Roll Handbook*." He points a finger up for greater emphasis. "Ah-ha. Everybody seems to have one handy. The stereotypical edition." He gives her a tight-lipped smile, rocking back and forth. "I'll tell you. I have no exercise routine. I walk a lot. Sometimes I jog, and sometimes I've been known to join in a friendly game of volleyball in California or Florida."

"Ooh." Connie coos, wiggling her body at the same time she takes a sip of soda.

"Now, if you're asking me if I go to the gym? No. I'm perfectly happy with my body, and I believe my stomach will be thrilled with that burger." He points down.

Connie asks, "Isn't that a lot?"

"Not for me, it isn't. I can handle the whole thing."

"But, wouldn't something lighter be better for you?"

"What? Like a head of lettuce? Connie, do you know what starving musicians would eat at the beginning of their careers? Nothing healthy. Absolutely nothing of nutritional value. A box of macaroni and cheese would be considered a luxury item. This burger would be more precious than gold at the time. And I have the privilege to devour it now."

Just as he's about to eat it, Connie says, "I wonder what the calories are in that thing?"

"You're not going to make me feel guilty," he insists.

He takes a big bite, then steals a fry from her plate.

Connie looks on in a state of shock at his brazen thievery.

"Mmm," Philip answers with a moan of approval.

After filling their bellies from a good day's worth of walking, Philip and Connie set off into the night. Once they reach the Ed Sullivan Theater between Fifty-Third and Fifty-Fourth Street, Philip stops. Connie looks at him with concern.

Looking down, he continues to inform her of historical facts.

"Over here is where history was made when the Beatles touched down in America and played this exact theater for their first appearance in sixty-four..." his voice trails off. "I think...," He glances up at the building and says, "...this is the end of the road."

Connie looks at him, slightly surprised at how fast he cuts off the conversation.

Philip shrugs.

"I have to get things ready. Go through rehearsals with the band. Kind of rusty," he answers with some guilt. "All those things that go with preparing for a tour of any size."

Connie nods her head with a reluctant agreement.

"So..." he says in a pause of awkwardness. Tight-lipped, he answers, "Yep. That's...about it."

"OK," Connie again nods.

"Hug?" he suggests innocently.

She can't resist the opportunity, even though a little disappointed at the thought of losing her buddy.

"Sure," Connie answers in a stoic manner that hides her pain.

They hug.

Just as quickly, the two disengage. Neither attempts to do or say anything that indicates sadness. At least not in front of each other.

Philip faces her.

"Bye, Connie," he smiles, sweetly, stepping back.

"Goodbye, Philip."

The two begin to walk their separate ways.

"Connie!" Philip calls out.

Connie turns around quickly.

"Not that it matters. I'm taking off on Friday. About noon. Probably twelve fifteen. Around there. Look for a large indigo Prevost bus. It's called *Vagabond.*

Connie stares as he turns back and begins walking away. She does the same in the opposite direction. As soon as she crosses to the next block between Fifty-Third and Fifty-Second, pedestrians crossing from the adjacent side of the street fill the sidewalks. Between people and the neon lights of Broadway, Connie's eyes scan for Philip, who has disappeared from her view.

Giving up, she heads back south.

On the far corner next to Fifty-Fourth, Philip turns around to see people flooding the sidewalk, moving north and south. He looks to see if Connie is anywhere in sight. Several groups of pedestrians swallow up his view.

Giving up, he heads back north.

The clock on the wall shows it's five of twelve. Connie blinks in anticipation as she looks up. All around her, computers click away in unison. A few co-workers giggle at the sound of someone's stomach growling. Connie remains oblivious. Her stare remains fixated on the twitching hand. At long last, noon arrives. She gets up, careful not to look overly anxious.

She would have to make up an excuse.

Her eyes turn to the left, then the right. Tapping on Ted's shoulder, she says, "Hey, if the boss comes by, tell him I'll be right back. I need to do something."

"Alright, but I can't guarantee he won't get angry."

"Ted, it's for a few minutes. Look, I'm serious. I'm just about done."

"You know lunch will be in about half an hour."

Connie looks up at the clock again. Two minutes have already gone by.

Quickly, she leaves the workroom floor to head over to the elevators. Her anticipation grows as her patience thins. The button lights up.

Time is of the essence.

Once she reaches the first floor, Connie dashes out the door, her brisk walk turns into a full run. Onlookers watch as she zips past them. They wonder what anybody can be in a hurry for when the city moves in fast motion enough as it is. Past the shops, restaurants, banks, and all other businesses, Connie glances down at her watch. The time runs as fast as her fleeting feet. Crossing the street becomes an obstacle. A group of people moves at a snail's pace. Cars beep when a taxi suddenly pulls up, creating gridlock. Everybody has to walk between the vehicles nearly mushed together.

Again, Connie takes off running as though sporting wings on her feet. She puts on the brakes, stopping immediately at Fifth Avenue. The street of so many adventures with Philip. Taking a deep breath, she rubs her sore ankles. Her heart pounds like a ticking stopwatch. But she can't take her eyes off the traffic. If she were to blink, she might miss it.

The northbound traffic moves at an even pace. Not too fast. Not too slow. Connie awaits like a child anticipating a parade. Cabs group together or ride separately. Several transit buses shine against the noon sun. A box truck rolls by, as she checks the time on her watch. Mickey's hand lands precisely at the fifteen minute watch line. Another taxi goes by. A Mercedes coup follows behind, with wheels indicating the driver wants to hurry up. Connie takes a second look. Several vehicles behind trails a large coach bus. As it gets closer, she sees it's a dark blue color — navy or indigo by all estimations. Above the windshield reads the word *Vagabond* in silver letters. The forty-foot coach eases through with its black top half and indigo bottom. On the side is a silhouette of Manhattan's skyline in black. Lettering in fancy scripture bears the words, *Vagabond Skyline* underneath.

Connie feels relieved she could see it with her own eyes. However, there is a sense of disappointment deep down inside. Maybe, for now, she could chalk up her adventures with a rock star as a one-in-a-million chance — a brief moment in time.

She watches the bus move along with the flow of traffic. Turning around, prepared to walk back several blocks back to San-San, she suddenly hears a commotion of horns honking. A barrage of beeping causes Connie to look back. Vehicles stop among the gridlock. Drivers impatiently drum on the outside of their doors, waiting to move again.

Connie spots a lanky black man in dreadlocks carrying a bag as he walks towards her. Again, she stretches to see what might be stopping the traffic. She makes eye contact with the man.

"Excuse me, sir?"

He smiles at her with teeth of white, gold, and darkened, empty spaces.

"Yes, ma'am."

"You just came from there. What happened?"

The man turns his head. His dreadlocks swing along.

In a thick Jamaican accent, he states, "Da big blue bus over dere. Gas cap was off. Dey get off and put back on." He illustrates the action, giving a hoarse laugh. Shaking his head, he keeps walking.

Connie looks ahead.

"Figures," she smiles.

The traffic resumes. The *Vagabond Skyline* disappears with the northbound flow.

CHAPTER 6

Several days of crossing the nation take Philip and his band through the west. They consist of five top-notch studio players he's retained for several years, with one new member. Mitch Evans and Perry Leonard provide the backbone as the rhythm section, drums, and bass, respectively. The blondish baby-faced newcomer of Philip's group is rhythm guitarist, Tim Grann, who has a resume that could put him in front as a leader if he wanted. The no-nonsense, Jheri curl-haired, Ross Johnson fills in on additional guitar. The lone woman in the band, Claire Bennett, a wavy-haired brunette who dresses in the trendiest stagewear, and modern make-up styles, completes the band's different look.

They start at Red Rocks Amphitheatre in Golden, Colorado, opening up for one of the single hottest pop bands of '84, Spandex Shades' *Radical Moon* tour. After conquering the venue and giving a performance full of energy and showmanship, Philip falls into a groove of enjoying the live scene once again. Wanting to prove his worth in a world of competition filled with fresh-faced electronic wizards in their twenties, he chooses not to let them forget about the voice of a guitar.

August seventh, the *Vagabond* reaches Phoenix, where they check into a nearby hotel.

Mitch pulls back the shower curtain, with Tim looking over his shoulder.

"Yep. It's good," Mitch answers, looking in the tub.

Ross plops down on the bed.

"Can't get used to these bus trips." He looks over to the bathroom. "Whatchoo two doin' in there?"

"Checking for scorpions."

"Scorpions?" Ross catapults up. "Aww, hell no! I'm not gonna share space with any damn scorpion."

"This is how it goes, Ross. Rats, mice, and roaches are New York. Alligators, snakes, and insects the size of your hands are Florida. Scorpions are Arizona."

Ross stares at his hand.

"We're not scheduled for Florida, are we?"

"No. We're only doing west gigs."

"Oh, good," Ross answers with more ease.

On the eighth, the band performs a knock-out show. The main act, Spandex Shades, turns out to have some sound problems.

The tenth, Philip and his crew head over to Albuquerque, much to Ross and Mitch's satisfaction. It's a decent show at Tingley Coliseum, even if the audience isn't as receptive.

The eleventh, they arrive in California. Set up at a better hotel, the band split three rooms. Philip has his own, Claire has hers, while Mitch, Ross, Perry, and Tim share one space.

In the early morning hours, Philip receives a knock at the door. Half asleep, he answers it. Mitch greets him with tired enthusiasm.

"Hey man, I need to crash. Perry's driving me crazy with the smell of that nasty lotion he slathers on, and Ross sounds like a chainsaw when he snores. I need my beauty sleep. Thanks, man."

Before Philip can utter a word, Mitch walks right past him. He drops on the bed, much to the exhausted dismay of Philip.

"This will do. Just remember, I'm the engine of the band. I need to make you guys upfront look good."

Philip shrugs. He has no rebuttal. Letting out a giant yawn, he returns to the bed on the opposite side, where sleep immediately overcomes him.

The twelfth, they play the Greek Theatre in Los Angeles.

The thirteenth, at a small though pleasant hotel, Philip signs in with the band.

Ross looks around. "This place is a bit tight. Remind me why we've got this hotel and Shades' got a Hilton or Four Seasons?"

Philip says, "We're openers. Their label allows them more. But, they'll pay more when it's part of the advance. I pay you guys, so it doesn't matter."

"Think it'll pay for the crib, Andrea, and I need?" Ross asks.

"It'll pay for that and half a year's worth of diapers."

"I can dig it then," Ross nods back.

The receptionist says, "Oh, there's one thing you need to know. Your rooms will be right above the honeymoon suite."

"Ah-ha. I see. And are there any occupants at this time?" Philip asks with charming innocence.

"Um..." she checks the computer system. "There is one couple. They haven't come down here since last night when they arrived."

"Thanks," Philip smiles, picking up his guitar case and luggage. The other band members trail behind.

With irritation, Claire says to him, "Since last night?"

Arriving at the set of rooms, they hear various thumping noises.

"We're never gonna get sleep," Perry grumbles.

Philip looks up, pointing at the ceiling with one brow raised. "Neither will they." He sighs. "The best thing we can do is go out and eat and see how things wind up by the time we get back. Maybe they'll be doing something uh..., different by then."

After hanging out at a reasonably quiet restaurant, the band returns to their rooms. Philip goes to his and looks down at the skinny black rubber bracelet that accompanies his watch. Glancing around, he feels satisfied by the performances, but there is a sense of loneliness in his heart.

Back in Manhattan, the nightlife is just beginning to awaken with all of its neon splendor. DJs prepare to spin a variety of tunes that will be certain to get people out on dance floors across the city in only about an hour or so.

At Scribbles, lights are checked, the sound system gets wired. People begin to populate the venue slowly. Several sit at the bar, chatting to kill time while sipping on drinks.

The phone rings incessantly at the bar while Prince's voice is piped through. Above "Little Red Corvette," a man slowly peeks up from behind the sound system. He glances around, realizing nobody is there to pick it up. Nearly tripping over a couple of cables, he races over to get it.

"Hello, Scribbles? How may I help you?" He looks around slightly nervous, knowing he has no right to be behind the bar.

"Finch?" comes the voice on the other end.

"Yeah, this is. Wait. Phil?"

"Finch!"

"Phil! Long-time, no see! Ya know, we keep running around in the same circles but never into each other. I heard Gretchen asked you about a thousand questions from the past."

"Yep. Anyway...." Philip begins. "Hey, can you do me a favor? I was wondering if there was a woman there. I'm looking for a brunette with green eyes."

Finch furrows his brows as he says, "There's a ton of women who are brunette with green eyes. That's a needle in a haystack! You sure she's here and not somewhere else in the city? On a Monday night? How am I ever going to..."

"You'll know it when you see her. Just check. This call is going towards my advance, and I still need to pay the band after. Her name is Connie. She said she's there often."

Finch grumbles, "OK. What are friends for, besides asking of favors? Hold on." He puts the phone down, glancing around. Cyndi Lauper croons "All Through the Night" in the speakers overhead. Finch goes up the small set of steps to the DJ booth, overlooking the dance floor to get a better look at the sparse crowd. There is a group of blonde women talking with a few guys. A dark-haired couple dance nearby. Finch leaves the booth, going back to the main floor. Glancing around, he sees two women at the bar. He's instantly drawn to them. One is a frizzy-haired redhead. From the back, he sees a stylish brunette with volume to her hair. He stops to listen when she speaks.

"I can't stand macho guys. It's like one time when I was at the bowling alley, and this young guy was trying to get any girl's attention. He's throwing balls and winking at them. Then he realizes he can't get a strike to save his sorry ass. The more he tries, he gets frustrated — ridiculous hits. The girls begin to leave, and he's throwing a fit because he can't get lucky. I look over at the ball he was using in the ball return. Guess what?" she takes a sip of soda through a straw.

The redhead grins back, "What?"

The brunette leans over with quiet emphasis.

"He was using a thirteen-pound ball."

"Oh! No way!"

"Gina, I'm telling you. It was one of the most pathetic things I have ever seen." she giggles, picking up her soda again.

Finch steps around the two women, staring at the brunette. His eyes meet her green-eyed wary glance.

"Connie?"

"Yes?" Connie answers straightforward yet uncertain of the stranger's acknowledgment of her.

"Phone call."

Connie's eyes swing to Gina, letting her know how odd it is receiving a call at the club.

Connie follows Finch as he walks behind the bar. Uncertain of being in a place where patrons never go, she stops. Finch waves her over, holding the phone.

She mouths to him, "Is it OK?"

"Go ahead," he nods back.

Connie picks up the receiver, licking her lips, before answering, "Hello?"

"Hey, Connie. How's it going?" Philip asks.

Startled by the voice at the other end at first, she quickly calms down.

"Hey, yourself." A smile creeps across her face. Turning away from the bar counter, she says, "How is it so far?"

"Fine. As it turned out, our set of rooms is right below a honeymoon suite, so we get to hear plenty of action."

Connie laughs, which makes Philip giggle.

She asks him hesitantly, "Have you met anybody?"

"Sure."

He pauses for a few moments.

Connie feels a rush of disappointment run deep throughout her body.

"I've met a lot of people so far," he answers mischievously.

"You know what I mean," she smiles with a thankful tone.

His eyes meet the floor.

"No. No somebody. I haven't had much time to wander around looking for company. It's not like the seventies, where fans lined up like it was a box office, waiting for their turn."

Connie laughs hard. At the same moment, an unhappy bartender shows up. Finch tries to hold him off at the pass, talking with the man. Connie turns to see the finger-pointing and raised voices above the sweet angelic delivery of Cyndi's throughout the club.

The bartender makes his way in the back of the bar, stating, "You need to get off the phone. It's not for the public. This is an employee-only area."

Philip enjoys hearing the sound of her voice, no matter the situation. He overhears her talking away from the phone.

"I'll be off in a minute," she tries to answer calmly.

"No. You have to get off now. Whoever told you it was OK? They were wrong," the bartender insists.

"Give me a second.

"Boyfriend time ends now."

Philip hears a click on the other end.

The phone goes dead.

He slowly puts the receiver down, staring at it. Creaking from above makes him eye the ceiling.

Philip shakes his head.

At the Santa Barbara Bowl, both bands blow away the audiences. They head off to San Francisco a day later, where Claire and Philip go shopping.

On the sixteenth, the band is to play a solo show in Sacramento.

Philip, decked out in an all-black ensemble of T-shirt and pants, except for a shiny silver vest, instructs his band, "This is make it or break it time," as they walk through the hallway. The rest of the members are equally dressed up in everything from leopard print, pink and black zebra, metallic blue pants, and suspenders. Older folks dressed conservatively stare at the odd six-piece band as though they landed by spaceship. Mitch's eyes swing to the side, taking notice of a couple, arm in arm, with disapproving expressions. Ross sees a woman give him the look-over from head to toe. Claire walks directly behind Philip, who is cool as a cucumber. He knows what needs to be done.

They stop in front of the double doors leading to the main hall.

Again, Philip instructs, "Let's do this," before donning his Ray-Bans.

The other five members pull out their pairs of cheap drugstore sunglasses of various colors behind him.

Showtime!

They throw open the doors.

Philip immediately peeks over the rims, while the band looks on in shock.

In front of them is a fanciful banquet room suited for something far and away from rock and roll. Older people walk around, some with walkers, and a few in wheelchairs, assisted by caretakers. Only about a dozen younger individuals populate the space.

They close the doors before entering.

Philip is on the phone, trying to get things straightened out with Barbara.

Tim says aloud, "I want to go home."

Mitch folds his arms. Ross goes to lean against the wall next to Claire, who tries to keep her wits.

Perry tells them, "Maybe it's not so bad?"

Mitch advises, "Oh, it's bad."

Philip answers into the phone, "I know. It's a three hour time difference.., What happened to our gig? We came here for the stand-alone show, and these people are lucky if they can even stand…, Uh-huh…, No. Not a fun, young audience who are going to get off on what we play…, Yeah…, Out in the hallway there was something amiss. We got that idea of how people were staring…, I honestly don't even know if these people are familiar with the Beatles…, Maybe swing?" he glances at the unhappy band members sheepishly.

Claire throws her hand to her face in embarrassment.

"This is more awkward than the Thanksgiving I spent with you at your parents' house a few years ago."

Philip continues into the phone, "Barb, we didn't even see an ad anywhere in the papers..., A venue...? Yeah, that would be great..., Right. In the meantime...," He looks up thoughtfully. "OK..., Everything else was fine."

Ross shakes his head.

"Man, I will never be able to play another gig in the state of California after this. I won't want to show my face here ever again. Ya know, I could get behind a white guy diggin' Motown. Even the whole pink guitar thing. Having my career destroyed for this shit? No way." He paces the floor, putting a hand behind his head. "So much for my future children thinkin', I was cool."

"Maybe it's not that bad like Perry said," Tim answers in optimism.

Ross shakes his head, "Look at you, Tim. You've got a three-page list of credentials, and you're here in metallic blue pants at some old people's gig."

"You look good in leopard print," Tim says with unaffected confidence.

On the phone, Philip tells Barbara, "Yeah. I got it. Right... OK. I'll let them know... Yeah. I'll do something. Thanks. Yep. Bye."

Philip hangs up the phone, glancing down at Mitch, Claire, and Perry sitting on the floor.

Claire gets up and says, "You remember that time I first met your parents for Thanksgiving three years ago? On a scale from that to worst, I'd say this is worse."

Philip thinks.

Mitch fingers his suspenders, "You know the story of the Titanic? It didn't sink immediately. This show has. I say we take a vote on leaving and not turning back. Who's with me?"

Perry says, "What's it gonna be, Boss?"

Philip answers quickly, "We rock."

All of the band turn their heads his way immediately at his lunacy.

Again, they stop in front of the double doors leading to the banquet room. Philip flips on his Ray-Bans like a gunslinger ready for a duel. The other five members pull out their pairs of colorful plastic sunglasses behind him.

They throw open the doors.

Philip and the band walk through as though they own the venue. Getting up the small set of steps, everybody takes their places. Mitch eyes the silver Slingerland drum set on the stage. Perry goes to his regular spot, hooked to his bass. Ross and Tim bookend their fearless leader with a pink Stratocaster. Claire looks around, noticing her instrument is missing.

Perry glances back at her.

She says, "There's no keyboard."

Philip has a delayed reaction, taking a second look at the set-up of no keyboards. He spins back to face her.

"What?"

"There's no keyboard," she answers thoughtfully.

"Something? Anything?" Philip says, slightly losing his cool.

Mitch says, "Over here." He hands Claire a tambourine sitting in the back of the drum kit. "It's the only thing."

Perry leans Philip's way to ask, "What's the plan?"

"Like every other show. Same set. Deacon, solo, and a couple of fillers. Whaddya say? Beatles? This is gonna take me back to those prom gigs I did. We'll start with Beatles because they won't know what the hell we're playing from the back catalog," Philip answers, unsure if he's making the right decision. "Let's do it."

He walks up to the microphone, making his introduction.

"Hey, just want to tell you I am Phil Reinhardt and welcome to *The Afterglow!*"

Older folks stare at the six band members attired in bright, shiny, metallic, and animal print. Several shake their heads at the sight of a guy with dark blond hair, sporting a pink guitar. At the tables, groups chew on bits of steak and mashed potatoes. They look around, unable to figure out what is going on.

Philip and the band kick into the Beatles "Drive My Car." Claire begins to get into playing the tambourine. As they play, the banquet tables shake violently — glasses of water and wine seesaw from the disturbance. Groups of people look at each other with more curiosity at what they're hearing. The more attendants sip wine, the antsier they get sitting in place. With each song, excitement flows throughout the room. Some of the women get up closer to the stage, entranced by the leader of the band. Philip knows he has them under his spell. A smile creeps across his face. A curly grey-haired woman grins wildly at his response of eye contact with her. The band sways and swivel their way through ten songs. More people get up to dance, trying to keep up with the pace. Even those in wheelchairs and walkers turn within confinement. The ladies up in front let their inhibitions go, acting like twenty-year-olds that can't stop moving.

So much joy!

The band catches the fever, playing as if to a venue holding ten thousand screaming fans.

Philip takes full advantage of the audience's enthusiasm, which he feeds off from. Grabbing the microphone, he lets Caddy swing freely while getting down to floor level. Joining the women for a rousing rendition of "The Afterglow," he follows it up with two songs from his Deacon's Alley days. The words! His moves! He makes them swoon! One woman puts a hand to her chest as he places an arm over her shoulder. An older man gets up and starts clapping along, with another at the next table. A group sways their heads in unison. A strawberry-blonde with tears in her eyes shakes and wiggles as though she were transported back to being a teenager at an Elvis concert.

The audience gets into the vibe. More people dance, clap, and join in the merriment from a rock-pop singer and guitarist from Allentown, who turned a boring banquet into the time of their lives.

After the show, Philip and the band celebrate at a restaurant, laughing and loving the experience of what happened. Nobody is disappointed. Ross finds his complaining from earlier hilarious. He and Mitch toast to the crazy night.

The following show, riding high from the previous fun-filled gig, the band conquer the much larger Sacramento Memorial Auditorium. Happy to go back to being an opening act, they surpass the energy of Spandex Shades' slightly sloppier set.

On the eighteenth, Philip and the band head up to Portland, Oregon. Issues arise with members of Spandex Shades, complicating morale for the tour nearing its end.

The next day, in Manhattan, Connie jogs upstairs to her third-floor apartment. Putting the key in the door, she drops a large bag. A neighbor is alerted to her arrival. The woman in her sixties looks on with interest. Connie turns around briefly to see the prying eyes.

"Hi, Mrs. Whittaker."

"What have you been up to lately, Connie? Find a man yet?"

Connie sighs, "No, Mrs. Whittaker. Just came back from doing laundry."

"OK. I haven't heard any odd noises coming from your place."

Connie rolls her eyes.

"Good day to you, Mrs. Whittaker," she answers, rushing into her apartment, throwing the bag over her shoulder. Dropping it on the floor, Connie goes over to check the messages on her answering machine. The first message starts with her mother.

"Hi, honey!"

Connie answers as though she can hear her response.

"Hi, Mom."

"Listen, you need to visit your grandma. You know how she reacts. She's been throwing food at nurses and making the orderlies feel uncomfortable. She loves you but nearly hisses at me. Please, go see her."

Connie looks up at the ceiling, "I will, Mom. I've been so busy with work lately. Next Monday I have a day off. Labor Day."

"OK. Well, that's about it. I don't like these silly machines," Connie's mother grumbles before hanging up.

"Love you too, Mom."

The next message starts up. It's Sally.

"Hey, Connie! I've got a great idea. How about Jeff and I with you and Phil for dinner one of these nights at our place? But, what do you feed a rock star?"

Connie shakes her head.

"Oh, I don't know. Throw some goldfish food at him?" she rolls her eyes. "Come on, Sally. Human food. Like you and me. What do you feed, Jeff? What's good for the Jeff is good for the gander. Ridiculous."

Connie punches the button on the machine after hearing enough. Plopping down on the couch, she drags the large bag near her legs. Picking up the remote control for the TV, Connie turns it on. Digging through the laundry, she looks up to see there's a video of Elton John's "Sad Songs Say So Much" ending. Emptying the contents of the bag onto the couch, Connie starts folding clothes. Keeping her eye on the TV screen, she watches as a male host makes comments about the video.

"Elton John just kicked off his *Breaking Hearts* tour two days ago at the ASU Activity Center in Tempe, Arizona, to a crowd of nearly eleven thousand eager fans. This will be the latest tour for the extremely prolific John since his *Too Low for Zero* tour that kicked off in February. The back-to-back tour ends in mid-November. And, on the subject of tours, Spandex Shades is enjoying their time on the charts and currently on the road for their latest album, *Radical Moon*. Opening up for them is Phil Reinhardt, who is experiencing some well-worth noted success on the charts with his latest album, *The Afterglow*.

Connie tends to her laundry, when hearing Philip's name attached with "interview" and "Seattle." Slowly lowering the garment she's been folding, her eyes meet the screen.

Philip sits across from the young female interviewer. He waves to the camera.

She asks him, "This is the first time in some years you've been on the road, why is that and what are your impressions on how it is now?"

Philip grins, "I haven't been on the road in seven years. It's not because I didn't want to. It's just that the music I made a couple of years ago would not have translated as well live. I was deep into New Wave with the last record. I was trying to be the male version of Debbie Harry. I had bleach-blond hair and wore skinny metallic ties. There were a lot of keyboards, and I'm more about the guitar. So that wouldn't have been as good, even with a band. The whole experience I have now is a thrill. I get to play with some top-notch guys and a lady. We have a lot of fun on the road, not only onstage but off as well. The difference between the years of seventy-seven and eighty-four is, there's more equipment to consider and for the trucks to load. The venues have gotten a lot larger over the years."

"This is one of the last dates of the tour. What is your impression of Seattle and the contribution it made to the music world?" she says.

Philip raises a brow, "Contribution?"

She nods back.

"Hendrix, of course!" he giggles. "I'm sure there's far more, but he was the main reason why I got into the whole rock and roll thing - him and George Harrison. That's who we followed in the sixties. They were our guitar heroes. Every kid playing in a band wanted to be those two."

"Why do you have a pink guitar?"

"To make the long story short, I used to have another guitar like Caddy." He picks up the guitar next to him. "It was a Fender Stratocaster like this one, only in sonic blue. George Harrison has one that he repainted into the iconic Rocky. Um, one night after a gig, all of our equipment was stolen. So, I needed another instrument, and I wasn't making much money in those days. I went to a pawn shop in lower Pennsylvania and saw this guitar. It was the only Fender Strat available, and I wound up trading a Martin acoustic for this one. And, that was it. Caddy's the one for me. She's my girl!"

"Do you think you'll have a second leg for this tour?"

Philip shakes his head.

"I honestly have no idea. It all depends if an audience wants to see me. Let me put it this way, the charts dictate if you're a success or not, and in turn, that translates into if somebody's worthy of going out on the road and the record labels financing it. The fans own us. They determine what gets played on radio airplay, videos like what you host, and how many seats we can fill. That's the way it goes."

She smiles, "I want to thank you, Phil, for your time, and wish you lots of luck on the rest of the tour."

"Thanks," he nods in acknowledgment.

"The remaining dates are here, in Seattle, at the Coliseum today. Tomorrow the twentieth at the Showbox...,"

"Yeah. That's a solo show. It's just my band and me there — no other act. I've been told the venue had some infamy after World War II, so it's the best place for some sex, drugs, and rock and roll," Philip raises his brows, then laughs. Toying with his hair uncomfortably, he realizes his form of humor might not pass with younger viewers. "It's all OK. We'll give them a great show."

"OK," the interviewer giggles. She turns back to the camera. "On the twenty-first, Phil and his band will once again take the stage before Spandex Shades for their tour finale at the Pacific Coliseum in Vancouver."

Philip puts on his sunglasses and looks at the camera. He points.

"We're comin', so be ready."

Unable to remain serious, he bursts out laughing.

Connie drops her head.

Closing her eyes, she utters, "God, I miss you."

Philip and his band once again give a high-energy performance the same night in Seattle. Spandex Shades shows signs of cracking as tension builds among band members.

On the twentieth, Philip and his band take advantage of having their solo show, after the Sacramento fiasco. It only proves the six-piece rock and rollers could perform for any audience. At the Showbox, Philip pulls out a list of songs sure to get the audience excited, mostly from his solo and Deacon's Alley catalog. Claire gets to show off her skills on a cover of the B-52s "Planet Claire."

A man in the audience pays special attention to the performers.

The next day, the band packs their bags. Philip carries a suitcase in one hand and a guitar case in the other. He puts the luggage in the lower compartment of the bus. Claire rushes over to place hers in the same place. She looks over at him, his right wrist specifically.

"What is up with you wearing that thing?" She picks up his wrist to briefly examine the skinny black rubber bracelet next to his watch. "Is it like a Madonna phase you're going through?"

He stops what he's doing.

"No. It was given to me by a friend."

Mitch comes up from behind.

He asks, "So, what happened with the Vancouver gig we were scheduled for?"

Philip says, "Spandex Shades has run into some unfortunate problems. Alex was caught drinking, and Donny freaked out over it. They got in a bad fight at their hotel, caused a scene. In a nutshell, Donny left."

Ross, Perry, and Tim arrive.

Perry answers, "Donny left the band?"

"Yeah. They have no lead singer. I don't know if it's separate planes or buses they're taking. Donny went solo. I'm guessing back home. The other guys, I have no idea what they'll do. Seth was pretty upset about the whole thing. Can't blame him. They climbed the charts, and drinking and drugging happened. The same story that's been written thousands of times." Philip shrugs. He closes his eyes for a second. "We're ready to go home, right?"

Ross, Perry, Tim, Mitch, and Claire either nod back or answer, "Yeah!"

"Let's rock then," Philip says before boarding the bus.

Everybody else follows.

The *Vagabond Skyline* prepares for departure and a two-day journey back to New York.

CHAPTER 7

Two days later, back in Manhattan, Barbara talks on the phone. Outside the office, several women stare at the stranger as their jaws drop.

One says, "Whoa."

A knock comes at Barbara's door.

"Come in!" she answers loudly.

The door opens.

She fails to look at who has entered her office. On the phone, she's turned to the side as someone plops down on the seat across from her.

"Yeah..., I think that's a done deal. Right..., What do you think should come up next? Promotion? I thought Tower was great for the exposure..., No, I think they should do that before the tour. Yes. That's what I'm saying..., Well..., What do you think promotion consists of? Exactly! Uh-huh. OK. Let's...," she finally turns her chair to face the front. Uncertain by what she sees, the conversation winds down, "Let's talk about this tomorrow..., OK? Yeah. I have to tend to something. Yep. Bye."

Putting the phone down, she blinks back.

"When did I take on Judas Priest?" She looks Philip over. "What the hell did you do with my client?"

Philip laughs, enjoying his manager's not-so-subtle reaction.

"Hi Barb," he answers, adjusting his Ray-Bans.

Barbara shakes her head at his outfit consisting of a black leather fringed jacket, matching tight leather pants, studded star belt, black button-down shirt, and black boots to go with the ensemble. No longer sporting two-toned hair, it has since returned to a natural dark bronze.

Philip pulls off the sunglasses, standing up so Barbara can take in the full outfit.

She shakes her head.

"Claire, put you up to this?"

"No. She tried to talk me out of it. We were shopping in San Francisco, and I told her I was looking for something different."

Barbara pinches the bridge of her nose as though to ward off a headache.

"Phil, drastic is not the same as different. You traded zoot suits and Lacoste shirts...," She puts her hand out. "...for this? Look at you. You're pushing thirty-five. I know you're mighty determined to have commercial success, but do you honestly think this is you? Am I going to see a Harley parked in your driveway the next time I come up?"

He glances down, not knowing how to feel other than awkward.

"You know what goes through my mind seeing you this way? What club membership are you with? Anvil or Mineshaft?" she asks.

Philip closes his eyes, dropping his head in disappointment.

Barbara asks him, "Do you think you can be taken seriously?"

"Come on, Barb. It's not like I'm gonna wear this grocery shopping. I'll probably only wear—" Philip gets interrupted by the phone before quietly finishing his line as he goes to sit back down. "...onstage."

Barbara picks it up, answering, "Hello? Whoa. Gerald, you're going too fast! What...? No. I don't know. He's what...? Wait. Wait. Uh, no. Did you ask Hal...? What are you yelling at me for...?"

Philip listens to her, not feeling as confident as when he walked through the door.

She continues, "He didn't..., No. I didn't know that. I knew about the LA appearance. Wait, that one too? Come on. Gerald, all I'm saying is I didn't..., No..., No..., Now, wait a second...," Her voice rises. "Don't you go off..., No. I know he's obnoxious. Now you are too! Don't you dare say things like that! He's your client too! No..., No..., He signed a contract with you! Stop saying that...! What is he?" Barbara turns to face Philip, who's eyes meet hers. "He's a human being. Treat him like one! I don't care who he sleeps with! Gerald, call me back when you learn some manners."

Barbara drops the receiver back on the hook in bewilderment. Philip can tell she's a bit unsettled by the conversation.

Quietly, she says, "That was Gerald Verlaine from Genuine Records. Al Shockley is missing. Petunia Prank is supposed to be the musical guest on Saturday Night Live. It's Thursday already, and he hasn't made it for any of the rehearsals. Hal, the music producer, doesn't know what to do. Then I'm told Al never made it to Chicago or Miami for the meet and greets. Nobody knows anything. It's like he just vanished off the planet."

Philip takes a slow breath. He looks down, shaking his head.

"He's not missing. Al's been in the hospital for a few weeks now."

Barbara stares at Philip.

"You know this?"

"Somebody told me he wasn't feeling well for a little while."

"How long?"

"As far back as when we were here talking with you last month."

"Oh, God," Barbara puts a hand to her forehead.

"His partner did not take it well."

"How many will it take until something gets done?"

"I don't know any more than you do, Barb. Nothing, other than Al didn't take this seriously. He believed he was immune to it all."

"We don't know if this is it, though, right?" Barbara asks in the sense of hope. "What about you? Have you had any checkups recently?"

"I have, and I'm OK so far. Haven't been with anybody in six months."

Barbara furrows her brows.

"Isn't that a long time for you?"

"Yeah. It is. I've survived so far. I have thought about joining the priesthood."

"You're not serious?" Barbara asks, bewildered.

Philip grins, "No." He looks back down, not knowing what else to say.

For a moment, both pauses until Barbara breaks the silence.

"So, I just want to say how sorry I was in not going to the west coast to see you. I've been swamped with other clients. You know, everybody wants representation now. I'm only sorry you got stuck with that gig in Sacramento."

"What exactly happened?" Philip asks.

"As you know, I can't call the offices of any label after five. They're strict about that. The solo show you were supposed to have in Sacramento was a no-go from the start. Nobody set it up. No advertising, as I'm sure you noticed. Nothing was done."

"We did a gig anyways. The folks there weren't expecting it, and neither were we. It was fun, though. Everything worked out."

"What kind of audience did you get?"

"Mmm. An interesting one," Philip answers with one brow raised. "Yeah."

"I'll take your word for it. Anyway, when you were playing the real solo show at the Showbox in Seattle, you may not have noticed, but you were being watched."

"Uh, I get watched by a lot of people, Barb."

"True. Although it's not every gig, you get a scout from England. He wants you to play at the Marquee. It's specifically a Friday gig. They're open every day, but he feels you're worthy enough of playing the best night of the week. He knows your label, and in turn, I received the call. I told him, OK. I figured since you have the promotional tour for *The Afterglow* in England, it would coincide with your schedule and make for a worthy conclusion." Barbara pulls out a pack of papers. She hands them to her client.

He looks it over.

"You've got your tour starting on the twenty-eighth of this month. That's when you go to London."

"I didn't know the guy from Duran Duran hosted a show," Philip giggles.

Barbara snickers, "He doesn't. It's a different John Taylor. Some guy with ITV or the BBC. Whichever."

"*Top of the Pops*? Is that kind of like *Bandstand* or *Solid Gold*?"

"Yes."

"Does it include lip-synching?"

"That would be affirmative."

Philip nods in understanding, leaning in to see further down the calendar.

"How many do you think will be going?" Barbara asks.

"Um, myself, Claire, Perry, Mitch, Tim, and Ross. Six."

"Alright. I will set it up for six." Barbara takes another look at Philip with his leather outfit. "OK. I'm just thinking of what you're wearing and Caddy."

Connie wanders over to the Xerox machine. Placing a page face down on the scanner, she closes the lid. Her fingers press several buttons as she waits for it to warm up. The machine stubbornly shuts off by itself. Connie turns it back on. Again, it resets. Not wanting to stare at the damn thing, she walks over to the nearest window, where she glances down at the usual foot traffic. Something makes her study the people's movements below. They seem occupied by an unseen force as they point southward. Groups gather in small bunches, turned in the same direction. Connie furrows her brows, then thinks of the stupid machine she needs to tend to. Nodding, she goes back to check. Again, the copy machine has puttered out and shut off by itself. She rolls her eyes. Quietly she mutters under her breath, "You've got to be kidding."

She checks the paper feeder, where everything looks to be OK. There is that continued beckoning of the window. Connie steps away from the machine. The force on the streets somewhere out of sight southward grabs her under its spell. People are far more interested in walking towards it. Even those who walk northbound, stop, and turn the opposite direction.

A voice breaks her concentration.

"What's up? Copier break down again, Connie?"

Connie swiftly turns to Ted.

"I don't know what's going on with this stupid thing. I checked the paper feeder, and it's fine."

"How about the toner?"

"No. There's some type of mechanism in there that seems to be malfunctioning. At least that's my guess."

A young man races into the office, nearly out of breath.

"Hey, you guys need to see this!" he emphatically crows.

Everybody in the office turns around.

Bryan turns in his chair.

"What is it, Dave, a state of emergency?"

"No. I've never seen anything like it before. Outside our window in front! Come on!" Dave waves his hand for everybody to see what he's talking about.

Denise says, "Can't we just see it in about a half an hour when we break for lunch?"

"They might be gone by then! Come on!"

All the workers glance at each other. Of course, an opportunity to get up from their seats is positive, but nobody wants to get in trouble. Several leave the office, with another group following out. They come across Dave's co-worker, Janna, who is leading a group from another office.

Soon, the corner office fills up with workers from various departments looking out the windows. Some go over to the lobby window to view the commotion. Looking down, those who stand by the window move their hips in a rhythmic motion.

Maria and Denise stretch to see what is going on.

"Oh, wow! That is so cool!" Maria answers in awe.

Ted and Connie soon join in to see what is so important for workers to come out in swarms. Connie wonders if it's what was luring her attention to the window in their department. It certainly was the same southward direction she witnessed people moving in.

Below, she views five black men standing in a row, moving in a synchronized manner similar to the groups of Motown. A crowd surrounds them, only growing in size. People walk the streets but are soon grabbed by the overpowering sense to dance. Men dressed in suits, ties, and loafers sashay along the sidewalk to the music. Women attired in their finest of work-wear show no fear in Bert Geller, Thierry Mugler, Fendi, Zodiac, and even last year's trend of Bandolino. They move to the beat like everybody else.

Perry Leonard and Tim Grann arrive to take in the atmosphere. Placing their instruments and amps down on the ground, both shrug to each other. Perry walks inside San-San, managing to find an electrical outlet near the door. Attaching the cord to where he stands near the outside wall, he plugs in and thumps out an adjoining beat on bass. Tim follows his lead. Both synchronize their playing with the singers out in front, giving the music more heft.

People pour out of buildings to the sweet sounds capturing their ears. An older black man preoccupied with a sales rack of shoes across the street begins moving rhythmically to the beat, and a cappella styling of the group singing. His wife looks at him strangely, until he provocatively wriggles his brows. Taking her hands, he dances with her on the spot. Other people pop their heads out of windows above, viewing the commotion across the way. A hot dog vendor rushes his wagon over the bumpy terrain of old tar and potholes to catch the enormous crowd gathered in hopes somebody will want to eat after all that wiggling and jiggling. A Chevy Impala taxi pulls up from the passing traffic, nearly clipping the sidewalk. Its driver emerges from the yellow door. A tall, lean, clean-shaven man pops up. Ripping off the knit cap from his head to reveal a receding hairline, he takes everything in with arms spread out.

In a thick Russian accent, he shouts to the sky, "I love this country!" Without thinking he might get in trouble for leaving the meter off, the cabbie joins in the gathering, getting swallowed by the crowd.

Other cars pull up behind the taxi, getting out to join in the street party.

Connie stares fixated on the five young men singing. She squints, noticing something incredibly familiar about them. Seeing everybody preoccupied with the commotion below, it gives her the perfect moment to dash out. Connie makes sure the coast is clear before running down the stairs. Pushing the front door open that's already ajar from the two cables running up to Perry's bass and Tim's guitar, she gingerly steps over them, careful not to trip. Rushing out the door, Connie meets a massive crowd of both men and women. She glances around, side-stepping her way around the joyous revelers on the left side.

Suddenly, she gets picked up and spun in style, befitting a fairytale.

Philip laughs.

"You came back!" Connie shouts.

He puts her down.

"I thought the tour ended in a few more days."

"The band broke up."

"Oh, I'm so sorry," she answers, putting her hands on his shoulders.

Philip grins, "Not mine. The band we were opening up for. My band wouldn't quit on me like that." He looks at Perry and Tim with a tight-lipped smile. "Ah, they can't hear me." Looking back at Connie, he shrugs. "Anyway..." He puts his sunglasses on.

"I thought you would've found somebody while you were on the west coast," Connie suggests.

A slow smile appears on Philip's lips. Again, he shrugs. As a distraction, he pulls her to join him. She won't budge at first, looking up at the window containing her co-workers. Could they see her? What would they say? Eyeing Philip, she decides to join him, whether anybody from above notices her or not.

Stepping out from the crowd, Philip spots the abandoned taxi sitting curbside. Getting up on the hood, he invites Connie to join him. Yet again, she wonders what they'll say in the office. Philip holds his hand out, waiting for her to take his offer. She takes his hand firmly into hers, getting on. Both look down, cautious they have little room to move. A blending of Capezio and scuffed Brogues use the yellow metal dance floor. With a view from the hood as her platform, Connie oversees everybody dancing around the five men singing, accompanied by Perry and Tim in the back. Even the hot dog vendor moves to the music near the corner of the sidewalk.

Connie bathes in the joy, sliding to-and-fro, hip-twisting, arms flailing. Philip does his own thing mostly in place.

High above in the offices of San-San, Connie's co-workers continue to watch. Gary spots her.

"Oh! No way! Is that our Connie?"

Maria asks, "Where?"

"Over there. On the taxi, with that guy."

"Ooh. He's cute!"

Philip slides off the hood.

Behind the two, drivers begin to get antsy, beeping their horns in the creeping traffic, swerving not to hit the illegally parked vehicles.

Connie glances around, feeling awkward being alone. Philip helps her off. Both laugh, realizing how ridiculous, crazy, and fun it has been dancing on a cab in the middle of the lunchtime rush.

She holds onto his shoulder, and asks him, "Is that what it's like to be on a stage?"

"Kinda," he turns to look back at the taxi. "Higher stage."

Connie closes her eyes in a dream-like state.

"Oh my God. This has been so much fun...," She glances at the San-San building before her. "...but I have to go back to work. I shouldn't even be here. Our break doesn't start until one."

"Ah. Coach turns back into a pumpkin?" he grins, leaning against the side of the taxi, putting his Ray-Bans on for added coolness.

Connie laughs, "Yeah. You could say that."

For a moment, she stares at the musician. Snapping back to reality, she nods, then says, "Bye."

He nods in understanding, pulling the sunglasses down to peer at her from the rims, watching as she gingerly steps over the cords sticking out of the door.

A siren puts everybody on alert. Philip glances over quickly to see an NYPD police cruiser pull behind the fifth car parked against the curb. The doo-wop singers look up startled by the commotion, with the oldest finishing picking up tips from revelers grateful they spread joy. He motions to the others they need to look busy. The crowd quickly disperses, spreading out, walking away as though nothing happened. All four vehicles leave the scene, vanishing down the street.

An officer steps around the parked taxi cab, in which he pulls out a small writing pad as the cab driver runs towards him.

"Oop! Oop! I'm moving! I'm moving!" he announces.

Clumsily, he places the knit cap back on his head, getting into the cab.

The officer watches the taxi drive away, still holding the pad. He puts a hand out in shock. He glances at Philip a little ways away.

"Excuse me, sir? Did you witness anything abnormal here?"

Philip turns around, adjusting his sunglasses.

"No. Nothing out of the ordinary, officer."

The officer nods, glancing around puzzled.

"OK," he pulls off his cap, scratching his head while returning to the cruiser.

Another NYPD car pulls up next to his — the officer motions for the others to leave.

He takes off.

Philip notices the doo-wop group at the hot dog stand. He approaches the five of them individually, shaking their hands.

"Roy, Frankie, Ethan, Isaiah, Xavier. Great job."

The leader of the group and eldest, Roy, steps forward.

"Hey, you're a pretty cool cat for a white guy. We had a lot of fun." He picks out a wad of cash from his pants pocket. "I do believe this is yours."

Philip glances down at the handful of bills.

"Nah. It's yours. You guys earned it. You told me you wanted to help send Frankie to college. Here's a little start-up cash for it." He puts a hand on Roy's shoulder. "Education comes first. He'll do better than I ever did. I never went to college. Not enough money, and I didn't have what it takes. Frankie's got a great big brother to look after him. Be proud."

Roy looks at the other four guys enjoying hot dogs and talking about the performance. He eyes Philip in half confusion and shock.

"What about you? You don't need it?"

"No," Philip glances back at the San-San building with a satisfied smile. "I got what I wanted."

Standing outside of a large department store, Connie mentions to Philip, "There are some things I have to look for."

He grins back wildly, "Shopping's not my greatest forte."

"You don't have to join me then," she answers with a tight-lipped smile, opening the front door.

Immediately he says, "Not that it's all bad."

They walk inside. Philip scans the surroundings while the escalator is ahead. Both wait for the metal stairs to take them down.

In the meantime, he eagerly asks, "Was everything OK afterward?"

"Yeah. I didn't get in trouble or anything. Generally, the boss doesn't care about some distractions. It happens in a city like this. You never know what you'll see here."

"A little bit of a *West Side Story* vibe?" he asks with one brow raised mischievously.

"I was thinking more like a Lionel Ritchie video."

"Mmm. I can see that too," Philip considers thoughtfully as the lower level comes into view.

Connie shakes her head, still thinking of the fun she had on Friday.

"I truly hope that the cab driver didn't get in too much trouble."

"He'll be fine. Hey, he did get out of a parking ticket."

"Really?" she asks, shocked.

"Yeah. It happened after you left. After most people left."

She laughs.

"You came up with the whole thing. You were the mastermind behind it all," Connie says, taking a small step forward that brings her to the floor.

"I'd like to think of the title as music coordinator," he answers, hopping off the escalator.

Connie thinks for a moment before saying, "Mr. Music Coordinator, I can't figure you out sometimes." She shakes her head.

Duran Duran gets pumped through the PA system in a portion of the beauty department, they pass. Philip finds it necessary to grimace and shuffle tightly past the ladies spritzing potential customers with the latest perfumes.

Connie fans the scent away, wanting to leave the area as quickly as possible.

"Not a fan?" he giggles.

"No!" she states emphatically. "Not at all. Of course, all department stores put the perfumes near the accessories section, which annoys me like crazy."

Philip walks along with confidence, mouthing the words to the music.

"So, what is it you're looking for?"

Connie comes to an aisle full of hair accessories. Picking off one from a metal hook, she says, "Hair stuff. I'm pretty sure I lost one or two when I went to the laundromat. Dryers full of static, and they swallow up anything." She thinks for a moment. "So, what's with your aversion to shopping? You're like every other guy I know who hates shopping and loves muscle cars."

"Like every other guy, except for the one thing, you mean," he answers her with a crooked smile."

"I wasn't thinking of that," she says, noticing his demeanor.

"You asked me about shopping? I never had a real problem with it until more recently. My parents would pile all of us kids in the car and go down to Hess's. It's this massive, fancy department store in the middle of Allentown. We'd go there mostly for Christmas shopping. My older sisters would hang out in an area like this or check out the latest fashions they couldn't afford. My older brother and I would check out the electronics department for radios. When my younger sister came along, then it was toys, toys, and more toys. My second older sister, Angie, really loved the large Christmas decorations. So, one year when I was making a sizeable amount of money with Deacon, I bought this six-foot toy soldier figure for her. My folks were a little freaked out, having this thing standing in the corner of the kitchen. When I went to visit them the same year, my dad said, 'You're in a successful rock and roll band, and you got this?' They had no idea what to do with it. The thing took up too much space in the house, and eventually, I got it. It's in my basement. Thankfully, it fits."

Connie shakes her head, putting a hair accessory back on the hook.

Philip bites his bottom lip in thought.

"Maybe shopping isn't such a bad idea, considering I'm going back on the road."

Connie immediately turns to him.

"You are?"

"Well, it's not really on the road as much as it's promoting. Yeah. There is a live gig mixed in."

"Where is it at?"

Philip takes a fluffy hair accessory off the hook, with an enamel British flag glued on.

She looks over the item and answers, "England?"

"Yep."

"That's pretty far," she says with surprise. "When is it?"

"Beginning of next month. It's the end of this month we take off. Then on the following Monday comes the whole promotional blitz, interviews, TV appearances..."

"Sounds exciting."

"Yeah. I guess. It's a week of insanity. So, I'm searching for a new look. Something different than what I've worn for the past seven months."

Philip puts the hair accessory back and disappears. Connie continues to look at items. He returns, holding a small black plastic earring card with outrageously long neon pink mesh dangles.

Putting it up to his left ear, he asks, "How's this?"

Connie snorts back a laugh.

"Uh. No. Unless you're trying to compete with Elton John for outrageousness. Then, the next thing you'll do is wear a Donald Duck costume."

Philip says, "Oh, but it would go great with your Mickey Mouse watch."

"Oh, you are bad," she answers dryly.

He bursts out laughing from her reaction, then walks away.

She continues to mutter to herself, "Then I'll have a visual locked inside my head of you wearing that stupid costume for days. Like when you told me about your Tom Cruise outfit for Halloween, which wasn't so bad," She shakes her head. "Nope. Don't need it."

He returns empty-handed when Connie is checking out an aisle of gloves.

Picking a pair, he says, "How about something like this with the fingertips cut off?"

Connie looks over at him peculiarly. "You're really serious about this punk thing? I wouldn't figure you for it. I thought you would look for something a little more conservative."

"Conservative?" he questions with peculiarity.

Again, he disappears.

Two middle-aged women attired in fancier fashions eye Connie, noticing the untamed bronze-haired guy wandering about in the ladies' accessory department. They watch to see what will transpire next.

Philip comes back, wearing a long flowing scarf wrapped around his neck.

"You know, these were all the rage about ten years ago. All the guys were wearing them. You could go totally crazy. Wear polka dots, stripes, metallic, leather, and about anything. Uh, wait. Anything that is, except tie-dye. Nothing goes with tie-dye." He shakes his head. "Ah! I think I know." Whipping off the scarf, he disappears into another aisle.

Connie smiles to herself.

She can't wait to see what he comes up with next.

So can't those two busy-body women hanging around.

Philip zooms out from the aisle, jumping out in front of Connie like a rambunctious kid, wearing a red bandana around his head. He tries to display his bottom teeth for added effect.

Connie groans, "Oh, good grief. Yeah. OK, Rambo."

Philip looks up, rolling his eyes.

"No. Not that."

Quickly, he starts rolling up his sleeves, displaying his less than toned arms. Moving around with arms swinging back and forth, he quietly sings.

Connie giggles at his display of spontaneity. She puts a finger up.

"I thought of somebody else. Loverboy. The band. The lead singer who wears them."

Philip drops his head shamefully.

"It was supposed to be the current Springsteen. I can't copy his underbite," he giggles.

"Oh! I was wondering what song you were singing!" she laughs back.

He unties the bandana, walking away.

The two middle-aged women talk to each other, loud enough for Connie to hear.

Philip returns, unaware of what has just happened. He smiles until noticing Connie's awkward reaction.

"Let's just get out of here," she shakes her head, walking away briskly to the nearest door.

Philip looks at her puzzled, knowing she was laughing and having a good time. He follows her out the door.

Connie's eyes meet the sidewalk while pushing back her hair in frustration. Taking a deep breath, she swallows hard. Philip immediately senses something wrong.

"What's the matter?" he asks in concern.

Connie hesitates before answering, "Nothing."

"We were in there, and you looked like you were having fun. Then, this."

"Those two buzzards had no right!" she says aloud.

Philip's eyes dart back and forth, trying to figure out what she's talking about.

Connie takes a deep breath, "There were two women in there, and they were talking loud enough I could hear them. The things they were saying." She stomps her foot in restless anger.

"I don't get it. But, OK."

She breathes back, shakily, "I just wish people could understand differences."

Philip nods his head as he sees things clearer.

"Ah. I think I got it now. Did they say anything to you directly?"

"No," she sheepishly answers.

"But you heard them?"

"I knew what they were talking about."

Philip fishes in his pocket, grabbing out a pack of Newports. He taps out a cigarette, putting it in his mouth. In the same pocket, he produces a lighter. The tiny orange flame dances as he lights it in a single motion. Dropping the item back into the depths of his jacket pocket, he inhales to get his nicotine fix or chill out from her anxiety.

Connie stares at him in disbelief, her mouth agape.

"A cigarette break?" She turns away from him in disgust. Blinking back, she goes back to face him. "You truly are like every other guy. Look at you. Cool as a cucumber. I'm sorry that I bored you." She says in a pissy tone.

Philip's eyes roll in the form of drama. He holds his cigarette out, tapping out the ashes. Looking down, he utters quietly, "Yes, dear."

Connie's eyes narrow. "You think this is funny."

With disinterest, he says, "I'm not laughing."

Flaring her nostrils, she blinks back while shaking her head.

"Unbelievable."

Finally, she gets a reaction out of him.

"It bothers you more than me. I didn't hear it. Sometimes it's better that way. I don't know what they said, but I think you're taking it too personally."

Connie's eyes gaze down in defeat.

"I've simply learned how to ignore things. You know better, so use your judgment wisely and don't rely on others." He takes another drag on the cigarette. "Besides, buzzards feed off of the dead. Show them you're alive. That's all."

"I hate when you're right," Connie answers thoughtfully.

Philip mocks her frown, "You look like a sad Muppet when you do that."

Connie stifles a laugh.

He leans over with a grin, "Attagirl." Surprising himself in thought, Philip tells her, "Remember how I was telling you about Hess's? I didn't tell you about what has kept me going there since I was a kid. It's their Mile-High Strawberry Pie. Fresh strawberries with an obnoxiously ginormous amount of whipped cream. Every time I go home to visit, I have to go to Hess's and get that pie. For the holidays or anytime. It's that good. But, I don't think there is such a thing in Manhattan. I haven't looked lately. Wanna hunt around for a good strawberry pie?"

"If it's as good as you say, why not?" Connie shrugs.

They begin walking down the street.

"I do have to tell you I tried making one myself."

"You're a chef?"

"Far from it! I had one of the background singers over my place. She said it would be no problem. We got as far as making the pie dough."

"What happened?"

"Well, we got into a flour war. We were bombing it at each other. Clouds of white powder flying everywhere!"

Connie laughs.

Connie walks along Tenth Street, under the watchful eye of the sun. Summer begins to fade as she dons a light jacket. She's taken by surprise, seeing Philip trot over to her.

"Your sense of timing is impeccable," she giggles.

"That's what happens when you have sessions, or I should say one or two lines as back-up on a chorus." Philip quickly changes the subject as they cross onto Fourteenth. "So, what's going on with you?" he asks.

"I have the day off, seeing as though it's Labor Day. I promised my mom I'd visit my grandma. You know, life can get pretty hectic. It's not like I was purposely neglecting to see her. She's meant so much to me growing up. I'm closer to my dad's side of the family anyway. She's been my greatest support. Sometimes more than my mom. I know it's going to hurt seeing her deteriorate mind-wise. But I need to do this." Connie looks at him, awkwardly. "So, it's not like I was going to ask you to tag along for something like this. It's not like we're—"

Philip hears his name called out. He looks over.

"Keep going. I'll catch up with you. I gotta go see what this is about."

Connie walks ahead, seeing her friend go to the man on the corner.

Philip looks over, seeing that Connie is away enough not to see anything. His demeanor and actions turn softer, taking on a slightly effeminate approach. With a smile, he says, "Hi, Doug."

"Gene is doing fine," Doug answers without being prompted. "When I first saw him a few months ago, I thought he was back with you."

Philip looks at him, puzzled.

"I'm not saying you have a twin, but from a little distance away, I honestly believed somebody else was you. Lighter hair like you had a few years ago and about the same height. The only difference is, he's not afraid to be seen with Gene. I've seen them together numerous times, and they are totally in love."

Philip's eyes meet the sidewalk as he nods in agreement.

"So, have you found anybody?" Doug asks.

"I recently got out of a nearly year-long relationship."

"That's pretty long, considering your record."

Philip rolls his eyes with a small smile. "It is what it is," he takes a deep breath, rubbing the back of his head while scanning the area. "Listen, I'm sorry, but I need to get going. You know, the guys at the studios can get on my case if I'm not there on time."

Doug senses Philip's awkwardness at their meeting.

"It was nice seeing you again. You look well and don't take this as some snide remark, but I truly hope you find happiness. When you do, it will feel natural."

Philip glances down and nods back.

"Mmm. Yeah."

Tight-lipped, he turns and walks away. He reunites with Connie a few blocks down. Immediately, she can tell his demeanor is solemn, unlike before. With hands in his pockets, he looks down in disappointment.

"I feel like shit, but I'll survive," he answers, picking his head up.

"I'm sorry," Connie says with sincere empathy.

"Sometimes things happen for a reason," he shrugs.

"That's a positive way of thinking...I guess," she answers awkwardly.

Philip takes a hasty breath with thought.

"Let's do it."

Connie looks at him, a bit confused.

"Do what?"

"Let's go visit Grandma," he angles with a nod.

"What?" Connie questions in shock. "You don't have to do it."

Philip steps in front of her with a look that she's grown accustomed to seeing when he's sure.

"I want to."

With the same expression, Connie says, "OK." In a moment, she adds in, "But, you need to understand it's outside the city, and I take the train up there unless you prefer a taxi?"

"It's your call," he answers.

"Somehow, I think a taxi would be best."

Almost an hour later, the two get dropped off at a large building in Westchester. Philip opens the door for Connie. They walk inside to the sights and sounds of caretakers chatting. Connie signs in with the visitor information desk. The assistant instantly recognizes her.

"Oh, hello, Ms. Ayers. Irene is in her room," she answers before looking at Philip. "Who's with you? Never seen him before?" She raises a brow with interest.

"Cousin."

"Half brother," Philip answers at the same time, causing Connie to glance at him.

She shrugs, "The same for him."

Philip says, "It's a southern thing."

The assistant says, "Irene will be glad to see you. And, the more, the merrier."

Connie smiles back, "Thank you."

As she and Philip walk down the hallway, Connie turns to him. "Half brother? You can't even get your lies straight!" She shakes her head. "You don't even have a southern accent."

"I figured it was no big deal. Aside from that, didn't—" Philip is suddenly interrupted by an object whizzing by his path, hitting the adjacent wall, skittering to the center of the floor. He gives a quick hop over the bowl, while a flurry of commotion comes from one of the rooms.

A man yells, "I don't want it!! Keep your damn slop!"

Philip looks back in concern. "Are you sure we won't need hard hats for this visit?"

Connie shakes her head again.

"My grandma isn't that bad. Come on."

They stop at a room with a closed door. Connie knocks. Upon opening it cautiously, the two are greeted by a young black nurse who sports a name tag showing, 'Cherese,' who smiles at them.

"Just finished getting her tidied up, and she ate. She's been a little feisty today. It's tough when they're struggling with thoughts. Not quite there. Other than that, she's been OK lately," Cherese answers while cleaning up a few things. "Gotta watch out for Bingo night. A few of the guys get her stirred up, and you can't shut her down. She loves a challenge! I try to stay out of it. Anyway, I'm going to leave you alone. I gotta go check on another patient." She looks at the old lady sitting in a comfortable chair, "Irene? Honey? Your granddaughter is here to see you."

Irene remains listless, staring far and away, talking to herself as if in a conversation.

Philip looks at the old lady, studying her features, which resemble her granddaughter's. The same expressive greenish eyes, and cheek structure. The only difference besides her well-worn age lines is the short silver hair. He considers this is what Connie will look like in her twilight years. A small smile broadens on his face.

"It's so hard to see her like this," Connie says, looking sadly at her grandmother. "I always feel so guilty about having a life while she's stuck here."

She steps up to Irene. "Hi, Gramma."

Philip spots a small bowl on a nearby table.

He mumbles, "Green gelatin. I'd be cranky if I were fed that."

Connie's distraction gets broken.

"What was that?"

"It's green gelatin." He turns to her with a puzzled expression. "What makes anybody think this is a good idea? The staple of every hospital. I don't think any schools I ever went to served it, thankfully."

"Me neither."

"It's like green slime when you think of it. I mean, cherry or orange is fine. Even grape. But, something about that color is rather unappetizing," he emphasizes, "green."

Irene looks up at Connie and asks, "Where's Sammy and Ralphie? Are they back at the house?"

"Gramma, I'm Connie. Your granddaughter."

"But, but Sammy and Ralphie are at the house, right?"

Philip's glance bounces from Irene to Connie and down to the floor uncomfortably. He closes his eyes, hearing Connie struggle to communicate with her grandmother.

"Gramma, Sammy, and Ralphie aren't home," Connie cautions.

"Where are they then?" Irene asks with growing concern, grabbing her granddaughter's hand with the weakened grip.

Connie looks at Philip for some reassurance. He's of no help, though.

"I don't know where they are. They both left the house a while ago. Sammy married Alice, and Ralphie married Catherine."

Irene becomes more insistent.

"No! No! Ralphie was going on his paper route! He was there! I saw him myself!"

Philip grows somewhat uneasy from the conversation. Without looking at either of the two women, he states, "Connie, she's going back further than what you're talking about." Shaking his head while turning away, he spots a large portable radio on the countertop. "Wow. You don't see one of these every day."

Connie says, "What? A boombox?"

He checks the titles of some neatly stacked cassette tapes off to the side.

"So, this is where you get your love of Tony Bennett."

Rather than pleased, Connie gives a huffy breath at Philip's frivolous interest in radios and choice of music at such a time.

She stiffly answers him, graciously as possible, "Yes, I left those for her some time ago."

Cherese returns to the room.

"Is everything alright in here? I just came by to see how things were doing."

Connie answers quickly, "We're doing fine."

Philip asks, pointing to the boombox, "How long has this been here?"

"Oh, one of the previous nurses brought that in months ago, I think. She didn't want it anymore and got a new one."

"It's a Panasonic RX five six hundred LS. They're called National in Japan. You don't find these at Kmart."

Cherese is both shocked and impressed. "Nah. Yeah. Not any Blue Light Special I've ever heard," They both laugh. "My brother's a DJ in Dayton. How did you know about this model? 'Cause, I was gonna say, you know your stuff!"

Philip grins slyly, "Occupational hazard." He raises a brow. "It's also one of the best models ever made, so far." Glancing down at the boombox, he asks, "Has anybody thought of using it?" Holding up a cassette of Tony Bennett's, *I Left My Heart in San Francisco*, "Like this?"

"Oh, we've thought about it, but she's in her own world most of the time, and a lot of us keep forgetting." She checks the time. "Would you please excuse me? I need to get to a few more patients. I'll sneak by if time permits."

Cherese leaves them alone.

Philip looks through more of the cassettes. "What will it be? We've got, Tony Bennett—" He stops immediately, looking at a title. His voice deepens with a low groan. "Pat Boone?" Shaking his head, he asks, "Did you have to put a paper bag over your head when you got this?"

In exasperation, Connie says, "It's not that bad."

He puts his hands up in defense.

"Hey, all I'm saying is, she's your grandmother, not mine." Looking at Irene, he adds, "Some things she doesn't have to remember." He looks around. "Um, is there a trash can handy?"

Connie tightens up in anger, shaking her head.

Philip says, "Tom Jones." Turning to her, he says in a severe tone, "You know this is grounds for abuse."

She flairs her nostrils and crosses her arms, staring at him.

"Tony it is," he says, noticing his antics do not amuse Connie. Growing more serious, he takes the cassette out of the case and loads it in the boombox. "Let's see what happens. Music has healing properties. A very spiritual nature. Not necessarily religious. You know, it brings out the joy in people when listening to it. It's expressive and powerful at the same time. Like the guys singing doo-wop on the street corners. The street musicians that hang around midtown or down in the subway. All the clubs. The break dancers who spin on sidewalks. A dance party on the street. Even what I've done in the past and present."

He presses the play button.

Irene's expression changes. Her eyes go big. The wrinkles around her mouth tighten as she smiles. She sways in the chair, listening to the piano introduction. Closing her eyes, she hears Tony Bennett's soothing voice. Irene's lips follow the words carefully. The following song, "Once Upon a Time," she looks up at Philip. Holding out her arms, he helps her to her feet. Immediately, she feels comforted being in his arms.

Connie stares at her grandmother, ready to tear up.

"Oh, Jackie. You always knew how to make me smile," Irene answers, joyously.

Philip holds Irene tightly as they sway to the music. She seemed to be in a whole different dimension. One of peace and tranquility. One of fond remembrance. He feels the warmth of her connection. Even if he wasn't the person she was thinking of, it felt right from experiencing the painful reminder of rejection he had only hours earlier. The expression of music and what it had brought an older lady who couldn't remember the beauty of life was all worth it. He needed a little light, and she did too. For a moment in time, he was who she dreamed of.

"You've always been a wonderful dancer, Jackie," she says with a smile, as Tony finishes up the lines to, "Taking a Chance on Love."

The tape stops.

Connie breathes back, holding in her emotions. She wipes a tear from her eye as Philip turns the cassette over and presses 'play' before the moment drifts away. Irene holds onto the top of the chair, awaiting more from the memories never forgotten.

"Jackie?" Philip quietly asks.

"Grandpa," Connie answers in the same way.

He nods back in understanding. Looking back, he sees Irene is still feeling the freedom from her trapped mind. Taking her hand, again, Philip leads her to the center of the small room. She looks at him with the youth in her eyes. Time had reversed course when the twenty-five-year-old fell for the young man on a dance floor that took her breath away, and eventually her hand in marriage. That was swing music, but this was Tony Bennett. Music that a husband and wife could slow dance to in the comfort of their living room. That's how Irene chose to think of her moment with a stranger.

Connie looks at the two who enjoy their time in each others' arms. It gives her a feeling of both melancholy sweetness and sadness. The sweet interaction between her grandmother was breaking free from her dementia, and a stranger Connie knew she could never share the same happiness with.

Philip and Irene part while staring at each other. Cherese returns to the room surprised to see the old lady on her feet.

"Did I miss something?" she asks.

The tape clicks to a stop, making her turn around.

"I think you need to use this more often. Music seems to jog her memory," Philip answers, tapping the top of the boombox.

Cherese takes Irene by the hand. "Irene, honey? I'm going to take you back to your chair. In another hour, you can see everybody else. OK?"

Irene answers with a smile, "Jackie took me dancing, and it was wonderful! He's such a sweet boy, and good looking too," she giggles. "He knew my feet were bothering me, but I wouldn't stop dancing. No pain, no gain! Jackie didn't have eyes for any other girl in the room."

Cherese looks at Philip, who nods with a small smile.

Connie takes a step forward and asks, "Is there anything she does here to stay active? Not that I don't trust the facility. We're still not used to this arrangement. My uncle's family was taking care of her until they found it too difficult."

"Oh no. Irene does fine. Like I told you earlier, she likes Bingo. That's where I was going to take her a little later on. She tries to do other things. I noticed that she's pretty good at poker."

"That was something she did as a teenager," Connie answers thoughtfully.

"She tends to recall how to play pretty easily. We tell new male orderlies to watch out when wearing all white. She likes to challenge them to a game of strip poker."

Philip lets out a hearty laugh.

Connie glances at him, then pay attention to Cherese.

"Sweetheart, don't worry. Irene is in excellent hands," Cherese answers.

Philip chimes in with, "Yeah. When she has a good hand." He giggles uncontrollably.

Connie rolls her eyes in dismay at his comment.

"I'm going to wait outside. Cherese, thank you for everything you've been doing for her."

"No problem. It's the job I do. You have a good day, Ms. Ayers."

Connie leaves the room, walking over to the adjacent wall in the hallway. She presses her forehead against the cold plaster, closing her eyes.

Philip gets over his giggling fit, putting an arm over Cherese's shoulder. Calmly, he says, "Do me a favor. Do you want to be a great nurse? Get her some better tunes. Keep Tony. There's a perfectly good wastebasket over there for the rest." He pulls away, digging in his front jacket pocket and produces a fifty dollar bill. "How much will Grant get you?" Cherese looks at him dumbfounded, as he hands the money to her. "Use your best judgment. Something with a little more soul," he arches a brow.

Cherese stares at him, not knowing what to say as she stands, holding the bill.

"Take care of Gramma." He gives a tight-lipped smile before leaving.

Outside the room, Connie crosses her arms with the look of unhappiness in her eyes. Philip goes to join her.

"Did you really have to try your brand of humor at a care facility? There's a place and time for that, you know?"

Philip's eyes meet the floor.

"I needed this."

Connie glances up at the ceiling. She lets out a stilted breath, shaking her head in disapproval.

He says, "Before we came here... Um, who I was talking with? I was told that I apparently have a twin."

Connie furrows her brows.

"There's only one you."

"I don't mean biologically." Awkwardly, he tries to explain. "Somebody from my past."

"You mean a past relationship?" Connie asks cautiously.

Philip slowly nods back.

"In a case of mistaken identity, somebody thought I was with this person again. They say everybody has a twin, and I didn't think I did. Anyway, they're happy." He nods back again, "I screwed up."

Connie brushes her hair back, "I'm sorry. I didn't know." She looks down in guilt. "No. Really. I'm sorry. I've truly acted immaturely lately. What you did in there...," she throws a glance towards the closed door to her grandmother's room, "...that meant a lot to me. Whatever rejection you experienced before we came here, you're very much appreciated. Your intuitive knowledge of what to do under stress is simply wonderful. And mine sucks." Taking a swallow, she continues with, "She hasn't mentioned Grandpa since he passed away seven years ago. She certainly never called him Jackie in years. I think maybe way back before I was ever born. I can't be sure. They met at a dance and hit it off right away. Depression-era. A cheap form of entertainment. It would have been fifty-three years they were married, this year. But, it was forty-six instead. She called him Jonathan all the time. I miss him. We all do. Oh, you would have gotten along with him. He liked music...a lot." Connie wipes her eyes, noticing Philip is merely staring at her. "We should get going."

They start to walk away when he looks back at Irene's room.

CHAPTER 8

Spinning on her heels, Connie faces Philip as she bites her bottom lip.

"Ever go roller skating?" she asks playfully, stopping in front of a nondescript building that bears the name, 'Lace Up!'

"A time or two. My younger sister had a birthday at one, and I had a gig at another. It was more of an experiment in sound. They normally played organ music, and uh, they wanted to get the kids to go 'cause skating was going lame."

"How about you?"

"Oh yeah, sure. It's not hard to do. Easy!" He shrugs, then takes a deep breath of uncertainty.

Connie puts her hand out, holding the door open. "Trust me. It'll be fun."

Philip follows her inside. Immediately, he's caught off-guard by the darkness of the interior, low-lighting, and loud music. Everything that would be ordinarily white has turned into a vibrant violet. Day-glow colors abound, against the back wall featuring an artsy mural of the city. Puffy orange letters resembling graffiti, announce the venue's name, LACE UP! A DJ booth sits in a far corner, facing the action of several dozen skaters on the crowded oak wood floor. Gloria Gaynor croons, "I Will Survive" over the PA system.

He looks around in a daze. "I don't remember it looking like Studio 54."

Philip follows the men's moves as they skate frontward and backward to the beat. Connie catches his stare, smiling to herself, thinking there are a lot of handsome looking guys. Surely one would strike his fancy. She heads over to the rental booth, where several shelves are stocked full of skates against the sidewall. Philip goes to join her. He starts to reach in his pocket when Connie shakes her head. She pulls out a wad of cash, plunking it down on the counter.

"My treat," she smiles. "You just go and enjoy yourself."

Both of them sit at a bench. Connie sits next to Philip but makes the room as soon as a young, fresh-faced gentleman needs some space. She lets him in between herself and the musician. Connie puts on her skates with no problems. Philip waits for her to finish as he slowly unties the laces to fit into the boot. He steals a glance at the guy next to him, like a kid trying to get the answers to a written test. His eyes bounce to Connie, getting up from the bench.

"I'm going to try these out a little before heading out to the main floor."

"OK," Philip nods back.

Again, he looks at the guy next to him.

Connie glances over, noticing Philip is chatting with the guy. She smiles, believing there could be a connection. There would be no need for her to play matchmaker.

Philip says to the young guy, "OK, so I have it right at this point. Then..."

The guy answers, "Then you tie it tight at the top."

"I don't have to bring the ties around the back, right?"

"No. You tie them like shoes," the guy grins, shaking his head. "First-timer, huh? I had a girlfriend who started me on this. Then, she quit skating and me. Now I enjoy it. You'll get the hang of it. When you get on the main floor, it's no different than getting onto an entrance ramp. You know, like the kind that's a little ways from the Hutchinson River Parkway upstate? The Merritt Parkway in Connecticut? That thing is like an autobahn!"

Connie hears the laughter of the two men sitting on the bench. She smiles to herself without looking back.

Philip shakes his head as he goes to join Connie, slowly rolling.

They stop at the floor's threshold leading to the spacious oak wood before them. Patrons dress as though they're in a club. It's a wide variety of fashions, from bright spandex on both men and women, denim, neon, bandanas, and even a few short-shorts present. Some spin in place, while others prefer not to be fancy. Disco lighting showers shards of red, yellow, green, and blue in dizzying motion.

Connie tries to get her footing as close as possible to the merry-go-round of skaters. Philip stares at the rolling traffic. He watches as both men and women glide by on four wheels. Connie notices his stare at the men in particular. So many young, athletic, good-looking men in outfits sure enough to catch his attention, especially the guys with short-shorts or tight-fitting pants with a visible bulge. It makes her feel good to know Philip might be interested enough to find a worthy partner for himself.

She waits for several people to whiz by when she gets enough nerve and accelerates onto the wood floor.

Philip exhales, glancing around again, until taking that one big move.

A baby step.

Connie rounds the corner when she sees him barely on the floor. She shakes her head in disbelief.

The other patrons wheel on to Phil Collins' "I Missed Again."

Again, Connie rounds the corner when she sees something that alerts her to speed up. She slows down when noticing Philip is sitting on the floor, holding his knees comfortably while skaters glide around him. Stopping, she looks down.

"What happened?"

"I like to be eye level with laughing kids."

"There are no kids here."

"I wiped out. And it was to a Hugh Padgham production," he answers with slight surprise.

"I thought you said it was easy?"

"Mmm. Yeah. Well, I never said I was an expert."

Connie closes her eyes, embarrassed by the whole thing. She puts a hand out to help him get up. Instead, Philip is dead weight and won't accept it.

"I would normally watch from a safe distance away while my sister or anybody was skating," he responds.

"What are you going to do? Wait to get run over?"

Suddenly, a young black man in a bandana rolls to a stop in front of the two and asks, "What might be the problem? Need some help, ma'am?"

Just then, a fair-haired model-looking type in short-shorts joins in.

Both lift Philip to his feet, like a wounded comrade in war. Slowly, they roll him back to the safety of the carpet.

Connie waits for him, flaring her nostrils in disgust as he rolls slowly.

Realizing the fool he's made of himself, Philip gives a feeble explanation to lighten the mood hopefully.

"To be fair, it was the second time I wiped out."

"Second?"

"Yeah. The first was when I got on the floor."

"Oh, God." Connie rolls her eyes.

After they change back to their shoes, the two leave quickly.

Connie reels around.

"I figured you were watching some of those guys."

"Yeah. I was. I was watching how they kept their balance and the way they moved."

"How about the fellow you were chatting with on the bench? I heard the laughter and figured I would leave you alone with him."

"I was wondering how to tie the laces. That laugh was from a joke. More like an analogy the guy made that I found to be funny."

"So, you weren't—" Connie stops.

"What?"

"You know? Interested?"

Philip shakes his head. "Yeah. Do me a favor and don't try to play matchmaker. I'm fully capable of finding someone myself."

"OK. So much for that experiment." Connie breathes out.

"What? Is that why we came here?"

"No. It was to have fun. Or at least I thought it might be." She glances at the passing traffic. "Why did you say it was easy?"

He looks down at the sidewalk, then back at her with a sheepish grin. "I guess I couldn't pull it off," he says charmingly.

"No." Connie stifles a giggle at his expression.

The two continue to walk down the street, further into the city.

"Who's Hugh Padgham?" Connie asks out of curiosity.

"He's a producer and engineer who's worked a lot with the guys in Genesis, starting with Peter Gabriel, and then his former band members. He's responsible for the gated reverb. It's hard to explain. You know it when you hear it."

At the next street, they come across a blocked section of the sidewalk. Two cranes are parked nearby. Another lifts a large rectangle item, dangling it from its grip. Philip looks way up at the building, realizing what it is.

Connie asks, "What is that?"

"That is a Neve console. I can't tell if it's an eight-zero-six-eight or an eight-zero-seven-eight from this angle."

"Yeah, but with a crane? Couldn't they just carry it in?"

"Some of the studios in these buildings don't have an elevator large enough, and nobody in their right mind is going to carry something that massive up several flights of stairs. So, they lift it to the roof. And in this case. It looks like they're doing just that."

"All for the sake of sound?" Connie asks.

"All for the sake of enjoyment." Philip gives a little nod. "Come on."

In the middle of September, on a nighttime stroll, Philip and Connie are on their way to a hip club. Attired in a fuchsia-colored suit, offset with a black shirt, Philip is amused by what Connie asks. She wears a long cobalt blue cardigan with subdued white and black underneath.

Philip turns to speak with Connie.

"Yeah. That's how these videos go. You stand around, hour after hour, while they get the set ready or the next shot. Then you're lip-synching to your own song, and sometimes the director will throw in some guitar at—"

He stops to see a commotion happening on the lower east side, where there is a row of apartment buildings. A police car pulls up behind another, as an older couple dressed in their pajamas appear at the doorway.

The officer says to them, "And you said, there was a man who lived alone in apartment thirty-six?"

"Yes, sir. The smell. When we were watching TV, it stunk to high heaven! A rotting stench."

Another officer already present inside, shakes his head.

The older man looks at the officer.

"What? He's dead?"

The officer refuses to say anything. Instead, he calls out to the other cop.

"I should have known. He was one of those," the old man quietly snarls.

"One of those?" The officer asks.

The man's wife says, "There was another man who died there a few months ago."

"He was one of those homosexuals. Knew it could happen. He probably had that gay cancer that all the news talks about," the old man answers.

She adds in, "I thought he was quite sick. He used to be so good-looking. Cy Vioskou. He was a fashion designer — a nice young man. His hair went completely white. His face became so pale. He lost so much weight over time. The suits he'd wear... Oh, it was terrible. Cy couldn't have been any more than thirty-eight or forty."

The officer at the foot of the stairs takes out his walkie-talkie.

Philip overhears him give a code, then announce how they will need rubber gloves for this DOA. He turns away from the entire scene as an ambulance pulls up.

The officer shakes his head.

"No. We need an M.E. This one's going straight to the morgue."

Connie holds onto Philip's arm out of fear. She says, "Oh my God. Is somebody dead in the apartment? That's awful!"

Philip responds with, "What's really awful is, they won't treat him like a human being." He takes her hand. "Come on. Let's get out of here."

The two briskly walk away.

Ten minutes later, they arrive in another neighborhood.

Philip points to a large, three-floor building.

"And, here we are."

Connie scans the building with her eyes.

"Looks abandoned," she answers dryly.

"Don't they all?" He waves his hand over. "Come on. I'll tell you about this place. It used to be a shoe warehouse back in the day. Then the sixties happened with the riots and civil rights. Businesses moved out, and the whole real estate market fell apart, leaving Manhattan in near-bankruptcy. The club opened a few years ago when this guy wanted to get in on the music market. FishKat has been jumping ever since."

"Is it the whole building?"

"No. The third floor. There are others, though. A Spanish club is on the first, and a modern darker New Wave type for up and coming artists on the second level. I think they call it gothic or goth. That one can get pretty crazy. Let's go in."

Philip and Connie enter the building. Music booms from a small darkened doorway. They watch as a woman attired in a frilly orange dress pushes through the narrow entrance. A young Puerto Rican guy in denim and a bandana wrapped around his head licks his lips at the sight of her. Philip turns to Connie, wondering what she thinks of the place so far. They walk over to a narrow hallway where there is a large freight elevator with a metal accordion gate. He slides it open.

"After you," he says.

They get on.

Connie looks him over.

"Could you have been a little less obvious?"

"Obvious of what?" Philip answers, puzzled.

"Obvious that you look like a neon sign."

As Philip begins to grin, a hand extended to display fingernails full of black nail polish juts out to catch the metal framework of the opened elevator. A small woman dressed entirely in black steps inside. Her jet black hair is more voluminous than Philip's. Caught off-guard by the fuchsia-wearing rocker, she's taken aback by his appearance. A man identically dressed like his girlfriend, steps on the elevator behind her. Noticing her expression of shock at the guy wearing pink, he reaches over to start kissing her. From Connie's angle, she can see a lot of tongue action going on between them. The pair rolls against the back of the metal steel enclosure with Philip and Connie bookending their romantic display of affection. Connie averts her eyes from them. Philip silently sings the words to his song, "Object of Affection." Connie happens to turn his way to see her friend is having fun with the moment. Her wide-eyed agitated gaze makes him look back mid-sentence of the song until he shuts his mouth abruptly.

Both Philip and Connie step to the side where they observe they are not moving.

"This is the slowest elevator...ever," Philip concedes.

The goth girl moans.

Connie says, "I hope we're not stuck."

Suddenly, the elevator jolts, giving motion under everybody's feet.

The goth boyfriend is too busy sucking on his girlfriend's throat even to notice when the elevator lands on the second floor. She lifts her head upon hearing the faint voice of Peter Murphy sing-speaking for Bauhaus' rhythmic "Spy In The Cab." The goth girl nudges him enough that he pays attention. They exit the elevator immediately, disappearing through a crowd of other black-haired guys and girls cloned among the smoky haze.

Philip rushes to the front of the elevator, shutting the gate before anybody else can join him and Connie.

"Yep. I think we've had enough of that," Philip answers in a quick breath, shaking his head.

Connie stifles a laugh.

"OK. So it'll be our turn," he says.

"What?" She answers in shock, thinking they'll be affectionate like the previous couple riding up with them.

"The next floor," he glances at the door. "When it decides to move, which I am predicting will send us up in about five minutes or more. Whatever it decides. In the meantime, I have to tell you where we're going. I sometimes think of it as Whitman's," he grins mischievously. "It's pretty exclusive and sweet, so I've been fortunate to get in."

"But, you're a musician. I figured you were plenty lucky."

"Not something like this."

The elevator gives a jolt. The two feel the motion take them up.

Philip says, "Just play along. OK, Constance?"

Connie breathes in rapidly, "Anything you say, Emmett." Her eyes widen.

Philip closes his.

"Ah. You talked with Gretchen." He nods tight-lipped. "She doesn't know everything."

Connie turns her attention, still wondering what Philip meant about Whitman's, and why he wore that silly grin.

Philip puts his sunglasses on.

Hesitantly, he says, "Uh, about that word? It's not something I would go around saying in public."

"I still don't get it."

"You will," he answers assuredly.

The elevator jolts to a stop, shaking up its two occupants. Connie gasps, as though she's been on an amusement park ride. They step off as a black couple gets on. Both exchange smiles. A black woman rushes off into a room off to the side. Connie immediately turns her head. Two black men of a lighter persuasion talk outside of an entrance. George Benson's "Give Me The Night" pours from the room. Connie stares. Her jaw drops. Giving Philip a look, she smacks his arm out of the blue.

"I get it now, and might I add, you're terrible," Connie shakes her head. "Whitman's," she quietly mutters.

Philip lets out a laugh. "Hey, it is what it is...a buppie club."

"A what?" Connie stares in shock. "I don't know which is worse? Whitman's or buppie? Where do you come up with these things?"

"Let's just go in. Remember, play along."

Philip clears his throat and adjusts his jacket. He walks up to the bouncer at the doorway, who looks to be the size of a football linebacker with big, broad shoulders and a massive neck. Dark as night, the man breaks into a smile, offsetting his brutish demeanor with bright white teeth gleaming.

"Hey! Hey! Phil!" The man says excitedly.

"Slim!" Philip responds joyously.

"Damn, man! You know style!" Slim answers, looking the musician up and down like a piece of art.

Connie can't quite believe her ears or eyes. She shakes her head behind him.

Philip takes Connie by the shoulder with a grin. "Oh, hey. This is my girl, Constance."

Connie gives a tight-lipped smile, shaking the big hand that swallows hers in a firm grasp.

She notices Philip's tone has changed to reflect a coolness that fits with the soulful crowd. Barely noticeable is the harder 's' she had been accustomed to hearing. It becomes apparent he was going to play things straight.

Philip and Connie walk past Slim, into a dimly lit space occupied by a sea of brown-hued patrons attired as though they belong on Wall Street, more than a nightclub. Not the clothing one would expect to sweat and dance in. The deep bass groove of "All Night Long" by The Mary Jane Girls gets people moving to a steady beat.

Connie turns to Philip. "You know style?" she asks him as distrust is in her voice.

A woman with black shoulder-length hair and an elongated face appears from the crowd yelling, "Phil! Phil!"

Philip turns to her with a smile. "Daisy!"

She rushes over to greet him with a big hug.

The musician coolly answers, adjusting his sunglasses. He puts an arm over Connie's shoulder, who glances at him knowingly.

"This is my girl, Constance," he says in a lower tone, tinged with hipness, holding in Connie tight.

Connie shakes hands with Daisy.

Daisy says in a thick Boston accent with scratchy voice, "Phil's welcome anytime! He's a cool cat! Cream and sugar, baby!"

"Ha! Thanks, Daisy," Philip smiles. He glances out at the packed dance floor. "How's it been?"

"Jumpin'! We got new people comin' in all the time. Oh, by the way, watch out for Brenda, honey. Bank teller over there. She's on the prowl. She broke up with her boyfriend recently."

Daisy looks over at the robust Brenda, jammed into a dress that's a little too tight for her size. She hangs around a lighter-toned black man who looks like he could be on a nighttime soap opera. Handsome, finely dressed, and a mustache. All the traits that make her more aggressive.

"Honey, I can cash your check," Brenda answers with a prominent gap between her teeth. Pressing herself against Mr. Hollywood-looking guy, she says, "but, I bounce." Her obnoxious laugh makes him turn away uneasily. Holding a drink in one hand, it shakes to the rhythm of her squeaky laughter. He slinks away.

"Aw, come on, buddy! I got the change rolls if you got the coins!"

Brenda watches him disappointingly. Soon, she disappears into the crowd, looking for the next victim of her overt affections.

Daisy shakes her head, watching the hapless bank teller melt away.

Connie says, "Um, Philip told me this was called a bu... Bup-py club?"

Philip removes his sunglasses.

Daisy answers, "Yeah. Buppie. Black Urban Professionals. We're all up and coming business people. A lot of Wall Street types. Bankers. Lawyers. Teachers. Engineers. Typists. Executives. You name it. We don't want to be street all our lives. Capisce? We want to move up in the world. Be respectable. Boys and girls in suits. Not ghetto."

Connie turns to look back at Philip, realizing he was right about the buppie reference. She turns her attention back to Daisy as the Dazz Band's "Let It Whip" plays.

"Has anybody ever told you, you look a lot like Donna..."

"Summer? I hear it all the time, sweetheart. It's either that or a black Joni Mitchell. There ain't nothin' wrong with that. I love both. People think I'm Donna's twin, or her sister, or that I'm secretly her. The funny thing is, we've got a lot in common. Notwithstanding, our names start with D. We're both from Boston, love New York, and a few other things. Only I have no musical ability. That girl can speak German! Really! I have a hard time grasping the English language and get all tongue-tied."

Philip glances around again, noticing that the girls are heavy into small-talk, which doesn't interest him in the least.

"I'm gonna go check things out with the DJ," he tells them, then disappears.

Connie says, "We were boring him."

"Men," Daisy responds with a nod. "So anyway... Yeah. I'm from Boston. I'm a business girl. I worked at Filene's Basement for a number of years. Then, I got this impression I really needed to come out to New York. With my background at Filene's, I got to work at Bloomingdales."

"You work at Bloomingdales? Wow!"

"Not on the floor. I'm billing. I'll tell you right now, whoever thinks the billing department is easy, that's bullshit. I get hassled plenty. It ain't because of the color of my skin either. It's how I talk. I get grief from some guys. They've got these heavy New York accents, and me? I've got mine. They get all angry at me when I'm tellin' them how much they owe. And I get, "You're one of those damn chowderheads. Listen, you two-bit Fenway broad. And then I hear them shout, 'Buckner's a bum!' Or, somethin' about the Celtics as if I know them personally. So, I gotta give it to them straight. 'Sir, you owe eight-hundred and forty-five dollars.' Obnoxious abuse!"

Connie says, "That's terrible!"

"I know. How about you? What do you do?"

"I do computer operations. I fill orders on electronics inventory for half the east coast within San-San Industries."

"No phones?"

"No."

"Oh, then you're lucky. I consider anybody who doesn't have to touch phones as lucky. Now, you got Phil. He's somethin' else."

"He certainly is," Connie answers wistfully.

Both women watch as he gets on the dance floor with some ladies who take them into their circle, dancing and swaying to "We Are Family" by Sister Sledge. Philip shows off some less-than-stellar moves. He puts one hand to hip, with the other outward in a feeble attempt at disco dancing. Waving his hand like the girls makes Daisy more aware of his softness, almost feminine at times.

"Constance, there's somethin' very different about him. Can't pinpoint it. He's not a good dancer, but the ladies sure like him."

Connie and Daisy watch him burst into laughter with the ladies enjoying his company. The two walk over to the bar, ordering up drinks and talking more.

"Like I was telling you about my specialty with department stores. Phil told me about Hess Brothers in Allentown, where he's from. It sounded like a dream! Five floors and an outrageous strawberry pie. Ooh!!" Daisy squeals in an already hoarse voice. "So, we went there."

"Wait. Philip took you to Allentown?"

"Yeah. It wasn't serious, like to visit his folks or anything. I'll tell you. One weekend I got the day off, and who do I see hanging around Herald Square? Phil! It's close to the holidays, and he wants to get out of there. So, he spots me, and he's like, 'Hey, Daisy! You're not at work today? I got a great idea since we're so close to it. How would you like to join me in going down to Allentown? I can show you Hess's. Make a day out of it." We were so close to Penn Station. There was no exact line to Allentown like he told me, but I think we caught a few different buses. It was crazy! We didn't even stay there that long. He never tried to make a pass or hit on me. A total and complete gentleman. All we did was bust out laughing at stuff, eat, and look at the decor. It was great! And we still got back to New York before it got really dark."

Across the way, Philip finishes talking with the DJ, who spins "Stomp!" by Brothers Johnson when somebody taps on his shoulder. Jimmy, a large, portly Italian man attired more like the age of disco, steps up to the musician. Nobody bats an eyelash at the sight of him. He takes Philip by the shoulder.

They walk to an emerald green-flecked restaurant booth. A young black man who easily fits in with the crowd sits looking up with both fear and excitement in his eyes. He licks his lips nervously. Getting up, he greets Philip with enthusiasm. The musician feels the trembling young man's greeting radiate through his handshake.

Jimmy steps through the crowd as willing patrons let him pass.

Connie watches with curious eyes.

She asks Daisy, "Who's he?"

Daisy takes a sip of her drink, then answers, "That's Jimmy. He's the boss. Everybody is on their best behavior for obvious reasons. Some people think he might be connected."

Connie gives her a puzzled glance.

"Mob. Yeah. Nobody can be sure because a lot of them have taken over so many things. Everything from food, entertainment, not sure about sports. Don't get me wrong. He likes sisters and gets along fine with brothers. No one asks him, and we're all happy here." Daisy looks over at Brenda, who remains on the prowl, trying to get the attention of any man. "Well, maybe not everybody."

The DJ yells, "Got to! Got to! Got to!" He then drops the needle on Cheryl Lynn's "Got To Be Real."

Philip continues his conversation with the young man.

He nods back, "Ah-huh. Yep. I gotcha." He breathes out, "After I got done playing with the band for seven years, I signed with a record company as a solo artist. One of the first things they wanted me to do was change my name. I've got Reinhardt, but they wanted me to remove the D. I told them no deal. There were a lot of things the company wanted out of me, and I refused. If anything, I made my own decisions. You have to watch out for the trappings. You know? If a label sees you're too eager, then they can mold you whatever way they want. You're no longer an artist. You're a puppet. There's a lot of messed up things with this business. It's not all about MTV and fancy videos."

Connie gets offers from a couple of men to dance. She refuses all of them while scanning the floor to see if she can find Philip somewhere in the crowd. As time rolls on, more songs play. "Get Down On It" by Kool & The Gang spins as patrons groove.

Philip emerges from the crowd. He lands directly face to face with Brenda, who licks her lips. Immediately, he backs away in avoidance.

"Well, well, well. Look at you, sweet thang! Want some cocoa in your cream? I can show you a good time," she answers, lasciviously dipping a blue nail-polished tip into her drink, then sucking on it.

Daisy shakes her head at sight, informing Connie, "She doesn't know when to give up. She'll go after any guy. And I do mean any. I've seen her try to interest a couple of guys who were gay. She'd say, 'I can change them.' Believe it or not, she would get one or two. Yeah, she turned them. Turned them straight away from her! They didn't mind being with a woman. I don't know if it was a conquest thing or what? But, they wanted to stay clear away from her in particular after."

Brenda continues her flirtation with the musician.

"You know, you look like pink Chinese sauce on ribs," she says, edging closer to him. "Not that I wouldn't mind nibbling on yours." Her tongue flicks out like a reptile. "The things we could do. We could have an X-rated barbecue."

Philip doesn't know whether to burst out laughing or stay perfectly still, in hopes she'll move on and pursue another victim. He chooses to remain quiet but takes a step back, which aggravates her.

"You're gonna be back-stepping me? You mean you ain't interested in a nice thick...," she drags her hands down her sides for further emphasis. "...chocolate shake?" In a disgusted tone, she raises her voice. "What's the matter? You gay, boy?"

Philip stares at her in shock. He hid it. He thought he hid it well enough nobody could tell.

Brenda suddenly feels a tap on her shoulder.

"No. He's with me," Connie answers stiffly.

Brenda makes no effort to fight for him. She gives up, walking through the crowd.

Philip looks at Connie, jaw agape. He raises his brows, still in shock over Brenda's shameless flirting.

The next song breaks through the room in the form of Earth, Wind & Fire's "September." It only gets louder.

Connie hesitantly says, "You disappeared for a little while. I figured it was about the DJ since you mentioned it when Daisy and I were talking."

"Yeah. I was introduced to a young kid. Well, twenty-three. He wants to be famous. Who doesn't? I had to bring him back to Earth and tell him not everything is about MTV, mansions, and Rolex watches."

"Do you think you got through him?"

"He'll be snorting cocaine with one hundred dollar bills in no time," he shakes his head in disgust. "Can't save them all."

"That's depressing."

"That's life," Philip answers, tight-lipped. "Let's just enjoy what we came here for."

Connie gives him a lost expression.

"The music!" he exclaims.

Connie lets out a laugh, noticing how badly he tries to dance among all those keeping a rhythm. It's almost embarrassingly adorable.

Awkwardly, she says, "Why not?"

"There ya go!" he eggs her on with hands to hips.

As they move around in their style, other patrons watch them. A couple shakes their heads. Philip and Connie continue to dance, forgetting about the different club they inhabit. Soon, they ignore the fact entirely neither can keep a proper rhythm. Connie laughs as they enjoy Diana Ross's massive hit, "Upside Down." Philip moves in such a way that looks awkward, bopping while standing in place. Then he goes for a conventional disco maneuver, which resembles a chicken dance. He mouths the words to the song. Philip puts his hand out for Connie to spin. She nearly bumps into someone else. He laughs, and that makes her laugh all the more. His moves change into playing air guitar by the end of the song. Connie bursts out in joy with some embarrassing snorts.

He indicates semi-quietly, "You're oinking again."

Connie has tears in her eyes from laughing even harder. She wipes them while trying to calm down.

Shaking her head, "Oh God. That was too much."

They hear the beginning of a drum pattern, soft keyboard trailed by rhythmic guitar strumming that makes every couple around them stand close to one another. The two see a woman's head on her man's shoulder or resting against his chest for a slow dance.

Connie's laughter ceases as her eyes canvas the dance floor. She takes a deep breath. Pushing her hair back nervously, she takes a step back from Philip, as though some power blocks her from getting close to him. His eyes stare at her before dropping to the floor with a sense of shame. Connie notices his energy fade, shoulders collapsing in defeat. Glancing around again, she sees all the happy and satisfied couples swaying to Michael Jackson's "Human Nature." It would be a terrible time to show the two were not a couple, as she rescued him yet again from danger. She saved him at the video arcade a few months earlier, and neither was to forget it. For them, not to dance during a slow song would never sit well with this crowd. They were the only white couple there. They hadn't cared who was watching them, no matter how badly they danced together during the last song. Now, it would ultimately prove they were comfortable to be seen together despite their differences nobody else knew and the intimacy it would present.

Something makes Philip attempt to put his hand out, to which Connie agrees timidly. Slowly, she puts her hands on his shoulders, easing into his tender hold on her.

He answers her concern, "Just imagine the person you really want to be with."

Connie leans her head against his chest, swaying to the soft beat.

She didn't need to pretend or imagine.

She had the real thing.

One week later, on a Sunday afternoon, Philip stands at the usual corner of Seventeenth Street in a black jacket. A hunter green AMC AMX hatchback Spirit pulls up. Philip takes a step back.

Connie stretches over the passenger's side. "Well? Come on!"

"In that?" he asks.

She rolls her eyes. "Oh, sorry to disappoint you that it's not a Buick or Mustang."

"I mean, is that thing safe to be on the street?"

Connie closes her eyes while answering, "Yes. Now, will you get in?"

Philip looks east and west to make sure the coast is clear before entering the car.

"I'm going to lay down some ground rules," Connie says, staring straight ahead. "Buckle up."

"OK," Philip answers with understanding.

He situates himself, leaning over to grab hold of the strap.

"No smoking. No touching the radio."

"Oh, now that's a bit of a deal-breaker, you know?" he smiles.

"My car. My choice of music."

"Boy, are you tough!"

"You haven't met my mom yet."

She stuffs a cassette of Human League's *Dare* in the tape player while staring at him confidently. Glancing at traffic, she pulls away.

Philip utters, "This is going to be a long trip."

Along the way, while entering the Saw Mill Parkway, Philip asks, "So, what made you decide that asking me to come along was a good idea? We didn't even have a proper date yet." He grins mischievously.

"It wasn't like I asked you at gunpoint. You said, alright. This isn't the first time you've met anybody's parents before, is it? You know, like past..." Connie hesitates. "...partners?"

"No. I don't make a habit of it. But it is awkward every time. Wondering if I'm good enough for that person."

"Just tell them you're a rock star."

"Never," Philip takes a deep breath. "Connie, it's not about gender. It's about class. I'm not a lawyer or doctor. Hell, I'm not even a fashion designer! I get asked all the time. I broke up with someone because their parents thought they could do better."

"Momma's boy," Connie darts her eyes at the passenger. "I mean him, not you."

"Pretty much."

"You were better off without somebody like that. I'm sure the next time you found someone else, it was good."

Philip looks down, "Yep." He glances out the window at the passing traffic. "It was better, but it didn't last long."

"Well, when I asked you last week after going to FishKat, it seemed like something you were willing to do pretty quickly. I wasn't sure if you would go for it."

"It's a good thing you got me now. I'll be pretty busy with rehearsals for the trip."

"Oh, that's right. England?"

"Right," he nods in agreement.

"Anyway," Philip looks away, uninterested, but then notices something that catches his attention. He picks up a small case on the edge of the backseat. "What's this?"

Connie keeps her eyes on the road, at the same time attempting to look at the rearview mirror. "What's what?"

"I'm not Indiana Jones, and I don't do archaeological digs, but I do believe this is a cassette case. Tell me right now, am I going to find anything by Fabian in here?"

"What are you doing with my case?"

Philip laughs, "Nothing…yet. Is this your Pandora's box? Come on. We're friends, aren't we? You can tell me."

"You know I'm driving."

"So, I'll check. I wonder how many webs I'll find here."

"You're terrible."

He opens it slowly as though something might jump out. Peeking in it, he surveys the titles.

"Let's see what's in here. Thank God you didn't just bring that Human whatever tape."

"Human League, wise guy. No. It's not the only one, either."

"Oh, James Taylor's Greatest Hits, Survivor…, Yeah, I'm surviving this trip! The Police. I'm hoping we don't get pulled over for having these tapes! Culture Club? Um, I don't know exactly what culture this is," he snickers. "Ah! I knew it. Every lady I've ever known has a tape or album of KISS."

"That's my laundry music!" Connie answers defensively.

"Your laundry? Oh, that explains it all!" Philip giggles. He continues to check titles. "ABC? And, DEF…GHI…JKL… I wonder how they get some of these names? Here's another one, Billy Idol. He's the guy who does the Elvis sneer. It's not an easy thing to pull off." He tries it out, with Connie cracking up laughing. "Told ya!" Looking down at more titles, he stops when he comes across one. "Oh, hey, hey! Now, here's something." Philip picks up a cassette.

"What's that?" Connie asks.

"*H2O.*"

"Oh, Hall and Oates. I should have known, considering the obvious." Philip shakes his head.

"Not true."

"It's not?"

"Only one is. Daryl is from Pottstown. That's close to an hour away from Philly. He started with a soul group called The Temptones and got to hang out with Smokey Robinson and The Temptations early on. John was born here in New York, specifically the city, but his family moved to the North Penn Valley. That's where he grew up."

"Gee, you probably know everything about them!"

"I know a good amount of their music dating back to *Abandoned Luncheonette*, which was their second album."

"That was around what year?"

"Seventy-three."

"I was twenty-one then."

Philip taps the cassette tape against his free hand.

"Yeah. I was thinking of maybe taking things more into a Hall and Oates direction the next time." Tilting his head, he says, "If the record company lets me." Glancing at the tape, he adds in, "Let's fire it up."

They listen to the first song, "Maneater."

Immediately, Philip locks into the smooth groove.

Connie shoots a glance without him noticing.

"I just thought of something," Philip remarks. "If I'm not mistaken, Hugh Padgham was the engineer on this record. The guy I told you about when I wiped out at the rink."

"Oh." Connie gives a disinterested nod. Her eyes turn his way again. "I've meant to ask since you brought it up... What do you mean by if the record company lets you? You've brought up the subject of how you have to protect your professional life. Does it tie in with the personal side? I mean, I hope it's OK to ask?"

Philip turns the volume knob lower when he says, "It's a loaded question. Um, OK. When an artist creates a song, they tend to have a specific reason for doing it. An experience that leads them to write that particular piece. When you listen as a fan, you have your idea of liking it. And it goes deeper than, 'I like the beat.' It speaks to you. Ya know? It's all about bridging consciousness with experience. I'm thinking of what Dick Clark has said. 'Music is the soundtrack of your life.' There could be no more accurate words. It's all how you relate to the song. You probably think of it differently than how the writer did. And, I'm not talking about some promotional video you find on MTV." He stops to think. "Here's an example, I have an attachment to Blondie's 'Dreaming,'" and I'm sure it's not the way Debbie Harry or Chris Stein intended. But, that's how I think of the tune. It's something I went through.

"When I've mentioned to you about mixing privacy with business, or how I don't want to lose the professional side? What I mean is, the record label wants particular things. To put it bluntly, they're in the business to make money. We help facilitate what the record label is trying to sell. If I were to come out to the public and say, 'Hey, I'm gay,' then I stand to alienate much of my audience. I'm only catering to a small segment of the population. Those who might have loved one of my songs and related to that tune will think differently. They probably won't be able to attach their experiences of say, a guy dancing with his girlfriend, or their first date. You know, something along those lines. It's all because they would only think of why I possibly wrote it and for whatever reason, whether it's religion or their dislike for what I am. They'll say, 'He wrote this for a guy.' And, won't want to bother with my music anymore. No more buying records or concert tickets. Eventually, other people would be the same way, and my fan base would dry up. It could translate into the record label dropping me, and nobody else taking a chance. My career would be dead."

"I've heard things about Boy George, but I figured he liked makeup and the whole look. Just like the keyboard player in Duran Duran," Connie suggests.

A smile broadens over Philip's face as he says, "Um, yeah. Well..., Just because the blinds are drawn, doesn't mean there's no sunlight."

Connie shoots him a glance.

"So, I should think differently of 'Do You Want To Hurt Me?'"

Philip shrugs his shoulders with indifference.

"Do you ever feel trapped from who you are?" she asks.

"You mean, do I feel trapped on a personal level? There's a difference between wanting and choosing not to. The answer would be no. I do what I want on my own time. That's not going to stop me. I simply choose to cater to a wide population. I love it when people approach me and say they enjoy my music. I wouldn't change that. Doing anything differently would be selfish on my part. Besides, it's not going to make a bit of difference. Relationships don't last forever. Music goes on to infinity." Philip adds in, looking down.

Connie looks at him in the sense of feeling guilty for the asking.

A half an hour later, they pull into the driveway of a Dutch Colonial nestled in a quaint neighborhood. The kind where kids play, ride bikes, and adults hold barbecues in their backyards.

Connie rings the doorbell. A middle-aged woman with dark hair answers the door. Beth Ayers gives a big smile to her daughter and an equally giant hug.

"Hi, honey!"

A taller man with dark hair, flannel, and black-rimmed glasses looms behind her. Roger Ayers waits his turn to give Connie an enormous hug, rocking back and forth with her.

"My baby girl," he smiles.

Philip stays still the whole time. Roger is the first to notice him.

"Ah! So this is Philip," he says happily, putting his hand out for a handshake. "I'm Connie's father, Roger. Nice to meet you."

Philip, genuinely nervous though pleased, answers, "Hi. Good to meet you too." He smiles, noticing Roger's traits have a similarity to his daughter's.

Beth's turn comes up. Philip feels a slight cooler reaction from her. She reaches her hand out, although her eyes probe him carefully. He picks up on the lukewarm body language. She's uncertain of what to make of him. Her eye contact nearly makes him want to step away. Instead, he puts his hand out for a handshake.

"Hi," is all he can muster from the introduction.

Roger says, "It looks like you two got here a little early. Dinner's not quite ready yet."

Connie answers him readily, "There wasn't any traffic on 9A or Saw Mill. Shocking."

"Not even in the city?"

"Nothing out of the ordinary."

Beth breaks in, "I'm going to continue preparing dinner. Connie, can you help set the table?"

Connie looks back at her, aware of the fact she wants Roger to handle Philip on his own. She glances at the musician, signaling to him with her eyes that things will be OK. Disappearing into the kitchen, Beth gives one more all-knowing look to her husband.

Philip keeps his hands in his pockets, slowly making steps to the living room decorated in an old-fashioned way. He blows out a silent breath from being nervous. Quaint, pastel walls, smoky hued La-Z-Boy recliner is adjacent from a large oak cabinet media center with a large TV situated in the middle. His eyes turn to a knick-knack shelf with a framed photo of Connie attired in her high school graduation gown between both parents. As he decides to double-back, it's then another object that grabs his attention. A large, rustic upright piano is against the wall. The instrument immediately entrances Philip. His fingers reach out to lightly touch the arm, as though it were a human in need of comfort. Two potted plants bookend a framed black and white photo of a young couple from above on the top board used as an extra shelf. It's tempting for him to touch a key. Then he would want to feel more keys. That would lead to further playing. In turn, it would result in him blowing his cover, exposing his true nature of being a musician.

Roger breaks his concentration. "You look like you're familiar with it."

Philip hesitates and shrugs, "A little."

He knows it's a full-blown lie. The make and model are incredibly similar to his dad's in the living room, as well. He'd only known that piano by tickling its ivories and learning the anatomy of the instrument from top to bottom, the same way a mechanic knows automobiles. He could pinpoint the problem and fix it, unlike his dad. Nobody else in the house knew how. Music, in general, became his secret friend and future mistress.

Roger grins, "Go ahead and touch at least a key. You know, just to see how it feels."

With the hesitancy of a small child, Philip gingerly presses a key down with his index finger. The hammer sends a rich-toned ring from deep within, reverberating throughout the first floor. It puts a smile on his face.

Inside the kitchen, Connie turns her head at the sound. Beth hears it too.

"Oh, it looks like your father is showing Phil that old piano."

Connie looks up from setting silverware on the table. She smiles to herself, knowing the truth that it's Philip who is showing her father.

Philip shakes his head slowly, surveying various parts of the piano.

Roger grins, "She's nice, ain't she?"

"Yeah," Philip admits. "Really nice. She's got great punch when you hit the key," he answers, making a fist for greater emphasis. "Not like the electric ones now. They're more brittle." Glancing back at Roger, he loosens his fist, realizing his musical knowledge is becoming transparent.

Roger looks at him. "You certainly know more than me."

Philip figures it's no use trying to cover up his passion and asks, "What year?"

"I think it's a nineteen eleven, from what I remember." Roger steps around the other side.

"That was the year they sold the most pianos. They've kind of gone downhill ever since. Not as much demand, I guess?" Philip takes a look back and forth, trying to find something else. "I'll say it's a Marshall & Wendell."

"I wouldn't know," Roger answers, shaking his head.

"I'll check," Philip says while taking off a potted plant. "Would you mind?"

"No. Go right ahead."

Roger watches Philip meticulously place the planters on the floor, and gingerly pick up the framed photo of the young couple. He stops for a moment, noticing the young lady's face. She has an uncanny resemblance to Connie.

"Those are my parents, Jack and Irene. This was my father's piano. He didn't know how to play it too much, though. He got it when I was a kid. Thought it would be a great investment at the time. He met my mom at a dance. You know, so it was music-oriented, and they both liked it a lot."

Philip picks up the top board, and releases the front, revealing all of its innards. Clear as day, the mark reads MARSHALL & WENDELL, ALBANY NY.

"Looks clean. Restored?"

"Yeah. I believe when my dad bought it, some parts had been restored. Like I said, he didn't know how to play much."

Philip puts everything back as it was. In finishing placement, he sits the frame back on the top board.

Roger looks at it with fondness.

"When my dad passed away seven years ago, Mom didn't want it around anymore. I didn't want to get rid of it simply. As you can tell, it's a fine instrument. My older brother didn't want it either, but he helped me move it here to this house. We had to shuffle around a few things to make room. It was worth it, though." He taps on the arm, the same as Philip had. "As you can see, she's more of a secondary shelf. Probably seen more potted plants than action." Solemnly, he says, "I wish I could do more with her, but I'm just not musically gifted." He takes off his glasses to wipe his eyes. "It's a part of my father I can't give up." Placing the glasses back on, he eyes the floor.

Philip nods back in understanding the attachment to family.

Connie pops her head out of the doorway.

"Dinner's ready."

Later on, once everybody has had their fill, Beth gets up.

"Anybody up for dessert?"

The responses range from nodding heads to hands waving for a pass.

"You know these brownies aren't going to sprout legs and walk away on their own. They're best when warm. Phil, are you sure you don't want to take any home?"

Philip reaches for his glass of Chardonnay, taking a sip.

"No, thank you. The pot roast was great, though, and the potatoes, and the wax beans."

Roger answers quickly, "Phil, you don't have to suck up to her."

Connie snickers.

He continues, "You can be honest about those wax beans."

Beth returns to the table, placing two brownies in front of herself.

"So, Philip, where are you from?"

Philip thinks for a moment before answering, "I'm from the east coast."

"And what do you do? Job-wise?"

"Uh, public relations."

Beth turns to her daughter, "Would that be for San-San, Connie? Or for your sector?"

Connie eyes Philip, "That would be a different location altogether. Actually, we met on the street corner."

Philip says, "True."

"PR for anybody special?" Beth asks.

Connie stifles a laugh while toying with her napkin.

"Not really. The usual. Really, there's a lot," Philip shrugs. "Actually, they prefer to stay private."

Beth takes a bite of brownie.

She then asks, "What was your last name again?"

"Reinhardt."

"Hmm. Interesting." Quietly she talks loud enough for everybody to hear. "Connie Lee Reinhardt."

Connie rolls her eyes, flaring her nostrils at the same time. She gets up out of frustration and grabs a brownie from the counter, bringing it back with her to the table.

Beth notices something she finds peculiar that her daughter wears.

"You still have that Mickey Mouse watch? Honey, how do you ever expect to be taken seriously with a kid's item? I know you're a Disney fan but in public? You're still wearing it?"

"Mom."

"Maybe when you have children, you can pass it down to them."

"Mom, I've told you already numerous times. I don't want kids."

"You say that now, but you might change your mind with the right man. Connie, you're thirty-two. I know you're feeling the biological clock ticking and figure there's no time."

"Mom," Connie says a little more sternly.

"I was reading an article in *Woman's World*, and they said it's not too late."

"Mom. Not right now," Connie gives her mother a look she'll understand.

Beth asks, "So, Phil, what team do you like? I know Connie was into basketball at one time. Who was the guy that brought you to a Knicks game? Danny?"

"Denny," Connie corrects her.

"I remember you had a great time," Beth says gleefully. "He taught you about different positions and points. You were studying it for at least a month."

"Mom, that was a long time ago."

Beth turns her attention back to Philip while Connie takes a bite.

"Are you into basketball at all, Phil?"

"No."

"Interesting," Beth answers, staring down at her partially eaten brownie. "Baseball? I'm sure you're one of those guys who has to have it either way. Yankees or Mets?"

Philip takes another swig of Chardonnay before answering, "Nope."

"Surely, you're a Giants fan. It is football season now. Roger can't get enough of it. Every Sunday." she giggles.

"Nope."

"Hockey?"

"No."

"Soccer?"

"No."

Beth stares at him with intent to intimidate.

"Golf?"

"No," he answers back, leaning forward with a challenging counter stare at her prying eyes. "But I can tell you're into fishing," he smiles back.

Roger notices Beth and Philip's frosty exchange, changing the subject.

"Oh, I know what I was thinking of when remembering about the piano. I went to visit Mom at the care facility. I don't like seeing her there, but..., Anyway, when I went, I couldn't help but notice the variety of music she has. I can't believe the great taste my baby girl has. You certainly learned! Marvin Gaye, Stevie Wonder, Smokey Robinson, Sam Cooke, Otis Redding..."

Connie slowly turns to Philip. Her nostrils flare. She kicks him under the table, then puts on a sweet smile for her father.

Roger continues, "Yeah. Some great soulful stuff. Of course, Tony Bennett. I thought you were mostly into the new kind of music. What do they call it? Something related to beaches or ripples? Not new ripple?"

Philip leans down, rubbing his sore shin from being kicked, "New Wave?" he manages.

"OK. That's what it is. Yeah."

"Oh. A lot of things might surprise you, Dad," Connie answers with certainty.

As the sun goes down, Connie and Philip get ready to leave. Beth rushes over to the door.

She gives her a big hug, whispering, "I just want you to be happy. I don't want to see you get hurt."

"I'm fine, Mom," Connie says back with equal strength in her hug.

Philip steps towards the door.

Roger shakes his hand and says, "It was great to meet you, Phil."

"Same here. It was my pleasure."

"Hope to see you again soon," Roger answers in a way that pleases Philip.

"I'd like to."

Connie goes over and hugs her father tightly.

"Take care, baby girl," he breathes into her hair.

Beth gives both, a lukewarm, though a sheepish expression of gratitude towards the guest.

"It was nice to meet you, Phil," she puts her hand out for a handshake or a truce.

Philip accepts, knowing she only wants to look out for her child.

They exchange smiles.

Beth then remembers something. She races into the kitchen for a moment, returning with a large tray of brownies covered in plastic wrap.

"I want you to have these," she presses them to Connie.

Philip arches a brow, "All of them?"

"Yes."

Connie tiredly answers, "Mom, you don't have to."

"I know. I want to."

"Thanks, Mom. I love you," Connie looks over at her father, "And of course, you too, Dad." She opens the door. "Bye."

Roger and Beth wave. They wait until the two make it back to the car and pull out of the driveway.

Roger thinks while turning to face the living room. "I think I should get some music books. Maybe even to check out the *Yellow Pages* for an instructor."

Beth crosses her arms, "Honey? What did you think of Phil?"

Roger exhales deeply, "Report card time? I liked him. He struck me as mature, respectful, nice, polite. Not like one or two of the other guys. You mentioned Denny. I did not like him. He had that pretense about him like he was God's gift to women. Phil struck me as an average, old-fashioned guy with good values. His parents obviously raised him right."

"You didn't notice anything off about him?"

"Off? No. Nothing out of the ordinary," Roger shrugs.

"You didn't notice that not once did he and Connie make physical contact? Hand over a shoulder at the dinner table? No kiss or hand-holding at any time?"

"Beth, he was probably nervous. Let's not kid ourselves. You grill all of Connie's boyfriends. You can be harsh."

Rather than being insulted, Beth is lost in her suspiciousness.

"He was quite vague with some subjects. Where he's from? Public Relations? No sports?"

"He's probably a busy guy," Roger offers up. "You know, having to deal with clients who have different needs and keeping them in line."

"I think he's lying about what he does as a job."

"Well, he certainly knows music."

"What makes you say that?"

"He knew his way around my father's piano. Not to mention, the choice of tapes for my mom at the facility changed to something far better a couple of days ago. You don't think Connie has that kind of capacity when it comes to music? I certainly don't."

"I don't think we have to worry about this one. Phil's gay."

"I thought he was from Pennsylvania?" Roger answers puzzled.

On the road, Connie remains silent, only keeping her eyes on what she needs to. She shakes her head.

Philip turns his attention to the backseat.

"You sure you're going to eat all of the brownies," he giggles.

"I can't believe you did that. Did you really? I should throw those brownies at you!"

"Did I what? And why would you want to waste your mom's perfectly delicious brownies?"

"Did you have the nurse throw away the tapes I got for Gramma Irene? My dad didn't say anything about Pat Boone or Tom Jones. Only Tony Bennett.

I spent money on those tapes. You know, just because you're some big rock star, you think that money is no object? You can just buy whatever you want, while some poor schlub like myself works hard to earn a paycheck. I'm pissed off."

"That's obvious," Philip answers calmly.

"Is someone's record collection a deal-breaker for you?" she huffily asks.

"I'll let some things pass. Others? Not so much," is his nonchalant response.

"Where would I fit in?"

"Your collection would be a roadside pickup."

"Oh, thanks!" Connie snaps back sarcastically.

Philip looks at her. "Notice I said your collection, not you."

"You know what you are? Roadside pickup!"

"What?" Philip turns to her, confused.

"You heard me," she says, pulling over angrily.

"Wha—, Come on, Connie. You're not serious?"

"You can take the brownies with you."

Philip glances outside, noticing it's virtually pitch-black. He turns back to face Connie when he hears her stifling laughter against the steering wheel.

"Throwing brownies? she wipes her eyes. "I actually said that? Over my hideous taste in music," she laughs harder.

Philip looks at her in concern, "Uh, maybe I should get out?"

"Absolutely hideous music!" She sits back in the seat. "The only reason I ever got the Pat Boone and Tom Jones tapes was because I thought that's what older people liked! I don't play stuff like that at home! Never! God! All this time. I hope I wasn't making my gramma sick!"

Philip opens his eyes wide at her cracking up.

"Did your mom put something in the brownies?"

"No. She associates that kind of behavior with dirty hippies."

He continues her line, "And rock and rollers."

Connie glances back at him more seriously.

"I never said that," she turns the wheel onto the main road.

Philip remains quietly deep in thought. The humor. The brownies. Even the music is far from his mind.

"What did your mom mean by what she said? Connie Lee Reinhardt?"

"I did not put her up to that. She does it to me all the time. Connie Lee Brooks. Connie Lee Alvarez. Connie Lee Timmins. Connie Lee Bradford. It goes on and on. She does it to embarrass me. She thinks that women are past their prime by the time they reach thirty. You heard her about the watch. I shouldn't be wearing it because, how in the world can I be taken seriously? A watch." She shakes her head, disgustedly. "I've told her to get with the times. 'It's nineteen eighty-four, Ma. Not nineteen fifty-four.' Whatever goes on, I have to reassure her that I'll find a good man who can help weed her garden or fix a leaky toilet. Besides, I know why she went after my watch. She knows I don't have much for a chest. She can't say, I wear low-cut things for action." Her eyes briefly turn to Philip. "Anyway, don't worry. It's her way of looking out for me when she can't play matchmaker. You know the truth. I know the truth. Nothing like that can happen. I wouldn't even dream it."

Philip's eyes meet his scuffed brogues in hidden disappointment. In his heart, he feels inadequate for either sex. Not enough for a man. Not enough for a woman. A disappointment for all of his desires.

The piano conversation with Roger gave him a great feeling of normalcy, which he craved. It was warm and natural, sort of like what he could imagine of having a father-in-law. Many family encounters by past partners had felt awkward. Some would understand but, others stepped on eggshells, leaving bad feelings in their wake.

It was different with Roger Ayers, though. He was not aware that a man of an alternative lifestyle sat next to his daughter at the dining room table. But, Philip was tempted to come out as a musician. He nearly did, and it started to feel good to reveal some actual part of himself. He might even be able to soften Connie's mom, Beth. There was nothing evil about the intentions of her daughter to find true happiness. She was only looking out for her only child's best interests. It was the same old paradigm he went through with his mom, who was waiting for the perfect girl for her younger son.

Connie continues, "I'm sure somewhere down the road, my folks will get the son-in-law of their dreams, or maybe never. You know, it's my decision. But then, as you've said before, I need to be more positive and stop putting myself down."

Philip still studies either his shoes or the floor, under lights that flash like switchblades in the dark.

Lost in thought, he answers, "Yeah."

"So, we'll take the same way back we came?"

Philip comes out of the spell, and says, "I'll take the train."

"You will? I mean, it's OK. None of my business where you go. I could drop you off wherever you need...if you'd want?"

"Naw. I'll be fine."

Several minutes later, they arrive at the train station.

Philip exits the car.

"Hey!" Connie calls out. She reaches in the backseat, handing over the large plate of brownies. "Take these. All of them." Her eyes look up in all sincerity. "I'm sorry about earlier. You didn't do anything wrong. You have better taste. You're a pro, and I'm not."

He gives her a small, gracious smile in return.

"Thanks."

Walking off with the large plate of brownies in tow, Philip shines brightly under the lights.

Connie smiles warmly at sight.

A rock star.

A plate of her mom's best brownies.

A memory for her to remember.

CHAPTER 9

Nearly a week later, Philip, Claire, Mitch, Perry, and Tim convene at Nom Wah Tea Parlor. At the diner-styled restaurant, a waiter begins taking away the empty plates.

Tim says, "What are we gonna do about this upcoming tour, or whatever you want to call it?"

"I can't call it a tour, per se," Philip corrects Tim. "More like promotion, and a gig," he answers while toying with a fortune cookie.

Claire asks, "We're going to play the famed Marquee Club? How did you manage to finagle that?"

"The label," Philip raises a brow.

"Of course!"

Tim adds in, "Let's hope it's not like that Sacramento show we had last month."

"It was some scout who saw our gig in Seattle. They got a hold of the record company, and we've got it."

Mitch says while picking up a fortune cookie, "Not with the five of us."

Philip looks at him, puzzled, "Five? There's normally six of us. Who's not going?" He glances around the table.

"Ross," Mitch answers as though Philip should know already. He sees the lost look on the leader's face. "You didn't know?"

Claire pipes in, "He only lives closest to you. We figured you already knew. Ross can't make it because his wife went into early labor."

Philip looks out into the distance, "I forgot about that."

Perry says, "We'll chip in and get some baby stuff."

Mitch sarcastically intones to Claire, "There is one good thing about Ross not coming along. Now you can play 'Planet Claire' to your heart's content."

"What, he never liked it?"

Mitch snickers, "Didn't you ever see him cringe when you played it? There's an advantage from the drum stool. Oh yeah. He's whimpered and whined about 'Playin any fucking B-52's song.'"

Claire's jaw drops, "He never told me anything."

"Yeah. Ross has been playing with that band that he does at Bitter End or Bottom Line. The one where they use 'Private Idaho' like every other band plays 'Mustang Sally.' Mitch puts his hands out. "You never noticed when he'd turn to you? What did you think he was doing? A gas bubble?"

Philip giggles slightly, shaking his head.

"I never noticed either."

"Of course, you didn't. That's when you let her take over." Mitch picks up the fortune cookie. "Are we gonna check to see if these things are any good?"

Perry asks, "Who's going first?"

Tim states, "You started, so, go ahead."

Perry cracks open the cookie. "Let's see. 'You will be hungry again in one hour.' That's it?" he shakes his head in disgust. "Tim, you go next."

Tim crushes the cookie open, grabbing for the little slip of paper.

"He who expects no gratitude shall never be disappointed."

"That's a pretty good one, Tim," Claire advises.

Mitch says, "Alright, I'll do the honors next and see what this bad boy says." He unravels the slip, reading it aloud, "The fortune you seek is in another cookie."

The whole table erupts into laughter as Mitch drops his head.

Claire announces, "OK. Now that Mitch has gotten the bad luck cookie, I'll tell you mine." She situates herself straighter, cracking the cookie in half. "I've got, 'Remember the birthday but never the age.' Ooh. Now there's one I can live with." Smiling, she turns to Philip. "It's your turn."

Philip says with hesitation, "I've never believed these things. More of a novelty item. You know, these things aren't even Chinese?"

Perry interrupts him, "You're stalling, Boss."

Philip cracks open the cookie reluctantly.

"OK. OK."

Mitch taps out a drum roll on the table in anticipation.

Philip begins reading the slip of paper, "A beau..." he goes silent, shakes his head. "Oh God, that's not going to happen. 'A beautiful, smart, and loving person will be coming into your life.'"

Claire offers up, "Oh, that's sweet."

"See? I told you I didn't believe in these things," Philip answers, rolling the slip of paper between his fingers into a ball. Dismissively, he tosses the tiny paper ball over his shoulder. "Don't need it," he mumbles under his breath.

Claire's jaw drops.

"Oh my God! Do you know what you just did?"

"What?"

"Your garbage landed on that man's plate!"

Philip turns around to take a look briefly.

Claire admonishes, "You are going to get it."

"W...," Philip starts.

Mitch, Tim, and Perry shake their heads.

Perry says, "Nope."

Philip glances back at Claire.

"Don't even look at me that way. You threw it," she answers.

Philip gets up and walks over to the next table consisting of an Asian family. The young girl pulls back her long black hair at the sight of the tall, bronze-haired stranger.

"Excuse me, but I'm just checking to see what you think of the food here. Everything's alright?" Philip asks, noticing the balled up piece of regret sitting on the man's plate of pan-fried noodles. He nearly goes white when the man digs his chopsticks into the noodles, flipping them around, not aware of the non-edible. "So, you new to the city?"

The woman answers in broken English. "We are from Sapporo, Japan. We are here to experience America and food. So far, so good!"

Claire looks at Philip in disgust.

"He's never going to get this done." She digs in her purse, shuffling some things around quickly.

Immediately, she gets up, walking over to the other side of the same table across from the band. The young girl glances over at the brunette, who searches for something on the floor.

Claire calls over the drummer, "Mitch, help me find the pill."

Mitch gives her a confused expression. "Pill?"

"Yes, Mitch." She nods in a jerky motion.

"Oh! That pill! Yeah. OK," he answers, quickly making his way over to her.

Claire gestures to Philip with a slight nod of the head to make his move.

Mitch looks around on the floor, as do the family, who take the opportunity to help.

The woman asks, "What color?"

"It's a little light green pill."

The man puts his chopsticks down, lowering his head past the table. Philip grabs the balled up piece of paper and makes his way back to his bandmates.

Claire digs in her purse again.

"Oh, wait! I think..." she shuffles her hand inside. "I think I've got it. It never fell out! I thought I dropped it, but it must have bounced into my purse."

She and the family laugh at the predicament.

"Thank you so much for your help. I hope I didn't bother you too much. Clumsy me! Please enjoy the rest of your time in Manhattan and the food."

The young girl glances up to see the cute bronze-haired guy has returned to his table.

Just as Mitch and Claire make their way back, the man leans over to his wife and daughter.

"Know who that is?"

The wife shakes her head, "No."

"That Rod Stewart! Yah!"

Mitch and Claire snicker, returning to their table. They can't entirely hide the amusement of the moment, looking at each other before laughing again.

Philip raises a brow in the peculiarity of their humor. He then flattens out the piece of paper, studying the words, lost in thought.

Mitch asks Claire, "So, what was the magic pill?"

Claire picks it out of her purse. Proudly she announces, "Tic Tac." She pops it in her mouth with a smile.

Tim asks, "What are we going to do? We've got one open spot for England? Saxophone? Another guitar player?

A distracted Philip stares out, toying with the piece of paper between his fingers, deep in thought.

***

Later, the same night, Connie holds a wrapped Nestle Crunch bar between her teeth, while dropping the work badge into her purse. She starts to walk to the corner and hails for a taxi. One pulls up. Before she can get in, the back door is held open for her. She looks at the driver, realizing he's still sitting there.

Confused, Connie turns to see Philip has his hand on the door.

"We need to talk," he tells her.

She places the candy bar in her purse and says, "It's only Monday. I thought you said you would be busy in rehearsals all this week?"

"How would you feel about going to England?"

Connie puts her hand on the door.

She angles to the driver, "Go ahead." Closing the door, she gives a lost glance to Philip. The taxi speeds away.

"Don't you take off on Friday?"

"Yeah," he bites his bottom lip. "One of the band members can't make it. I can't simply call the union and have somebody fly out with us on such short notice. It would take some time to break them in. So, there's five of us already, and I think we'll do fine with what we have. But, yeah, there's enough room for one more. The record company doesn't know. They set it up a few months ahead of time. As long as they get their money, they don't care who I bring."

Connie eyes the sidewalk.

"Gee, that is short notice." She looks back to see the disappointment, but understanding in his eyes. "It's Monday, and you go on Friday. Four days in between. Shaking her head, she says, "I don't know if my boss would ever go for something like that."

"If you choose to… Jeez, now I sound like *Mission Impossible*." He changes his tone to the narration. "Your mission, should you choose to accept it…" Giggling from his spontaneity, it makes her join in. He gets more serious. "If you want to, just be out here at seven. We don't take off until about ten or eleven, but Friday traffic can be brutal. 'K?"

He doesn't even wait for Connie to answer, leaving her frozen where she stands. When she's able to get her wits back, she looks around near the building.

Philip has disappeared like a dream.

Connie rushes back to the main door of San-San, running to the double set of elevators when she comes across the maintenance guy, Richard.

"Forget somethin', Ms. Ayers?"

She hops in the elevator and says, "Yeah. I hope I'm not too late!"

The doors close behind her.

Reaching her destination, Connie rushes down the hall. Luckily, the door to her sector is unlocked. She briskly walks by the bank of computer desks. Once she gets to the door of her boss's office, she knocks. The door unlocks.

Mr. Edwards is already seated at his desk and says, "Connie," in a surprised tone.

Connie drops her hands on his desk to steady herself while trying to catch a breath. He can tell something urgent is on her mind, to come back to the office and speak with him.

"I need some time off," she exhales.

"OK," he slowly tries to understand. "And what are you looking for, because if it's the holiday season, I can't promise you anything. The workload is going to be enormous. We'll probably have to hire seasonal help with the way the electronics market is booming."

"Friday."

"Friday?" he arches a brow. "This Friday?"

"Yes."

"That's a bit short notice."

"I know it is, but I'd truly appreciate it, Mr. Edwards. It would mean so much to me. Besides, I barely ever use my vacation time."

Mr. Edwards takes a deep breath, "And how much time off are you looking for?"

"One week. The twenty-eighth to October fifth."

"Friday to Friday?" he peeks over the rims of his glasses.

"Yes, sir. That would be correct."

He nods back, noticing her anticipation.

"Sign the slip." Scratching the back of his head, he says, "I'll get back to you tomorrow or Wednesday at the latest."

She immediately signs the vacation slip in front of him. Sliding it over, she clasps her hands together in a gesture of grateful prayer, backing away.

"Thank you so much, sir."

Mr. Edwards nods, "You are welcome, young lady. Now, I have to get back to this," he points down to a packet of papers.

Connie puts her hand up in a motion that he doesn't have to say anymore. She leaves the office.

Mr. Edwards walks over to the door, shutting it, then returning to his desk where he eyes the slip. Jotting something down, he takes off his glasses, looking ahead at the door. He shakes his head and returns to his work.

The next day at the office, everybody tends to their usual duties. Keyboards softly sound off in unison. Words get scanned with eyes. Breaking the silence, Ted starts up.

"Hey, has anybody else been watching this new show, *Miami Vice*? It's awesome! It's got this guy, Don Johnson. He's like, one of those TV actors that makes the rounds. You've seen his face but couldn't remember his name. He's one of the stars. The other guy is this cool black dude. I don't know his real name, it's like three names, but on the show he's Tubbs. So, they're Crockett and Tubbs. The first episode was recently on."

Maria turns in her chair, "*Miami Vice*? The guy with the three names is hot! That's Philip Michael Thomas. I'm gonna tune in for every episode. As long as he's on? I'm there!"

Ted continues, "Yeah. So, the beginning has this great scene where Tubbs, er, Thomas is sitting in the car, doing surveillance. These gang rat kids start harassing him, and Tubbs says, 'Beat it punks.' The kids push their luck, and one pulls out a switchblade. Tubbs pulls out a double barrel, and he's like, 'Can it wait? I'm a little busy right now.' Such a great scene. Listen, I'm tellin' you this show is a real winner."

Denise says, "I'm gonna stick with *Scarecrow & Mrs. King*, and *Cagney & Lacey*."

Ted turns to Connie.

"How about you, Connie?"

She continues to type, attempting to ignore Ted's questioning.

"Connie?" he asks again.

"What?" she answers, looking up.

"What shows are you looking forward to seeing this season?"

Connie says, "I don't know. I don't watch too much TV."

Ted leans in, "Ah, I know. You're glued to MTV all the time. It's like you have this love affair with music."

Connie stops typing and rolls her eyes.

He continues, "That's right! You use KISS as your laundry music!"

Connie shoots Maria a glare.

"Bigmouth. That was supposed to be confidential."

Maria innocently replies, "Sorry! I didn't know it was a secret!"

Gary adds in, "Just give me *Dynasty*. Great catfights! Raow!"

Denise responds, "You know what Gary? It just occurred to me that you're a pig. Catfights. You probably go see mud wrestling too!"

"I'm going to have to check the listings. Thanks, Denise."

Denise shakes her head in disgust.

Gary gets up and walks over to the Xerox machine. He starts whistling a tune. While placing a page on the scanner, the whistling turns into him entirely singing the lyrics to The Eurythmics' "Sweet Dreams (Are Made Of This)." He notices nobody is paying attention except for the new girl, Gina, who finds everybody's antics amusing. It's enough to persuade Gary to take things further. He sings more dramatically.

The Xerox machine makes a clicking noise. A hiccup of a flash explodes under the scanner lid. A deathly silence makes Gary aware something is wrong. His pseudo-lounge act finishes as quickly as it started.

"What the hell? No! No! Come on! I need copies. You can't do this to me!" he begins yelling at the machine. "You betrayed me!" He coughs, holding his throat, Gary sputters, stepping backward, shaking. In a choked manner, he utters, "Bastard," before dropping to the floor.

Another worker from in back yells out, "No copier?" He too chokes and croaks, landing his head on the desk. His neighboring co-worker feels the ripples of the Xerox copier's hold on herself. Her head drops the opposite way. Several more workers sputter, cough, make choking noises, and splat their faces onto desks.

Denise yells out, "No!" just before she goes silent, sliding down in her chair with eyes wide open.

Bryan and Patti follow her lead.

Ted sputters back, grabbing his throat, "No Xerox? How am—" He makes a choking noise while his head drops to the desk. His tongue rolls out.

One of the few left, Connie chokes back, unable to speak. She reaches out her hand and manages, "Help us." Slowly, her head slides on the desk until it stops moving.

Maria's head nearly hits the floor as her body goes limp in the seat.

Gina is the last to go, but can't control her giggling while keeping her head against the desk.

Mr. Edwards steps out of his office, realizing it's too quiet throughout the workspace. He walks in to see all of his workers have dramatically croaked. Tongues out, eyes stiffly wide, limp bodies in chairs, heads against desks.

Shaking his head, he dismissively murmurs, "Copier's down again, I see." Stepping around to get a better look, he nearly trips.

"Talbot, go back to your chair and die respectfully like your colleagues."

Gary gets up and rushes over to his chair.

Mr. Edwards walks back to the front and talks aloud.

"I've got a room full of adult kindergartners," he grumbles. Looking over at Connie, who's head is still down, he is unaffected by her dramatization. "Ayers, in my office."

Connie lifts her head, realizing the boss means business. She gets up and follows him back to his office.

Maria holds her head, slowly sitting in a normal position.

"Ow! Does anybody have any aspirin?"

Denise removes her head from the desk. She looks over at Ted with a gross expression.

"Ted, were you drooling?"

In Mr. Edwards' office, he closes the door and goes to sit at his desk.

"Ayers," He taps the vacation slip on the wooden table. "You're one of my best employees, if not the best. Hell, you do overtime when others run away from it. I don't ask anybody about their business. Everybody has bills to pay."

"I like my job, sir."

"I know you do. I've noticed a difference in you over the past several months — something I've never seen before. You asked me earlier to cut you some slack for overtime on Thursdays and Fridays specifically. I heard about your little disappearing act before lunchtime last month. And, your guest spot for *Fame* out in front on top of a taxi."

Connie grows uncomfortable under the line of questioning.

"You, Connie? Doing all these things?" Edwards shakes his head in disbelief. "I can see this kind of behavior coming from Delgado or even Anderson, but you?" He can tell she's deeply embarrassed by her previous behavior. "It can give me time to break in the new gal, Gina Caffrey."

Connie looks up at him in surprise.

"Ayers, do me one favor. Find yourself a prince, not a frog, like my half-brother. God only knows why I'm related to him. I adore Arlene. I can't believe he would screw up like this. I'm sure you can do better."

He passes the slip on to her.

At night, Connie exits the doors of San-San Industries. Running out to the corner of the sidewalk, she looks back and forth with deep breaths. She hails a cab, which instantly pulls up.

***

Connie walks through the door of Scribbles, where she encounters a few people hanging around on a Tuesday night. She makes her way past a group of twenty-somethings with drinks in their hands. The bartender eyes the determined woman walk by the bar as Flock of Seagulls' "Space Age Love Song" blasts through the PA system.

Finch turns around to face Connie.

"You're Pete Fincher. Finch," she says to him.

"Yeah. Do I...," he cocks his head in remembrance. "You're the phone lady."

"You're Phil's friend. I need you to do me a favor."

Finch feels slightly uncomfortable, as he tries to look busy. He begins to walk, but Connie follows him.

"Look, it's nothing personal. I know Philip's your buddy from way back. I just need you to do this for me," she repeats. "Please take this," Connie pleads with a piece of paper between her fingers. "You're the only way I know how to get this to him."

The music turns to the electronic beat of Yazoo's "Situation."

Finch reluctantly takes the item and asks, "You don't know how to contact him? He never gave you a phone number? An address?"

Connie glances down in embarrassment while uttering, "No. I figured you knew him better."

"I can't get him on the phone myself. He's never home lately."

Finch sees the desperation on Connie's face.

"He doesn't normally come around here. I know he frequents other clubs. We can hope for the best."

"He did call here before. Just, can you please give it to him? In case?" Connie pleads.

Finch takes a deep breath and nods back, "OK."

"Thanks!" Connie answers with a beaming smile. Quickly, she makes her way out the door.

***

Philip clutches his long dark coat, crossing under the dilapidated former West Side Elevated Highway. A piece of roadway badly destroyed by years of deterioration. The street itself is one of isolation and desolation. Like a scene out of a film about dystopian America, this section of Manhattan offers no promises. On the western fringes of the city, gay men populate the Chelsea Piers at any given time. Whether cruising, or in search of finding that one diamond in the rough, a soulmate to love forever. Various piers provide the perfect location for trysts. Nobody who enters the buildings cares about the state of disrepair. Bullet-hole-riddled windows, with spider web cracks filling the empty spaces, resemble streaks of lightning in an open sky. Busted Venetian blinds, twisted and tangled, give no privacy, however, it is an oasis of pleasure for a man seeking company. Oddly, and miraculously, there is some dim light, filtering through what's left of the blur of windows.

Philip finds himself wondering about that life. That part of town. He had been used to the cleanliness of dance clubs and singles bars, although nothing like this. Not the dirt and grime. Not the possibility of having a one-nighter on the hardness of cold cement, or using wood-splattered crates to create some sense of comfort. It's too bleak for him. Waking up to the sight of New Jersey come sun-up, doesn't hold any romanticism. The unknown. The danger of possibly being found by an angry heterosexual man, who in a fit of rage, destroys the life of another human being, leaving behind nothing but destruction, and an outlined crime scene.

He steps over to see the seedier side of life. The only sound present comes from his shoes clacking against asphalt, echoing in the darkness. A car pulls up, letting out a long-legged woman in a tight mini skirt. Her high heels make a louder clap against the street than his. It's then, Philip realizes, that she is a he, returning home to the piers. A safe haven used by young transsexuals and the newly initiated, seeking refuge after coming out only to being thrown out by their families.

Philip watches as he feels a strange thin lump under his heel. He lifts his foot to reveal the pinkish tail of a deceased rat. The rest is badly mashed into the street. Immediately, he hops back, wiping the rodent remnants from his heel. Shaking his head, he walks over to another building. Pulling out a cigarette from his pocket, he puts it in his mouth. Before he can fish out his lighter, the end of his cigarette has magically been lit. A young, good-looking blond man in a satin jacket and tight pants looks back at Philip, eying him with a slight smile. In turn, Philip stares but gives no indication he wants to follow.

In time, the musician has seen several young men of various ethnicities converge at the beckoning call of the piers.

Two men off to the side make it publicly known of their desires for one another, barely able to disappear into the darkness of lust.

Philip thinks long and hard about what he's seeing. It neither interests or disgusts him. He has no feelings for what is supposed to be his community. Tossing down the remains of his cigarette, he feels the black rubber bracelet next to his watch. It's a reminder of his friendship with a woman he met earlier in the year. It's an odd yet comforting expression for a deeply closeted gay man.

Confusion gnaws his soul as he realizes something like the piers are supposed to be the comfort, not some trendy little piece of cheap jewelry given by a woman. He thinks of what Al Shockley had teased him about, and his state of concealing his true identity. The asphalt is full of cracks from disrepair, and the dilapidated buildings should have seen a bulldozer years ago. The rat had no intention of being crushed to death during the day. The men continuously seek love among the ruins in a hidden part of town, oblivious to the dangers of the rapid plague killing them by the dozen. The sounds, smells, and even the eerie breeze carry a sense of danger and death to Philip.

He walks away from it all, seeking to find a different location that challenges everything he is.

Among the darkest shadows, Philip emerges into a part of town that's full of rejection. Only the hardcore patrons are allowed here, hidden among the warehouses of the West Village's Meatpacking District. 835 Washington Street. The gritty, sleazy, darkness would make any unknowing individual hightail it and run in the opposite direction. Philip knew it only by name and reputation. This part of Manhattan remains closed off to people like him. The deeply closeted would be ostracized and made to feel they did not belong.

The Mineshaft had been the epitome of gay men's culture. By far, the most well-known and infamous of all clubs. A nondescript building with a black front, no name, other than the address and block lettering painted in white, reading "private club." The club had become the central location in fulfilling every men's sexual desire behind closed doors. It was the male Disney World of the adult set where even kinky dreams came true. A sinister doorman protected it.

Overwhelmed with curiosity, Philip walks up to the door. The doorman eyes him sharply, noticing the musician's physical appearance. Although he wears a long dark coat, many traits would never gain him admittance. Far more Barneys or Bloomingdale's, Philip would be deemed too pretty for such a place. Collar length bronze waves and curls made to perfection hidden in the coat. His face is too well-shaven and groomed to pass within the sea of men in Castro-clone form consisting of mustaches and short-cropped hair. Physically, he was too soft for the hard, beefy bodies tucked into leather and western wear.

The doorman, also in clone form, takes a step forward, letting the musician know his presence is not welcome. Philip takes the hint and steps back to read the notice on the door stating approvals and rejections of the dress code.

MINESHAFT Dress Code

THE DRESS CODE as adopted by the membership on the
first of October 1976 will apply during 1978 & 1979.

APPROVED ARE CYCLE & WESTERN GEAR. LEVIS. T-SHIRTS.
UNIFORMS. JOCK STRAPS. PLAID & PLAIN SHIRTS. CUTOFFS.
CLUB PATCHES. OVERLAYS & SWEAT.

NO Cologne or Perfume or DESIGNER sweaters

NO Suits, Ties, Dress Pants or Jackets
NO RUGBY STYLED shirts or DISCO DRAG
NO COATS in the playground
NO LACOSTA ALLIGATOR SHIRTS

Philip edges away, looks at the doorman, then is just about to cross the street when the door flies open. Two men with mustaches and western wear squeeze out of the entrance. One of them aggressively leans in for a kiss with the other man against the wall. The slightly younger one puts his hand to the other's chest. He coyly responds to the advance.

"Save your energy for the next dance, cowboy."

Both men begin laughing. The aggressive one takes his denim jacket and slings it over his shoulder. He spots Philip in the darkness. Tossing his head to the side, the man puckers his lips and gives a wink, before he and his partner walk into the night arm in arm, laughing and chatting among themselves.

A happy couple. Although in the confines of a dark and sleazy setting, they have each other.

Philip watches them as they quickly get swallowed up into the Manhattan night. Eyeing the sidewalk, he shakes his head and moves along slowly.

The musician makes his way through Fourteenth Street. A woman runs by in a long coat with half spikey hair. She then hurriedly goes to meet up with a man in a letter jacket.

She grabs onto the man with insistence.

"Where were you? I was looking all over and couldn't find you! Don't scare me like that, OK?"

She throws her arms over his shoulders, getting lost in his embrace and finally a lengthy kiss. It's a sweet scene that unfolds — a happy ending without fear and frustration.

Another happy couple.

Even among the more seedy offerings of triple-X theaters with glowing promises in the dark, there remained posters of couples together. A harsh reminder for the lonely. Sex shops nearby offer up every ounce of adult toys and gear for the most eager and kinkiest of couples. Under the glow of dim pink light is the reflective glory bouncing onto a pair of black lambskin gloves and masks in the window display. Indeed, somebody would be getting lucky soon.

Walking past the various neon signs of all-night diners and coffee shops, Philip can't help but notice the warm smiles from men and women sitting across each other while sipping on coffee and eating late-night fare. Laughter can be heard even through the thick plate glass.

Philip continues his journey past darkened buildings, graffiti that seems to take every wall in the city hostage, and storefront gates. It's an ubiquitous sight. Deciding to hail a cab, he doesn't notice a middle-aged couple doing the same. A taxi pulls up, just as a man starts to walk up to the door.

Philip nods to him, "Go ahead. You take it."

The man thanks the musician before taking the lady's hand. They hurry into the waiting taxi.

Who knows where they were going? They were together on a journey.

Philip puts his hands in his pockets, watching the cab speed away. He continues his journey down the street until finding a taxi for himself.

He soon finds himself at the Brooklyn Bridge Promenade, overlooking Manhattan's skyline from afar. Quickly, he lights a cigarette.

A light breeze catches his hair as he wonders.

How many times can a person's heart get broken? Does it become tough, maybe leathery, like a tortoiseshell, to ward off the pain and rejection? Does it crumble under the lack of trust? Love lives like birth and death. It has an expiration nobody is ready for. Philip thinks about how many times those he loved, left him because he refused to go public about his affections. He couldn't blame them, though. He struggled between a thin line of fame and personal gratification. Leading a life not everybody approved of. He chose his priorities, and it was never his love life. Career came first. So many guys thought they would have it with a successful partner. What they could not anticipate was how quickly Philip could retreat into hiding his true self. He shielded his heart in the dark. In doing so, his companions felt alienated.

Never did he allow hand-holding or even a kiss in public. There were never formal dates at restaurants, since anybody could spot him out and alert the media. If aware of a photographer's eye, he would quickly separate from his partner, or insist on book-ending with others. He was always willing to accommodate a picture with a lady. Often, it would include her arm over his shoulder, with the other hand pressed against his chest. Philip didn't mind it at all but left his partner bewildered at how easy he made it look. He would only refer to his partner as a buddy, which suited him just fine. It would create friction at home, though. Squabbling, generally from the present partner, would give way to punishment through the act of taking the couch or staying in a different room. It was hurtful to the musician, but nothing would change. He stood firm with his relationship boundaries.

Then there was Connie.

She had been completely respectful of that fine line. Connie made sure never to be seen holding hands with him. It was her own decision of not displaying anything, which may be perceived by anyone as a relationship. Her touch was careful, wary of the bounds she set with him after he revealed he was gay. The fame part was nothing to her. She didn't treat him like a rock star.

She never tried to change him.

The only issue had become; she was a girl.

Philip sighs, thinking about his upcoming promotional tour of London in three days. He takes a long drag on the Newport, letting the smoke lift past the hazy gray of the night like an airborne balloon.

What was he thinking, asking Connie to join him in London? He made things clear women were not objects of his desire. His friendship was just that, a platonic buddy. Why would he even consider her for such a trip? He knew the whole thing was awkward. She'd be too busy or make up some excuse why it wouldn't work. He begins to consider the entire thing was a bad idea. Hopefully, she would ignore his stupidity. Maybe that way, he could indeed be at peace with who and what he was. But, he couldn't help think of the disappointment and rejection that became a regular part of his life. Lost in thought, he hears his name.

"Phil?" A woman's voice calls out.

Philip turns in her direction to see it's Barbara.

She walks up to join him, overlooking the skyline.

"So, you come down here too?"

Philip angles with a nod. "Perspective."

Barbara stares out at the buildings across the way.

"Yeah. That's why I like coming here myself. Funny how this crazy city has us in the palm of her hand, and for better or worse, we run back to her. Seeking. Searching for that perfect world full of promises." Barbara can tell her client is distracted by his thoughts with the lack of response. She continues with, "I just came back from a business dinner here in Brooklyn. Nobody's heard from Al." She thinks for a minute. "You know Jack, the Chinese guy at the deli on St. Mark's? His son Ron, or I should say, Rhonda, ran off and was working the streets after his parents threw him out. He had been bartending at one of the clubs but then disappeared. Same as Driscoll at the antique shop on Third, the shoe guy on Fifteenth. Bobby, the tailor on Tenth Avenue. They all vanished like it was some alien abduction you read about in those crazy papers. They're all so young."

Philip props his arm up on the railing. He rolls the Newport between his thumb and forefinger, looking directly at Barbara.

"I'm next," he reveals.

Barbara immediately says, "Oh, Phil. I'm not saying that."

Philip looks down.

"What if I've been lying…to myself?"

"Over what?"

"Life in general."

"I don't follow you," Barbara blinks back.

"Maybe there are no certainties in life. You know, cut and dry? Exactness?"

Barbara shrugs then gives him a vote of confidence.

"I'm sure you'll figure things out," she smiles.

Philip takes one last drag on the cigarette, looking out at the opposite side of the skyline.

He looks down again and states, "Some players get traded."

Barbara glances at him, puzzled. She shakes her head.

He looks back at her with a tight-lipped smile.

Barbara puts a hand to his arm.

"It's getting late, and I'm going to get out of here. Promise me you won't vanish like the others."

He briefly watches her walk away, nods, and snuffs out the rest of his cigarette. Gazing out at the skyline again, he thinks of everything he's heard and experienced for the night.

***

At Scribbles, Pete Fincher enjoys the fruits of his labor, listening to Anne Clark's "Sleeper in Metropolis." A mix of heavy electronic beats overlaid by the singer's poetry.

Several young men talk among themselves, holding drinks in their hands, listening to the curious music. Philip makes his way through them, setting his sights on the soundman.

"Finch!"

Finch looks up, broken from the spell of Clark's voice, as his name gets called. He glances around, trying to see who said it.

Philip stands directly in front of him, with hands in his pockets.

"Phil!" Finch gleefully announces. He gives him a big hug. "Jeez, I haven't seen you in a while. Gretchen told me she ran into you a couple of months ago here. Is Dill's ex still your manager?"

"Yep."

"How did the last album go? I didn't hear much about it, other than the one video you did."

"It went," Philip nods his head. "I can't say it was a total failure, but I'm sure you can find it in the discount rack of any record store...that's willing to stock it. It's not like there aren't other things to worry about in this world. Starving people in Ethiopia, bodies thrown in the East River, bombings over religion..."

"Aren't you a happy sunflower," Finch intones with sarcasm.

"Anyway, my true intentions were to ask if you were doing anything next week? Uh, starting with Friday. That is, this Friday. In like three days from now. I can use a sound guy. It can be like the old days."

"That's such short notice. Where are you going?"

"What makes you think I'm going anywhere?"

"Phil, you don't do anything in one day."

Philip turns his head in defeat, "London. It's not quite a tour. More promotion than anything. OK. One gig at The Marquee."

"You're playing The Marquee? Damn, man! You used to play Toledo, Detroit, and Madison Square Garden. Now, you're playin' closets? School gymnasiums are larger than that place."

"I don't mind the smaller venues. Sometimes they're more fun."

"Always an optimist," Finch scratches the back of his head. "You know I'd love to relive those old Deacon days, but I gotta pay the bills. Strangely enough, I have vacation time next week from the day job, but I already promised Gretchen we'd go up to Vermont for leaf-peeping season."

"Ah, I see," Philip gives a tight-lipped look, hiding his disappointment. He turns and begins to leave.

Finch puts his hand in his pocket. Immediately, he calls out, "Wait! Phil!"

Philip turns around, seeing his buddy rush over.

"I forgot to give you this," Finch reaches in his pocket, handing over a small folded piece of paper.

Philip examines it between his fingers.

"You're giving me a receipt from a video store?"

"What? Give me that!"

Philip teasingly holds it away, not allowing Finch to touch the receipt.

"Wait," he chuckles. "What have we got? Oh, *Halloween*? That's not exactly what I would consider a good date night. You'll give your girlfriend nightmares with this stuff."

Finch swipes it away.

"That was the wrong one." He shoves the slip back into his pocket and digs further. Quietly he mutters, "She was the one who wanted it."

Philip eyes him oddly, "Do you keep a Rolodex in your pants?" He giggles.

Finch takes out a piece of paper the size of a business card. He hands it to his friend.

Philip scans the paper with his eyes.

Finch says, "She came by earlier, wanting me to pass it on. You know, she was..."

Philip briskly walks away, leaving Finch talking to himself.

"...the one on the phone. Yeah. Nice seeing you too," he shakes his head.

An exhausted Connie walks up the stairs to her apartment with an overloaded basket of laundry.

As she walks to the door, a woman calls out, "Is this yours?"

Connie turns to Mrs. Whittaker. She holds up an oversized red jersey.

"Are you pregnant?" she asks.

"No!" Connie yanks the shirt away, tossing it back in the basket. She turns towards her door, rolling her eyes.

"Oh, before I forget, I've got some extra gefilte fish you're welcome to have. I don't want this stuff to go bad. I can leave it for the feral cats around the neighborhood, but what the hell? Why do that when I've got a nice, young, single gal next door?"

Connie tries to hide her aggravation towards the nosey neighbor. She smiles cheerily, rather than gritting her teeth.

"That's very kind of you, Mrs. Whittaker, but I'll be out of town next week. I know fish doesn't last that long without going spoiled in a few days. I don't want to leave it in the refrigerator to stink so bad that somebody might call the police department thinking there's a dead body in my apartment."

"I'll leave it for the cats," Mrs. Whittaker smiles in agreement.

Connie begins to put her key in the door.

"Where are you going?"

"Outside of the city."

"Going with anybody special?"

Connie glances up at the ceiling in the thought of what she wants to say.

"Just somebody I know. Not that well. Nothing more than that."

Mrs. Whittaker leans towards her with a gleam in her eye.

"Er ken makhn dem kholem greser vi di nakht. He can make the dream larger than the night."

Connie stares at Mrs. Whittaker as her key unlocks the door. Startled by her motion, she walks inside.

Through the door, she hears, "Have a safe trip!"

Connie lets her tongue hang out as she drops the basket of laundry on the floor. Shaking her head, she goes to the turntable and pulls out an album of Tina Turner's *Private Dancer*. Placing the needle on the vinyl, she folds a few items.

"Looks like it's you and me, Tina," Connie announces to herself.

Pulling over a large suitcase, she fills it with sweaters, warmer jerseys, pants, and undergarments. She grabs a variety of items from the bathroom, tossing them in a carry-on bag. In her bedroom, Connie picks up more things to bring with her.

The phone rings.

Connie picks it up.

"Hello?"

"Hey, Connie!" Sally answers. "Wanna go to Scribbles tomorrow?"

"Oh, I can't. I'm leaving for about a week."

"You? Is San-San sending you to headquarters in Japan for one of those meetings or conventions?"

"No. I'm going to London."

"England?"

"I was asked a few days ago. My boss let me do it at short notice."

"Wait. Why would you go there? Asked?" Sally, let's out a halted breath. "He asked you? Oh my God! Phil asked you? I'm guessing it's Phil, because why else would you, of all people, want time off at such short notice, other than to spend time with a rock star?"

Connie closes her eyes.

"Yes, it's Philip. It's not the two of us. It's his band too. So, no. We won't be spending much time together. He has a lot of promoting to do, and with everybody having their own rooms, it'll be tough to have fun. I'll make the best of it. Right now, I'm getting packed and ready."

"When are you going? Sally asks.

"Tomorrow night. That's why I've done a ton of laundry, cleaned out the refrigerator, finished up the accounts at work. I know as soon as I get back, the holiday rush will happen. It'll be madness until New Year's."

"A week, huh? A lot can happen within that amount of time. You. Him."

"No. Nothing will happen. I can guarantee it. I am not Philip's type."

"So you say."

"I have to get going and finish packing."

Friday night, Connie drops her luggage on the corner of Seventeenth, watching the traffic. Many cars pass, making her wonder, how will she know how to find him. Philip only told her to wait on the corner. She checks the time on her watch. Seven thirteen. She knew Friday traffic could be rough. The endless line of bright headlights continues. A cab pulls up to the corner, releasing an occupant.

Philip steps out. A sight Connie is only too happy to see. He grabs her suitcase, placing it in the trunk.

"Sorry to be running late," he says in a slightly gruffer tone.

After shutting the lid, he slaps the car, indicating he's ready.

"Got it!"

Philip turns to Connie and states, "Friday traffic can be brutal." He checks his watch. "Seven twenty. Usually, it takes under an hour."

The taxi driver says, "About forty-five minutes normally. More on a Friday night."

"I think we'll be lucky to get there by nine," Philip answers sheepishly. "Come on," he puts a hand out to Connie, allowing her to get in the cab before him.

She gets in, nearly jabbing herself with a long obstacle in the way. Connie then realizes what it is.

"Oh, hello, Caddy. Nice to see you again."

Philip notices how carefully Connie tries to get around the guitar case.

"Let me move her for you."

He gets in and shuts the door behind him.

Afterward, they finally arrive at JFK Airport.

Philip checks his watch and says, "About eight fifty. Come on. I hope we can find everyone on time. I'll introduce you to them when we get there."

Connie lugs her suitcase while the carry-on bag slips from her shoulder.

Philip picks up her suitcase with one hand, holding his own in the other with the guitar case and a garment bag.

"You don't have to do that, Superman."

He turns to her.

"Here, we'll switch. You take Caddy and a bag. We don't have time for you to drag your suitcase at a snail's pace."

Connie picks up the garment bag, seeing the dark item under the flimsy transparent plastic.

"Is that a leather jacket? It weighs a ton!"

"Do you want your suitcase back?"

"Never mind. I can handle this."

The two of them walk through the TWA terminal. A futuristic cavern made up entirely of a white and red interior, winding staircases in mid-century modern style. Passengers wait in the all-red seats.

Philip tells her, "Let's get this baggage out of the way before anything else." He walks over to the black rubber bag carousel, heaving over one suitcase. "Yargh!" Then he does the same to the other. "Yargh!"

Connie glances at him, puzzled.

"Yargh?"

He stifles a giggle, shaking his head, walking back to the lounge.

She asks, "Is that caveman or pirate?"

Philip giggles. It spreads contagiously to Connie, who follows suit.

As they walk, Philip notices his bandmates up ahead, sitting on the red lounge seats. Claire, Mitch, Perry, and Tim talk among themselves.

Mitch looks around and says, "Every time I come here, it reminds me of a peppermint candy that's melted all over."

Tim states, "There could be worse."

Claire checks her watch when she spots Philip.

He goes over to them with Connie following a few steps behind. Mitch recognizes her, giving Perry a nudge. Perry, in turn, peers over the rims of his sunglasses.

Mitch quietly says, "The same chick from earlier in the year."

Perry nods in agreement.

Connie glances around nervously, not knowing if the band members will accept her.

"We've got room for one more," Philip tells his crew. "I'd like to introduce you all to Connie Ayers. First up, we've got Tim Grann, guitar."

Connie nods.

Tim puts his hand out for a shake. He says, "Nice to meet you, Connie."

Philip puts his hand out, introducing the others. "Perry Leonard, bass. Mitch Evans, drums, and Claire Bennett on keyboards."

Connie takes a long hard look at Tim.

You said, Tim Grann? Where have I heard that name before? You're on a record I have."

"Probably," Tim gives a funny pulled face and slight nod in recognition. "I've been on a few."

Claire adds in, "He's modest. Tim's been on a lot of records. His resume is double mine, Mitch, and Perry's all together."

Mitch snickers, "Timmy burns through business cards. I'm saying that with the utmost respect."

Philip points to them with a grin, "See? I know how to pick them." He tells Connie with arched brows. Checking his watch, he announces, "We've got about a half an hour."

Mitch asks, "Couldn't we have gotten something faster for a red-eye to London? These overnight trips are killers."

"You're starting to sound like Ross. Bitch and moan." Philip answers him.

Mitch nods sheepishly.

An announcement comes over the loudspeaker for boarding flights. Philip prepares all of the ticket information set by the record company.

Onboard, Philip and his crew talk about what they'll be doing in London.

Perry stretches as he says, "Ah, London. There's a lot of freedom in Europe. They do things differently, right, Boss?"

Mitch leans forward to ask, "This freedom you're talking about? What do you mean they do things differently?"

Tim leans his head back. "It means you can be yourself. There's a lot of sexual freedom over there. They don't judge you like here in the states."

Connie gives Philip a glance without his knowledge.

Mitch asks in curiosity, "You mean like they have a lot of nudie beaches?"

Claire rolls her eyes. "You, of course, being piggy would think of something like that."

"It's an honest question."

"You're getting an honest answer from me."

"Would you go?"

Claire sits up in disgust. "Oh, that's it. I want a different flight!"

Several of the members snicker.

Mitch advises, "On another note when we get to the hotel, I'm going to crash. There's like a five-hour difference between here and there. So, we've got what? Eleven? That makes it four in the morning in London. And it takes about seven hours to get there. I figure we'll get there around six. Add on five hours, and we'll make it right about eleven."

Tim tells him, "Nice problem-solving!"

Perry asks, "What hotel are we staying at?"

"Let me check," Philip looks at a folded page from his pocket. "We've got the Columbia Hotel. Anybody know where that is?"

"I think it's near Hyde Park. Pretty close to the royal palace," Tim answers. "It's a rock and roll hotel. A lot of bands get assigned there for their TV appearances in town."

"A rock and roll hotel, huh? They want to contain us? That's not going to happen! We'll trash the place. Throw out the TVs!"

Mitch pipes in, "Tear off pieces of wallpaper. That grandma wallpaper."

Perry adds, "Take out the feathers from pillows!"

Tim grins, "Terrorize guests. Wear underwear on your head."

Everybody turns to face him.

Mitch keeps things tame by responding with, "Take out all the brown M&M's from the candy dishes."

Philip pointedly says, "Yeah. What's with that? Did you hear it too? Van Halen is notorious for the story. Brown M&M's are no different than any other color. They're still chocolate. It's not like black jellybeans."

Claire groans in disgust.

Philip points to her, "See? She knows!" He laughs.

Perry thinks for a second before giving his opinion. "Maybe it's some weird color thing? I don't know? They don't match?"

"But they're candy. Do you stare at M&M's rather than eat them? Come on!" Philip answers.

Tim shakes his head.

"There's some weird road rituals out there."

Philip says, "When it comes to food, we left tables empty. Our drummer would suck up the crumbs like a vacuum cleaner!"

Everybody laughs.

"It's true!" he giggles.

Perry changes the subject.

"So, I'm guessing Mitch, Tim, and I split a room?"

Connie sits up after being quiet for a duration of time.

"Excuse me. I'm sorry, but I thought everybody gets a room?"

Philip looks at her with some hesitancy.

"It does not work that way." He shakes his head. "The record label pays for our accommodations. Sure, I get an advance. But in the end, I'll have to pay them back. It's reimbursement. I'll get whatever profit after the label receives the full amount that they fronted to me. When it comes to hotels, we have to split them. Paying for individual rooms is a bit costly. I'm not that rich."

Connie thinks aloud, "So, you're saying if there are three rooms, then the three guys will have one, like Perry said, you'll have one to yourself, and us girls, Claire and I will split the third."

Philip remains silent.

She looks for reassurance.

"That is what you're saying?"

His eyes fall on her in such a way that's both charming and unnerving to Connie. Awkwardly, she eyes the floor, not knowing what to say in her estimation of the subject. She gives him a stinging glance with nostrils flared.

Several more hours into the flight, Philip slumps against the window with Connie facing the opposite direction. Claire is across the aisle. Mitch nearly rests against her. Perry curls up behind them, with Tim leaning his head back against the seat.

A little after six in the morning, the plane lands at Heathrow Airport.

Mitch checks his watch with a yawn. "Six eighteen."

Tim stretches in back, leaning forward.

"If we're in London, then it's eleven eighteen. Not six eighteen."

He hears Perry snoring loudly and nudges him. The bassist snorts in awakening.

Tim says, "We're here."

Claire blinks herself awake.

Connie wakes up to the sensation of Philip's head nearly against her arm. Not knowing what to do, she remains confused about how to get his attention without being too abrupt.

Claire advises, "Nudge him. Go ahead. He won't bite."

Connie uneasily glances at Philip. She lightly nudges him. He awakens with eyes widened, blinking to a state of consciousness. With a partial smile, she says, "We're here. We have landed."

Inside the men's room at the airport, Philip gets done washing his hands when Mitch steps up to him to do the same.

"Does Connie know your engine won't run hot for her?"

Philip looks directly in the mirror, "Yes. She's aware."

"Just want to make sure there's no unnecessary drama. The way she acted not too pleased about the hotel arrangements. I take it, she wanted a room of her own, not to share with Claire."

"Yeah," Philip answers, awaiting Mitch's exit. He then looks in the mirror again, reflecting on his thoughts.

CHAPTER 10

After picking up their baggage, Philip and his crew are whisked away to the stately Columbia Hotel.

At the check-in desk, Perry and Tim drop their luggage, flopping down on chairs nearby. Perry lets out a yawn. Mitch stands next to Claire. Connie wanders over to check out an adjacent room.

Philip stands at the desk, awaiting an answer from the receptionist.

"What's the name?" she asks.

"George and Louise...Jefferson."

Perry and Tim turn to each other with a nod, while Mitch sputters out in laughter. Claire shakes her head.

Philip grins wildly. "Uh, it's Phil Reinhardt."

The receptionist puts everything on a computer in front of her. "OK. You are all set, Mr. Reinhardt."

Philip calls Claire over. "Be sure to get two keys to your room. You know. In case Connie wants to bail on me."

Claire nods back in understanding.

The receptionist says, "Here are your keys."

Connie steps up in time to see the exchanging of keys. Her jaw goes limp. She wants to say something, but no words escape.

Claire steps up, "I'll need two." She arches her brows in a flirty way, angling to Mitch.

All six members climb up the stairs, carrying their luggage. Tim lets out a yawn. Claire slips the extra key to Philip, while Mitch talks about planning out the night.

"Hey, so we'll go out to eat after, right? I'm wondering what side you'll take? Do you prefer the left or right, Claire?"

Perry unlocks the door to the assigned room with Tim following close behind. "I'm hungry."

Tim nods back. "Me too."

Philip and Connie take the room next door.

Claire unlocks the door to hers, closing it before Mitch can gain entrance. He looks around, realizing he's the only one still out in the hallway. Everybody else has gone to their rooms.

Connie surveys her surroundings. Fancy wallpaper, bureau, a TV set, something that looks like closet space, and the one thing her mind dwells on, a single bed. "No way." She stares. "This whole arrangement is bizarre. I know that nothing is going to happen, but I'm not sharing a bed with you. I honestly don't care what you are — green, blue, purple, alien. To me, you are of the male species. I am female. Therefore, sharing a bed is a no-go. I'm an old-fashioned girl with old-fashioned values."

Philip plops down on the bed and pulls a sad face.

"Did I sprout horns overnight?"

Connie giggles back, "No. But, you never know if a long pointy tail might grow." She grabs a pillow from the bed, dropping it on the floor.

Philip drifts off quickly.

Glancing at him, Connie decides to relax below.

Time passes when the two emerge from the room attired in what they arrived in. Philip lets out a yawn, rubbing his eyes. He checks his watch.

"Six seventeen? Were we out all that time? Jet lag can be ugly."

She says, "But it can feel good to rest!"

"True," he nods. "I'll tell you what else can feel good — going out to eat. I'm starving. Plane food at thirty thousand feet above ground doesn't do much for me."

Philip leads her out. He gives a quick knock to his bandmates' rooms before heading down the stairs. Mitch, Perry, and Tim emerge, yawning and blinking. Claire steps out bleary-eyed. They all follow their leader.

Thirty minutes later, they all sit at the Golden Hind restaurant, over fish and chips. Philip takes out a notebook, looking it over.

Mitch says to Philip, "So, what we were talking about on the plane? You said you guys always left the tables backstage empty."

"Yeah. There was a band that shall remain nameless to protect the innocent," Philip giggles. "While we were busy devouring everything on the tables, this band had their own thing they'd do. They would pick out stuff from the buffet like the rest of us. That's where the normal behavior stopped. This band would take plastic forks and fling whatever was on it at the wall. Usually, these were the white plaster walls of arenas. Take a forkful of something cooked. Squash, mashed potatoes, and they'd catapult it right at the wall. It was to see who could reach the highest. Sort of like playing darts, only with food."

Connie says, "And you were all angels," as she eats.

Philip grins, "Maybe we had manners when it came to food, but I can't say we were angels. There was plenty of rock and roll behavior going on, which we won't get into." He looks back at the notebook. "Anyway, this is what we have for the week. Today and Sunday, nothing. So, we can do all of our sightseeing tomorrow. Monday I've got a TV interview. Tuesday is another TV interview, then after that is a magazine interview. Wednesday, we've got *Top of the Pops*. Thursday is when we film the video, 'cause you know MTV wants it."

Mitch responds with an exaggerated macho voice, "I want my MTV!"

Philip giggles before continuing, "The video will be for 'Object of Affection.' I'm taking care of that with Claire. We'll probably be out most of the day, filming. Then, Friday, I've got a bunch of interviews for various newspapers and magazines."

Perry asks, "Any *Rolling Stone*?"

"No. No *Rolling Stone*. They don't like me," Philip puts on a mock sad face before laughing. "OK. After the barrage of interviews, gotta get ready for our big show at the Marquee. And, on Saturday, we have some more jet lag to look forward to as we return home."

Once they finish, the crew returns to the hotel, retiring to their rooms.

Philip emerges from the bathroom in sleeping attire consisting of a T-shirt with New York emblazoned across the chest, and sweatpants. Connie silently admires his slightly defined physique, which had been covered up by suits, jackets, and baggy shirts whenever she's been in his presence. Connie dresses in a long T-shirt with pajama bottoms.

He picks up a pillow and flops down on the bed in the opposite direction, holding a remote for the TV. "OK. Let's see what's on the tube."

Connie corrects him. "I think they call it a telly here."

"Eh. Whatever." Philip widens his eyes in mock interest. Turning on the TV, he remarks, "We've got power."

Connie looks at him with hesitancy, unsure if she wants to join him on the bed.

Philip notices her apprehension. He taps the mattress and gives the nod. "Come on. I don't bite."

Connie grabs a pillow and lies next to him the same way on her stomach. Both look at the TV in front of them on the stand. He presses the button. Neither are impressed by what they see.

Philip quietly announces with each press, "Weird movie. Weird movie. Weird movie. Strange show. And…, Whoa. What's this? Who's…, Check to see the guide. It looks like a game show of some type. The contestants are, Ian McNabb, Dave Edmunds, and Thomas Dolby. Wait. Edmunds was with Rockpile."

Connie checks a small guide. "BBC1? It says here *Pop Quiz* with Mike Reed."

Philip says, "This is where we stop. I like the host's shirt!"

They listen intently, as they say at the same time as a song plays, "Cinnamon Girl."

Philip remarks about the next question to listen for, "Stray Cat Strut. Come on. This is too easy!" The next one stumps him a little bit. "That's the Faces or Small Faces."

Connie asks, "What's the difference?"

"Size difference," Philip giggles. "Rod Stewart or Steve Marriot." His jaw drops. "Hank Marvin is on here? Oh, wow!" He listens to the next quiz question. "What? No. No. It's Hendrix. 'The Wind Cries Mary.' Come on. He's gotta get this one."

Connie says, "He looks lost."

"He shouldn't!" Philip says at the screen. "Come on, Hank. Now's not the time to screw up. Of course, it's the end of a well-known song by a well-known guitarist. He's going to lose this one."

They listen to Mike Reed say the answer is Jimi Hendrix's song "The Wind Cries Mary."

Philip puts his head to the pillow, then comes back for air. "And every rock and roll guitar player bows in shame of this once-great six-string virtuoso.

Big disappointment. How anybody cannot remember a Hendrix song is beyond me. To think, we don't forget about 'Apache.'" He shakes his head.

Connie watches the TV. "Maybe there's some consolation. Somebody else might score the points on his team."

"Yeah. Someone half Hank's age and more knowledgeable."

Philip lets out a yawn that Connie doesn't catch. Slowly, he looks down.

"Dolby got Squeeze right. They're British too." Moments later, Connie sees guest Lulu become confused by an answer. "So much for Marvin's team. They've got six points while Edmunds has ten."

Connie fails to notice her jet-lagged roommate sinking fast against the pillow. "Third round. Uh, over half of these are English bands I don't know. What about you?" Connie turns to Philip, who is fast asleep. She picks up the remote from between them. The voices and cheers fade as she lowers the volume until the screen goes black. Carefully, Connie gets up from the bed and picks up her pillow. She looks at the contentment on Philip's face as he sleeps peacefully. An attractive, bright, humorous, fun, and unusual guy who the computer-operator managed to meet in front of an office building. He was a rock star by many accounts, yet she did not care. Connie loved his very different traits and spontaneity. There may have been no romantic inclinations, but being in his company opened her world up in a way she never imagined — a true friend, male, and strictly platonic. Connie doesn't think of what could have been if circumstances were different. If they had been, maybe he wouldn't have that special bond with her. Perhaps he would prefer hanging out with someone far more glamorous. Maybe a lady ten years younger. All of Connie's insecurities come rushing back to her even though she knows she can't change him. And why would she? He was perfect for her.

Connie looks at the dark lashes covering his unusual brown eyes. The bronze waves of hair scrunched up against his elevated shoulders. His oval face with soft features. The full-frame of his body taking up the length of the bed.

She clutches the pillow tightly against her chest and silently mouths, "I'm sorry I don't handle things better. You deserve more, and I hope you find it. Goodnight, Philip." Connie walks around to the other side of the bed. Turning off the light, she makes herself comfortable.

Sometime later into the night, Philip opens his eyes to shooting pain, indicating how stiff his whole body feels from the way he was sleeping. He then realizes while half asleep, Connie is not on the bed as he remembered. Crawling over to the opposite end, he hears light snoring. The sound makes him quickly look over the right side. He sees Connie curled up in a fetal position asleep. Philip yanks up the first layer of blankets, twisting himself around to place it over her gently. She reacts with a twitch, then huddles within the covers until her light snoring resumes. Philip tucks himself into the second layer of blankets before his head hits the pillow.

On their first full day in London, Philip, Connie, and the band explore the sites, finding music-related attractions at the top of the list. Everybody hops onto a red double-decker bus. Philip commands his crew to ride on the second level. They look out the windows to see where the *Old Grey Whistle Test* is filmed at Shepherd's Bush Empire Theatre, recalling various artists, and Philip's own experience.

"We had a great time filming there. Everything went without a hitch! They let us play live. Some of the studios won't because of the poor sound system they possess. They're not all made for the live experience, only TV. Luckily, Old Grey was, and they dealt almost exclusively with rock music. It worked great for us!" He grins.

Afterward, they head over the A219 route to the Hammersmith Odeon.

Tim asks, "So, this is where you burned it down?"

Philip's eyes turn to Tim. "I didn't burn anything down." He pauses for a moment. "Almost."

Perry pipes up. "Just what kind of guitar was that?"

Philip closes his eyes, agonizing over the story. "It was a cheap guitar...and it sounded that way. I'd rather not divulge what kind it was."

Tim looks on in shock. "Don't tell me it was a Fender?"

"Guys, there's Fender, and then there's Fender. You have to understand that all of mine were made before the big switch in sixty-five."

Claire pops up from the next seat over. "Is this the famous story where you thought you lost Caddy?" She turns to everyone else. "So, he was given a loaner by a stagehand, and chaos ensued."

"That's about it," Philip agrees. "Um, really, there was more to it. I didn't want the same thing to happen that happened to the blue Strat I had before then. So, one of the stagehands gives me a guitar which is like, severely out of tune. I'm about to play, and I hit one chord, and it's the worst sound you can imagine. It made me sound like an amateur. Instead, I grab the microphone and ask the audience, 'Anybody got a lighter?' Somebody up in front hands me over a lighter, and without playing anything, I put the flame to the headstock of the guitar. This thing is going to be torched in seconds because there's lacquer all over it. The fire grows, and I'm staring at it. Not even afraid if my fingers are going to get burned. Two road crew guys come out and douse the flame, pulling the instrument away. I get yanked off backstage, and I'm given the third degree on safety in a theater. The show had to go on, and they gave me another guitar. They had these guys watching me throughout the whole show to make sure I wouldn't do the same thing again. Later, I went back to the hotel room and discovered Caddy was where I left her. Nobody moved her. I was high as a kite and forgot her. That's when I started to realize rock and roll could be hazardous to one's health."

He looks out the window.

A few minutes later, Philip and Perry look over a map of the city. Perry points to another place. "Hey. Hey. We gotta check this one out."

"What's that?" Philip asks.

Perry begins humming the Beatles, 'With a Little Help from My Friends.'

Philip tries to figure it out. "Beatles?"

"Abbey Road. The studio."

"Oh, yeah! Of course. The studio. Where is that on here?"

Perry points to it on the map. "Right here."

Fifteen minutes later, Philip, Connie, and the band get dropped off nearby the studio.

"Claire, have you got the camera? We need to do this!" Philip calls out.

Claire pulls out a small camera from her pocketbook. "Yeah. I've got it. So, you want to walk across like John, Paul, George, and Ringo?"

"That's about it," Philip says, unable to think of any other reason.

"OK. You let me know when."

Philip immediately grabs Connie's hand unexpectedly, taking her across. She reacts, stunned.

"Me? I thought you would...,"

Philip calls out to Claire. "Now!"

Claire snaps the picture and starts laughing. The other bandmates cross, with her snapping their photo too.

"If you want, I'll take a picture of all of you. Claire can be part of it too." Connie offers.

Philip shrugs to his bandmates. "Back, we go."

They all walk back. Claire hands the camera to Connie, showing her how to use it.

Connie waits to take her cue and snaps the picture while they're midway across the street. She lets out a laugh.

Later in the day, Philip, Connie, and the band wander around Carnaby Street, taking in the atmosphere of shops, boutiques, theatres, restaurants, pubs, and services. What's even more interesting are the people who populate the famed street. Young men look like a throwback to ten years earlier. Others take on the image of a porcelain doll punked out with caked-on bright-colored eye makeup. It's a mish-mosh of styles, much like Manhattan, consisting of smartly dressed men of all ages in ascot or cravat, slicked hair, and Paul Smith or any suits that are of haute couture. Some even look like models wearing chic BOY of London jackets. Young women are no different in varying styles. Punks wear leather and studded moto jackets. Their hair resembles that of a cockatoo, feather duster, or wild mohawk. Each one tries to vie for the attention of any onlookers as the heights of hair are more outlandish. Philip feels comfortable as nobody looks his way or recognizes him. Tim immediately turns his head when he sees a short-haired blonde walk past them.

"Was that Paula Yates?"

Philip answers with little interest. "Could be? I don't know?"

Tim keeps an eye on her.

"Looks like it."

"OK. So, it looks like her," Philip answers mockingly.

Perry adds in, "I didn't see a Geldof type of guy with her."

Claire says, "Don't encourage him." She turns to Tim. "So, what if it was? She's got a boyfriend and a baby. That's like practically married."

Tim says, "But, she's not."

Claire sputters, "What is with you guys?"

"I'm gonna go check out something." Tim points. "I'll catch up with all of you later."

She says back, "Betcha will."

Tim disappears into the crowd. Philip looks back.

The group continues walking the street.

Mitch looks into the window of a very hip clothing boutique.

"I'm stopping off here. I need to check it out. Oh, those jackets! Yep. I'm goin' in.

A little further ahead, Perry's attention goes to a record store where the latest albums put on display are in the window. The group stops to look. Philip sees the titles.

"Bastards. They don't have it up."

Claire asks in exasperation, "Whaddya gonna do about it?"

Philip immediately opens the door to the shop.

"Shit. I should know enough by now, not to encourage him," Claire grumbles.

Connie asks, "What?"

"He's going to do something. He always does. I swear, sometimes I feel like I'm among kids. Oh well. Boys will be boys." Claire shrugs.

Claire, Connie, and Perry watch the window. They see a hand slide a record over one already displayed.

Claire folds her arms, shaking her head. Philip soon remerges from the shop.

"That's better." He says with a bit of pride.

Claire says, "You have no shame. You're going to piss someone off with that no-name artist you put your record over."

Philip answers casually, "Oh, come on. It was just the Sugar Lovers new album *Uranus is Mine*."

He turns to look at Perry, tight-lipped, holding in his emotions. Both look down, then back up at each other. It's a fight to see who can hold it together, the longest. Neither can. Philip and Perry burst out laughing, nearly falling over.

Claire looks at the two with disdain. She admits to Connie, "See what I mean?"

Philip puts his arm around Perry's shoulder, trying to save him from himself. It doesn't work. Both break into laughter again. "Hey. Hey." Philip attempts to calm down long enough to say a few words. "Can you imagine if somebody named their band, Bladder Control?" Another eruption of laughter follows, this time with tears streaming down their faces.

"You two are terrible," Claire tells her bandmates, shaking her head.

Perry catches his breath, wiping the tears from his face.

"Seriously, I was thinking of checking out that place."

Philip says back, "You were? I would have had you do it instead."

"Uh. No way would I put your album out front like that."

Philip answers him with, "Traitor." He gives a slight nod to Perry. "Go ahead."

Perry immediately disappears into the record store. Philip, Connie, and Claire move along down the brick covered street.

"And then there were three," Philip acknowledges.

Soon, Claire finds a boutique that catches her attention with mannequins donned in scarves and hats. She stops and looks back. "The two of you can keep going. I'll meet up with you later."

Philip and Connie turn to each other. He puts an arm over her shoulder. She doesn't quite know how to react but goes along with their cozy situation until it feels too awkward. Then she breaks free of his casual arm hang and walks alongside him. After all, he was the one from the start who did not like her hand on his arm. He looks down, realizing his contradiction. They continue to glance at the numerous retail attractions or people on the street and their various state of hair and apparel.

At night, Philip and Connie walk along Old Park Lane in the Mayfair district, where they come across the Hard Rock Cafe. The two look up at the gray-beige, seven-floor wonder. Connie admires the outdoor plants set in rectangular fashion next to the main entrance. They walk inside together, only to be greeted by a crowd of patrons who sit at various booths and tables. Nik Kershaw's "Wouldn't It Be Good" is pumped throughout the restaurant. Philip starts to get into the beat. Connie gives him a big smile when he starts mouthing the words. Both look around at the walls covered in rock and roll memorabilia consisting of tour costumes, photographs of various sizes hung in gold-toned frames, signed guitars, and gold records given by the RIAA.

Philip points to a black and white Les Paul on the wall with Pete Townshend's name on a plaque next to it. "Hey, it's not broken!" He bursts out laughing.

Connie shakes her head. "You are so bad!" She then joins him in laughter. A large clock outlined in red neon shows the time to be about a quarter after eight. Turning to him, she says, "Maybe we should order something now." Looking around, Connie adds in, "If we can find a seat. It's pretty packed."

They walk around, looking for a table. The Rolling Stones play in the background with Keith Richards and Ronnie Woods guitars getting entangled in a funky groove of "Slave."

A couple nearby talks with a waitress when a woman says, "Blimey! Is that...? Honey, is that him?" She discreetly points a finger Philip's way, who has his back turned, seeing who else is grooving to the Stones. Connie catches the woman's finger point.

She taps on Philip's shoulder. With gritted teeth, she says, "I think you have been spotted."

The woman smiles at her husband, pointing the musician out. The man says softly, "Christ, almighty!" He makes a small squeak of noise before going silent — his jaw drops.

His wife stands dumbfounded, lost in thought. "He's a bit of a dish too!" She takes her now non-verbal husband by the hand, guiding him towards the two people. "Come now, Walter."

Walter follows his wife with short, stiff steps as though he's gone through physical therapy to get his footing correctly. The couple steps up to Philip and Connie.

"Excuse me? Aren't you, Phil? Phil Reinhardt of Deacon's Alley?"

Philip answers quickly, "Yeah."

The woman says with glee, "My husband and I are big fans. We saw you at the Odeon in seventy-two and Royal Albert Hall in seventy-six. Wonderful shows, and you, sir, were amazing! Very much like Hendrix!" She looks at the two, realizing how much she's been talking but never bothered to introduce herself or her partner. "Oh, where are my manners? I'm Shelley, and this is my husband, Walter. We're big fans. Walter said you were like Hendrix. He got to see him back before being famous at…" She turns to Walter. "Darling, what was that club you said?"

They listen to hear him sputter an inaudible squeak.

"Oh, wait. Bag O'Nails? No. That was Scotch of St. James."

Philip says in astonishment, "Here? In England?"

"Yes! He played often enough for several months before returning to America. Walter here is a guitar player himself. Not on caliber like you."

"I wouldn't say I'm that high on anybody's list. Not like these guys who've got axes in this place." Philip points around to the guitars on the walls. "Nowhere near the legends." He giggles back.

Shelley says to Walter, "Hear that? He's not a legend."

Philip rolls his eyes.

Walter lets out another inaudible squeak again.

She looks at him, slightly disappointed her husband has gone silent. "You'll have to excuse him. He's done this before. It happened when we met Toyah."

Philip looks at her, then Connie, who exchanges glances with him. Shelley notices their eye contact. "Oh, I'm sorry. That would be Toyah Willcox. Singer and actress around these parts. A lovely lady. Not overblown in the head, conceited. Just a lovely person who's been through a bit."

He grins back, "You take the fame thing really well. You've probably had better luck than I did at first. When I was starting with the band, we were playing in Los Angeles, and there was a band touring around there, that will remain nameless to protect the innocent." I grew up on their stuff. Being where I'm from, it was normal. It was in seventy-three, and I thought, 'This is going to be great. I'll go over there and tell him what his music means to me.' How they mixed players by putting two worlds together. I'm seriously tripping on this opportunity. So, I go over to the lead guy, introduce myself, and right away, I could tell this wasn't going to be good. He wasn't in the best of shape, and everything I wanted to say to him, I couldn't. He wasn't feeling it. These guys were hanging around him that looked like they could hurt you, and I thought better of it. There's this saying of, don't meet your heroes because you might be disappointed. Yeah. Sometimes that happens. We're not all spaced-out and inflated, or overblown in the head as you put it."

Connie stands by, listening, and entirely taken by how Philip treats his fans. Pat Benatar starts singing, "You Better Run," as the crowd gets a little louder.

Philip tells Shelley, "We all have our moments. Some good. Some bad. Ah, I think Walter will eventually come back to this planet."

Walter lets out another loud squawk. Philip looks at him with a smile. He puts a hand on his shoulder. "You'll be fine, Walter. OK?"

Walter makes some progress as his jaw moves up and down, but there is still nothing audible coming out.

Shelley says, "Would you ever donate a guitar as Clapton or Townshend have here?"

Philip answers quickly, "No. I use all of mine."

"Do you still have the pink one?"

"Caddy? Yeah. I used her mostly for the latest record. She's been with me so long I could never give her up! A guitar that's not played simply becomes an antique." He puts a hand out earnestly, raising his brows. "Speaking of which, if you want to see more of her, I'll be at the Marquee on Friday."

Shelley asks excitedly, "A show?"

"Yep." He turns to look at Connie as if he knows something she doesn't.

Shelley eyes her husband. "We'll be sure to check it out! In the meantime, since he can't say anything, and we should be going, would it be any trouble if I could get a little written account of our meeting?"

Philip lights up. "Sure!"

Shelley looks around. "Um, this is a little embarrassing. I don't know what you could sign?"

Connie suggests with some apprehension, "A napkin? It's sort of soft paper." She winces. "Kind of?"

Shelley pipes up. "Great idea!"

Connie says, "I'll get it." She steps away.

Philip and Shelley watch her retrieve napkins from the bar.

Shelley says, "Lovely lady."

Philip nods back in agreement.

Connie returns with two napkins. She holds them out. "I figured two would be better. One for you and one for Walter."

Shelley puts a hand over her heart. "Oh, what a sweetheart you are!"

Connie fishes through her pocketbook until her fingers produce the one item necessary. A pen. "I have one." She hands it to Philip, putting a hand on his shoulder. "Do your thing."

He leans over the table and asks, "Shelley, with an E and Y?"

"Yes."

"And to Walter." Philip finishes signing both, before handing the two napkins to Shelley. "There you go."

Shelley says excitedly, clutching the napkins to her chest, "Oh, thank you so much. I'm so sorry my husband has been gobsmacked to silence."

Philip smiles and shakes his head. "No problem."

The couple walks towards the door. Shelley takes Walter's hand as he slowly shuffles away.

Philip has already gone off to find a table. Cyndi Lauper's "Time After Time" pours through every speaker. Connie watches him when she receives a tap on the shoulder. She turns around to face Shelley, who says, "Luv, he's arse over elbow for you!" Shelley arches her brows and gives her the thumbs up. Walking away, she joins her husband. They leave.

Connie slowly turns Philip's way to see him looking around. She stops to think, furrowing her brows in the thought of what Shelley told her. What did she mean? Connie walks over to the booths set with brass-topped railings. Taking a seat across from Philip, she looks through a menu.

Upon arriving back at the hotel, Philip and Connie get settled in for the rest of the night. Philip drops on the bed. Connie walks around before sitting next to him, pulling at her ear.

"I can't believe how loud it got in there!" She says in astonishment.

Philip puts a hand to his stomach. "I feel so full."

Connie looks back at him. "What do you expect? You ate that entire mega-sized burger and every fry! Then you really had to do it, and dance your ass off right after that. Didn't your folks ever tell you not to exercise until a half an hour after you ate?"

"Yep. Then I went and jumped on the bed," Philip smiles back proudly.

Connie rolls her eyes, "Oh." She shakes her head.

He turns over on his side with impish charm. With one brow arched, he asks, "So, what side do you want?" He gives a big Cheshire Cat grin.

Connie instantly propels herself off the bed. "Oh, no. No. No. Nope." She shakes her head. "Mr. Rock Star, you need your rest more than me. You've got a full schedule ahead of you."

"Compromise? How about we'll both take…," Philip starts to suggest.

Outraged, Connie sputters back, "What? No! There will be no compromise. I will not sleep with you! No. Absolutely no. I don't care what your preference is. I do not sleep with men casually!"

Philip plays innocent. "You make it sound so dirty." He lies back down, having his head leaning over the side of the mattress in upside-down fashion, where he can keep his sights on her. "Aww, come on, Connie. Cuddling never hurt anybody. Just think of it as a stuffed toy. Something all squishy and adorable without fur."

Connie looks at him, shocked. She quickly picks up a pillow. "What is wrong with you?" She then throws it at him, before picking up another one, holding onto it tightly. "No! No! No!" Connie runs into the bathroom, still clutching the pillow and shuts the door behind her.

Rolling over onto his stomach, Philip holds the pillow while laughing madly.

Connie cracks open an eye, seeing everything through a blurred vision when hearing a noise that barely raises her from slumber. The noise is a little louder, receiving enough attention to fluttering her eyes open for all but a second. Again, she doses off. A third sound gives her concern with a lazy eye partly open to the vision of the showerhead above. She never notices the hand turn the faucet on clockwise.

"Aaaaaaaaaaaaaaaaaaaaaaaggghhhhhh!!!!"

The door to the bathroom flies open. Connie appears, soaking wet, with the most stunned and miffed expression.

"You couldn't use an alarm like a normal human being?" She states as her nostrils flare.

Philip takes one look at her and laughs hysterically, dropping his head onto the pillow to muffle the sound.

Connie answers to his laughter with sarcasm. "Oh, I'm glad you find this so funny." She realizes in a split second how ridiculous she must look. It doesn't help that she's wet and her oversized T-shirt is a bit revealing. She has a small frame, her barely-there breasts peek through the skin-tight material, nipples standing full attention. Any hot-blooded male would be turned on by such a sight. A feeling she would accept if it had the makings of a romantic interlude. Philip was no ordinary hot-blooded male. Connie looks down, dejected. Letting down her guard includes her prudish anxiety not to cross her arms. Nothing to worry about or feel excitement over.

Philip is curled up, still laughing hard, like he's just executed the best prank in the world.

Connie looks down, shaking her head. "Let it all out of your system," she answers dryly.

He doesn't stop.

She looks up at the ceiling. "How does anybody put up with you?"

Philip pulls himself away from the pillow, long enough for his eyes to peer at her. Another wave of laughter hits him.

"That's right, laughing boy." She looks directly at him rigidly.

Again, Philip pulls away from the pillow. He wipes his eyes and reduces his laughter to sporadic giggles. He says with raised brows, "Norwegian Wood?" He gets up and picks out articles of clothing from a drawer.

Connie throws her arms out. "Oh, great! Now it's about Beatles songs!"

Philip walks directly over to her. He says with one brow raised, "Hey, it's not like I accused you of not sleeping in a bed like a normal human being," before going inside the bathroom and shutting the door behind him.

Connie shakes her head, knowing he makes sense. She walks over towards the bed as he tosses the wet pillow out of the bathroom. The door shuts again.

Connie picks it up.

***

Later in the morning, Philip sits across from the host of the BBC's talk show, *Here With Nigel Taylor*.

"Welcome to the show, Phil. Now, should I be calling you Phil or Philip? Everybody has a preference."

"Phil's fine. How about you?"

"Oh, I reckon people call me things I can't say on television."

Philip lets out a laugh. "Fair enough. I won't ask."

Nigel looks at his notes. "However, it's not the first name I want to ask you about, but it's the last."

"Here it comes." Philip grins, shaking his head.

"Sorry?"

"I get asked this all the time. The answer is, no."

They say it at the same time. "Are you related to Django Reinhardt?"

"I've become a pro with this line of questioning. No. I'm not. A previous record company wanted me to sign my name without the D. I told them I wouldn't do it, simply based on principle. If I were to change my name, what else would they want me to change? Besides that, I'm happy with the way it's spelled. No shame. I don't have anything to hide. Don't I wish I were related to Django, though! He was a pioneer among guitar players. But, no luck. No relation." Philip gives a tight-lipped smile.

Nigel says, "Now that you've revealed that bit, I'd like to confess. People sometimes confuse me with John Taylor."

Philip looks at him, puzzled, "Bassist from Duran Duran?"

"Yes. We have the same name. He uses the middle one, 'John.'"

"Ah. I see."

"In turn, when it first started happening, I was receiving a letter a day, and I thought, 'Great! I've got fans! They do like me! And it grew to somewhere between three to five letters per day. I was chuffed to bits! Then I read one and saw stuff about some girls having fantasies of being with Nick Rhoads and myself. I thought, What is this? Some bit of sex fantasy as ménage á trois? Then I read the words, 'I heart Duran Duran.'"

Philip bursts out laughing.

"That must have been a disappointment."

"To find out, a bit of a clanger! Let me ask you something. Groupies. I'm sure you've got some stories to tell."

"I'm...," Philip hesitates, gritting his teeth through the shame. "I'm not into groupies."

"You're not?"

"No."

"Looking at my notes...," Nigel picks up a page. "...says here, you were inspired by particular instance about a lady."

"True. Yeah. I wrote 'Oxblood Blues' from something that occurred with a fellow bandmate in the group I was with about ten, twelve years ago." Philip thinks before defending his decision. "You can get inspired by a lot of things in life. All you have to do is look around. It doesn't always mean the subject of the song has to be about you, personally. There are a few autobiographical songs I've written. Um, but that one is not."

Nigel looks at Philip in shock.

"No groupies, though?"

Philip shakes his head.

"No. I don't know. Maybe I'm a little bit old-fashioned? You see how your parents are, and you kind of learn from their behavior. I'm into the whole giving of the heart and soul. All or nothing."

Nigel then asks, "Now, what about this? *The Afterglow*? What's the meaning behind such a record title?"

"Well, it's about the feeling you get. Ecstasy. When you're in love, and your heart beats like a drum. It's uh, those thousands of butterflies set free from deep within. OK. So, maybe I'm not that old-fashioned." Philip admits with raised brows and a growing smile. "Sometimes you have an angel on one shoulder and a little guy with horns on the other. There's always a feeling of telling the angel to take a hike. That's rock and roll, though. I've learned through the school of rock and roll, if you're not doing it, then you're thinking it. If you're not thinking it, then you're writing about it. So, it kind of is part of the grand scheme of things. The nature of the beast."

"So, how is the record doing?"

Philip has to think for a second. "It's going well. We still have the rest of the week of more promoting and stuff."

"Got any videos?"

"Yeah. As a matter of fact, we're filming one in a couple of days. I can't remember who's directing it."

Nigel asks, "Aside from videos, anything else planned?"

"Yeah. The band and I are playing at the Marquee Club on Friday night.

"Are you going on tour?"

"We just did a partial tour of the west coast in the states. That ended in later August. If the opportunity arises, I'd like to get back on the road and continue it. A European leg wouldn't be out of the question either."

Nigel takes a cue from the stage director off to the side.

"We've come to the portion of our program where we pick a lucky member to ask our guest a question."

A man runs up the steps to where a crowd of a few dozen audience members sit. He puts a microphone in front of woman's face.

Nigel calls out, "What would you like to ask Mr. Reinhardt?"

The woman can't wipe the smile off her face.

"I'd like to know what kind of music do you listen to while shagging?"

Audience members snicker and laugh. Connie sits among them, confused by the wording.

Philip looks down, genuinely puzzled with the most quizzical expression as he repeats the words. "What kind of music do I listen to while...? Shag...?" He turns to Nigel, hoping to get the meaning deciphered. "Vacuuming? Haircut? What? In America, we have, I should say, we used to have shag carpeting growing up. That and the hairstyle famous for about two decades."

Nigel says, "You never heard of the word?"

"No. I'm not familiar with it."

"Shagging means having sex over here."

Philip is immediately overcome with embarrassment and shock by the forward question. "Oh, no. I can't answer something like this."

Neither Nigel nor the audience helps him. Connie looks on, feeling sorry for her friend.

Philip knows he has to answer the question. He thinks for a moment after giving the host a look. "I choose to go between the grooves of my own rhythm."

Nigel asks, "That is?"

"I don't like to listen to music when making love. It ruins the mood of everything."

Connie leans over to see if the woman who asked the question showed embarrassment by her line of questioning.

No.

She simply sits back, savoring every bit of awkwardness from Philip.

Connie is slightly put-off by the scene. She glances down, shaking her head.

Nigel abruptly says, "Oh, we've run out of time, but I'd like to thank our guest, Phil Reinhardt, who will be performing at the Marquee Friday night." He turns to Philip. "Thank you for being a good sport."

Philip giggles back, "Part of the job requirement. Thanks."

The two men shake hands.

The stage director calls out, "And, we're off!"

Audience members get up to leave. Connie does the same, looking around for directions. She sees Philip talking with the stage director while taking off his clip-on microphone. Connie holds her jacket, waiting for the final audience member to leave. When the coast is clear, she heads down the small steps.

The stage director says to Philip, "The bit about the Marquee? Your episode won't air until a few weeks into the month. We're going to leave a line on the bottom of the screen. That's to let viewers know this was taped before your appearance there."

Philip nods back. "OK. I kind of figured that would happen."

He senses a pair of eyes watching them. Looking out at the bottom of the shallow stage, Philip makes eye contact with Connie, who stands by patiently.

The stage director looks at her, knowing he needs to give the two time alone. He walks away.

Connie says nothing.

Philip looks at her pleased, but almost shy. "Hey!" He brightens up, not wanting her to see how awkward he felt, knowing she was in the audience.

She notices his reticence.

"You did fine."

"I did? Because I didn't feel it. Of course, I didn't see that one coming."

Connie shakes her head. "Crazy women." She grins.

Philip giggles back, loosening up. "Yeah. It's alright. All part of it."

Connie says with amazement, "I guess they do things a little differently here."

Philip lets out a laugh.

They leave the stage together.

Later on, Philip, Connie, and the band enjoy dinner at a trendy restaurant in central London, where they enjoy the ambiance of dim light and people milling about. At their table, the band trades studio stories. Mitch, in particular, reminisces.

"I remember when we did the *No Bounds In Love* sessions, there was a background singer. She was a hot ticket that could really sing."

Perry sits up straighter as he asks, "What? Now, I know I would have remembered that."

"Oh, this was a little before you got hired. It was me, Ross, and a few others. Phil had the perfectly coiffed light blond hair then."

"OK. I remember the hair, just not the woman."

"So, she introduces herself as Poppy Seed."

"Poppy Seed?" Perry asks, taken aback.

Claire adds in, "I'm starting to pull this out of my memory bank. She was a brunette, right?" A moment later, it hits her. "Oh, I know now. She was on the song, 'Hopscotch Heart.'"

Mitch points to her and says, "You got it." He turns to everybody else. "So, you can imagine Ross's reaction to this lady. Then we're about to do sessions with Frankie James—"

"The sax player? I think I've worked with her," Tim pipes up.

"You've worked with everybody," Mitch answers dryly. He continues his story. "The two women meet each other, and it's not too cordial. Poppy Seed has this attitude already since she's been on a few disco albums. She's like, 'Hi. I'm Poppy Seed.' And then Frankie introduces herself. Poppy Seed says, 'What kind of name is Frankie? Then Frankie answers with coolness, 'What kind of name is Poppy Seed?'

Claire turns to Philip and asks, "Wait, was it Poppy Seed you brought to your cousin's wedding?"

Philip picks up a piece of the straw wrapper, toying with it between his fingertips.

"Nope. It wasn't her. It was Nicki, who I graduated with."

Connie listens silently to the conversation, with hidden confusion as she turns to Philip.

"OK. I wasn't quite sure." Claire answers.

Mitch responds with, "This chick gets to sing on the song, and I don't know what happened, but the next day she's super happy about being with someone. I don't know, maybe a boyfriend or something? God, but I have no idea what her real name was. She even went by Poppy Seed on the credits."

"Lisa," Philip answers while continuing to ball up the paper between his fingers in preoccupation. "It was Lisa Goodstein."

Mitch slaps the table.

"Of course, you would know! You're the bandleader."

Philip stops what he's doing and looks in disbelief.

Connie can't be sure if his expression is one of guilt, sly admission of something more, or both.

***

At night, everybody returns to the hotel. Philip sits at the small desk, writing then picks out a grape from a bowl of fruit at the far corner. Connie flips through a book.

"I got this book about British slang before we went to the restaurant." She flips a page back and forth. "OK. So, some of these words are incredibly weird. What was that one Mr. Taylor said when you guys were talking about names and fan mail? It started with a C?" Connie's finger runs down a list of words and their meanings. "I think it was CH. Oh, wait! Is this it? Chuffed? As in 'Chuffed to bits?' Wow." She lets out a laugh. "Says right here, it means to be pleased with something. Well, that explains it all. What else is in this crazy book?" Connie's eyes scan down, then back up the page when she stops to see the slang term Shelley mentioned at the Hard Rock Café. She looks back up at Philip, who continues to write, oblivious of her glance. The phrase puzzles her so much, Connie quickly puts the book down but thinks about the background singer and the numerous other women in Philip's life. She shrugs it off, switching her emotions back to the book. "Moving on." She raises her brows. "I still can't get over that terminology. Shag? I thought the same thing as you did! It confused the hell out of me! Good thing my Aunt Myrna doesn't get to see the show."

Philip asks her while staring off in distraction, "Why's that?"

Connie walks over to him. She picks up a grape from the bowl and eats one.

"She still has shag carpeting. Ugly green and a putrid patterned couch to go with it."

Philip lets out a giggle.

"Your aunt's couch was probably the same pattern as my parents' wallpaper."

Connie quickly changes the subject. She asks, "So, you have another TV appearance tomorrow? I wonder how that one will go?"

Meanwhile, Philip zones out, thinking about things instead of listening to Connie.

She says, "Hopefully, there won't be questions, but if there is, then let's pray they aren't like that lady's. I can't imagine what goes through somebody's mind... Anyway, I'm sure you'll do fine. You know?" Connie looks over at him, noticing his frozen state. "Philip?"

He blinks back to reality. "What? Sorry about that. I was kind of thinking of stuff. Got a lot on my mind."

"I'm sure you do. You've got a full schedule." Connie sighs. "An interview tomorrow. An appearance Wednesday."

"I've thought about a lot of things over the past few months." Philip looks at Connie with concern in his eyes.

Connie says, "This isn't about the show either I take it?"

"No." Philip looks down. "It's something far more complex I've been going through, about life, changes, and the future in general." He looks back at her. "Sometimes, we visit the darkest parts of our soul."

Connie takes a deep breath. "And sometimes we need a friend." She steps around to him. "I think you need a hug."

Unlike other times, Connie wraps her arms around his shoulders to provide warmth that's uninhibited and more inviting than previously when they attempted to connect. He does not pull away. Instead, she feels the pulsation of his whole being in the embrace, hoping to will away all of the storm clouds in his soul. He clings to her like a leaf hangs onto a bare tree's winter awakening. Not out of desperation, but out of familiar comfort.

Leaving the hotel room, Connie races down the patterned carpet stairs, trouncing her way to the landing. Philip is lightning fast, giving chase into the lobby, past the check-in desk. They skitter across the tile floor. Running into the stately common area, Connie grabs hold of a comfortable chair by the back, steadying herself, breathing hard. She laughs when Philip is across from her the same way. Connie makes a move. He makes a move. Slowly, she creeps around the chair, partly hiding behind it. Above them is a large chandelier, throwing off light in all directions. Connie tries to distract him. He wags his finger as he's not falling for it. Their playful romp is placed on pause as they hear several voices nearby. Philip drops onto one of the chairs as if it were musical chairs. Connie grabs on, throwing herself onto a couch. An older couple enters the room. With legs crossed, Philip eyes the floor. His foot taps to an imaginary beat. Connie eyes the couple who are unsure what area they want to be in. Philip's eyes swing over to the right, where the couple talks. Connie peeks at them, patiently waiting for the two to leave.

The lady says, "Charles, I think we want the bar."

Philip rubs under his chin in a preoccupied state, when he breaks into a broad smile. He mouths to Connie, "Charles?" Raising a brow, he continues with a backward thumb point. "Diana?" He holds in a small giggle.

The couple leaves the room.

Connie finds it the perfect opportunity to run out. In shock, Philip races out after her. Both run past the lobby again.

Two receptionists watch. One says to the other, "Honeymooners."

Connie goes up the stairs as fast as she can, with Philip hot on her heels. They round the corner upstairs. Connie jams the key in the keyhole to their room as quickly as possible. She runs in, not realizing how close he is to her.

Philip tackles her on the bed, rolling over while holding her. They laugh at their spontaneous action. Realizing her position of being right on top of the musician, she looks him in the eyes. He does the same before lowering his sights. Their laughter ceases. For a moment, neither does anything. Connie pushes off of him, feeling awkward.

"OK. Time out." She says in a breath. "I can't believe we just ran down there like that. We must have looked like kids racing around like mad! Can you imagine?"

Philip rolls over to his side, hand on head.

"I'm sure they've seen worse. Eh, broken TV sets, smashed windows. A toilet seat cover on the hood of a parked car. A streaker. Cleaning lady who sees too much." He raises his brows devilishly.

"A what?" Connie laughs out loud. "Wait. Did I hear you right? A toilet seat cover…"

He finishes it for her. "…on the hood of a parked car. Mmm, yeah. That can happen. Not that I ever trashed a hotel. You would be surprised at what goes on in places like this. Full-on rock and roll decadence and bad behavior."

Connie says, "What was the worst thing you ever did in a hotel?"

Philip tightens up at the question. "I like to subscribe to the code of honor. We don't kiss and tell."

She arches her brows at his answer. "Oh, so you were a bad boy."

He hesitates, sitting up. "I did a few things on the road that are better left unsaid. Yep."

A few hours later, Philip sits in another chair across from the far more brazen, Chuck Gilbert. A musician-wannabe who gets off in asking questions that satisfy his insatiable fantasy of living through guests vicariously. The TV cameras roll as the two converse.

"You were with band…," Chuck checks his notes. "…Deacon's Alley."

"Yep."

"That must have been quite an experience?"

"Yeah. It was. For seven years, we got to see a lot of things. A lot of traveling from town to town. Buses at first, because we didn't have the budget to get a plane. Eventually, we did. There were, and continuously are, lessons in life we learn.

"I'm guessing with seven years there were plenty of birds!"

Philip glances out to the audience, unsure of the foreign wording to him. Again, Connie sits in on the taping. She watches as everyone else does.

He turns to the host in slight confusion. "That is?"

Chuck quickly wakes up to the fact his guest is unfamiliar with the wording.

"Oh! What you might say in America. Foxes? Chicks? Women."

"Ah-huh. OK. I gotcha," Philip answers with understanding. "Yeah. Ladies is what you're talking about."

"It's all the same. Seven years' worth, though. What might have that been like, besides great?"

"It wasn't everything," Philip turns to the audience uncomfortably. "Should we be talking about such things filmed for a morning program?"

"Oh, the people at home don't mind a little zest in their tea!"

"I see. Well, it's more than seven years. I mean, yeah, it was seven with the band, but I was playing with another one before that. We played high school dances, proms, auxiliary halls, backyard barbecues. Anywhere people wanted to hear us."

"But the women!" Chuck enthuses.

"There were some. Don't you want to know about the record?"

"Oh, yes. But, it's always good to know about these experiences on the road."

Philip grins "For research?"

"Well, personal and professional," Chuck says, unabashedly straightforward. "What do you look for in the opposite sex? What is your type?"

Philip's eyes bounce around in thought. "My type?" He looks up for a second, trying to conjure up an answer like a spirit. "I would have to say a lady with movement. The art of dance is a major attraction for me. If she can move, she moves me," he laughs.

"Where do you find such ladies?"

"The Upper West Side of Manhattan. Julliard is a great place!" Philip answers, mischievously. "A lot of young dance students. Ballerinas, theater, Broadway. Professionals who know how to move," he arches a brow and laughs.

"I thought you might say clubs or discotheques?"

"No," Philip grins. "That's amateur stuff."

"I take it that a fine fellow such as yourself has no problem in catching a lady's eyes?"

"Single...for now," Philip glances down with a smirk on his face.

Connie stares at him, unamused by his antics or how he's acted in front of the host.

Chuck and Philip continue to talk.

After the show finishes, Philip walks outside to be met by Connie's back turned. Her nostrils flare as she stares out at the passing traffic.

Cheerfully, he says, "I was wondering what happened to you after the taping? You didn't try to approach the stage like yesterday."

"I didn't feel like it," she stiffly answers.

"Not that you had to."

Swiftly, Connie turns to face him.

"What's up with you and women? What gives?" She stares at him, seeing he's caught off-guard by her line of questioning. "Taking Daisy with you on a whim down to Allentown for a show-and-tell of your favorite department store. You and some background singer baking. Is that some kind of code? That Poppy Seed girl. And what was with that look?

"What...?" he tries to keep up with her rant.

"Oh, and then I'm sure Claire has hung out with you, and can't forget about Nicki. 'I went to school with her and brought her to my cousin's wedding.'"

"Why does this conversation sound familiar? I'm thinking of the scene in *Lady & the Tramp* where Lady starts grilling Tramp and reels these names, 'What about so and so and her, oh, and that one.'" He starts chuckling.

Connie becomes angry at his teasing.

"You think everything is a joke!"

"Well, you are putting me in the doghouse. You know, you really do act like one of those actresses in a teenage movie."

"And you know what? You can sound like a real creepy jerk! 'If she can move, she moves me?' And, 'Clubs are amateur stuff?' The jokes about women at Julliard? Upper West Side? The tone. It didn't even sound like you."

Philip shakes his head, "I had to say something to get him off my case. You saw how he kept on the same subject. He wasn't going to be happy until he got an answer from me."

Connie shakes her head in disgust, giving a sour expression.

Philip becomes more solemn as he sees she's not buying into his jokes or affinity in referencing films.

"There was nothing that went on between myself and Poppy Seed. Lisa. I felt genuinely bad for her because the guys in the band were giving her a hard time. She wanted to be treated like a human being. I knew how she felt, and it was common courtesy on my part. I was in a relationship at the time. I mean, I can ruin that without any woman. The deal with Nicki was, I graduated with her. My cousin was getting married, and there was no way in hell, I was going to bring a guy with me as my date. I wasn't going to come out to all of my family and friends in Allentown like that. Plus, there was no way I was going to do it with the priest who was officiating because he was the same guy I saw at church every Sunday as a kid. Daisy happened to be hanging around on a Saturday and we decided to do something completely spontaneous. Like a road trip with a buddy. The same thing goes with the background singer when we were baking. It's not some euphemism for sex or anything. It was genuinely to hang out and have fun. Yeah, and I've hung out with Claire plenty. She's not only a great keyboard player but good company."

Connie remains unaffected by Philip's explanation.

"I just don't get it about you — these stories. My accommodations at the hotel with you." She shakes her head. "It's weird. It's not right!"

Philip grins while answering, "Connie, I don't hate women. It's just that I don't connect with them the same way. As for the hotel room, you're free to leave anytime."

"No. Of course, you don't hate women. That's too obvious. You told me back in June...," Connie glances around to make sure the coast is clear. "...you were gay. The odd thing is, after all this time, I've never seen you make eye contact with any men in a romantic gesture. I never witnessed you getting cozy with any guys. It's as if you say one thing and show another. You told me not to play matchmaker with you at the skating rink. You probably don't even have pictures of past boyfriends, partners. Whatever the hell you call them." She gives an untrustworthy squint. "How am I supposed to believe what you say is the truth? All I've heard is how you hang out with women specifically. It leads me to believe, well, I don't know? It's just odd. It's like you avoid being with your own kind."

Philip furrows his brows in confusion. "Own kind? Jeez, Connie. You make it sound like I'm a rare species from a zoo. Yeah. I'm different. I already know that."

Connie squints angrily, "Why did you ask me to come with you to England? So I could hear you lie? You know, you're the one who could dole out all this advice and tell me to 'Just be yourself.' Yet, you can't do the same.

Instead, I get to hear along with everybody else in this country your lies. What was it you told me a few months back? Something about how the worst thing you could do is be fake because it leads to being miserable. And you can hide it from everybody but yourself." She points a wary finger.

Philip tries to speak, but no words will come out.

"You guys were talking about having more freedom in London than in the states."

"That's not what we were referring to," Philip shakes his head. "I can't just say in an interview what I am. Not here either. Information can travel fast. Somebody can watch my interview over here, and then tell their friend back in the states, "Phil Reinhardt is..." he raises his brows to make Connie aware. "Then, my family would find out. I don't want to lose them. They mean too much to me. I can't do that. And then the record label would get a hold of the information, hold it against me, and have these expectations I don't want to give them because they won't treat me as a serious solo recording artist, which I want more than anything. There's a lot more to it."

Connie rolls her eyes. "Oh, boo hoo."

"Look, my way of living isn't up to everybody's standards. You saw what happened the night we went to FishKat. What happened to that guy at the apartment. They're calling it a plague of sorts, a gay cancer. There are thousands of guys in my situation who are dying for love. What we all want is time. Not everybody has that."

"You're talking about AIDS." She thinks about a solution. "It doesn't have to happen if you're careful."

"There's always a chance somebody will mess up. Sure, for somebody like you, you don't have to worry. For guys like me, it can be a death sentence." Philip sees how frustrated and confused Connie is. "We're seen as immoral, delusional, unnatural, possessed. I've heard it all how we deserve to die for our sins. It's God's way of teaching us a lesson. Hospitals and doctors treat patients like they're toxic. Young guys are dying in a sterile, empty room without family or friends because they've abandoned them, thinking it's contagious. So, lying? I don't know? If lying is to save our asses, then yeah, I'll take it."

"You rather hide who you are?" Connie asks, not feeling any compassion for him.

"It's complex," he nods while eyeing the sidewalk.

Connie cannot comprehend what he's saying as she shakes her head.

"That doesn't even begin to explain things."

Philip bites his bottom lip when he answers more assertively, "It's complex."

"So, you're OK with pretending?"

The two stare at each other, knowing they are at an impasse with their friendship.

Connie knows not to push him any further as she advises, "You have another interview to do. You should go and do that."

He walks away while she watches.

***

At night, Philip returns to the hotel, talking with Tim before entering the darkened room. He lets out a slight laugh, then turns a lamp on a low setting. Tossing down his jacket, he ruffles his hair. Curiosity gets the better of him. Crawling onto the bed, he takes a peek over the side.

Connie lays on her side, sleeping snuggly under the covers.

Philip's thoughts are firmly focused on their talk. He thinks about her confusion and frustration in trying to understand him. In how mixed up she felt in the refusal of matchmaking. Her willingness to let him go at various times. His selfishness of not wanting to be alone. The sense of truly having a friend felt like home. Of course, she felt confused.

So did he.

Getting up, he goes to pull up a chair near the window. Plopping down, he leans back, taking a deep breath.

CHAPTER 11

On Wednesday, Philip and the band head back to Shepherd's Bush, where they play on the music chart television program, *Top of the Pops*. BBC TV Centre fills up with eager kids wanting to smile and dance for the cameras. Connie squeezes by some people to get a better view. Everybody waits for the stage lights to turn on. Many hold balloons with the *Top of the Pops* logo prominently displayed. A cue is given. Everybody cheers. Two hosts welcome everyone to the show.

The female host excitedly says, "We have six new chart entries this week. Starting things off with number twelve is, Phil Reinhardt with 'Object of Affection.'"

Philip is already on the stage, dressed similarly as to when Connie had first met him. The backdrop comes alive, consisting of flickering fluorescent tubing — symmetrical circles and squares of neon flash in green and purple. A rotating disco light provides strobe-like action, flourishing the stage with omnidirectional power. A large screen in the back reflects what's going on in front. The steady beat starts up, urging the crowd to move. Claire sways along while she expertly presses on the keys of an unplugged keyboard. Perry does the same with his bass. Tim tries to keep with the timing of the rhythm guitar. Mitch makes it look like he's adding power to the drums. Philip takes the lead on both vocals and guitar. Fans surround the stage, holding balloons, and dance in place as the studio is incredibly crowded for anybody wanting to let loose. The track is pre-recorded, while Philip mimes to the song. Nobody in the audience seems to mind. They're accustomed to the studio's advantages and disadvantages. Some artists simply didn't like to sing live with the sound provided. For Philip, he didn't mind. He had to save his voice for Friday's show at the Marquee.

Connie finds herself enjoying the company and all of the atmosphere. It's not like back home in Manhattan, where guys would pester her and be all macho. Several simply move like her, and some girls follow along. Philip scans the floor, hoping to catch a glimpse of Connie. He plays up to the TV cameras as much as possible, putting Caddy up to the lens, or flashing a broad smile. A few times, he even winks at a few girls in front for good measure as they wave balloons and smile back in recognition of the guitarist's flirty ways. The audience enjoys the song, down to the last faded note on the track.

Right after Philip's performance, the show focuses on the many other chart-toppers of the week, mixing up positions, then featuring an artist to either mime or sing live. Sporadically they air a promotional video as a hit. Balloons bounce around the audience, often making their way to one of the several stages, only to get kicked off during mid-performance. The dizzying array of different colored lights resumes until the program finishes.

The lights come back on. Everybody stops dancing and begins to walk away. Connie looks around at the steady stream of foot traffic passing her.

"Excuse me?"

A young blond guy stops in front of her and smiles.

"Yeah?" he answers in a London tinged voice.

"When does the program air on TV? How many weeks?" Connie asks.

"Tomorrow. Airs on Thursdays at seven thirty-five on BBC1," he answers with a smile.

"Tomorrow?"

"Yeah. There's not much to edit. What you see here is pretty much what you'll get on-air."

"Thanks," Connie says, half-stunned by the news. She quietly says to herself, "Tomorrow. Wow."

At night, Philip and Connie retire to their room after having dinner with the band. She steps out of the bathroom in her usual sleepwear of T-shirt and pajama bottoms. Plopping herself on the bed, she turns on the TV. Philip tosses his suit on the chair and begins to unbutton his shirt. He sits on the opposite side to change.

Connie remarks while looking at the screen, "I swear there are only four stations. You'd think there would be more by now. BBC1, BBC2, ITV, and some..., I don't know? Irish or Welsh channel."

"You don't honestly expect them to have all the cable stations like back in America?" he answers.

Connie starts to turn around when she sees his bare back facing her. For a moment, she's caught off-guard. Stifling a breath, she turns quickly to see the TV. Her eyes swing back and forth. She mouths to herself, "Don't turn around. Please don't turn around." Biting her bottom lip, thoughts race through her mind. She would love to look again.

No. She couldn't think that way.

Suddenly, Connie feels the pressure of the bed change. Quickly, she buries her head in the T-shirt.

Philip gets up, attired in a printed T-shirt and dress pants. Holding a pair of pajama bottoms, he steps around when he looks at her with one brow arched at the sight of Connie's head buried within her T-shirt. He taps at the top of her covered head.

He mumbles, "And people think I'm weird?" Breaking into giggles, he asks, "What's goin' on in there?"

Connie emerges from her buried state.

"Oh, I was checking to see if this shirt smelled funny."

Giving a nod of understanding, it hits Philip in a delayed reaction. He shakes his head while walking into the bathroom.

Connie waits until she hears the door shut. Then she drops her head in a sigh of relief.

In the grasp of autumn's hues of brown, orange, yellow and fiery red, Hyde Park is covered in splendor. On a bench, overlooking the expanse of the Serpentine Lake. Connie and Claire converse. Claire carefully holds a lighter, flicking it on for the Benson & Hedges between her long, graceful fingers. After lighting the cigarette, she sits back, savoring the taste and lingering breeze.

Connie says with a bit of amazement, "It sure is beautiful here."

Claire nods back, straightening herself up. "Yep."

The two remain silent.

Claire breaks the silence. "He's complicated." She looks at Connie. "Phil." Taking a long drag, she thinks for a second. "He's a lot like the city he loves, New York City. Full of contradictions. Even his hair isn't what you think it is. He's not a natural blond by any stretch of the imagination. That's the weird hair color he keeps getting done. It's naturally brownish." Claire flicks some ashes to the ground. "Phil is different, though. Yeah. He can be very much a typical male sometimes, especially with the terrible jokes." She exhales the smoke, shaking her head slowly. "Really terrible jokes. I don't know if you've ever noticed or gone with him anywhere, but he cannot dance. Some of the moves can give away him being different. That's why it's better when he has a guitar strapped on, or he's behind a keyboard. It's a more natural fit." Claire faces Connie to ask, "Have you ever seen Phil play live?"

"Uh, no. Last night was the first time I ever saw him with the guitar in any manner."

"You're in for a real treat then — just about every girl who's watched him love it. But, that's only a small part of who he is. He's seen more goodbyes than hellos. Phil wants a simple life, not a merely chaotic one. He's more a romantic than a realist. He's not impressed with fame and doesn't like the whole rock star shtick. Only, some other people seemed to enjoy it more than he.

"I went with him to visit his family in Allentown, and they were great to meet. His oldest sister, Emma, and younger one, Paula, were as crazy as him. A lot of fun! You could tell his parents were so happy to have the whole family home for Christmas. One night, before we went to sleep, he turned to me. It was just the two of us in the room. He got serious and said, 'I wish I were normal.' It was heartbreaking to hear him say those words. I had to reassure him, 'You are.' I think I had to hide my tears that night." Claire turns to Connie with a slight smile. "Anyway, Phil invited you, right?"

"Yeah." Connie looks down. "I don't know why?"

Claire responds with, "Phil does not like to be alone, especially on these European jaunts. He likes familiarity when he's out of the US. Normally, it would be with another man, in separate rooms. Not that he wouldn't visit them. He's always aware of the possibility he could be outed, and he tries to avoid it. I'll admit him with a girl is different, but he figures it's safe." She grins. "A lot of people think he and I got something going on the side. His manager, Barbara, thinks the same thing. Yeah. I have accompanied him to a few events here and there. That's what he wants if the cameras are around. I'll guess the same goes for you too."

Connie stares straight ahead, half-listening to Claire, and the other, to her thoughts.

Claire continues while putting out the rest of her cigarette.

"Well, let's enjoy the rest of the time we have here." A moment later, she asks, "Are you ready to see how a music video gets made?"

***

Afterward, Philip, Claire, and Connie converge at a studio on the set of a filming location for the creation of the "Object of Affection" music video. Philip leads the two ladies through various doorways.

Connie looks around.

"So this is where the magic happens we get to see later on something like MTV or *Night Flight*?"

Philip answers her with, "Yep. It's not all fun, though. A four-minute video can get stretched to nearly twenty hours of filming. These guys get picky."

"Twenty hours? I know you told me there was some time in between."

"Yeah. Patience is required. They do these things like mini movies. Of course, I've never experienced it being that long."

Connie turns to Claire. "Have you ever done a video?"

"Once," Claire smiles back. She leans in, quietly adding in, "He's a little dramatic with the time frame."

Connie mentions to Claire, "It'll be interesting to watch."

Philip walks by a few people. Claire is approached by somebody on the set, disappearing into the crowded space. Connie glances around at all the cameras on tripods and dollies. Several people surround her.

"Oh, I'm here to watch," Connie advises.

The crew surrounds her, gradually leading her away.

"Philip? Philip! I'm going to get you for this!"

A man walks up to the guitarist with a clipboard. Philip stops to see it's a consent form.

He asks Connie, "How do you spell Ayers?" Glancing in back, he blinks and shrugs, writing it down. "C. A-y-e-r-s. That should cover it."

The man says, "She's a little feisty."

"She'll get over it."

Philip continues to walk onto the set, where he finds the shaggy-haired British-born Scandinavian director, Zigmond 'Siggy' Dyuman.

"Philip, right?" Siggy asks.

"Yep."

"We'll go over everything as we did on the phone, this time in person. As you can see, we lucked out and got word about this place. A soon-to-be-made film will be taking place here. If not, I don't have to tell you about the cost. Yeah. Panned out where the place resembled the storyboards best. We got the cages all set. Extras are prepared. Now, you said you had Claire. We came to an understanding she would be the one with you at the end."

"Yeah. Um, I have two ladies with me. The other is my friend." Philip stops for a moment. "Well, she's with me too."

"OK. That'll be fine. She'll be with the other girls."

Philip nods back in agreement.

Siggy turns to his assistant. "Bring in the girls."

All of the extras are brought in representing various origins and ethnic backgrounds.

Philip turns to Siggy. "Looks more like a Rick James video." He laughs, turning to the director, who doesn't get it. When he glances back at the girls, there's one he recognizes right away. Connie gives him an icy stare with her green eyes. She's made up in far more makeup than he had ever seen on her. Philip can't turn away. He knows he's in trouble.

Connie looks down in defeat.

All of the women are put into cages in groups of various ethnic colors. A dark wall further away gets covered by churning smoke machines, making the room seem fuller than it is. The dungeon-like cells include metal bars put into painted foam and rubber to give a right look. On the floor is a track for the camera dolly's tracking shots. An Arriflex 35 IIC film camera is set up.

Philip looks at the script with Siggy, figuring out what changes need to be made, to heighten the excitement of the video. A woman dressed as a correctional officer makes her way onto the set. She walks over to Siggy. Wrapping her arms over his shoulders, she gives him a long kiss. Philip glances down, awkwardly at the affectionate display.

"We'll play that game later, Stephanie," Siggy says suggestively.

"Oh, that sounds good," she answers with flirtation before walking away.

Siggy looks back at Philip. "Bartered labor."

Philip gives a smile. "I can see that." He raises his brows. Pulling out a cigarette from his pocket, he looks for a lighter.

Siggy says, "Need to light your fag?"

"A what?" Philip answers in shock.

He looks at Siggy, who holds a lighter.

"Oh, sure." Philip leans in for the offer. Exhaling a puff, he gives a lopsided grin. "Back where I come from, we sometimes call them a ciggie."

In a delayed reaction, his eyes go wide. He quickly walks away.

Shortly afterward, filming begins as the countdown is called.

The introduction starts with Philip entering the darkened room. Stephanie, as the officer writes down something, then motions for him to follow her. They repeatedly retake the scene several times to make sure it's right. When Siggy is happy, they move on. A curtain of smoke obscures Philip's vision as he's led where the women are kept. Outstretched arms in various flesh tones reach outside the bars. Philip looks to the side where the cells are, pulling down his sunglasses. The smoke lifts, revealing a dozen women in each cell, dramatically looking, nearly climbing over each other like kittens waiting to be adopted. Some are pushed against the bars. Hands reach out again as he sings to them. One woman's hands reach the bottom of his jacket. Philip springs into action as the music continues by pulling out an object from the correctional officer's holster, revealing it to be a small handheld mirror. He shines it on the prisoner, who gets caught in the reflection and turns to stone. The other female prisoners take the opportunity to knock her down, shattering pieces of ceramic look-alike to the cell floor. Three takes are made with various camera angles, whereby they will be pieced together. Another woman in a different cell reaches her hand out. Philip takes hers, and before he knows it, hers turns to sand falling away. The other women look at the pile of sand in the center, undeterred at receiving his attention. He coyly sings the bridge to Stephanie, the officer, allowing her to believe she is the object of his affection. That is, until he comes across the dark-eyed brunette sitting on the floor. Claire stares up at him in dramatic fashion. Connie is behind her, looking up as well. Wearing the sunglasses, Philip smirks, with her reflection seen through them. The cell door opens. Philip and Claire walk arm in arm away from the camera, through the smoke.

Shots are filmed separately of Philip playing Caddy, or close-ups of the guitar, to later be interspersed with the storyline.

Hours later, once everything is complete, Philip talks to Siggy while holding a page consisting of script notes. All of the women walk by, leaving the studio. Claire walks by him, grazing her fingers over his shoulder and winks. Connie is the last to leave. She gives a sarcastic smile. Snatching the paper out of his hand, she rolls up the item and firmly slaps him on the shoulder with it. Handing it back, she walks away.

Philip watches her with one brow arched.

Connie looks at the small theater's awning, the famed letters of The Marquee Bar & Club. She carries Philip's guitar case containing Caddy. There is no doorman. Stepping inside, she checks her watch. Mickey's hands are on the six and twenty-five dots. Perfect! She's not late. Looking around, she says to the guitar, "Well, we're here, Caddy. You just have to wait for Daddy to arrive." Hardly a soul is in sight. She hears plucking of a bass nearby. Glancing at the stage, she sees a man setting up hardware for the hi-hat on the drum riser. She asks, "Excuse me, sir?"

The young gentleman turns to her, seeing the guitar case in her hand. "Yes?"

"I don't know who I'm supposed to talk with, but um, I'm here to drop off Mr. Reinhardt's guitar?"

He squints his eyes, not quite believing her, "What kind it be?"

Connie is a little taken back at his questioning. She answers matter-of-factly. "It's a nineteen sixty Fender Stratocaster originally Shell Pink. He had it custom painted Cadillac Pink in nineteen seventy just before joining Deacon's Alley."

The stagehand's mouth opens.

Connie stares at him. "He needs to get her refretted, but doesn't know when that'll happen."

"Uh. That'll be fine. Just give her over here, and we'll hook it up."

Connie smiles back. "Thanks."

He watches her walk away. "Eh, yeah." Shaking his head, the man continues to set up.

People begin to line up outside. Connie overhears someone say that things are looking pretty good out there. A doorman is dispatched immediately to take money from eager fans. Several people walk in, taking their place directly in front of the stage. Mitch comes through. Connie recognizes him.

"Mitch!"

He hears his name but doesn't know from where.

"Mitch!" Again, he's called.

Walking over, he notices Connie waving to him.

"Hey, Connie."

"Where is everybody?"

"I just got here. Nobody else has shown up yet?"

"No."

"I'm sure they'll all be here really soon. It's crazy outside. There's a line that stretches out from the ticket window, all the way down the street." He checks the time. Putting a hand on Connie's shoulder, he says, "Listen, I'd love to stand around and chat, but I have to check on some of the important aspects of this gig. I'm sure Phil will love how many people are coming. I'll talk to you later."

"OK," Connie says with understanding.

Mitch hops onto the black stage, overlooking the drum kit on a small riser. He asks a stagehand where the backstage area is. A finger points to the left side of the large yellow Marquee sign on the wall. Mitch opens the door. "Oh shit." He closes it immediately. Rushing off the stage, he looks around and spots Connie. "Connie! Connie!"

She turns around, surprised at the immediacy of the drummer's calling.

"What?"

Mitch says, "I know Phil rarely is ever in a bad mood, but this time I think he's not going to be happy with something." He takes her hand, leading her up on stage. Opening the door to the dressing room, Mitch gives her an acknowledged glance of I-told-you-so.

Connie's jaw drops.

"That's why." He answers, closing the door again.

Mitch leads her off the stage. "Hey, did you bring Caddy?"

Connie nods back immediately. "Yeah. She's next to the riser. That was the first thing I did after getting here."

Mitch looks around. "Good. Maybe that'll soften him up a little." He then goes back up to check on the drums and placement of microphones.

Connie continues to watch the crowd. Glancing around as she had done before meeting up with Mitch, her eyes fall upon more people dressed casually. The club becomes packed. Music pours out of the speakers. Attendees walk away from the bar, carrying drinks to their designated section of the room. Somebody taps Connie on the shoulder. She turns around quickly to see Shelley and Walter. She greets them like old friends.

"Hi!" She lights up with a smile. "You made it!"

Shelley answers first. "Oh, we wouldn't miss it for the world!"

"We're very excited!" Walter mentions.

Connie looks at Shelley. "He speaks!"

"Why, yes!" Shelley giggles back. "Oh, I know that bit of excitement got him to shut off. Luckily, he's back. Is Phil excited about playing?"

Connie looks around. "I haven't seen him all day. He was out of the hotel before I ever woke up."

Mitch walks up to Connie. "They just got here. Back entrance." He smiles. "Get ready." He then disappears into the crowd.

Connie tells the couple. "He's here now."

Shelley says, "We thought if you had time after the show, we could grab a pint. Not here, of course."

Before Connie can say anything, Walter adds in, "I promise I won't be gobsmacked."

Connie thinks for a moment. Philip hates beer. Awkwardly, she says, "Philip's not a beer drinker."

Shelley laughs back, "Oh, well, neither am I! I'm a gin and tonic girl myself!"

Walter says over her shoulder, "I'm a scotch!"

The two of them laugh, putting Connie at ease. They continue to talk.

Philip, wearing a long, dark coat, holds a large duffle bag, making his way past the back entrance, looking a little more rugged than usual. Claire, in a long beige coat, holds a dry cleaning bag slung over her shoulder. Perry, followed by Tim come in directly after them. Someone from the club leads a guiding hand to the backstage dressing room, opening the door for them.

Philip's jaw drops slightly.

Over his shoulder, Claire utters, "Holy shit."

Perry and Tim look on in a state of shock.

Philip answers a matter-of-factly, "Yep. Don't let anything touch the floor."

They walk inside the small, graffiti-covered room. Graffiti on the half vaulted ceiling. Graffiti on the room-sized bench. Perry pulls up his jacket over his nose from the stench of liquor, sweat, stale cigarettes, and funky odors of a dubious nature.

A man from the club comes up from behind.

"Will you be OK?" he asks.

Philip continues to look around the room, wondering where to put his belongings. He says, "Uh, yeah. Got a fold-up chair?"

"I don't know. If there are any chairs, they'd be upstairs in an office."

"OK. That'll do." Philip smiles back.

"I can't simply go and get one for the band and bring down here. The boss would kill me."

Philip says, "I'll pay for your burial."

Perry snickers.

Out in the main room, Connie continues to carry on her conversation with Shelley and Walter.

"Today's the last day before we fly back to the states."

Walter looks at the club floor, which is becoming packed by the minute. He tells Shelley, "Darling, we should think of trying to grab a spot. I don't know if they'd be willing to make room?"

Connie thinks for a minute, noticing the couple wants to get going and move to the next room. "Shelley, can I ask you a question?"

"Yes, dear? What is it?"

Connie hesitates at first. "Um, when you said that phrase at the Hard Rock on Saturday? What was it? Ass over...?"

Shelley corrects her. "Arse over elbow?"

Walter says to Shelley, "Darling, you need to speak American. They don't know the expression." He turns to Connie. "Head over heels."

Connie nods back. "Yeah. Head over heels. How did you come up with that? I just never...," She wants to tell Shelley she's wrong. There is nothing between her and the rocker. That would seem weird, though. He brought her along with him on the trip. They shared a room. They were strictly platonic.

"Dear, it's obvious the way he looks at you. The way he includes you in the chit-chat. You may not see it yourself, but others can. I know the feeling because Walter has done it to me many times."

Walter looks at Shelley with fondness. Connie watches them.

He says, "Sometimes she picks up on it, and sometimes she doesn't."

Shelley tells Connie, "You make a darling pair." Peeking out of the room, she checks to see what the club floor is like at this point. "Speaking of darling..., darling, we must be going now. I don't know where we'll go. Hopefully, nobody too tall in our way. We'll see you later, Connie. Our offer still stands. Bye."

Connie watches them walk into the other room. "Bye." She then wonders what the night holds for her while thinking of what the couple had told her.

Philip and the band start to get ready. Claire places her garment bag on the hook. She looks at the bench, and then the chair Philip had been given. Perry and Tim quickly get ready. Philip looks at Claire, who remains reluctant while the other two sit on it.

"Hey, you're welcome to sit on that thing. I'm not." He pulls up the collar of his black button-up short sleeve satin shirt under the black leather fringed jacket. Philip then quips, "Nothing a little bleach can't fix."

Mitch comes back to join the rest of the band, tapping out paradiddles on his knee.

Perry glances at him. "Hey, look who decided to come back."

Philip says, "Not enough room in here now. Where were you?"

"At the bar. I had a soda. I needed to replenish my energy. Plus, I had to spy on how it is out there."

Tim asks, "So? How is it out there?"

"Packed!" Mitch answers excitedly, flipping a drum stick.

Claire turns around to see how Philip has his look. Her eyes scale him from head to toe.

"Wow. You definitely look good. I mean really good. Is that the outfit you were talking about that you got when we were in San Fran?"

"Yeah," he answers with a proud grin. "I showed it to Barb."

"And?"

"And? She called me, Lady Killer."

"That about sums it up." Looking back at what she can see of the crowd, Claire informs the rest of her bandmates, "I need to get ready."

Tim says, "There's enough room."

"I am not changing in front of you guys." Claire snatches the garment bag off the hook. "Where's that bathroom?"

She walks out.

Philip checks his boots, tying the laces when the club's soundman comes by.

"Do you want me to check monitors on the guitar?"

"Yeah." Philip answers while tying one of his bootlaces. He looks back up. "Wait. Did you get her?"

"There was a good-looking bird that dropped 'er off." The soundman replies.

"I've only had her for fourteen years." Philip answers in a puzzled tone.

The soundman furrows his brows in confusion.

Philip says back to the man, "The guitar. I was kidding you." He finishes up with his boots, standing back up.

The soundman continues, "The bird knew everything about the guitar. She knew the year. When you had it custom painted. She even started talking about refretting."

Philip nods back in acknowledgment.

"I'll check monitors," the man answers, then leaves.

Smirking with satisfaction, Philip quietly says to himself, "Atta girl."

People pack into the already crowded club. Two young men attired in flannel approach Connie with beers in hand. One, a blond, puts his arm around Connie's shoulder.

"Hey, wanna watch the show with me? Then we'll hang out after and see where it takes us."

Connie pulls his arm away from her shoulder. "Not interested."

"I don't see anybody claiming a fine bird, like yourself." He says in a suavely macho tone.

"This bird is flying." She walks away.

Right at that moment, she hears the strumming of a guitar, and it's not just any guitar. It's the chiming bright tone of a Fender Stratocaster. Alerted by the sound, Connie looks at the stage, seeing a soundman check the monitors. He tests an effects peddle, stepping on it to make the sound swell. Grabbing a cable, the man takes out one, exchanging it for another, connecting it into Caddy's jack. He retunes, checks the lead cable and strums again.

Audience members pay attention, knowing it's getting closer to showtime.

Backstage, Claire comes back wearing a strappy slinky red metallic dress. She slips on long fingerless black mesh gloves. "I don't know which is worse, that bathroom or the dressing room?" Grabbing an item out of a shopping bag, Claire puts on a long velvet-like purple cape, attaching it to the straps of her dress. She gets Philip's attention. "Now, I look as pretty as you."

He grins.

She sticks out her tongue.

A man from the club stops by the dressing room, giving everybody notice.

"You're on in five."

Philip nods back, putting his hand out. "OK." He mouths back. While primping his hair for last-minute adjustments, Claire walks up to him with a small shopping bag in hand.

"Hey, not so fast, Mr. Reinhardt. I got something perfect for the occasion." She places a long Union Jack flag scarf over his neck, careful not to touch his hair. He looks down at it as she adjusts a loose knot in front. "Now, you're ready. Gotta show that you're one of them."

Philip turns to the rest of the band, and asks, "Are we in agreement over the setlist?"

Perry answers back quickly, "Yeah."

A club representative asks, "Ready? You're on."

Philip answers readily, "Yep." He turns to the band. "Let's rock and roll."

Mitch comes out first, followed by Tim, and Perry, who hands the club announcer a note. Claire waves to the audience with cheers, and some wolf calls from the people gathered in front as the stage goes dark. Philip comes out last to a roar of approval. Picking up Caddy, he plugs her in, slipping on the guitar strap and waits for his introduction by a club representative, who looks at the note.

"From the east coast with the most, will you please give a round of applause and a warm welcome to Phil not-related-to-Django Reinhardt!!"

The stage lights turn on, while the audience cheers.

Philip lets out a laugh, pointing to Perry on bass. A crescendo on the cymbals follows the bass lines, before the count-off on drum sticks. "two...three...four!"

The band kicks into "Object of Affection." Claire sways in a slinky motion behind the keyboards. Several audience members move to her beat.

Philip comes into full view, causing some fans to look on in shock and confusion. Whispers abound, and some talk out loud in back, over the song. Connie hears somebody say, "Oh my God!" She stands on her tippy-toes, trying to get a view from beyond the mountain of shoulders in the way. The audience tightens up, making things tough for those in back. Several guys hold up their beer bottles in rejoice of the music they witness on stage. Connie attempts to squeeze past a few groups, but pulls back when things get too rough.

Once the song finishes, Philip makes some small talk with the audience.

"Yeah! We just did a video for that one last night, so be sure to keep your eyes peeled for that one on MTV."

Somebody shouts something to him.

"What? Huh! I stand corrected. BBC." He laughs back, "Got to remember where I am!" Looking back at the band, he says, "We're gonna take you back…,"

Perry says something that makes Philip shake his head.

"Like I was saying before, we're going to take you back to the velvet-wearing, jet-setting, free-loving ways of the seventies.

Perry yells out, "For some!"

Philip laughs back, "For some. This is a little song called 'First Time Lady.' True story. I won't elaborate."

The band gets into high gear, with the audience clapping along. Connie makes another attempt at moving closer to the stage. It's not until at least four more songs she makes progress. There would be no way she could find Shelley and Walter. Who knew where they were among a sea of four hundred fans packed in tightly? When edging in, she overhears two women say how surprised they are at how he looks compared to the latest album cover. More curious, Connie becomes determined to see what people are talking about. It gets hot among the crowd, and in some places, a little too unbearable as arms wave up in the air. The closer she gets, her eyes focus on the parting shoulders, allowing her through as she shouts out, "Excuse me?" Finally, she gets close enough to see what the chatter has been about. She gives a long, hard stare. It was Philip Reinhardt. Or was it? He didn't look anything like the guy she had met in April at the corner of the San-San building. Gone were the trendy suit jackets, T-shirts, button-ups, and three-tones of blond. They were all replaced by an unrecognizable volume of bronze collar-length hair, partly hidden under the collar of a black leather fringed jacket, tight-as-can-be black leather pants, and a pair of black lace-up boots. The soft features of his face she had grown used to, took on a slightly rougher appearance, including a slight five o'clock shadow. All of the black apparel had been off-set by a red, white, and blue Union Jack scarf, and that Cadillac pink Stratocaster. Connie shakes her head, trying to make sense of it all.

Then he gives a big smile that Connie recognizes immediately. It makes her watch intently. The audience cheers him on, and he basks in the glory of their love and appreciation. It's a feeling he had not experienced for some years. Philip goes over to Claire at the keyboards, playing the chords while she takes on the keys. Flashbulbs pop in the middle of their performance. He pulls at a button of his damp shirt under the scarf. The heavy volume of hair becomes more wilted as time goes on. Claire sashays with her cape in a wagging motion alongside the guitarist's movements. Philip says something to her while she plays. Claire nods back.

Philip goes back to the front microphone and says, "And here we showcase the lovely Claire."

Perry turns to him.

Philip turns back to the microphone. "And the lovely Perry." He laughs.

They launch into Sly and the Family Stone's "Dance To The Music," followed by "Thank You (Falettinme Be Mice Elf Agin)." Philip is only too happy to play sideman to catch his breath and dry off, while the keyboardist and bassist take over for the time being. The audience eats it up, becoming hyper. Claire finishes up with her showcase piece of the B-52s "Planet Claire."

Getting his second wind, Philip comes on even stronger to the audience. He runs from one end of the small stage to the other, garnering attention from both sides at any given time. Philip twirls, holding Caddy like a dance partner. He pulls out the pair of Ray-Bans, putting them on and steps close to the edge of the stage, egging those with cameras to shoot. He pulls them off immediately after, seeing as though he can't view too much between the extreme contrast of the dark club and a super bright light shining on him. In his peripheral vision, one person grabs his attention among the flailing hands and moving bodies. Connie stands in awe. Suddenly, he turns back to one side of the stage, and runs up an onstage monitor, ricocheting off of it to the crowd's sheer delight as they cheer. Connie takes a step back, startled by his burst of energy, but heavily attracted to his passion for playing. She never saw him like that, and it was doing something to her. Philip goes over to the far left side of the stage, teasing a bunch of ladies gathered below. Their jaws become agape as he flashes them a big smile, raising his brows in a charming manner.

One woman flutters her hands in fast motion, trying to catch her breath.

"Oh my God! He's such a doll!"

Connie tries to peek over from where she stands.

Philip returns to the middle of the stage, calling out into the microphone, "Remember when?" He snaps his fingers with a sea of finger snaps from the audience.

Connie looks around, joining in snapping her fingers.

By then, the band kicks into high gear with "The Afterglow."

Connie overhears two women next to her talking about Philip and the album cover. She steps up to the front of the stage, watching Philip in a trance-like state, shutting herself off from everything except him.

In the middle of the song, Philip goes into a solo worthy of any rivaling moment seen at the club. Picking up Caddy with raised shoulders, and fingers on the fretboard, Philip puts himself behind the guitar. He gives a long glance to the center of the audience until there is the connection he was in search of. Arched as though he's about to reach for the bottom fret, his brown-eyed stare directly matches against Connie's green-eyed trance. Both lock into vision on each other as if under a spell. Philip throws a hand up, signifying a finishing move with the chord singing on its own. He closes his eyes, and pulls back immediately, joining in with the rest of his band.

Connie feels a hard thud inside her body, making her motion to step back, as though drunk. She becomes engulfed within the sea of hands outstretched in the air and hungry cheers for rock and roll guitar solos. Her heart gives powerful blows to the inner cavity of her chest wall, much like a boxer strikes an opponent. A heated surge of electricity courses through her body. Catching her breath, she wonders if it's the onset of a heart attack or fainting spell. The thudding is foreign to her senses. She looks up at the stage, beyond a few fans ahead. Her heart races while attempting to watch him. Pushing her hair back in front, Connie glances down at the dark floor. It hits her that she's not in danger of a medical episode. She shakes her head, uttering, "No. No. Connie, calm down. Don't do this to yourself. Remember." Taking a deep breath, she looks at the other members of the band. That is, anybody but the lead guitar player.

After the song finishes, Philip pulls off his jacket, much to the audience's approval. He frees another button from his shirt underneath the scarf. Starting a song called, 'East-Western Boulevard' from his days with Deacon's Alley, Philip launches into a guitar intro accompanied by the assistance of a delay pedal. The sound creates a double and sometimes triple effect, leaving the crowd in awe. He plays Caddy behind the back of his head, expertly knowing every chord.

Several guys jaws drop in wonder, as they try to keep up with him while playing air guitar.

A young man in the front says an emphatic, "Bloody hell!"

Philip goes up to Tim, telling him, "Cover for me. I'm gonna need to wrap myself in about a dozen heated towels and soak in Lysol for a few days after this."

Tim nods and laughs.

Philip signals the band to takes things down low. Perry follows his lead with sporadic bass notes.

Dropping to his knees, Philip wrings out the chords on Caddy in dramatic fashion. The audience eats it up, yelling and cheering, clapping in unison to an almost invisible beat. Letting himself go limp, Philip lands against the stage's floor, still playing. He breathes hard from moving around so much and the hot lights. Fans in front watch in shock, tapping their hands against the edge. It's a floor filled with history from famous footprints, and sweat, among gifts of nature. On his back, Philip continues to do a mixed bag of showy guitar maneuvers including, double-stop bends, pinch harmonics, palm muting, ghost notes, volume swells, and whammy bar dive-bombs. The guys watching in front of the stage rejoice in unison over the testosterone-laden display of musical hot-rodding. Fists ball up, punching the air, egging Philip on his showcase. Connie watches from a safe distance at the lead guitarist's insane antics. She shakes her head in the sense of awe.

Philip dislodges himself from the floor's hold, getting back up without missing a beat. The audience continues to cheer. Once he finishes up the song, he does one more to keep the fans going. Philip then announces all of the band.

"On rhythm guitar is Tim Grann. Perry Leonard on bass. Mitch Evans on drums. And I'm saving the best for last. The lovely Miss Claire Bennett on keyboards!" He follows the finale with a hearty though rough-voiced, "Thank you!" The band takes their bows to rapturous applause before exiting the stage.

All of about ten minutes later, Philip hangs out at the bar in back, making small talk with patrons, giving them road stories, and signing things. Mitch comes up from behind him, handing over a towel. The band leader puts the item over his shoulders, adjusting the scarf over his half-buttoned shirt. The audience disperses into the night, fulfilled from a worthy showcase of talent. Philip gets his picture taken with a couple of girls. He holds them tight, giving a sly smile to the camera. Again, he chats with various people.

Connie checks the time on her watch while walking in the direction of the bar. She stops when she sees Philip holding court and instead quickly turns in the opposite direction. Closing her eyes, she begins to head back towards the stage.

"Hey, Connie!" a voice calls out that is familiar.

Tim smiles, catching up with her. "How did you like the show?" he asks cheerfully.

Philip walks back towards the dressing room with someone from the club in tow. Mitch joins them minutes later.

Connie manages to see him walk away.

"Oh, it was great! The audience really ate it up!" she answers.

Tim asks, "Really?"

"Yeah!" Connie says, excitedly.

"Be honest. Phil was the great one. We're there to back him up. He's the name." Tim grins back.

Connie is left speechless as Tim walks over to the bar. She says to herself, "He definitely was great."

After nearly a half an hour, the club clears out. Only a few stragglers hang around at the bar, talking with the manager, and an assistant. The sound crew is busy pulling apart cables and disassembling the drum kit and riser.

Backstage, Tim and Perry finish getting ready. Claire puts her cape back under plastic. Philip sits on the chair, while a wound-up Mitch taps a beat on his knees with the drum sticks.

He says, "Hey, wanna go check out The Wag?"

Claire asks, "What's The Wag?"

Philip puts a hand to his head, ruffling his hair. "It's another club."

Tim adds in, "Yeah. It's not that far from here. Listen, if you can walk some fifty blocks to wherever in Manhattan, then this is a piece of cake!"

Philip makes a face showing his uncertainty. He shakes his hand in a lukewarm fashion, indicating 'maybe.'

"OK. I'm going to leave now and check it out. I'll see you guys later," Mitch tells them.

"We're going too," Perry says, pointing to himself and Tim. "Enjoy your time in this rat hole of a room!"

Philip and Claire are the only ones left. She finishes placing items in a bag. Taking down the cape covered in plastic, she looks back at Philip, who remains quiet. "You gonna be alright?"

"Yeah," he nods back.

With certainty, she states, "You were hot tonight."

Philip grins back, "I know I am."

Claire shakes her head at his quick-witted response.

Connie looks at the empty black stage and the door necessary for her to walk through. She closes her eyes, bracing herself for what is to come. Taking a deep breath, Connie steps up onto the stage and goes over to the dressing room tucked away in the back. She stops when she overhears Claire. She thinks of what to say. How to act? The look probably meant nothing to him, but it struck her hard. Now she was left to face the music.

Claire walks out, then notices Connie outside the door. She smiles at her, leaving with the bag and plastic covered cape over her shoulder.

Connie slowly steps inside the dressing room, ignoring the dingy, graffiti-riddled atmosphere. There she finds Philip, leaning back on the chair, legs splayed out. Closing his eyes, he loosens the scarf a little more. The door creaks ever so slightly, placing him on alert. He turns his head.

"Hey," he says in a pleased tone. Sitting up, he puts his hand out, wanting her to take it for a grasp or even merely a touch of comfort. Connie doesn't reciprocate. He pulls his hand away, noticing her distance. "How ya doin'?"

"Fine," she answers with her head bowed down, not wanting to even look at him.

"Heard you did well when bringing Caddy here," Philip answers, impressed with raised brows.

"Yeah," Connie finally looks up, not wanting to be too obvious. She can't help notice how incredible he looks. So many factors of his transformation to a rocker. The idea he took on a slightly scruffy appearance. His hair in that wilted state from an hour and a half of playing his heart out, raw energy which was thrilling and utterly amazing for her to watch. The fact his shirt was unbuttoned entirely underneath the scarf, partly displaying a slender physique. It didn't help her nerves. If it wasn't the bare flesh that stripped her of confidence, it had to be the incredibly soulful brown eyes that bored straight into her heart. She was terrified, that with his keen sense he could tell of her trepidation, which had never before existed between them.

Philip's creeping mischievous grin appears as he asks, "What's up, Connie? You look like you've got something on your mind."

Connie turns away from him abruptly to collect her thoughts. Her eyes meeting the dark floor.

He arches over, holding his hands together out of comfort. "I figured we would be able to talk about anything by now."

She swiftly turns back to him.

"I think it's time I changed rooms. I know it's the last night. Um, hopefully, Claire won't mind the company."

Philip rocks back and forth in a nodding fashion. Taking a breath, he tilts his head at an angle, "OK." He answers in his charming, non-combative way.

Looking at him in a manner that she hopes will not hurt him, she attempts a faint though guilty smile. Turning back, she exits the room quickly, leaving him alone.

Philip glances down at the floor, tight-lipped and raising his brows. He turns his eyes towards the doorway. Straightening his posture, he mulls things over. Seductively biting his bottom lip, he points his finger at the entranceway, mouthing the word, "Gotcha."

***

Shortly after, Connie returns to the hotel. She packs everything in her bags and suitcase, leaving the extra key on the bureau. Heading over to the other room, where Claire had been staying, she unlocks the door. Stepping inside, she drops her belongings in a corner. Walking over to the door, Connie closes it with her whole body. Taking a long breath, she looks up at the ceiling. Holding a hand over her throbbing chest, she tells herself, "I'm in trouble." The tears start to flow. "No. No. No. I can't. I just can't." A feeling overtakes her body. She then realizes her heart has betrayed her.

***

Following their performance at the Marquee Club, Perry, Mitch, and Tim reconvene a few blocks away at The Wag. Philip and Claire arrive. They walk inside, where it's packed with patrons of all types. David Bowie's version of "Criminal World" is heard through the speakers. People move to the rhythm of the music. Fans who had been at the Marquee, choose to hang out here as well. Several people congratulate Philip on an excellent performance. Others ask for autographs, which he's content to sign. Tim talks to somebody at the bar while ordering drinks. Mitch goes over to some girls standing around towards the back. Perry watches some entertainment. Claire goes to the bar, ordering a drink, then rejoins Philip.

"Nice place, huh?" She takes a sip of her drink.

Philip has his head turned away from her as he answers quickly, "Yeah."

"Aren't you going to order a drink?" she asks him, puzzled.

"Nah. I don't feel like it," Philip answers, looking around.

Taking another sip, Claire says, "Phil, you've been acting strange lately. Ever since we did the gig tonight, it's like your head is somewhere else. I don't know where that is."

Two young women sashay their way over to Philip, wanting to dance with him. Claire watches him shake his head.

Culture Club's "Church of the Poison Mind" gets people to dance. Several patrons whoop and holler above the crowd. Young, rowdy revelers step directly in front of the uninterested Philip, who walks around them. Claire goes to follow him.

"Phil? Phil? What is...? You just passed up dancing with those two ladies. You don't usually do that. You're the life of the party." Getting serious, she winces, trying to look into his eyes. "Wait. The way you're acting. I've seen that look before."

"What look would that be?"

"When you were with particular people."

Philip takes a deep breath, glancing down.

Claire stares at him, coming to a realization. "You're in love."

He looks away at the mention of her guess.

"I don't know when it happened, but you've had that distracted look on and off since we came here to London. I'm guessing it occurred right before then." Claire shakes her head. "Phil, when will you learn? How many times does your heart have to get beaten up repeatedly? I'm not suggesting for you to give up on love. Maybe be a little more careful in who you give it to? You're very intuitive, but then again..., Well, you go too soft, and get trampled on. Does this one know what you do? Is he aware of how guarded you are?"

Philip's eyes meet the floor. He digs in his pockets for an item. Fishing out his sunglasses, he puts them on. "Let the guys know I'm going back to the hotel. I'll pick up Caddy on my way."

Claire asks, puzzled, "What should I tell everybody else?"

As Philip begins to walk away, he turns around in a twirl. "Tell them you know everything." He answers with a put-on smile, along with a wave of his hand in dramatic fashion. Turning back in an exaggerated feminine manner, he sashays to the exit. Philip opens the door, pulls off the sunglasses and leaves, walking out in his usual masculine yet determined gait. He blends back in with the nightlife of Wardour Street.

A half an hour later, he arrives back at the hotel with a duffle bag and guitar case in hand. He stops at Claire's door. Glancing down for a moment, he takes a swallow and glances at the black rubber bracelet on his wrist before moving on and pulling out a key. Stepping into the darkened room, he puts on the lamp, drops the bag on the floor, and places the guitar case on a chair. He spots the extra key on the bureau, then walks back to the front of the room. Placing his hand against the door, with head bowed down, Philip closes his eyes.

An empty room.

No companionship.

A full heart that cannot keep secrets any longer.

At Heathrow Airport, people mill about, either arriving or leaving. Philip stands, overlooking the windowed wall of glass at Terminal 2. Claire steps over to him.

"She knew this could happen." Placing a hand on his shoulder, Claire briefly looks out with him.

Further away, Connie crosses her arms, staring motionless out the same window. It would be great if she could admit her time in London was amazing. Yet, her thoughts are relentless. The betrayal of her heart. Shame in feeling that she crossed the line. Embarrassment if she were to even look at him

Connie closes her eyes in the defeat of her thoughts.

Claire leans toward Philip. "She likes to sleep on the floor."

He swings his eyes to her.

Glancing over at Connie, Claire shakes her head and walks back to join the other bandmates.

Philip bows his head down in thought, before realizing he needs to do something. Looking back up, he has Connie in his sights. He starts to walk towards her.

Over the loudspeaker comes a voice who announces a plane number.

Philip stops, realizing their flight is ready.

Perry and Tim meet up with him. Perry says, "Ready, Boss?"

On the plane, everybody takes a seat. Philip sits with Perry, while Claire and Connie are across the aisle. Tim and Mitch are seated in the back of Philip and Perry.

A half an hour into their flight, Claire finds Connie's carry-on bag. Pulling it over, she picks out a small book.

"There it is!" She waves it in front of an uninterested Connie. "I knew I saw it on the dresser before we took off. It's called *Brit Speak*. OK. Guys, we're going to play a little game. Guess what the British term means in American."

Mitch leans over. "I'll bite! Go for it."

Claire says, "OK. The first word is aggro."

"Aggro? What kind of word is that?"

Claire looks back at Mitch defiantly. "You said you wanted to play."

"OK. OK. Aggro? A growing thing. I don't know."

"Nope. It's short for aggravation. No points for you, Mitch. Next one, anybody's guess. Bespoke."

Perry answers quickly. "I think I've heard of this one before. That would mean, custom made. You hear it a lot when they talk about the tailoring of suits."

Claire raises her brows, looking at the answer. "You would be correct. One point for Perry. How about this one. Bite your arm off."

Mitch looks on puzzled, "What? Bite your arm off? That sounds a bit hostile."

Claire lets out a laugh, "None of you will ever get this one. It means someone who is over excited to get something."

Philip looks over and states, "How romantic."

Mitch turns to Perry. "Excited? What? Maybe if it's applied to a film by Wes Craven or John Carpenter. I could see that. Other than them, no, it's not something I would want to use unless I wanted somebody to run in the opposite direction."

Claire says, "OK. Here's another one. Dog's bollocks."

Perry furrows his brows, "Sounds obscene."

"Well..." Claire hesitates. "The answer would be something fantastic."

Mitch shakes his head in confusion, "What the hell? What kind of warped language..., Come on. You're making these up!"

"No, I'm not!" Claire insists.

"Pick something not so...weird."

"Party pooper. Killjoy. That's you, Mitch." Claire rolls her eyes. "OK. Gobsmacked."

"Oh! I've got this one!" Perry says. "Amazed!"

"Two points for Perry!" Claire announces. "Alright, gentlemen, how about this one? Her Majesty's pleasure."

Philip says, "What you find in Times Square."

Claire lets out a laugh. "Phil, that's not it, but thank you for playing. Anybody else wants to take a jab at this one?" She looks around. "No? The answer would be, put in jail without a release date."

"I liked my answer better," Philip says with a smirk.

"OK. Wiseguy. Try this one. Pardon me."

"Excuse me." Philip shrugs, unable to think of any other conceivable answer.

"No. It's what you say after a fart."

All four guys burst out laughing.

Tim asks, "That's for real?"

Claire nods her head, "Yep." She turns to a random page. "OK. Snog."

"That's easy!" Perry answers back. "Kiss!"

Philip asks him, "Just how many times have you been to London?"

"I pay attention to things. Plus, you're not the only one I've played for. I've been here a few times."

"Uh-huh. I see."

"Three points for Perry. You guys are falling behind very quickly. The three of you are still at zero each." Flipping back pages, Claire announces, "I'm going to go back towards the beginning of the alphabet. Oh, here's a fun one. Arse over elbow.

Connie stares out the window at the clouded carpet in the sky.

"Head over heels," she answers without a glance towards the others.

Mitch is quick to notice her answer.

"Of course she knows. She bought the book."

"Someone told me...," Connie slowly turns her head to face everybody else. "...earlier in our trip."

Claire looks at Philip with curiosity.

She answers, "That would be correct. We now have Perry with three points and Connie with one. Um, OK. We'll go back to the letter S. We have shag."

Philip raises a finger, "Sex."

Perry shakes his head, "I guess you've paid attention too."

Philip grins back, "Fast learner."

Claire raises her brows, "Alright. We've got Perry with three points, followed by one point each for Phil and Connie. Let's see who gets the next one. Chuffed."

Connie says, "Pleased."

Philip thinks for a minute. "That sounds familiar."

"You weren't paying attention when I brought it up." Connie glances out the window again. Thinking about something, she gets up. "Excuse me." Leaving the aisle, Claire lets her through. Connie walks away with all eyes on her.

Claire looks directly at Philip. "She's pissed off at you."

Perry glances at the guitarist. "Did I miss something?"

Several hours pass. Philip looks out the window at clouds. He turns to see Perry is asleep, as well as Claire and Connie across from them. His attention turns to Connie, who, even in sleep, looks pained. He knows something is deeply on her mind, but she won't say what it is.

Eventually, he gives into rest.

At night, the plane lands at JFK Airport. Everybody is happy to be back on the ground. Mitch lets out a yawn, looking out at the vastness of the airport's pick-up area. A fleet of New York cabs parks in a line, awaiting eager travelers.

"Home sweet home. All I want to do is get back to Jersey and sleep in my own bed!" the drummer exclaims.

Tim drags himself and his guitar case over to the next available cab, walking by Mitch. "If Registry tries to call me until Wednesday, I'm not answering it. Let somebody else get a paycheck. Feed the damn cats, water the plants, and decompress. That's all. I'm out of here. I will see you, ladies and gentlemen, at no particular time. Goodnight. Goodbye." He waves to the crew, then gets whisked away.

Mitch watches the cab disappear. "Huh. Well. I know how he feels. Phil, if you need me, I'm your man! Hey, I'm not going to turn down a session, even if it were tomorrow. Need the money." He walks over to an awaiting cab, placing his luggage in the trunk. Shutting it, he says, "It's been fun. London was a real trip! Gotta do that again sometime! Connie, you were great company. Hope to see you again soon."

Connie bows her head down with a smile of recognition.

"You too, Mitch."

Mitch announces with a wave, "Au revoir!"

Another cab leaves the pick-up area.

Claire steps out of the doorway with two suitcases. She notices Philip and Connie standing far apart.

"Baggage nearly lost the suitcase carrying my cape. I had to wait around until they found it. Perry's still inside. He said he was going to look for some food. Probably snacks or something." She rushes over to a cab, dragging over the luggage to the back. The driver helps her out, placing both suitcases in. All the while, she continues to address Philip. "I have to get as much rest as I can because I've got to catch a red-eye to LA tomorrow night. I forgot to tell you, since her name came up earlier this week. Frankie wants me to do sessions. I promised her I'd do them right after London. So, I'm going to keep to it."

Philip asks, "Frankie James?"

"Yeah. Frankie thought I would be a perfect fit for the sessions. Then, I think we're heading over to the Twin Cities. Wouldn't it be something if I ran into Lisa Coleman? That would be a hoot! Nobody could say we were one and the same if that happened. Who knows, maybe I might bump into Prince himself! He hangs out plenty at First Avenue. If that happens, I'll get you one of his garter belts."

"Uh, yeah. Thanks, Claire." Philip shakes his head with a grin.

She walks over, planting a kiss to his cheek. "I'll see you in a few weeks. Don't get into too much trouble without me."

Philip grins back, mischievously, "Just promise me you won't go to Tom Jones' garage sale."

Claire lets out a laugh. She approaches Connie. "You were a lot of fun. I'm going to give you my card. It's the one I use for Registry, but all my information is on there. If you ever want to hang out, just call me. OK?" Connie nods back. Quickly, Claire gives her a hug and whispers, "There's plenty of fish in the sea." She smiles at her. "Take care."

Connie says, "I will. Thanks. For everything."

Claire winks at her. "You'll do fine." She gives Philip one more glance. "See you later, Phil." She gets in the cab, and just like her other bandmates, disappears into the night.

Perry strides out, holding a small package. He douses the contents into his mouth in one move. After chewing, he looks at Philip and Connie watching him. "Sorry about that. I got really hungry. Airplane food won't do it for me, so I had to search for something. I originally wanted a salad, but there was nothing. Instead, I got some trail mix. Raisins are the greatest pick-me-up snack, nuts too. The best!" He looks around. "Where did everybody go?"

Philip says, "They left already."

Perry walks from one side of the glass enclosure to the other. "Claire's going off to LA tomorrow. Oh, shit. No taxi's left?" He wanders away, leaving Philip and Connie alone.

Connie gets startled by a tremendous booming noise heading closer. The sound grows more volatile. Suddenly, a jet zooms overhead, with only four bright afterburners glowing in the night sky, dashing out of sight in only seconds. "Holy Jesus! What was that?"

Philip looks up. "Concorde."

"That was?" Connie answers in wide-eyed shock. She shakes her head. "I've heard them before, but never that close." Gathering her thoughts, Connie goes back to being reticent with Philip.

Philip glances around at the arriving and departing traffic while taking a deep breath. "So, what did you think?"

"Of London?

"Yep," Philip nods back tight-lipped.

"It was fine," Connie answers. The traffic distracts her. "I need to get going now. It's getting late." She reveals while scanning for a taxi.

"Hug?" he asks with a huge grin and raised brows in a display of friendly charm.

Connie tries to hide her nervousness around him by averting eye contact. She becomes overwhelmed with guilt. After all, he didn't do anything to her. She walks up to him with a change of heart. Looking him in the eyes, she feels her whole body pulsate in excitement. Connie throws her arms around him, giving the most passionate hug she can. Philip shuts his eyes. For those seconds, both feel like time has stood still. There is no traffic. No airport. Nobody around. Only the blankness of a new page in life. It was the right fit. The two disengage as though they were forbidden, teenage lovers. Connie looks at him as though she wants to say something. A pair of headlights from a taxi cab shines brightly. It takes everything in Connie's willpower to not act on her emotions. She swiftly turns around and goes to catch a cab nearby that has just arrived to drop off a passenger. She gets inside without turning back, not wanting him to see her in tears. Connie drops her head at the mercy of her emotions.

Philip stares at the red brake lights disappearing further from the futuristic architectural world of the JFK Airport. A yellow cab that resembles the furor of the afterburners glowing from a Concorde jet as he and Connie had just witnessed.

A cab pulls up. Perry pops out of the backseat. "Hey, Boss! Want a ride?"

Philip turns around. "Yeah. Sure." He picks up his luggage and guitar case, placing the suitcase in the trunk. Getting inside the backseat, he instructs Perry. "Make room for Caddy." Philip slides the guitar case carefully in the cab before they, too, become movement in the night.

Chapter 12

A few days have passed since the Afterglow U.K. promotion. At home, Philip sits in his studio, opening an envelope containing a bunch of photographs. He looks at several others of the same size. A folded piece of paper slips out. Picking it up, he reads it to himself.

Enjoy the pictures. Maybe I went a bit overboard! - Love, Claire.

"Uh, maybe you did." Philip remarks as he begins to look at the photos. Everything from a past session they did and the band's trip to LA a few months earlier. He begins to open another envelope, realizing they are from their trip to London. A wildly mischievous grin spreads across his face while he looks through pictures. There are images of the band members unable to keep it together, laughing heartily. One where he's hiding behind Caddy turned upside down. Another of him holding the Strat, like a giant violin and Mitch's drum stick like a bow. The phone rings. He picks it up.

"Hello? Oh, hey, Barb. Yeah. I just got them. Claire gave them to Perry just before she took off for LA…, Yeah…, I heard. Frankie James. Right. London was great!" He goes through one picture after another at the same time. "Yeah? You heard, right… We sure did." Philip stops when he finds a photo with Connie and himself goofing on a Buckingham Palace guard. He flips to another with Connie and him at Hyde Park's Italian Garden. A third shows the band, Connie, and himself having fun. All the guys surround her in a playfully flirty manner. Then there is Abbey Road and the walk across the famed street. The next shows them making a run for it instead, laughing hilariously.

Barbara continues to talk, but Philip's mind is elsewhere while reminiscing of his time in London.

"Yeah…, Um…, I gotta go. Lots to do. OK. Bye." He puts the phone down, still holding one of the photographs. Looking at it, he picks up one of Connie and him at Hyde Park's Italian Garden. Going through a drawer, he picks up a framed photo of the same size. Unfastening the back, he pulls out the picture and replaces it with the new one. Biting his bottom lip, he flips the older image over to reveal a photo of himself and a previous partner, a slim, attractive man with dark eyes and a big smile hugging each other in a pose that closely resembles a Hallmark Card moment. He thought maybe he found the one. Just as he felt the man who made his heart melt before, that would be the one. Or it could have been another before that. All failed him, or vice-versa. Pulling the photo away, he holds it at arm's length, then drops it into the wastebasket next to the desk. He places the newly framed picture of Connie and himself next to the mixing console. His fingers lightly graze the black rubber bracelet on his wrist.

Connie walks from her kitchen to the living room with a container of leftover Chinese food. She throws down a small pile of mail on the couch. As she munches on reheated rice, her eyes fall upon the carry-on luggage she hasn't touched since she left London. Connie reaches over to unzip it. Immediately, she picks out a toothbrush wrapped in toilet paper, a small plastic baggie full of tan nylon socks, and assorted makeup. The book *Brit Speak* sits at the bottom of the bag. She pulls it out, then gives a double-take, noticing something else is underneath. Connie pulls out a folded item. It is Philip's Union Jack scarf, the same one he wore at the Marquee. Confused by finding it in her bag, she looks inside again.

"How did that get in there?"

She plops down on the couch, dropping the scarf next to her. Picking up the container of food, she goes for another bite. Again, her sights fall on yet another item. This time it's the mail spread on the vacant cushion that gets her attention. She picks up a letter from San-San Industries, then rushes to open it. Unfolding a letter, Connie checks the contents of what's written. Grabbing the scarf like it's her best friend, she goes to dial the phone.

"Hi. Yeah. I'm calling about the letter I received... Yeah. Please put me in for the position. Tomorrow?" She looks down at the scarf. "Yeah. I don't have a problem with it at all. The holidays will be here shortly. Yep. I appreciate it. Yeah, you too. Thanks. Bye."

Connie eyes the scarf once again. She picks it up, inhaling Philip's very essence and whatever the Marquee had to offer.

"Philip, I'll have to give this back to you. Whenever that will be."

She picks up the letter again.

Later in the week, Philip waits by the front of San-San Industries, hoping Connie will exit the building. He checks the time on his watch. Looking out at the bright lights of traffic zooming by as a distraction, he gets antsy waiting. The cooler air makes him rethink his strategy of sticking around any longer.

It's a second night of waiting, with the same results. Only this time, he spots somebody leaving San-San. His eyes follow them until they disappear down the street, catching a taxi. Philip looks up at the building. He walks away, shaking his head.

Shortly afterward, Philip visits the same diner he and Connie had gone to after seeking shelter from the rain, and him shattering her dreams. He pulls out a small pad from his jacket pocket and clicks on a pen. Lighting a cigarette, he jots down a few words. A waitress delivers a cup of coffee to him. He looks out the large panel of glass, watching people pass by in front of the soft neon glow of the shops across the way. Ah, Manhattan. Beauty. Splendor. Yet, a sense of unattainable love lingers in the air. What is one to do under her presence?

Taking a sip of coffee, Philip thinks about things that pertained to his time with Connie. Their talks in reflecting on life's little things. Bursting out in laughter from being spontaneous. The sights and sounds of all that surrounded them while carrying out journeys together. Racing across the streets before the traffic started. All the things that made two human beings connect. He couldn't help it. Drawn by life's ups and downs, happiness and loneliness were his bread and butter. It's what he did as a songwriter. Getting inspired was his connection between emotion and communication. If one is upbeat or in love, they reflect it as such. If one is down or broken-hearted, that too is reflected in a somber tone. Either way, it was an all-encompassing form of the human spirit.

A Friday night brings Philip back to facing San-San. Again, he looks up at the many windows lit from above. For a split-second, he thinks of what to do. Opening the door, he walks into the narrow corridor. On the left side of the wall is a large greyish plaque that reads, SAN-SAN INDUSTRIES: Computer Technologies and Data Processing. Underneath a pewter-colored directory are individual businesses listed. Philip's eyes scan the three rows of names assigned to all four floors. They are all listed as Co, LLC, departments, associations, groups, or Inc. Philip couldn't remember the name of Connie's workplace, let alone what type of business listing it was. Defeated, he leans his head against the wall and slams his hand to it out of frustration.

The following Tuesday, Connie stops by a record store at St. Mark's. People are busying themselves, flipping through the racks of albums. She rubs the back of her head with some slight hesitation in searching for specific titles. Glancing around, she finds the new releases available on a forty-five single. Flipping through, she finds one that grabs her attention immediately. Pulling it out, Connie looks at the sleeve picture. It's Phil Reinhardt's latest single release, "Object of Affection." The glossy cover shows Philip and Claire in one pose, overlaid by several others that are faded, making it look like the steps of their perceived attraction to one another. Taking a closer look, Connie quietly says to herself, "So, that's the photo shoot." She realizes that the sleeve photo was taken before the Marquee show, seeing as though Philip looked the same as he did that night. The fluffier hair and his slightly rougher unshaven appearance show, even though he's dressed in a nice suit, not leather. Connie closes her eyes, remembering everything about the Marquee gig. She holds onto the forty-five, continuing to seek out more musical treasures. In the album area, Connie parks herself in front of the racks, flipping through LPs.

She sees a woman placing albums in the correct areas, figuring she works there.

"Excuse me?" Connie says.

"Yes?" the woman answers.

"Do you have anything by Deacon's Alley?"

"Yeah. Let me show you. That would be under, D. Are you looking for a specific album, because if you can't find it, we can order it."

"I'm looking for the first one."

"Oh, *Moorestown!*" the sales lady excitedly answers.

They walk over to a section of the aisle.

"I know we have them. Let's see, though." The sales lady flips through records. "*Dreaming Is Believing, Altar of Deception,* and *Red Light.* Wait just a minute." She pulls out an album. "Ah! Here it is. *Moorestown.*"

Connie says, "Oh, thank you! You've been a great help."

"No problem. If you need help with anything else, don't be afraid to ask."

Connie smiles back, "That'll be all." She smiles, then goes over to the register to ring up her purchases.

The gentleman looks through her purchases on the counter. "OK. What have we got here? Oh, Deacon's Alley. Nice choice! We don't get too many people who even know about this band, and yet they've played worldwide. How did you get into them?"

Connie smiles back. "A friend..." She stops to think for a moment, thinking of what Philip meant to her. "A friend suggested them to me. They were going on and on about them, and I figured, what the heck? You know? Expand my knowledge."

"Nice. Ah! The guitar player for the band." He glances at the forty-five. "We just got that one. It's a UK import. I see a pattern here. WLIR got a hold of it. Found out it was a big hit in England, had it dropped into their shipment, and started playing it. People called them up and said, 'What are you doing? That guy's from Pennsylvania!' It was like the station didn't even know about Phil Reinhardt. Crazy. He has that one big solo hit currently, "The Afterglow," and it's like they don't even know it's the same guy. Weird how things happen."

"Yeah," Connie says in agreement. "It's not like LIR only plays artists from the UK."

"You gotta feel bad for guys like that, though. You know? I mean, he was with that band, Deacon's Alley, and now it's a solo career. Those aren't easy to come by." He looks at her. "Hey, I'm gonna show you something." He reaches into a pile of magazines and pulls out a newspaper. "Here we go. It's under the *Entertainment* section. Check this out. A London paper." He shows her a half-page review on Phil Reinhardt's appearance at The Marquee, with an accompanying picture of the guitarist playing dramatically. "Look at this guy. He comes back on the scene with this new album, and he kind of looked like another Billy Joel. Before that, he had a whole New Wave thing with bleach blonde hair going on. Goes to London, and you mean to tell me this is the same guy?"

Connie looks at the picture, playing dumb. "I guess anything is possible."

He marvels at the image. "Record companies are weird sometimes with what they expect." Stopping himself, he folds the paper. Glancing up at her, he says, "I think you can use this more than I can. I'm sure you're interested."

She stares for a minute.

A woman in her mid-twenties goes up to the register, breaking Connie's concentration. She notices the forty-five sitting on the counter. "Hey, I think I've seen that guy. Pink guitar? Ray-Bans? He's been at a club or two in recent times. His smile is like, so adorable. Yeah. My sister kissed him. He was so totally not into it."

Connie looks at the young woman. "You mean she just went up to him and kissed him?"

"Yeah."

"Well then, of course, he wasn't going to be into it. Your sister was a total stranger to him. How would you feel if some random guy just put the moves on you? Oh, wait. Or is it because you or she figures he's a guy, so it's no big deal?"

The girl defends her sister. "He was cute. Not to mention he's a musician. I mean, what did he expect getting into music?"

"So, what he does as a career justifies her actions? What if he were, say, a plumber? Would she have done it then?"

The girl looks at Connie in annoyed confusion. "What does that..., What are you, like one of those Gloria Steinem followers?"

Connie turns to her. "No."

All the while, the record store owner watches the conversation unfold. He places Connie's items in a bag.

She takes it and the folded newspaper. Before leaving, Connie turns to the girl once more and says, "He's not that kind of guy."

The next day, headlights shine on a lone phone booth caught under the watchful eye of the streetlight. Immediately, the car's engine turns off. Philip gets out of the driver's side and looks at the booth. He steps in, checking the thick phone directory's cover. It reads, Bedford, NY. Philip flips through the pages, realizing the book does not serve his needs. He mutters quietly to himself, "Bedford. Dammit." He immediately goes back to his car and drives away to the next destination.

Philip walks into a restaurant in Mt. Kisco, where he goes to find a payphone. On the ledge is an ultra-thick phone directory. Screamin' Jay

Hawkins is half-yelling, half-crooning "I Put a Spell on You," as overhead music. Philip goes through the pages, running his fingers down over the last names that start with the letter A. Quietly, he scans. "Atwater, Attridge...Aubrecht, Aucott, Axell, Aydlett, Ayles." He picks up the phone, drops a dime in and dials immediately.

Philip hesitates for a moment. "Directory assistance?"

"This is the operator. How may I help you?"

"Hi. Yeah. I'm looking for a specific name in Mount Kisco. Ayers. Roger Ayers.

"Hold on a minute. I'm finding Ayers, but no Roger."

"OK. Let's go with the initials. How about R. Ayers?"

"Nothing is coming up for R. Ayers."

"Um, Beth? I mean, Elizabeth Ayers?"

"There is nothing listed for an Elizabeth Ayers."

"I'm guessing the same goes for E. Ayers?"

"No, sir. There is no listing for E. Ayers."

Philip bites his bottom lip. "Probably unlisted."

The operator responds, "Possibly so. Will that be it, sir?"

Taking a deep breath, Philip answers back, "Yep. That's it. Thanks."

Philip hangs up the phone in defeat. "Unlisted." He shakes his head.

***

Connie sits on the bed in her tiny apartment in the Village reading *Rolling Stone* magazine. While skimming through it, the phone rings. She picks it up.

"Hello?"

The other voice comes through as her friend, Sally.

"Hey, Connie! Where have you been? I want to know. So, how was England?" Sally asks.

"I've been swamped lately. England was fine." Connie responds.

"Fine? That's all?" Sally prods.

"Yeah," Connie answers plainly.

"What about Philip? What was it like being with him?" Sally suggests.

"Things were fine. We had fun. We wandered around the streets of London, went shopping, hung out at the Hard Rock in Mayfair. I was part of a studio audience three times. One was kind of like *Solid Gold* or *American Bandstand*, where they lip-synch. The other two shows were interviews. Some of the ladies in the audience there were crazy. The things they asked him. Um, I got to be an extra in a video."

Sally stops her. "Wait. You mean to tell me you're going to be on MTV?"

Connie smirks back, "It'll probably show up there."

"Oh my God! Holy shit, Connie! You are so freaking lucky! That is so awesome! And he's like, such a babe!"

Connie answers back, thoughtfully, "I need to let him go."

"Yeah... You what? Did I hear you right?"

"I have to let him go."

"You want to dump a rock star? You are crazy! You are batshit crazy! Look, I can hook you up with an excellent therapist. I know you're insecure. Boy, do I know it! The Cuban guy at the bowling alley you turned down. The fellow who looked liked Rick James that knew how to dress. That guy at the club last year. The cutie with the spikey hair. And now, Phil Reinhardt, an adorable, beautiful dreamboat of a musician, who has given you these adventures beyond your wildest dreams! Connie. Doesn't that mean anything to you? You're thirty-one."

"Thirty-two." Connie corrects her.

"OK. So, you're thirty-two going back to sixteen. You act like a scared little teenager when it comes to guys. You don't simply let things happen."

"Sally, I'm not like you. I'm glad though you and Jeff are doing well. You don't understand. I just need to let Philip go."

"I do understand that you are batshit crazy."

"Sally, do you have any advice on what I should do?"

"I don't know? What are you supposed to say to a rock star when you dump him?" Sally answers sarcastically. In a hasty breath, she says, "Look, I'm sure you'll think of something. I have to check on dinner."

Connie nods back in understanding. "OK. I'll talk with you later. Bye."

She hangs up the phone, takes a deep breath, then falling back on the pillow. Her hand rests on the nightstand, where she grabs for Philip's scarf.

"Sally, he's gay, and I'm falling for him badly. He doesn't care, but I do. I need to stop feeling this way. I need to let him go."

Connie squeezes the scarf in a moment of loss.

At Grand Central Station, through the large cathedral windows, light cascades onto the cavernous cement floors like Heaven's showers. It presents a romantic atmosphere and nostalgia of an old-time black and white Hollywood film. Commuters wander the main concourse. Their footsteps echo, high heels clicking, flats shuffle, traversing the semi-glossed floor. Connie finds herself one of those commuters, among the dizzying display of human traffic. She looks up at the dark green Mediterranean sky on the mile-high ceiling as though it's a fresco in an Italian cathedral. The gold-plated art deco clock at the information kiosk points to nearly eleven o'clock.

Connie closes her eyes, taking in all of the sounds. Somewhere among the hustle and bustle is a voice echoing throughout the building, announcing the New Haven line at Track thirty-five. It's here that she believes she can find the same magic as that fateful night when her eyes fell upon the stranger in Ray-Bans and a sports jacket near San-San Industries. The same guy who gave her so many feelings. It had been a world he introduced her to of music jargon, crazy mythological tales, adventures where the human heart fears to tread, the child-like wonderment of life, romances which went awry, dancing until dawn. It was his compassion that grabbed her. It's how he threw aside his heartache and lifted her grandmother's spirits. Or how he reacted in London to Shelley's awkwardness of husband, Walter's ability to freeze up, offering his own story of expectations as a fan. A thousand other things flash through Connie's mind regarding Philip. His charm, mischievous nature, the ability to be so male without macho overtones. She steps forward, stone-like in the center of all the action. Her eyes fixate on the lit-up departure times listed for the New Haven and Hudson lines.

The mental connections she makes between departing trains and those arriving leads her to believe maybe that next line will hold the person with whom she is to spend the rest of her life. A man on the hunt, perhaps a lost soul like herself, heart tangled with what he cannot obtain either. He didn't have to be a musician, just fall in love with her as a man should. He didn't have to be the stereotypical tall, dark, and handsome. They were some beautiful traits, but not necessary. What was required was for him to have a heart. Perhaps a sense of adventure, spontaneity, charm, fun-loving, compassionate. No. That was expecting too much. That was Philip. He embodied so many of the things she cherished and longed for in a man. Somebody so different that it took her breath away.

More people pour through the doors from Vanderbilt Avenue to forty-second Street, making their way down the stairs. A family rushes through with kids trying to catch up. Others quicken their pace, not wanting to miss the next train. Connie witnesses a man racing through the concourse. He drops with a slide on his knees up to a woman, immediately pulling out a small velvet box. Several people turn to look, nodding with approval over the proposal. The man picks up the woman for a spin. It's just like they would in the movies, or kind of like when Philip caught Connie upon returning from his west coast tour. She shakes her head, knowing fairy-tales happen, but not for her. One thing she notices is that people have lives and move with a purpose. Nobody looks lost. They appear to be determined, whether it's to reach their destination or bury themselves in a magazine while sitting against the wall. Passengers arrive with kisses and hugs.

Connie begins to think twice about being there. Nobody showed any concern towards her. If she was worried about Philip, or his not reciprocating feelings, then this felt even colder. Complete strangers couldn't make eye contact with her. It makes things worse. She was the only one who seemed to have nobody on a Saturday. A day that was supposed to hold fun excitement and adventure, away from the daily grind of working. She was wasting it and trying to find something or someone who wasn't there for her.

Studying a variety of men, Connie realizes Philip is the right guy for her. Not in a romantic sense, but as a friend. An exceptional friend. One in a million. She couldn't simply let him go like she told Sally. Taking a deep breath, Connie closes her eyes. She thinks of how foolish she's been since London, avoiding Philip, missing out on whatever he did that could lift her spirits. Instead, Connie focused intensely on specific signs, and what people thought they saw. Although it was cute, she knew better. He wasn't playing games with her heart. It had been all about how she wanted to see things. She wasn't looking to change him. She needed to change her thoughts, or else she would lose him by her selfishness. All she had to do was reset her heart. Think about the goodness he provided, but at the same time erase any romantic expectations, even the flirting. Connie nods to herself. Feeling it's the right thing to do. Eventually, she would find the guy of her dreams. Not this day, though.

Instead, she would go back home to her little apartment and take in the sounds of what Philip had been. Her ears would open up to something other than her regular staple of pop, top forty, and New Wave.

Connie opens the cellophane, uncovering the album, *Moorestown*. Her turntable does the rest. Sitting back on the sofa, she looks at the cover of a green silhouette tree—a rather bland and not so rock and roll image. Checking the back cover, she finds a black and white photo of the band. It's a motley crew of four guys with longish hair, and their outfits reflect exactly Philip's words to her from a few months earlier. They wear what looks to be velvet suits. She recognizes the dark feather-haired fellow with a soft smile. A smile creeps across her face. Connie listens to the music while reaching for the scarf, in the form of fond remembrance, toying with it between her hands.

The lyrics are about female companionship, having good times, subtle innuendos, traveling, and being a musician in general. It's all accompanied by raging guitar chords, pedal swells or wah-wah action, keyboards dancing in between, beefy bass lines, and a variety of drumming patterns. It's more of a hard rock buffet with the usual suspects at play used as inspiration. There is some Deep Purple mixed in with Zeppelin, a pinch of Hendrix, and a dash of Cream or Beatles.

Connie studies the lyrics on the inner sleeve. Much to her surprise, all of the relationship songs are written exclusively by Phil Reinhardt. She is confused about how a man who had told her at various times about his male partners, could write such sensitive material regarding a gender he did not understand. Sweet songs, and singing in a way that seemed to ring true, or at least in a way she could relate to them. Whatever way she felt, she had to listen to the whole album a second time to digest it. Thinking about what she's heard, leaves her with the feeling of wanting more.

Not more than a couple of hours later, Connie goes back to the record store on St. Marks. Stepping inside, people wander about with albums in their hands. She sees the same gentleman at the register. Immediately, she goes over to the rack of albums and pulls out several other Deacon's Alley records, including such titles as *Dreaming is Believing*, *Altar of Deception*, and *Red Light*.

She looks in particular interest at the cover of *Red Light*, where it shows an image of all the band members engulfed in a red glow, surrounding a dark car next to train tracks. Then she realizes the car is Philip's Stingray he had mentioned from a couple of months back.

She makes her way to the register. The owner looks at her.

"The Reinhardt lady."

Connie looks down for a moment in awkward shyness.

The man says, "What have you got today?"

She puts the albums on the counter.

"Eager. I'm guessing you enjoyed *Moorestown*."

"Yep," Connie answers, rooting through her pocketbook.

"Uh, hey, I thought it was great what you said the other day, how you defended Reinhardt. Some people forget musicians are human. I don't know what kind of connection you have with him. It sounded personal. I couldn't be sure, but any lady that does what you did is good in my books. Truly special."

Connie cracks a small smile. "Thanks. It needed to be said." She makes her purchase. He places the items in a bag. She takes them and walks to the door. Just before she opens it, she hears him.

"Tell Phil the single is selling like hotcakes here."

Connie gives a slight wave of acknowledgment, then leaves.

With a brand new week on the horizon, Philip finds himself at his favorite place to meditate, the Brooklyn Bridge Promenade. He looks across at the Manhattan skyline, wondering about life or when the next time he'll see Connie? What if he never sees her again? What if that fantastic hug at the airport meant goodbye? She was unlisted in the phone book. Her parents were the same, up in Mt. Kisco. He couldn't complain though, so was he. Somewhere on that big, crazy island of Manhattan, Connie was there. A good many past relationships went badly, and one-night stands he wanted to forget about existed there too. Connie was a clean slate, though. He was going to lose her. London was a try-out to see how she would react to being somewhere other than 'The Big Apple' with him. Philip knew the Marquee gig was going to affect her some way, as she had never experienced seeing him play live. He just didn't anticipate how much.

While staring at the city of heartache and disappointment, he notices quick flashes of light that seem abnormal on a night like this. Aside from the usual light pollution and lit-up windows in buildings, it's as though heat lightning flickers. The sound of giggles nearby grabs his attention. Philip turns to look to his right, where a couple holds each other. A man standing further back snaps pictures with the flashbulb going off. Philip sees the couple holding white roses, staring deep into one another's eyes.

A proposal?

Engagement announcement for the *New York Times*?

Honeymoon?

It didn't matter. Philip felt like a third wheel, being so close to the lovey-dovey action of the happy couple.

Something he felt he could not obtain with any person.

Without words, he slips away from the promenade.

A short while later, Philip returns to Scribbles. Looking around through the crowd, who dances to the Thompson Twins' "Hold Me Now," he finds High-Top as he heads up to the DJ booth.

"Hey, High-Top, have you seen Finch?"

"He hasn't been around for a couple of weeks. The last I heard, he caught a nasty cold while up in Vermont. He calls it a transitional seasonal occurrence. I've had to tell him, 'You mean you're experiencing a change of the east coast, my man.' No need for some mumbo jumbo wording. College kids!" He shakes his head.

Philip grins back, "Uh, Finch never went to college. He was like me, too broke, and didn't have the interest."

"So, you here to boogie?"

"Nah. Hey, do you know a lady by the name of Connie who comes here?"

"Connie? I'm tryin' to remember what she looks like. I see a lot of people, especially women."

"She introduced me to you, remember?"

"I'm drawing a blank, man, " High-Top shakes his head.

"Kind of looks like an actress. Brunette."

High-Top giggles, "Just about every woman in Manhattan looks like an actress."

Philip glances out on the dance floor when he sets his eyes on a girl dancing. Putting an arm around the DJ, he points her way.

"See her? See the way her hair is? Kind of like that."

"Oh, wait! Now I know who you're referring to. Man, I couldn't remember names though. You're talking about the cute brunette chick with the green eyes. She comes here with her girlfriends sometimes."

Philip nods with understanding.

"Aw, man. I ain't seen her in a little while, like maybe last month or so."

Philip drops his head.

High-Top offers some comfort by adding, "Hey, I can tell her you dropped by the next time I see her, and I can tell Finch you were looking for him too."

Philip scruffs his hair out of anxiousness. He knows he'll have to continue his search.

"Thanks," he weakly smiles at the DJ, before walking away.

Several days later, Manhattan's streets become bathed in the formation of watercolor patches, illuminated by nearby shops and businesses from the rainfall. Brake lights of passing traffic glow a burning red. Neon signs become splendidly vivid within the night's eye. Drops sparkle like diamonds as they fall from awnings. Couples tuck under umbrellas, fearing to get caught by Mother Nature's wrath. The insistent tapping of rain only gets stronger by the minute.

In a long, black overcoat, Philip makes his way to an electronics shop. He tries to shake off the rain and cold since there is no umbrella in his possession. Stepping inside, Philip meets a salesman.

"Yes, sir. How may I help you?"

"I'm wondering if you can tell me who does your inventory processing?"

"Who does our inventory processing? We leave that up to the corporate offices in Miami. What is this about?"

Philip shakes his head. "Never mind. Thanks." He goes out the door, back into the rain, wandering along the sidewalks of the East Village. Letting out a column of breath in the cold, he looks around at the nearby shops. Another electronics store becomes part of his mission. He opens the door and sees customers waiting. Catching the glimpse of a salesman, he immediately lets his intentions be known.

"Who does your inventory processing?"

The salesman asks curiously, "Who sent you? Are you competition?"

"I'm looking for a specific company."

"We're out of Hoboken and headquarters is in Cherry Hill. Does that help you?"

Philip nods his head and answers, tight-lipped, "Yep. It does. Thanks."

Again, he walks out into the rain without care of getting wet. Looking up at the pouring sky, another breath of cold air follows. He starts to wonder how many of these stores he'll have to visit. Several people run by him, seeking shelter. A third time, he walks the streets further in search. Yet another electronics store greets him. This one has three letters burned out, making the sign look like ELE RON CS. Quickly, he reaches for the door, unable to handle the rain as he had—the coldness bites at his fingertips. Walking in, he takes a deep breath. A small TV set that a young man is watching plays in the back of the register. A middle-aged man of portly stature walks over to him. He turns to Philip, seeing him wet and eager for assistance.

"Yes, sir. How may I help you?"

The young man chimes in, "We've got TVs, computers, radios, and accessories. The best in technology!"

The middle-aged man turns to look back. "He's right. But, uh, you look like you're in search of something."

"Yeah. Can you tell me who does your inventory processing? Look, I'm not with any competing business or wanting to take anything away. I just need to know what company..." Philip loses his breath briefly from the cold air he had been breathing in. "What processing company does your inventory lists for the products you carry?"

"That would be Gary. Gary Talbot a few blocks away."

Philip produces a small notepad, flipping a page, and clicking on a pen. "Gary, you said?" He writes it down.

"Yeah. Gary. Let's see, and then there's Bryan, Ted, Lou, and a few ladies. They're at the San-San building. It's a few streets back up from here."

Philip continues writing everything down more eagerly.

The young man adds, "Ooh. They've got this lady working there with dark hair. She comes around here at four o'clock to make the delivery herself. She is such a babe. They're from the JLP Group."

Philip looks up, tosses the pad and pen back in his oversized coat pocket, and leaves quickly.

Picking up the pace, he runs through puddles while crossing streets. At long last, he reaches the San-San Industries building. He rushes inside, running to the lobby directory. Breathing heavy, he points a finger down the listed names. First floor. Second floor. Third floor. Fourth. In the center of names, he puts his finger on it. He makes a slow trot towards the elevator. At the same time, Richard, the maintenance man, makes his way from the opposite direction.

"Sonny, the elevator is out of order," he calls out.

Philip backs up, looking around. He spots the door to go upstairs. Rushing through the door, he looks up and begins his ascent up the stairs.

At JLP Group, Gary and Ted prepare to leave for the night.

Gary asks, "Did you shut all the computers off?"

Ted answers back, "Almost. This one's so slow. Connie was right. This thing is slow as molasses. It's only half processed. I've got to wait."

Gary grabs the pot of coffee in the corner of the room, filling his mug.

"Hey, where is Connie?"

"I don't know. Connie hasn't been back since going on vacation a few weeks back."

"Vacation? Connie? She doesn't go on vacation. Since when?" Gary grabs a page to look it over, then places it back on the table.

"I heard she wasn't alone. Somebody saw her get in a cab with a guy who helped her with the luggage," Ted advises.

Gary looks out of a window. "Oh shit. It's raining. Great."

The two hear a door shut. Both look over to see a sopping wet man in a long, dark overcoat standing before them. He does not attempt to dry off. His hair is a dark mass of dripping curls and waves flattened. His breathing is hard from running up four floors.

Philip asks with determination and calmness, "Excuse me, where can I find Connie? Connie Ayers?"

Ted and Gary exchange glances.

Ted answers back, hesitantly, "Uh, I don't know. Normally, she's here, but your guess is as good as ours."

They can see the utter desperation in Philip's brown eyes.

Ted thinks for a minute in how to calm the concern of the man before him.

"I haven't seen her since she took a week off for vacation. That was like four weeks ago. A month at the most."

A dejected Philip walks out the door. He goes back to the stairs where he takes on two flights. Leaning against the wall, he slides down to the floor in complete and utter exhaustion in a cold, wet, heap.

***

The thunder rumbles outside as the doorbell rings on the Upper West Side. Barbara shuffles over to answer it. She opens the door, surprised to see her client caught in the rain.

"Phil!"

He walks directly past her. She feels the cold steam rise from his long coat. Stepping into the dining room, he says, "It'll be a cold day in fucking hell before I become like Al."

Barbara raises her brows in surprise. "Of course you don't have to become like Al. You can be more careful with what's out there."

Philip puts his hands on a dining room chair, dropping his head, still dripping wet.

"It doesn't explain what you were doing out in the rain," Barbara says with some concern.

He lifts his head. "I'm in love."

A day later, at the same time, Ted looks out the window on the fourth floor. Gary helps himself to the copy machine. Connie rushes in.

Ted is the first to notice. "Hey! Will you look at that? Maybe theorists are wrong about the world being flat. You didn't fall off it after all."

Connie rolls her eyes while picking up a page. "Nice. Ted. No. I did not fall off the planet."

"Did you stay three weeks later for your vacation?" Ted asks with curiosity.

"For your information, I was transferred downtown to train incoming holiday part-timers. Ah, but you know what they say?" She looks over at her workstation, throwing her arms out. "Absence makes the heart grow fonder." Walking to the computer, she hugs the monitor. "I missed you, you stubborn, outdated piece of worthless metal."

"Gee, the computer gets more love than I do."

Connie looks back at Ted. "That's because I missed my computer."

"Aww! Thanks, Connie."

Connie smiles back. "I'm just glad to be back. I'm not too fond of downtown. Guess that's what I get for going away for several weeks."

"Speaking of which...," Gary begins. "How was that vacation of yours?"

Connie hesitates, "It was fine. Good."

"Where did ya go?" Gary asks.

"Europe. Um, London." Connie answers carefully.

"Wow! That's a bit far for you!"

"Yeah. Well..." Connie is almost at a loss for words.

"I mean, what did you do over there?"

"Ya know, typical things you do on vacation. Sightseeing. Restaurants. Shopping. All that stuff."

Ted asks, "Who'd you go with?"

Connie gives him a sharp look. "I liked it better when Gary was asking me questions."

"I went with somebody. No big deal." She looks at a file on her desk.

Gary changes the subject, knowing how uncomfortable Connie feels with their line of questioning. "It's great to have you back. Everybody missed you."

Ted says, "Yeah."

Connie gives a tight-lipped smile. "Thanks, guys."

Gary says, "You're quite the popular girl here. You had a visitor yesterday."

"Visitor?"

"Yeah, well, the two of us were a little surprised ourselves."

Ted takes over the conversation. "This guy came in, like super wet. Dark coat. About our height. Maybe five-ten or five-eleven."

Connie stops what she's reading, listening to her co-workers.

Ted adds in, "Blond."

Gary intervenes, "Dark blond."

Connie corrects them both. "Brownish." Neither hears her.

Ted continues with grander gestures. "He had this look that I don't know..."

Connie feels herself getting more uptight.

Gary takes over. "Yeah. It was like a scene out of an old black and white movie. He had...well, how do I put this? It was sort of a kind of magic about him. He was a pretty good looking guy. It's not like I'm gay or anything."

"THERE'S NOTHING WRONG WITH BEING DIFFERENT!!!" Connie shouts.

Realizing what she has just said, Connie turns her back on both men. She looks up and closes her eyes. Silently she utters, "Shit."

A shocked and stunned Ted barks back, "Jeez, Connie! Go easy! I think being overworked is taking its toll on you! You don't have to yell at everybody."

Connie pinches the bridge of her nose, feigning exhaustion and confusion while feeling relief that her outburst went over both men's heads. She turns back to face them, embarrassed.

"You're right. I'm...I am tired. It's been a long three weeks. But, I promise to be back home. Home base. Sorry about my outburst. I just came by to check on things. So, tomorrow will be back to normal. See you guys later."

Gary says, "G'Night."

Connie walks out, closing the door behind her. She walks away, muttering, "Why are you doing this to me?"

Inside the office, Gary asks Ted, "Wait. Was that guy the same one Dave and Janna showed us outside the window with those black kids doing the doo-wop?"

Ted shrugs, "Could be. I don't know. I wouldn't recognize him if it were, with the way he looked yesterday. Rough shape."

Gary admits, "Connie was kind of testy."

"Yeah," Ted nods back, looking at the door.

The next day, Connie returns to San-San. She looks at the elevator after leaving the JLP Group from a full day of work. The maintenance man waves to her.

"Richard? Is it working?"

"It should be fine now, Ms. Ayers."

Connie smiles back. "Oh, good. I don't have to take the stairs. Thanks!"

Happily, she gets on the elevator, where it whisks her down to the main floor. She walks through the lobby, realizing there's something she needs to do. Glancing down, Connie unclips her work badge as she exits the building. Picking up her pocketbook, she drops the item inside. While zipping it back up, a voice speaks up from nearby.

"Hey, Connie."

Connie gets startled. With a quick breath, she closes her eyes and turns around to face him. Quietly she answers, "Hi." Carefully, she tries to stay calm, keeping the butterflies in her stomach at bay. She flips her hair with nervousness.

Immediately, Philip can tell Connie is reticent by her body language.

He glances down for a moment. "I was wondering what happened to you."

Connie finally looks at him, replacing shyness with thinly veiled frustration. "Yeah. I know. You went to my workplace. Well, you made quite an impression on two of my male colleagues. Isn't that what you were looking for?" She gives him a hard glance until realizing what she's just said. Rolling her eyes, Connie puts a hand to her forehead and says, "That didn't come out the way I wanted it to." She looks out at the passing traffic, before turning to him.

"It's a crazy time for us at the office. Right after Halloween, it gets to be nuts. With this year, it's even worse as the electronics industry grows. There seems to be a new electronics store popping up every day somewhere in the states. Manhattan must have about a thousand of them alone." Stumbling over her words, Connie goes non-stop. Her voice trembles with nervousness. "There are so many computers for home use coming up, and with that big commercial from the Super Bowl in February... Everybody wants to compete with Apple. Just this year, we've seen IBM release their version, and the Commodore Sixty-Four came out. Anything and everything with 'DOS' and 'DIR' related. And it's not just computers. Everyone has an Atari, and that's another primary seller for the people with younger kids out in the suburbs, who don't have arcades nearby. The companies have us up the wall with this stuff." She puts her hands out in dramatic fashion, babbling on a mile a minute. "Pagers. Pagers are another thing. You know about those. Your band members have them. I saw the ones they had. It's a new way to communicate!"

Philip takes a step forward to her.

Connie takes one back. Her heart races as she explains further.

"Answering machines are huge for work-minded people. I'm sure you have one yourself. I can't forget about kids either. There are these toys. Electronic toys have to be inventoried too because who doesn't want to be on top of everything? Nobody wants a dumb kid." She feels herself nearly cracking up under the pressure of her own emotions. Pushing back her hair, she tries to think of something else to say but cannot come up with any ideas.

Sheepishly, Philip looks down at the sidewalk. "I kind of figured it was because you were trying to avoid me."

"There's just so much…"

"I'm not infected yet."

Connie's eyes go wide in fright. She shoots back, "Don't talk like that!" Putting her hands out, she pleads with him. "Don't say things like that. Not about people who are suffering."

"People suffer all over the world. It all depends on what you make of life."

"I know," Connie answers in a miserable tone.

He looks down as he says, "You said some things back in England that made sense."

She stares at him, puzzled and concerned.

Philip then tries to find the words for what he feels.

"I'm trying to be an adult, but it's not working. It's so much easier to be a kid. When you're a kid, you can play in the dirt, and nobody will say anything because they know you'll grow out of it. It's just a phase. When you're an adult, you can't do the same thing. People will think there's something wrong with you."

Connie swallows hard, trying to figure out what he's telling her.

"If this is your way of explaining some type of analogy—"

"Before I joined Deacon's Alley, like going way back to high school, I knew something was off. I would try and pick up magazines and look at the pretty girls, but then I'd find ads of these guys and wonder how they were and what they felt. What it would be like to feel their touch. I would shut the magazine, and it scared me. I tried to put it out of my mind, but then in my mind's eye that feeling would only grow stronger. I'd try to get along with the girls and act like my friends. After nothing would happen, people would simply say, I was a late bloomer. I dug myself deeper in music." He looks at her, hoping she'll understand. "When I would play shows, I'd see these guys with their girlfriends…" He closes his eyes to the memory. "All I could think was…I'm not normal. And I would hope for things to change. The guys in the band would have these make-out sessions in their cars or wherever, and I'd be with a girl and try for it, but my feelings… I just didn't feel it, and she knew that. The heartbreak would happen repeatedly, and there was nothing I could do."

Philip's glassy-eyed stare makes Connie swallow hard.

"I knew I could never have that kind of happiness. I wouldn't allow it. When I joined Deacon's Alley, I thought things might change with the whole rock and roll scene. I got excited about being on stage and getting this feeling of happiness playing in front of thousands. Then it would be back to an empty hotel room while the rest of the band found girls to be with or they had their girlfriends and eventual wives with them. I would see these guys out in the audience and wonder if I could talk with them. You know? Get to know them a little better? I'd stop myself because I knew if they weren't like me and found out my intentions, then I would be labeled a freak, fag, homo. Whatever way, they could hurt me. It would end my career that I wanted more than anything.

My music wouldn't matter, and I wouldn't. What I am would." He thinks about another memory, savoring the thought.

"At one point, long after the band broke up, I was myself and got to be with who I wanted to. I was going to bring Gene with me to meet my family. I knew how I felt, and he knew how he felt. We were in love. That's all that mattered. He thought we all needed to meet on neutral territory, not drop the house on my parents. Gene felt I was moving too fast, and I would regret telling my folks. Who knew what would happen? I could lose them..." He bows his head down. "...like forever. You know? What would happen if I lost them, and Gene? I'd have nobody. I mean like really nobody. I can't say I don't deserve it. I've wanted the happy-ever-after for a long time, but it's not available to me. I have sabotaged every one of my relationships for one reason or another."

"OK. You can stop." Connie wipes her eyes hard with a sleeve. "I get it." She sniffles back, "I get it, and I don't want to see you so miserable." She examines her wet hand. "Look at this mess," partially she answers through a bubbling nose. Quickly, she fishes through her pocketbook, searching for a tissue. Satisfying the needs of her nose, she chokes up her courage among the stream of tears. "I'm...I'm willing to let you go. I just can't stand the idea of being in the way of somebody's happiness. If that's what you're trying to...,"

"I'm not," Philip tries to tell her.

"I mean, I've enjoyed the time we've spent together." She laughs through her fight of heartbreak and strength. "So many meetings out here. I never expected any of this. I don't think I can look through my record collection the same again after what you taught me. I'll miss...," She reaches for fresh tissue. Before she can even put it to her face, he takes it instead, drying her tears. "I'll miss everything...," The tears start up again. "I'll miss everything, but never forget you. I couldn't do that. I don't know. Maybe somewhere down the line, our paths might cross, or maybe not?" She answers in grim cheer, breathing back heavily. "Why didn't you ignore me or walk away that night? It could have been so easy."

Philip leans closer, realizing the pain she feels from losing him. An overabundance of tears marks their territory, etched by his careless words of desperation. Losing a friend in such a way strikes him like losing his family to his secret. He couldn't reveal what he was, out of fear of rejection. He couldn't communicate properly in telling his feelings to Connie, out of fear of rejection.

His eyes meet the ground in shame as he wills himself the words necessary to release him from the agony in his heart.

"Give me one more chance."

Connie awakens from her misery.

"What?" She asks, puzzled through tear-stained eyes.

"Give me one more chance." He repeats with greater emphasis. "Give this friendship one more chance. If it becomes too much, then I'll accept it. We'll both move on, and that'll be it."

"I don't know what to say?"

"Say, you will."

Connie eyes the heavily used tissue. With hesitancy, she nods back. Softly, she says, "OK. One more."

Philip desperately wants to hug her and tell her everything will be OK. But, he's uncertain with her fragility, how she might handle it. Instead, he says with determination, "Next Friday. Same as usual. Eight o'clock."

Connie nods once more, wiping her eyes dry. She takes a step back and walks toward the edge of the sidewalk to hail a cab.

A taxi pulls over. Connie looks over her shoulder. She thinks about what her boss had told her regarding in finding a prince, not a frog. Philip had been a prince, but his true self was something she could not have. He needed to return to the pond.

A small smile crosses his lips as he waves goodbye to her.

Connie gets whisked away.

Philip puts his hands in the oversized pockets of his coat. He looks out at the street, then walks away.

A week passes. Attired in a robe, with a towel firmly tucked around her hair, Connie studies her reflection in the vanity mirror. She looks away, and, getting up from the chair, she goes to check on the clothes laid out on the bed. Several sets keep her wondering what to choose. Dressy? Casual? Formal? Fun? Overly fun? Less than exciting? She looks at one outfit, tossing them aside. "Ick. Too flashy." Eyeing a green top, she says to herself, "What do I want to do, look like a Christmas tree?" Connie throws the jersey aside. "Nope. Not going to work for this night." Two cowl neck tops remain. One is red. The other is grey. She grimaces at the red one. "Red? Too provocative. It's not a date." Connie looks at the final top left. "Stay neutral." Grabbing a pair of black knit tights, she puts them over her shoulder along with the grey cowl neck jersey.

Ten minutes later, her hair is fluffed dry. Again, she sits at the vanity mirror. Digging through an organizer of makeup haphazardly bunched together, Connie thinks still. "I must be stupid, crazy, or both." She grabs a handful of cosmetics and releases them on the table. The palm of her hand rests on a bottle of foundation. "Maybe that. Yeah. At least a little." She puts the tip of her fingers on a blush brush, then quickly takes them off. "No." Looking down, she picks up a bottle of mascara. "Do I truly need this?" She stares at the reflection in the mirror of her green eyes. "Nah. My eyes are fine the way they are." Connie tosses the bottle back in the organizer. She stares at a tube of lipstick. Picking it up, she twists the item up. In disgust, Connie drops her head in the palm of her hand. "Why even bother. It's not like I'm going to get my lipstick smeared." She peeks at the reflection. "Wait, Connie. What are you doing? Who are you trying to impress? Even if you go out, there surely are plenty of straight guys who would be interested." A thought crosses her mind. "Who am I kidding? It still won't get smeared." Reluctantly, Connie swipes the lipstick against her lips, then tosses the tube back in the organizer.

She takes the Union Jack scarf from the nightstand. Connie places it into her pocketbook next to the apology card Philip had given her months ago.

Fifteen minutes later, Connie finds herself at the spot of all her meet-ups with Philip. She checks Mickey's hands on the watch. A little after eight o'clock. What could be the delay? Taking a deep sigh, Connie looks around at the traffic zooming by. A black limousine pulls around the corner. It stops on the side of her. The driver's window lowers.

A middle-aged man calls out, "Miss Ayers?"

Connie cautiously walks toward the window, looking back and forth. "Yes?"

The driver says, "I'm here to pick you up."

"You are?" Connie questions. She steps around the side, noticing the driver is about to get out. "No need. I can let myself in." In the next breath, she mutters, "Boy, are you full of surprises."

Connie gets in the limousine. Immediately, her eyes scan everything from the slate-blue interior with six matching velvety seats, a small bar, a phone, and a six-inch TV screen.

The driver lowers the back partition separating the two of them. "Miss Ayers? It will be about an hour until we reach our destination. If you need anything, don't hesitate to let me know. My name is Michael. There's a TV on your left, with the bar next to it. The phone, if you need anything, is on the right side."

Connie answers back, "I'm fine."

Michael begins to raise the partition when Connie asks, "Does he always do this? Mr. Reinhardt? To send out for a limo that is?"

He responds with, "Only during the winter and maybe special occasions."

"OK. That'll be all for now. Thanks." Connie watches the partition slide upward until she's left alone. She says to herself, "Special occasions." While looking around again, she spots a small white envelope on the adjacent seat. Picking it up, Connie inspects it to see her name written out in small letters on the front. She examines the contents and flips open a card.

Enjoy the ride! - P.R.

Connie slumps back, placing the card off to the side. She closes her eyes, thinking of what has led her up to this point and why it all happened. Where was she being dropped off? An hour's drive could lead to a variety of places. Quite possibly, Long Island? That seemed to be an appropriate place for somebody of his stature. It had to be reasonably close enough to the city. Surely not the Hamptons. New Jersey? But, he said there were only two things he had in common with Springsteen, and New Jersey was not one of them, only Deacon's Alley started from that state. Connecticut? Nope, nothing there. Upper state? Again, nothing there. Where would this place be? Connie looks outside the window. It's nothing but piers and the deepest navy of the Hudson River, illuminated by the ripples created by city lights.

CHAPTER 13

A little over an hour later, the limo stops. The partition which separates herself from the driver lowers. Michael looks at her from his rearview mirror.

"Miss Ayers? We've arrived at the destination."

Cautiously, Connie exits the vehicle. She shuts the door, looking around in the darkness. The limo pulls away, leaving her alone. The only things she sees are the vehicle's brake lights and dim light in the distance.

She tells herself, "Great. That's just great. I'm stuck in the middle of nowhere." Her eyes scan the darkness of the evening sky. "I want to live. I want to live." Connie turns around to see a lone black car parked in the driveway. She steps closer, noticing it's a Corvette Stingray. Two overhead lights suddenly turn on. One is over the garage, and the other above the main entrance, illuminating a large-sized, powder blue house. Connie walks up the small stairway. The door is already a crack open. Slowly, she steps in.

"Anybody home?" She calls out. "Philip?" Walking cautiously, she says, "Hello?" Connie stops when a large display catches her eye. She turns and walks in the direction of the curiosity on the wall — a large glass case of museum quality, houses three certified gold plaques. Through the glass, she can partly view her reflection. Wanting to get a better look at the awards, Connie steps closer. Five small overhead studio lights illuminate the gold records, bringing their color to life. She steps back, startled. Upon further inspection, she is not the only one in the reflection. The dark eyes fixed on her from behind make Connie turn around. Philip stands, leaning against the doorframe. He looks the same as he did at the Marquee Club, from the slightly scruffy facial appearance, hair lightly puffed to perfection, and wearing a maroon button-down shirt over black pants and a matching belt. Maroon, of the red family. The color Connie thought was too provocative for something so casual, especially with a platonic friend. That exactness of his appearance is déja vu to her soul all over again. Her heart excitedly beats, and those one thousand butterflies join in, making her a bundle of nerves. She fights every one of them off with as much courage and dignity as a person with barriers can.

Taking a deep breath, she says, "I thought he was going to drop me off in the woods."

Philip chuckles back, "It's not wooded. It's just that nobody likes to keep their lights on in this neighborhood."

Connie thinks of something else. "I'm going to have a tough time getting back home if it's that dark out with no lights. How in the world does a taxi find this place?" She turns away, pointing to outside.

Philip glances down and quietly says, "They do fine in the daylight."

Connie turns back to him, unable to read him or what he just said. "What would... Of course, daylight is easier." Instead, she thinks of something else that crosses her mind. "A limo," she grins back with pride. "Thought you weren't into all of the stardom."

"Whatever's available," Philip answers assuredly. "It doesn't hurt to have some privileges."

She giggles back. Walking by him, into the spacious living room, Connie takes off her coat and plops herself down on a cozy black couch.

Philip puts his hands in his pockets, wondering what to say. Finally, he comes up with something.

"So? How was the ride?" He walks over to the couch and sits on the arm of it.

Connie is careful with her eye contact, not wanting to avoid him entirely, but keep her distance. Philip senses her shy demeanor.

She says back to him, "It's a big car. I didn't notice anything incredibly impressive about it. It's just space for an hour's ride." Glancing down, she feels the words leave her. "Total loneliness." She finally looks back at him. "Um, I have no idea where I am, even if I wanted to call for a cab."

"Brewster," he answers quickly.

Connie wakes up from her shy state. "What? That's only about a half an hour away from my folks."

Philip sheepishly grins. "Well, it's not Beverly Hills."

"True," she nods back, then pauses for a moment. "I couldn't help but notice there were no other cars parked out front. What did you do? Send all the hired help away for the night? I thought there would at least be more guests here. So, what's going on?"

"Oh, yeah. The circus left town," Philip grins.

"You're terrible."

Connie's eyes fall upon her pocketbook. "Oh! Before I forget." She reaches in, pulling out the Union Jack scarf.

"That's where it went," he answers in mock surprise.

"I don't know how in the world this got into my carry-on bag. I found it there when I was taking everything out." She begins to hand it to him when noticing his sly grin. "You put it in my bag."

"Come on now. I wouldn't do such a thing." He answers in bashful charm and innocence.

She angles to him. "You're a lousy liar."

His sly smile grows.

Connie throws the scarf at him, which he catches.

She shakes her head disapprovingly and mutters, "What am I going to do with you?"

Philip says with a quick nod, "Come on. I'll give you a tour of Big Blue."

Connie finally begins to loosen up, realizing how foolish she's been acting since arriving at the house.

"Big Blue? I thought this place would be called like, Chez Reinhardt, or something?"

"I'm not French." Philip answers.

They walk down a short hallway, past the large cabinet of gold record plaques.

Philip giggles. He shows her various rooms. "There's the master bedroom. Next to it are two guest rooms. And the one over there is the doghouse."

A shocked Connie replies quickly, "What?"

"It's a closet." Philip bursts out laughing.

Connie answers back, suppressing a giggle. She gives him a light punch to the arm. "Oh, you're bad!"

Philip laughs harder. Connie leans against him, unable to restrain her laughter. They hold each other, unknowing, and not caring about their physical closeness. At that moment, Connie lets her guard down, feeling like she's got her buddy back, not the guy her heart did somersaults for in London. Finally, they let go and continue the tour.

"I'll show you where the action takes place," Philip says.

Connie looks at him with confusion. "Action?"

"Yeah. The studio, silly!" Philip answers her with a giggle.

"Oh!" Connie pipes up.

He walks her over to the very back of the hallway, where they stand next to a door. Philip opens it and feels for the light switch. The room comes alive with a few cables on the floor, a mess of black wires connected from one piece of audio equipment to the next, an equalizer, a sequencer, and an Apple computer. A mixer hooks up to an outboard processor. Three guitar cases are on the other side of the room.

Philip says, "Ah, Caddy and her younger sister are over there."

"Caddy has a younger sister?" Connie asks with mock surprise, looking at the Cadillac pink Stratocaster. "I would have never guessed."

He picks up a brighter pink one with a black pickguard and headstock.

"Yeah. She's this one. I haven't had her as long as Caddy." Philip answers while giving Connie the same stare he had at The Marquee, that peek from behind the guitar's neck.

Connie breathes in hard, stopping herself from feeling turned on in some weird way. "Oh. A sort of bright flamingo pink, at that," she replies in distraction. A moment later, she asks, "So, why do you have a studio when there's one like every five blocks or so apart in the city?"

Philip carefully puts the guitar down as he says, "Easier access. Got an idea? Go inside the room — flick on the switch turn the power on, and instant gratification. Also, it gives me more artistic control. I get to keep my master tapes, rather than the label." He looks at her. "Everybody has a studio now. Whether it's at home, a guesthouse, an office somewhere uptown, or downtown. "They're everywhere because artists want full control of their music. When I first got the house a few years ago, I had the option of putting in a pool. But then I figured it wasn't something I needed. Instead, I got an addition added since there was an allotment of space out in the back for it. Essentially, what you see here is what you get."

Philip plugs in a wire and takes the other end to another machine. He thinks for a second before saying, "About fourteen years ago it was a different story. A lot of us were broke, and it wasn't unheard of if somebody traded in a van for studio time. That was for one day's worth. When I was with Deac, we had a routine. There were girls around, and they would want to spend time with the band. Some of us would play cards, and the prize would be one of these ladies. I became a pro at playing, so I racked up the wins." He raises his brows devilishly.

Connie says in complete disbelief, "What?"

Philip looks at her, then leans over, trying to cover up his uncontrollable giggling.

She nudges him. "You are such a liar! You made the whole thing up!"

Philip busts out, laughing. It's so incredibly contagious that Connie can't contain her composure and joins in.

"Great story, though!" Connie says back.

"What? Didn't you believe it? Man, nothing gets by you!" He laughs again.

She giggles, "You cracking up was the dead giveaway!"

Philip calms down. "I thought it would work," he shakes his head. "Come on. I'll show you what's upstairs."

They walk up the steps where there is a set-up of bookcases and a full entertainment system containing a TV, VCR, stereo system with massive speakers, and several rows of albums.

Connie looks all around. "Wow. This is quite the house!"

Philip says, "It works great for separations. Those times that company wants to ignore me completely or gets pissed off for one reason or another. It's a cooling-off spot or even just a place to unwind and think alone."

Connie says, "Another, doghouse?"

Philip answers with a hint of guilt. "One of many."

"That's sad," she says with pity in her voice.

"It's how things go."

Connie thinks for a minute, taking in what he's told her. "Still."

Philip tells her, "The rest is just another bathroom, and an additional room used for extra space. The second set of stairs takes you out to the garage," he gives a tight-lipped smile. "That's pretty much it." He thinks for a split-second. "Oh, wait! There is something else." He swings open a door slowly. Inside is a closet full of varying types of stage wear. It consisting of velvet suits — at least a dozen of them on hangers, in different colors.

Philip hangs his arm over the closet rod, as a slack-jawed Connie stares at the inside.

"In case you thought I was lying." He raises a brow in teasing fashion.

"I never thought you were lying." She looks at one. "Even silver."

"Yeah, well, we had to step up our style as disco was coming about. You know. Gotta try and fit in."

Connie stops to think. "What's different turns out to be all the same."

Philip lets out a laugh, recognizing the words. "That would be right. I guess you've been listening to some records. So, tell me. Anything else you've learned from *Altar of Deception* or any of the tracks?"

Connie looks up in thought. "Nope. Nothing else I can think of at the moment. I'll let you know if anything comes up."

Philip glances down, amused by the knowledge she has on her own.

They go back downstairs.

Philip points to a door. "Over there is the garage. And on the other side, where we're heading to is the kitchen, and just beyond there..." He starts to say. "That's the dining room."

***

Philip enters the kitchen, with Connie following behind.

She says, "OK. So, what's on the menu?"

Philip answers quickly. "Spaghetti. The only thing I know how to make without getting the fire department involved. Many times there has been some kind of drama resulting in Chinese food as an alternative."

Connie laughs. "Oh, that's bad."

Philip says proudly, "So, I know my grandmother's recipe by heart."

Connie leans over the countertop while he prepares the stove. "Wait. Now you're going to tell me you're part Italian?"

Philip thinks about something while grabbing a container full of dry spaghetti strands before revealing, "Uh, yeah. Part. Half. Whatever. My mom's side. There's a bit of a misconception where spaghetti gets its origins. Some say China and other places recorded are Greece and even the Middle East. The popular belief is Sicily." He breaks a whole batch of spaghetti in half.

Connie grins. "You're a walking encyclopedia of knowledge, Mr. Reinhardt." She giggles back, undoing her watch in anticipation of helping him.

Philip smiles back at her charmingly. "Now, back to that all-important question of my background?" He answers her while tossing the pasta in a pot, "Maybe a small bit of Greek thrown in," he says with raised brows teasingly.

Connie furrows her brows and rolls her eyes. "No. You're not. Get out of here. You're so full of it."

He giggles back. "I don't pick apart my heritage. All I know is, I wouldn't make a good chef."

Connie tells him in seriousness, "I can certainly see the Scandinavia or European influence. It's in your eyes." She briefly stares at him when he returns the glance. She looks away while answering, "I know I guessed you were a musician from the start. But, no way are you in any shape or form part Greek." Connie hesitates. "You don't even have the right body type. No way."

Philip picks up a bottle of Opus One, pours himself a full glass, and polishes it off.

Connie giggles back, pointing at the empty glass. "OK. Did you just guzzle the whole thing? Wow." She shakes her head in astonishment, not knowing what to make of his behavior.

Philip steps around the back of her. "Spaghetti is the language of lovers." He arches his brows, holding up a long wooden spoon.

Connie gives a puzzled expression. "Um. Yeah. Right, Don Juan. I think that glass of wine is talking now. Either that or you're an incurable romantic." Claire's words of Philip being a romantic, not a realist, enters Connie's mind.

Philip was acting weird, as though he was trying to grasp the concept of flirting. Maybe it was his version, if not a clunky one.

He smiles broadly, then goes to check the stove and places a sauce concoction on simmer. Checking on how the pasta is softening, he picks out a strand, letting it dangle from between his teeth. Leaning in, he shows it to her.

Connie tries to stifle a laugh. "Incurable romantic. Cute. Very cute."

He giggles while trying to capture the strand.

She shakes her head. "This has got to be the strangest possible goodbye I have ever experienced."

A thought enters his mind. "Let me ask you a serious question."

Connie eyes him peculiarly. "Serious? That's a change of pace for you. But, OK."

Philip asks, "What is the most important thing to you? What do you treasure above all else?"

Connie smiles back with a slight giggle. "You sure are diverse. From fun to philosophical." She thinks for a moment. "Um, but I'd have to say, trust. Yeah. Trust means a lot to me. Everything, when I think about it."

Philip gets distracted by a thought. "Yeah. Can you get the herbs out of the fridge?"

Connie looks at the refrigerator. "This thing is about five times the size of the little dinky icebox back in my apartment. What is...," She opens it. "Holy cow! It's full. Herbs, you said?"

While she looks for them, Philip takes the pot of spaghetti off the stove, bringing it over to the small table nearby. He becomes distracted, almost agitated by his thoughts. It's as though he's fighting something deep inside that won't let go. His eyes swing over while Connie's back is to him. "Do you trust your heart?"

Connie stops rooting through the refrigerator to think. She's dumbstruck by the question. "I...um... Nobody has ever asked me that before. Gosh. Jeez. That's hard to say." Hesitantly she answers, "Sometimes."

Philip closes his eyes, leaning his hands against the table's top, as though he needs to keep himself propped up. His fingers drum with nervousness. His eyes bob up when he hears the refrigerator door close.

Connie walks back to the table. She pushes the container towards Philip. He grabs her wrist tightly, yanking her up to himself for one long and aggressive kiss. She pulls away immediately.

"I think you need to get a prescription for real glasses."

"There's nothing wrong with my sight."

She slowly shakes her head with puzzlement. For a fraction of a second, Connie thinks of how this will affect their friendship. That moment of awareness breaks, as Philip makes his intentions known, kissing her again. She throws her arms around his shoulders, kissing him back, letting the feeling fill her senses.

Philip nearly dumps the pot of spaghetti on the floor in the middle of his uncontrollable desire. Acknowledging that the kitchen is nowhere proper for a display of affection, he guides her without disconnecting.

***

Philip throws his back against the wall, sending the glass curio cabinet of gold records a few feet away rattling. His passion leaves her a little surprised. The contradictions fly through her head. He's soft, though his kisses can be somewhat hard. He's rough, yet gentle. It's understandable, considering his nature, but doesn't hurt that he's a damn good kisser! Philip takes Connie's hand, guiding it to his thudding heart, running a mile a minute. She cups her hands on both sides of his face, pulling away to look into his eyes. Up close, they are like brown galaxies of the unknown. Mysterious and inviting. As enchanting as the windows of his soul may be, Connie can also tell there are stories and years etched in his gaze. So much pain, pleasure, fear, desire, and love.

His eyes shut as he goes for another kiss. Philip lets one hand free, unbuttoning his shirt in quick succession. It's still tucked in his slacks, though. Stopping, he puts a finger up, signaling for her to wait. He takes her by the hand and leads her a few steps into the first room. Shutting the door, he resumes in kissing her. He then stops again, long enough to turn a knob on the wall, bringing the light down to a low dim.

Philip untucks his shirt. Connie waits for him to finish as she bites her bottom lip nervously. Her eyes briefly leave him, spotting the pair of Ray-Ban Wayfarer sunglasses on the nightstand. He attempts to lean in for another kiss. She puts her hand out, holding the pair of sunglasses. It stops him dead in his tracks.

Philip answers the gesture with a growing smile. "If that's your idea of fun?" He puts them on, immediately doing an impromptu version of Corey Hart's "Sunglasses At Night." Connie nervously laughs at his spontaneity. The response is contagious as he giggles too.

His sleeves are up to the elbows and a shirt unbuttoned to display his bare, slender, yet impressive physique. Philip puts on the broadest smile while playing up to her, stealing a kiss every so often. He undoes his belt, taking it out of every loop, then puts his hand out. The item slides off his fingertips onto the floor. He gives a playful hip wiggle, then goes in for another kiss.

Prancing around to her back, Philip breathes in her ear so softly that she feels a tickling sensation. He holds her sides through the cowl neck sweater. She turns her head to face him. Quickly, he steps around back to the front, watching her laugh. He pulls up the top over her head, revealing Connie to be left with a bra and a bit of static-cling frizzed hair, accompanied by a pair of form-fitting black knit pants. He holds up his collar to hide half his face in a playfully seductive manner.

Connie breathes back, trying to hold in her laughter. "Good God. Never a dull moment with you."

With serious determination, Philip pulls off his shirt, dropping it on the floor. Connie looks him over in all of his bare-chested glory. He yanks off the sunglasses, kissing her trembling lips. She feels the back closure of her bra released. Closing her eyes, Connie slips one strap down after the other, letting the garment drop at her feet. She looks at him briefly, with her eyes gazing down in embarrassment at her flat chest. With a big grin, Philip grabs her for a tight hold against himself for some skin on skin contact. They continue to kiss. She slides her hand down the crease of his dark slacks, where she encounters a rigid sensation. Connie remains drawn to him, yet confused by his desire.

Closing her eyes, she sits on the bed. Philip pulls her shoes and socks off, allowing her bare feet the freedom to feel the hardwood flooring underneath. Leaning forward, he gently kisses her forehead, then the tip of her nose, followed by his hands running over the soft structure of her cheekbones. His eyes meet hers. Philip leans forward with a little more force. Connie finally gives in, pulling him towards her as she hits the pillow. She runs her hands through his hair, kissing him.

It's just the two of them under the guise of darkness.

Together, a unity in both body and soul.

When morning arrives, Connie wakes up to the feeling of bare skin and a content heartbeat against hers. They lay against each other, harmoniously bonded. Her motion stirs Philip from sleep as his eyes open. She looks up.

"Hey," Connie answers to his awakened state.

A sly smile creeps across Philip's face.

He says with one brow mischievously arched, "Rock and roll." Pulling her over to him for a tighter squeeze, he gives Connie a lengthy kiss, then nuzzles his face against her neck. She lets out a giggle.

"What are you running on? Duracell? Eveready? Definitely not generic."

Philip laughs hard. He pulls away to prop up his head against the pillow.

Connie leans up, landing her body on top of his. In assured confidence, she says, "I'm not the first woman you've ever been with."

He glances down in thought, picking his words carefully. "I am acquainted with the female anatomy." His brows arch up.

Connie smirks. "That's obvious." She looks down. "It's just that I figured nothing could happen between us."

"Um, there is no such thing as one hundred percent anything."

He taps her hand on his chest.

"No?"

"I don't know. Maybe it's different with other people who have other working situations. When you're on the road, and the band thinks everything is regular, well, you go with it. I'm not saying that I ever had an aversion to women — more like the opposite. I wrote about them, and sometimes I even sang about them. It's just what you do." He shrugs. "And, at the time, I didn't know what I wanted, other than to be in a successful band. I wasn't sure of who to love. I thought I was in love a few times while on the road, but then something would pull me away, and it felt wrong. The guys in the band didn't know what I was going through. The rock and roll lifestyle isn't conducive to what I am or what I perceive myself as such. Being single and lonely, no matter what a person thinks they are, is still single and lonely. That's not going to change. So, there have been some opportunities presented.

"When did your opportunities start?" she asks.

"Ah, sometime back," he answers carefully. "I can tell you about one specific experience I had that was memorable."

Connie giggles back, "Oh?"

"It happened after a gig in Cincinnati. I was almost twenty-two, and it was during our first tour. I was the only guy who didn't have anybody, and bandmates tried to play matchmaker plenty. Uh, this lady who was a friend of the road crew wanted to hang out, and all of us wound up having a big party in a hotel suite after the gig. I didn't feel like partying it up by drinking and drugging myself that night. So, this lady was hanging around, and she was sort of all over me physically. We split the party and went back up to my room. He shakes his head in the sense of wonder. A sly smile creeps over his face. "The sex was great. It was so great that when morning came, and we were asleep, neither of us heard the cleaning lady knock on the door. She showed up, and we were on the bed. No blankets. No sheets. Just us. She got to see everything, and I mean everything in full view. That cleaning lady couldn't high-tail it out of the room quick enough. She was freaking out in either Spanish or Portuguese."

Connie leans over, giggling.

"That was a day of broadening my horizons, and a cleaning lady became a nun." He tries to hold in a laugh.

Connie gives a sexy little wiggle. "So, you were a bad boy!"

Philip gives an unabashed, glorious laugh. After a few minutes to calm down, he hesitantly says, "Um, about that gold tooth."

"Uh-huh," she answers, gently grazing her finger against his bottom lip.

Sheepishly, he tries to get the words out. "It was um, an after-show encounter. An accident while playing a little too rough."

"I remember you told me part of the story."

"Her knee. My jaw. I felt something warm in my mouth. She turned on the light, and it was a total nightmare. My mouth was bleeding badly. I nearly swallowed this tooth, and my jaw was sore. We had a gig the next day, and nobody could be sure if I would be OK for it. It was cold compression packs, ice, and towels for several hours. The road manager found a dentist super fast the next morning, and I got this gold replacement. Cost a fortune for a starving artist! Yeah, so I learned I had to either be a more careful lover or bring a flashlight."

Connie laughs.

Philip grows serious again as he thinks aloud. "Just like what I told you last week. When the band broke up, I was on my own. That was when I had more freedom to explore who I was and what I wanted. Many of my serious relationships have been men up to this point. Ladies were more casual. Nothing serious. Just a one-night thing. As long as I didn't get a tooth knocked out." He smirks.

"So, you're—"

"Yeah," he answers before she's finished. "Surprise. I'm a double freak show. I told you things were complex. I have an affinity for guys, but it doesn't mean women are completely off the table. It makes life that much more complicated for me. When you think you know what you are, but then someone comes along and changes everything. I can't even categorize myself, because I hate labels, so I go with my tendencies. It's been challenging with men. They would find out and couldn't deal with it. So, here comes the sabotage and heartbreak." He thinks for a moment. "You know, I mean, I started out going to church every Sunday like every other kid on my block. I got in trouble in the first...second grade, when I kissed Ellie Sandheim. I did it because I saw my parents do it a lot. I wanted to try it out, and uh, I liked it. I've been striving to find the same happiness my mom and dad have had for the last forty-two years. But, I can't seem to get the same balance."

Connie looks him in the eyes, feeling sorry for his predicament. She toys with the lowest strands of his hair that fall in front. Reaching over, she leans in for a kiss. The Opus One has since dissolved, revealing his natural taste. Her mind wanders as she doesn't want the moment to end. Gently, her fingertips touch the light fuzziness above his upper lip. "You are beautiful and perfect in every way. That's why..., I..." she hesitates. "I think I'm in love with you."

Philip's eyes never leave hers as he states, "I want you to move in...," he nods. "...here."

Connie blinks back in shock. She looks into his eyes. It was the same expression he gave her when he entrusted her with his deeply hidden secret. She throws her arms over his shoulders and kisses him. He holds her tight. The warmth of her slender bosom creates a bonded experience as their hearts join together, beating in time.

Connie walks out of San-San to a brisk breeze threaded in between buildings. Only, this time she has a purpose. As night encapsulates the city, she throws her arms over Philip's shoulders, drawn into a kiss. It's the feeling of happiness that gets her through any day. His kiss is enough to light her up like a neon sign. Not like a cheap motel. Perhaps orange like a setting sun or a crazy yellow. She feels the electricity of just being with him.

He looks her in the eyes.

"Got the West Germany gig."

"You did?" She answers excitedly, giving his arm a little squeeze.

"Yep. Next year. And, back to England."

"Oh, well. You're going to have to brush up on your British lingo!" She laughs.

"What about you?"

"I finally got to tell my nosey next-door neighbor that I was moving out. Now, she wants to hold a big goodbye party. A girl who's in her twenties showed interest in the apartment already. Mrs. Whitaker will be so happy to find somebody new to torment. I called my parents and told them I was leaving the city. My mom was panicked at first, asking me where I would work. I told her it was the same place, and I adjusted my schedule. They were thrilled when I said I would only be half an hour away."

"Nice," Philip grins.

"Oh, hey, you're not off the hook. My dad said he wants you to show him more about that old relic in the living room."

Philip gives a sly smile, knowing he's content with everything.

He hugs her and gives a little nod. "Come on."

They walk arm in arm along the East Village, past the brick buildings boarded up, tattooed in graffiti and posted with theater bills, half peeling from time and weather. Litter embedded against the curb. Dimly lit shops closed for the night. A lanky man writes in his notebook under the moonlight, while several black youths set up headquarters under the awning of a shut down building covered in graffiti. They have a cache of spray paints in their arsenal. One shakes a can vigorously, working his way in the color red. The other two boys keep vigilant, making sure the cops don't roll by.

Philip and Connie head their way, through the griminess of New York City's night. The boys look at them, realizing it's just a couple. Yuppie white people, in their eyes. The two begin to pass through. Philip stops immediately and looks over the outside walls of the buildings as if it was artwork and not a nuisance. Turning to Connie, he waits for her to notice his absence. She stops and looks back.

He nods to the boys, seeing a can of spray paint in his sights. Reaching over, he picks it up and grins.

The boys shrug, wondering what this guy has in mind.

Philip scans the next brick building, looking up. He shakes the can vigorously and steps up to a surprisingly uncluttered section, free of graffiti. Among the artist tags, scrawled on names, and mini art installations, he goes over to spray on a heart and initials with P R + C A.

He hands the can back to one of the boys, who stares.

Philip goes back to Connie, giving her a long kiss before they continue their journey through the city's undercover of emptiness.

They are one story, of the millions in New York City's web of spun tales. With contradictions of the heart, like many other lost and found souls. A city that turns on its axis, between hedonistic glories to the bated breath and bell rung on Wall Street.

Acknowledgments

In honor of those who have inspired this story from the past and present.

To my dear, sweet friend, Kevin Levine who loved his childhood, growing up in the eighties as much as I did, and being the spark that ignited this story.

For my mom, Teresa who watched over the creation of this tale with the same enthusiasm I had.

To Mike Taylor, for helping me with whatever needed fixing and always a great friend.

For New York City, who became the muse of my tapestry that wove in between the characters and their actions.

www.ingramcontent.com/pod-product-compliance
Lightning Source LLC
Chambersburg PA
CBHW070559120726
47909CB00007B/2389